Güneli Gün was born in Turkey, but now lives in Ohio. She has taught creative writing and Women's Studies at Oberlin College and is the author of *A Book of Trances*.

BLACK SEA

Istanbul

Bosphorus

Scutari

Bursa ★

AEGEAN
SEA

T u r k e y

ANATOLIA

KARAMAN

Hürü's
Lagoon

★ Konya

T a u r u s M t s

★ Tarsus

★ Aleppe

★ Antioch

Cyprus

S y r

MEDITERRANEAN SEA

★ Damascu

★ Tiberias

★ Acre

★ Gaza

Locale of
ON THE ROAD
TO BAGHDAD

A r

The Ottoman Empire
—·—·— at beginning of reign of Sultan Selim I
— — — at the end of his reign

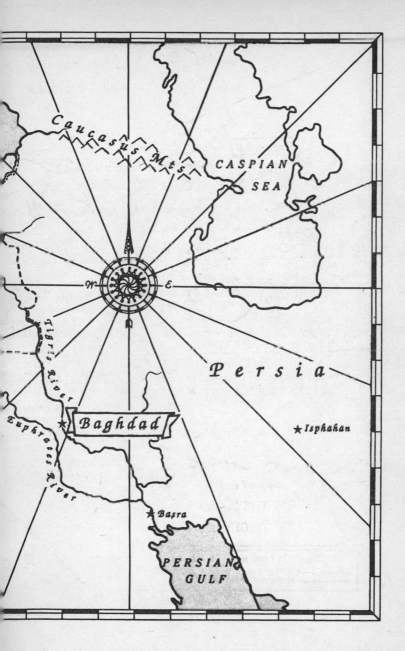

ON THE ROAD TO BAGHDAD

*A Picaresque Novel
of Magical Adventures,
Begged, Borrowed, and Stolen
from the Thousand and One Nights*

✦

Güneli Gün

PICADOR

First published 1991 by Virago Press Limited

This Picador edition published 1994 by
Pan Books Limited a division of
Pan Macmillan Publishers Limited
Cavaye Place London SW10 9PG
and Basingstoke

Associated companies throughout the world

ISBN 0-330-32463-2

3 5 7 9 8 6 4

A CIP catalogue record for this book is available from
the British Library

Printed and bound in Great Britain by
Cox & Wyman Ltd, Reading, Berkshire

TABLE OF CONTENTS

✦

PART TWO
INITIATION
WONDER JOURNEY BACK TO EIGHTH CENTURY BAGHDAD
AND THE BOOK OF A THOUSAND AND ONE NIGHTS

✦

PART THREE
RETURN
HÜRÜ IS SNATCHED BACK INTO REAL TIME
AND A LIFE WAITING TO BE LIVED

INTRODUCTION

*H*ürü was born in Istanbul (still called Constantinople by many a twit) in the year 1496, or in her own Good Time, year 900 of the Flight of the Prophet. For a short while, she was the greatest minstrel in the world, Moslem, Christian or otherwise. But she chose to throw away the gift. Why?—you might well ask. I certainly did. And I still am not sure if I like the result of my historical sleuthing.

The story takes place during the golden age of the Ottoman Empire when the Crescent of Islam ascended like a scimitar in the Western skies. The Ottoman armies were, in other words, on the move,—such a powerful force that Europe came close to trading the Cross for the Crescent. Our heroine, Hürü, cared little about foreign policy, yet Destiny, it turns out, had reserved her a blessed moment in the world of ideas.

Storytellers find it all too easy—as well as pleasant and profitable—to indulge in ironic hindsight so that we may all *laugh* at historic personalities who seem to us, now, too dumb to notice the obvious. That's the trouble with revisionist histories. For my part, despite my shortcomings as a historian, I won't make light of my heroine's existential woes. On the contrary, I hope to adorn myself with the admirable virtues that belong to this young woman called Hürü.

Hers is an odd name, Hürü. What does it mean? Difficult to

pronounce and track down, her name may be a Turkish rendering of *houri*, the Arabic word that designates those charming creatures bonded to serve worthy male souls in Paradise. When you come right down to it, Paradise is where we all belong, male or female, with only wonderful ideas to serve us all. Our Hürü was a truly liberated soul, not a handmaiden devoted to the pleasures of the opposite sex. For my money, I think it likely that our heroine's name was derived from the word *hür*, which, in Turkish, means *free*. In any case, the two interpretations of the name cannot be reconciled.

So, it's up to you, Good Reader, to go along with our heroine. See what you make of the fabulous adventures that Destiny had in store for Hürü, on the Road to Baghdad.

Oberlin, Ohio
1990

Part One

Departure

Call to Adventure on the
Road to Baghdad

Chapter 1

THE HEARTBREAK OF EDUCATION

Hürü hears the monotonous music of the World

Not only was Hürü not endowed with marvelous talents: she despaired of the gaps in her education. Hürü knew enough to know she didn't know. Oh, she'd memorized the Koran by now, but not with the same ease and verve as her girlfriends. On top of being stuck with a voice too low to be pleasing in a girl, Hürü mispronounced words in the Arabic text whose meanings she scarcely understood and, when stuttering, substituted words in her native tongue. But Turkish was condemned as being too straightforward a language to accommodate God's Utterances. Besides, Hürü stammered and stuttered the holiest verses into bits and shards.

When she faltered in her recitations, her tutoress (a slovenly tub of a woman who devoured sweetmeats all through the lessons) rapped Hürü sharply with the regulation size tutor's stick. This implement, long enough to reach the pupil without disturbing the lardy tutoress on her cushion at the head of the schoolroom, stung Hürü where she sat on her knees by the doorway. Because she proved so slow with her religious instruction, Hürü, at sixteen, still labored through the basics when her girlfriends had already learned to giggle together behind latticed windows, pushing, now and then, a needle through the linen stretched onto a communal embroidery hoop. And they were already watching eligible young men gallivant about in the street. But not Hürü. She had yet to earn a little praise. Still, her parents doted on her—as only parents can on a child who's a little out of hand.

Her tutoress, the ogress called Mistress Kevser, gave her parents good reasons why Hürü must be held back, since, in her estimate, Hürü was far from the model student. It wasn't so much that the girl's memory was faulty so that Hürü couldn't properly recite God's Inspirations: it was more because Hürü insisted on interpretation when the Word should be sufficient to the Faithful. Their daughter was too literal minded, so much so, Mistress Kevser feared, that the Seven Heavens would never open up for the poor child. Hürü wanted to know Why This, When That and How Is It Possible. Model students, and Mistress Kevser had taught many in houses far greater than this one, just sat down and recited, leaving arguments and interpretations to those whose business it was to argue and interpret.

"Who is Hürü," Mistress Kevser demanded, "that she must know the Z of it when she hasn't learned the A?"

Who, indeed? That's what Hürü wanted to know, too. When called on the carpet, Hürü intimated the tutoress was hardly a model teacher either.

"P-p-perish the thought," Hürü said, "but Mistress Kevser's very f-f-fat!"

"So?" her mother said.

"She stu-stu-stuffs herself."

"Do as your tutor says," her father admonished Hürü, "and not as she does. Remember what the Prophet said. He said, 'Let me be a slave to the teacher who's taught me a single word.'"

"In that c-c-case," Hürü said.

According to the Prophet, whose only instructor was God, teaching was a more sacred calling than the Call of God. So why hadn't God, in his Mercy and Compassion, provided Hürü with a more attractive teacher? She supposed there must be, somewhere in this marvelous world, a teacher so magnetically true that the pupil's mind gravitated to the teacher's as iron does to lodestone. But, she thought, maybe she was unworthy of a Real Teacher, seeing as everything about her was also imperfect and undistinguished.

Besides being slow with her memorizations, Hürü, who ordinarily stammered only a little, stammered hard when faced with the texts. Her tied tongue was a sign, her tutoress informed her, that Iblis, or a lesser *jinni*, had taken a keen interest in Hürü's peccability. Those repulsive beings, too, were peccable and proud of it. When God introduced Adam to the Angels and the *jinn*, He invited all to bow down before Man. The Angels, who were impeccable and created out of light, had complied; not Iblis and Co. They didn't want to bow down before any creature made of clots of blood and were immediately fired for their vanity. For it is written that mischief opened the hearts of men to Iblis, his sons and his perfidious troops who skulked and lurked in baths, latrines, wells, ovens, marketplaces, ruined houses, junctures of roads, the sea, rivers—waiting for a heedless and unaware person like Hürü to invoke them between her stutterings of the sacred texts. Girls like Hürü were the very meat of Iblis, whose food was whatever was killed without the Blessing of God being pronounced over it first, who drank whatever intoxicates, who was called to prayer by musical pipes, whose *Koran* was poetry, whose speech was falsehood and whose snares, women.

So, to Hürü's mind, the road to virtue didn't appear open. She was sinful already because she loved music. Yet she hated her music teacher. A woman of Arabic origin, the music teacher's breath was so foul, it wasn't hard to imagine her singing all night in the company of the *jinn* of the latrine.

Her parents didn't fret when Hürü turned away from her lute. They speedily dismissed the Arab instructress as Hürü had urged so often. But Mistress Kevser stayed. And stayed. Mistress Kevser's presence wasn't optional. The music lessons, on the other hand, had been instigated at Hürü's childish insistence and not because an obsession with music is suitable for a well-bred girl. Performing suited slaves, itinerant beggars and infidels who didn't have much choice in learning the unseemly task of entertaining others.

Looking with dismay at Hürü's two front teeth that had come in a little too large, her freckled skin, her truly red hair, the absence of two proper swellings on her chest, her bony height more suitable for an archer than a girl, her hips that seemed too narrow to give birth or please a man, her large hands and feet, her wide and full mouth, and her hazel eyes that stared too intently, her despairing parents thought their daughter might as well be educated so as to have something to do with her life when suitors didn't materialize. But the girl was hopeless as a scholar, too. Might as well tutor a rock! And

Hürü was their only daughter.

When the girl was told to bring a tray of drinks to serve the sort of women who make it their business to keep an eye on everyone's marriageable daughters, Hürü tried to refuse, saying she was too deep in study. But the daughter of the house must serve these hens who would otherwise maliciously cluck whenever they had been served by a servant instead of Hürü. Told to wash her hands of ink, Hürü would lumber in like a camel wearing shoes of sheer ice, her eyes intent on the glasses on the tray, which is a sure way of spilling the sherbet into the saucers. And she wouldn't be done until she managed drenching some gossip in ruby syrup.

"Keep your eyes off the tray," her mother instructed, "and on the horizon, as if you see a beautiful sunset."

"What ho-ho-horizon?" Hürü said, wondering what the horizon and beautiful sunset would be doing in a room designed to keep the outside out.

"Imagine it!" ordered her mother, who was big in a queenly way and carried her curves and heavy bronze hair with the lust of a purebred mare.

The model mind of the times was one that submitted, and the model of feminine beauty was the distilled essence of languorous Arabian nights. Her face must be like the full moon, fair and gibbous, and her hair black as the deepest hue of the night. A rosy blush must spread in the center of each cheek; a mole must provide a propitious accent as a globule of ambergris might upon a dish of alabaster. Her eyes must be black, large and almond shaped, fringed with long, dark silken lashes. Above her eyes, two thin black eyebrows must arch on a forehead wide and as fair as ivory. Her breasts must be like two pomegranates, high and firm, her mouth like coral, her teeth pearls, her waist slender with hips wide and large, her hands and feet small, white and not suitable for work. She must walk slowly, moving her body from side to side, her hips undulating as if she had a thousand years to reach her destination, without a care in her head other than pleasing others.

Although Hürü thought her mother beautiful, luxuriant and fragrant, the matriarch didn't comply with the model either. Lady Gülbahar was too much a daughter of the steppe just as Hürü's grandmother had been—a horseriding, campfollowing wife of a march-warrior, who'd arrived with her man to conquer Constantinople and remained, conquered by city life, allowing etiquette to replace the sincerity that had existed among the bronzed women of the steppe. Hürü remembered her grandmother's stories, true stories that happened under a big sky, on lands that stretched for miles, where the winds blew recklessly unimpeded. She still heard in her head her grandmother's ballads of heroes who'd become as gods; her lyric longings for a person, a campsite, a distant home; her praises of this creation, of God, of valor, honesty and justice; her satiric verses on the shortcomings of mankind, and, most poignantly, her laments.

Despite the family longing for lost places and lost climes, whose memory has been embellished by distance and the passage of time, Hürü, though slow in speech, was quick to perceive the natural graces that blessed the city of Istanbul. The air, sweet as the nectar of flowers and always refreshed with delicate breezes, the surrounding waters, both salt and fresh, shimmering like God's looking glass in many hues of blue, the verdant hills which gave the eye varied vantage could scarcely be imagined by those who imagined Paradise. The City could not but inspire its inhabitants to wake in the morning and declare themselves the happiest of souls. To say that one was a born-and-bred Istanbulite afforded one both honor and felicity.

The eavesdropping that Hürü managed under her father's roof informed her that the whole population, whether out of force or choice, had immigrated from other places. As soon as someone had finished giving thanks to the Almighty for the happiness of residing here, he would, invariably, speak of some other land, other customs, another language. Whether they were artisans from Persia, theologians from Arabia, shepherds from Serbia, archers from Crimea, beauties from Circassia, engineers from Magyarland, cooks from Armenia, farmers from Rumania, slavedealers from Judea or merchants from Venice, these people would immediately chatter in tongues which altered and enlarged the speech of Istanbulites. When Turkomans, whose Empire's capital Istanbul really was, visited the City of Cities, they felt like dolts, and, in defense, poked fun at the way Istanbulites minced their words, like some damn foreigners. Real Turks from the hinterland gave the citizens of The City the shudders. Hürü, a Real Turk on both sides, wondered what was wrong with being a Turkoman.

"Not fashionable," her father explained. Real Turks were, Hürü's father went on, the reason why the reigning Sultan no longer presided over the Divan as his ancestors had done from nomadic times, hearing councils directly and openly in tents where any petitioner was welcome to state his case. One day, as Mehmet the Conqueror sat on his elevated seat, a ragged Turkoman burst into the Divan and demanded in the gross dialect of his origins: "Well, then, speak up! Which of you fops is the happy Sultan?"

Hürü's father didn't know the fate of the ragged Turkoman with the rash tongue, but the Conqueror was so incensed with this affront to his sacred person that he thereupon ceded his seat to the Grand Vizier. That's why the Sultan sits viewing Divan meetings from a latticed balcony above called The Eye of the Sultan. He sees everyone but no one sees him. No wonder Hürü had never laid eyes on the present Sultan although her family lived a stone's throw from the Sublime Porte. But why was the Sultan so sacred? Wasn't he a man as had been all the sons of Osman?

"Mehmet the Conqueror's mother was Greek," her father said. "The Byzantine blood in his veins demanded its quota of vanity. Time was when the ruler ate with the people, rode out front to battle, staked his manliness in games and open tourneys. Not anymore . . ."

Hürü spread a big ear on her father's stories, her only real source of history, geography, medicine, political theory and common wisdom, which he delivered fresh and firsthand, most of it contradictory to prevalent opinions. Turhan Bey, Hürü's father, a wiry and stubborn gentleman approaching his sixties, was attached, under duress, to the Palace as a court physician—not, however, as the reigning Chief Royal Physician. That office was always held by a renegade Christian, or some Persian whose credentials as a medical man, according to Turhan Bey, smelled of gnosticism, superstition and downright incompetence. Yet the life of the Sultan could not be entrusted to a son of Turkomans, no matter how learned a physician or astute a humanitarian. A Real Turk might have tribal loyalties in conflict with his loyalties to the House of Osman. Turhan Bey tended to the royal household, mostly uppity slaves, and swore that the servants received better care than Sultan Bayezid himself, who neither exercised nor ate the right foods, and then wondered why he, the felicitous Sultan, enjoyed such poor health.

"What's the Sul-Sul-Sultan like?" Hürü asked. "Is he f-f-fierce?"

No, the Sultan wasn't fierce at all, more's the pity. The weak kitten in the litter, he was the antithesis of his father. He was a soft, sedentary scholar, a mystic and, in Turhan Bey's view, a reactionary. Bayezid's first act on his ascension to the throne had been to sell off the beautiful paintings done for his father by a famous Venetian artist called Bellini, including the Conqueror's royal portrait. Christian dealers and private collectors had fallen on the art treasures with such venal glee that the Physician said he wouldn't be surprised if the Conqueror's image weren't, right this minute, gracing some vengeful Christian's latrine. The Physician chuckled at the thought. He said the sons of Osman were so mean to each other that once the reigning Sultan bit the dust, the surviving son would never wish to be reminded again of the bastard his father had been, let alone allow his portrait to hang around ungraciously.

"B-b-but," Hürü said, "making images is ter-ter- terr . . . it's very bad." She meant that making images consigns the maker into the everlasting fires, but that was quite a mouthful for Hürü, for whom going to Hell was a much simpler task.

"It's not making images that's a sin, Sweet Idiot," the Physician corrected his daughter. "Making images is in the nature of man, a gift from God, so that man may celebrate God's creation. The more true the image, the more blessed the maker. Got that? Good. Remember, the sinful maker is the incompetent maker."

Hürü wanted to know why her father's opinions were in direct disagreement with the teachings of Mistress Kevser, but she couldn't fetch up the words to frame an appropriate question. Instead, she asked why they weren't allowed to visit Konya, the Physician's hometown, where he was a prince of a defunct royal house.

"Ah, for a glimpse of Konya!" sighed the Physician. "But I'm afraid it's not to be, Sweet Idiot! The Sultan isn't as harmless as he looks. He couldn't be! Someday, maybe someday, we will all go back to Konya."

Chapter 2

FAMILY ROMANCES

*Hürü loves the stories
her father has to tell*

*A*lthough a mere physician now,
Turhan Bey descended from the
House of Karaman, a former principality that revolted against the
Ottomans so regularly that the younger brother of the crown prince
always served as the governor at Konya, the capital of Karaman,
where liberal activities, both religious and political, might be surveyed and quickly curtailed. The Karaman princes saw themselves as
the rightful heirs to the Seljuk Empire, first broken into principalities
and now swallowed up in the belly of the insatiable Ottomans. When
the Ottomans were still a rude and shiftless bunch of nomads back
in Turkistan, the Karaman already enjoyed a full-blown civilization,
replete with scholarship, the arts, fine manners and elegant speech.
At the eleventh hour came their distant cousins, a mere three
hundred men led by a callow youth called Osman; pagan, raggedy,
bewildered, foul-smelling, looking for a handout. "Just anywhere at
all," young Osman petitioned the last Seljuk Emperor; "let us stay."

As any frontiersman knows, once you settle down and begin
enjoying a certain prosperity, nothing can keep your poor relations
back in the Old Country; soon they arrive in droves, asking for a
helping hand while you yourself had to do it all on your own. Well,
the Ottomans were allowed to drop their behinds in the most
dangerous border fief. Who would've guessed they'd survive their

first winter? Once the Ottomans acquired their first set of teeth, after sucking the Byzantine lords dry, they began gnawing on the Turkoman *Bey*s who didn't care for central authority, especially not the authority of rude newcomers still wet behind the ears. And, although the sons of Osman perpetuated their house with greed, they hated anything that smacked of other people's heredity. They created an environment where they might teach everyone how to turn Ottoman; no color, creed or language stood as barrier. In this multinational empire, the Ottomans only discriminated against their distant cousins, the Turkomans. And they trusted only what was foreign.

But the Karaman were the most rebellious of the principality. If the Karaman weren't revolting on their own behalf, they'd revolt for the sake of a younger brother of the Sultan-designate, conveniently nearby and serving as the local governor. The last, and most fateful, uprising had been for the love of Prince Jem, a man of action and romance, vigorous and valiant, and an accomplished poet who learned much from the poets and philosophers of Konya while he governed Karaman with a keen taste for the pleasures of life. The Karaman took Prince Jem to their hearts as if he were a prince of their own blood. Yet, Jem lost his bid for the empire, his life in self-imposed exile, and his supporters to the justice of Sultan Bayezid.

Turhan Bey's life was spared, since, as a younger and punier son of the House of Karaman, he'd studied medicine instead of war. But he lost the freedom to practice his science where he liked it. He also lost his elder brothers, his paternal uncles, cousins and his inheritance. Sentenced to live in Istanbul, not quite free yet not a slave, he arrived with an infant son whose mother his art couldn't save from childbed fever. In Istanbul he sulked. His life was a burden to him; he lived only to see his infant son achieve manhood.

Then, as now, new leases on life are always lurking around the corner. At the celebration of Spring on the Anatolian shore one day, he beheld the lady called Gülbahar gallop on her horse along the walls of the Boghaz Kesen Castle. An Amazon, if he ever saw one; natural, joyous, a head taller than himself. This girl wasn't, obviously, the sort whose father gives her away. She'd have to be won. Turhan Bey surveyed his diminished assets: a piddling job at the Palace, no more hope of ever making medicine stand on its ear, a physique not quite that of a he-man, a little snow already on his temples, and encumbered with a son left behind by a dead woman. He certainly wasn't as eligible as some. But he spoke elegantly and wrote verse which, if not inspired, he felt was eloquently penned.

He learned that Lady Gülbahar's father belonged to that vanished breed of free-born nomadic march-warrior, a retired Ghazi who'd stormed the walls of Constantinople, and claimed descent from the original three hundred ragged Ottoman horsemen who had arrived with no religion or wealth to speak of, but with plenty of will to learn and make good. Lady Gülbahar, then, was related to the House of Osman; therefore, she was the enemy. But what a marvelous enemy! In this hodgepodge empire of nations, the lady was probably as true an Ottoman as they came, considering the ragamuffins had scarcely brought along any women on their long march but acquired three hundred wives here, there and everywhere. They were not choosy as to whom they mingled their blood with, these Ottomans!

What with all the loot from Byzantium, Lady Gülbahar's father was reputed to maintain a generous open house, feeding and entertaining whomever dropped by without even asking the guest's name because one does not question a guest sent by God. So he would hand out clothing to the ragged, arms to the armless, horses to the unhorsed, solace to those with broken hearts and conversation to those who longed to confabulate. Feeling themselves above conventional and newfangled practices such as the seclusion of womenfolk, the women of the household went about just as they pleased, uncovered and unencumbered by attendants, partaking freely of the food, the wine and the conversation. This practice didn't appall Turhan Bey as it did his native Istanbulite informant; he came from Konya where the teachings of Mevlana Jelal-ed-Din Rumi had opened a new world of perceptions that released sincere students from habitual behavior. Turhan Bey had never considered that women were not people.

So, the Physician knocked on the door, announcing himself God's guest. They welcomed him with glad faces and fed him graciously, Lady Gülbahar strongly in evidence, but not paying him any more attention than any other guest. They poured him wine which he drank in moderation, were pleased enough with his conversation that they pressed on him a robe of honor, and invited him to spend the night. Over breakfast, apologizing for his untoward curiosity and only because he loved the guest so well already, the old march-warrior finally asked Turhan Bey his name and the trade he plied. He was very pleased that the guest knew the science of healing.

"See this rotten wart on my nose?" said the old warrior who was otherwise hale and hearty as a lion. "Appeared lately and, for the life of me, I can't keep my hand off it, worrying it all the time. Can you get rid of the wart, my son?"

Perdition! thought Turhan Bey, who no more knew how to get rid of warts than win the willful daughter of the household. But maybe he could convince the old warrior to get rid of the wart himself. Casting about for a quick inspiration, he spied a handful of laurel leaves on the breakfast tray with which the water in the washbowl was made aromatic. Solemnly taking up three leaves of laurel, the Physician passed each leaf over the old man's nose.

"The wart will be gone in three days time!" he decreed, looking hard in the old warrior's eyes as if he were giving the old soldier a command that couldn't be refused.

Then Turhan Bey took up a pinch of salt from the salt cellar and salted the old man's wart for good measure. The old soldier blinked a little at having his nose salted. But the Physician regained his eye.

"The wart will melt," Turhan Bey announced with the absolute authority of his art since he felt the physic was on very shaky grounds, now sprinkling a bit of water on the offending protuberance, "as salt melts into water."

Shaking with suppressed laughter, Turhan Bey could hardly wait to bolt. Salting the old man's nose, indeed! But once out on the street, his heart sank. What to do when the wart didn't vanish? He let several weeks lapse before he ventured another visit, afraid they'd call him a quack and bolt the door against him, hoping they'd forgotten the shameless practice he'd perpetrated on the old warrior's nose. But the Physician was welcomed with great rejoicing. The wart, as he'd suggested, had melted away!

He still had no scientific explanation for the miracle of the wart, except the great miracle of the human mind itself which, with a little guidance, will perform the inconceivable. Perhaps medicine was not only a science, as he'd previously thought, but also an art.

"Then what hap-hap-hap . . . ?" Hürü asked, although she knew the story by heart.

"The wart your grandfather lost, Sweet Idiot," Turhan Bey teased Hürü, "had to be born again in the form of a little girl."

"True," Hürü said sadly; "I'm a wa-wa-wa . . . a lump."

"No, you are neither a lump nor a wart," her mother said,

caressing her daughter's feet. "You are a wonderful child. Although I wish you'd hold your back straight."

Well, he'd enticed Lady Gülbahar with poetry. Just as he suspected, in the heart of every hearty, arrogant girl slept the longing for a kind of sickness. The more healthy they were and the more natural, the harder they fell for the malady called love, their joyous disposition changing into sighs, their openness into secretiveness. Since the miracle of the wart, Turhan Bey had become a regular at the house. The old warrior introduced him around as the Physician of the Age! And the Physician, he must use his foothold as the base from which to move this immovable girl. Twenty-three years old, an age when other women begin contemplating becoming grandmothers, Lady Gülbahar, aided and abetted by her father, would not marry. She loved her freedom in the house so much, she'd already refused every eligible and ineligible man in town.

He sat down and wrote a poem praising her, a very bad poem that harped on the lover who knows neither night nor sleep, longing for her who is slender as the cane and elegant as a twig of the willow and whose approach obscures for him the constellations in the heavens—nay, the moon itself! Etc., etc. Praying that she wasn't illiterate, he slipped into her hand the poem as he took his leave. And she was so unprepared for any advances from him, since he pretended not to take any notice of her, she took it and, to his gratification, hid the poem in her sleeve.

For six months, he versified diligently so that he could leave her with a poem every evening; she accepted each one without a word.

"I was curious," Lady Gülbahar protested, "to see what idiocies you'd come up with again."

"But you finally slipped a poem into my hand!" he laughed.

"Was it any g-g-good?" Hürü asked.

"Very good indeed!" Turhan Bey said. "Your mother had stolen an entire poem from Yunus Emre and scribbled it out with the worst hand you ever saw. It wasn't even a poem about human love but mystic love for God. At least she showed better taste than I, stealing the whole of a good poem rather than imitating a thousand bad ones. And it was in spoken Turkish. So simple, so clear, it broke your heart."

"We didn't have another book of poems around the house," Lady Gülbahar said in her defense. "And I didn't think you'd recognize my theft since you seemed to go for fancier stuff."

More than him, the Physician always said, she'd fallen in love with her new self who began to understand the mystical poems she copied out so painfully. She loved him for opening an understanding she hadn't expected in herself. Now sure of her love, he asked her father for her hand. The old warrior was outraged. Well, the impropriety of it all! The audacity! All this time while the Physician had been treated with courtesy and friendship, he was really making designs on the daughter of the house. He hadn't brought up his daughter to be wedded to some damn tribesman. Who did he think he was, the lousy Karaman Turk? A no-account physician who worked for *wages* at the Palace. Hell, no! And don't show your face around here again!

That's why Lady Gülbahar was forced to elope with her Physician, a shame that followed her to this day, after all these years of solid and harmonious marriage. The gossips still talked about ancient history; how she'd left home without the benefit of judge or clergy, without dowry or marriage contract, without wedding feast or presents, and consummated her nuptial night in the woods like some common peasant girl. Perhaps it was this history that compelled Lady Gülbahar to run her household with stricter and more conventional customs than she'd enjoyed in her father's house. No more evenings when men and women dined together in the courtyard, celebrating the gifts of this life, conversing on subjects too dangerous for the neighbors. No more galloping about on wild mares; no more copying out love poems, be they addressed to God or men. No more showing her face in public, uncovered and unencumbered with a thousand niceties. None of these for her only child either. Hürü must have religious instruction until it came out of her ears, blocking the heavenly music that tortured her with its beauty.

Yet, her parents were somewhat different than other men and women she came to know. Hürü didn't know how and why. She did know there was some force alive in her house which didn't live in other homes. When out visiting, she couldn't wait to get back so she could breathe again.

Whenever the story of her parents' love and courtship was related, Hürü's older brother always excused himself, saying he had studying to do. Hürü admired her half-brother Mahmut Jan, adored his easy and elegant manner of speaking, his dark and wiry good looks, his somewhat aloof disposition, and his self-assured walk. Mahmut Jan would've preferred studying at the Palace School of

Pages, where the instruction in liberal arts was combined with physical training, the sciences of warcraft and statecraft with the fine arts. But he had to content himself with going to the School of Theology and Islamic Jurisprudence. He loved the life of action, power and passion. But, he complained, he was stuck with making his way in this world through quibbling and nattering, sitting on his behind and watching nothing happen.

The Palace School of Pages was rife with slaveboys of Christian origin, captured, kidnapped, extracted and turned Ottoman. A smart and talented young man might rise to great distinction there. Several in each class could expect to become generals, admirals, ministers, even Grand Vizier, and lead interesting lives full of color and passion. Should a freeborn Turk demand equal opportunity, he'd better watch his head before it was chopped off for him, suspect as he was of ideas of his own, relatives and friends whom, if he came to power someday, he might protect and favor. Never was there a government, Mahmut Jan said, more hostile to its real people; this was the age for slaves and renegades. And he fussed. And he fumed. Mahmut Jan dreamed of an independent state called Karaman and believed he was next in line to its throne; in private, he had Hürü call him "my Lord." Talking with Mahmut Jan was an ordeal.

Hürü suspected she was a princess in her own right, although she never breathed a word about her suspicion, even if she could have without getting her tongue all tangled up. Still, the visage she beheld in her looking glass didn't look like a princess. Princesses were beautiful, talented, smart; they had winsome, demanding, coy and delicate ways. Sweet Idiot, her father called her; she could only pretend to the realm of Idiocy. She was awed by her half-brother's regal ways.

Yet, she worried about Mahmut Jan. She feared for him. He was so arrogant, he wouldn't rest until he got himself into some serious trouble. Her father's father, Karaman Mehmet Pasha, had been just such a man. Appointed the last Grand Vizier to Mehmet the Conqueror as a ploy to appease the rebellion in Karaman, her grandfather had been assassinated by the heartless Janissary corps. The slave soldiery had then borne her grandfather's head on a lance through the streets of Istanbul. Karaman Mehmet Pasha's crime had been his policy of financing foreign wars in devalued currency; whatever that meant, it hadn't been popular with the Janissaries.

Chapter 3

THE WISH

*Hürü longs for a Teacher
worthy of the Name*

They lived on the Golden Horn, just outside the walls of the Palace of the Cannon Gate. Three times a day, some big black eunuch, who acted as if he'd just finished creating the universe, brought them their meals on a tray; removing the silver covers with a flourish, he studied their faces. They oohed and ahhed properly. Soon as the eunuch left, the food was distributed among the mendicants who knew just when to arrive at the back door. Like everyone who was at all connected to the Palace, no matter how small or great a function he performed, Turhan Bey was obliged to receive the Sultan's food. No one could refuse the Sultan's bounty. Otherwise, the Sultan might feel bad and have one strung up.

One might think delectables cooked up in the Palace kitchen would delight the soul and nourish the body, considering how the best ingredients in the world—the rarest, the freshest, the most succulent—were procured as a matter of course. The most renowned chefs prepared the food, consulting with each other, ransacking recipes from people who invented new dishes, or adding personal touches to those already known. But Turhan Bey deemed Palace food unfit for consumption. He felt it was a pity to poison city beggars with so much fat, so much syrup, so many spices; and every time, the beggars were forewarned that the food was dangerous to their

16

health, life expectancy, good humor. They'd be better off with regular poverty food: a few olives, a couple of onions, yogurt and a loaf of bread. But who listens to reason when there's a tray of savories on which to fall?

Turhan Bey said we dig our graves with our own teeth; each time we eat, we die a little. Yet we must eat so we can live. Every food has its detrimental effects as well as its nourishment; one must be sure to eat a little of everything and never grow overly fond of any particular food. The Physician was an expert gardener. He grew many of his own vegetables and fruits and tended an herb garden so pleasing to see that the fame of his herbs spread throughout the city. He grew vulnerary herbs as well as the savory and his knowledge of the curative and preventive virtues of plants and roots was unparalleled. My knowledge is not so extraordinary, Turhan Bey said; for the man who could read, the ancients wrote extensively on their experiments with natural cures. He advised those who came to see his herbs to flavor their foods with herbs instead of spices. But people love their salt and pepper. To those who came seeking help with some magic drug, he advised long-term diets and exercise. But people love their pills.

Hürü, too, had a bed of her own to cultivate. She chose to grow roses for their clear blooms that unfurl on thorny stems. As she slowly learned the nature of roses, Turhan Bey introduced her to one of the Palace gardeners, all of whom were Albanians; it was this gardener who sometimes gave Hürü a cutting from some famous and rare rose to graft on her more humble breeds. She'd even seen the Palace gardens under the auspices of the gardener who constantly reminded her not to giggle or rustle too much, lest she disturb the *odalisques* taking their ease in arbors and elegant *kiosks* within the high fortress walls. The Palace gardens were vast and beautiful. There grew every imaginable plant and fruit; water, fresh, clear and potable, flowed out of fountains, pools, cisterns, over stones so cleverly laid out that the arrangement seemed God's handiwork instead of man's; flocks of birds, both game and ornamental, warbled and chattered in the trees; herds of domestic and wild animals browsed in the woods; and an army of Albanians toiled everywhere. Still, Hürü had eyes for naught but the roses. She hoped life was like the rose: an undistinguished little bush now, and full of thorns, but later, ah, what display!

During her sixteenth spring on this earth, Hürü awaited im-

patiently the festival on the Sixth of May, known and celebrated by
vulgar folk as Hidir-Ilyas. Ever since she learned where the name of
the festival came from, Hürü burned with an inner excitement; she
didn't dare ask her father, who seemed to know everything worth
knowing, fearing that he'd dismiss the truth of the Two Brothers,
called Hidir and Ilyas, as so much *hurafa* invented by the Arabs who
were fond of pleasant lies. This pleasant lie was one she'd rather take
Mistress Kevser's word for: the Two Brothers came from the world
of Wonder, which exists parallel to the one in which we live.

According to the cosmography lesson, beyond the Sea of Darkness, in the southwest corner of this earth, there's a place called
Zulumat, a place of terrors and difficulties, where the Fountain of Life
springs from disgusting and malodorous terrain. It was said Hidir
drank of this fountain, by virtue of which he still lives and will live
until the Day of Judgment. Hidir was a learned, just and saintly
personage who'd been transformed into one of the mysterious
Guardians. Another was his brother, Ilyas, who started out as a
prophet, known to the Jews as Elijah. Some stupid people confused
the two Guardians, saying they were one and the same. According to
Mistress Kevser, most people didn't know their ears from a hole in
the ground; she maintained that Hidir appears to those in dire
distress, clad in green garments. Ilyas, on the other hand, wore all
blue but couldn't be seen.

"If Il-Il-Ilyas can't be seen," Hürü asked, "how do you know he
wears b-b-blue?"

"Stupid girl!" Mistress Kevser snapped her stick on Hürü's
knuckles.

Mistress Kevser went on to explain that Ilyas wanders upon the
seas and directs voyagers who go astray while Hidir perambulates
the mountains and valleys, assisting travellers who don't even know
they're in distress, even before something terrible happens; at night,
the Two Brothers meet together and guard the ramparts of Gog and
Magog to prevent the impish beings who live there from intruding on
their neighbors. One night a year, the night of the Fifth of May, the
Two Brothers don't guard Gog and Magog; instead, they roam the
world by the dark of night and meet, sometime before sunrise, beside
a rosebush. No, no one knows what rosebush; it's a different bush
every year. But if they meet by your rosebush—and you've had the
foresight to hang on its branches a red pouch containing a message
to the Two Brothers—your wish will be granted, since the Brothers

are in a good mood on their only day off from the world's cares when, like everyone else, they, too, enjoy the most perfect day of spring.

"Has Hid-Hid-Hidir ever app-app-app . . . Have you seen him?"

"What do you think?" Mistress Kevser said. "Am I not a most pious Moslem? Haven't I been in terrible distress? Sure, I've seen him. He handed me a pouch of red-gold. For my dowry."

"But you never mar-marr-marri . . ."

"I never married," Mistress Kevser said, "because that brother of mine, God take him, took the pouch of red-gold Hidir gave me."

Somehow Hürü didn't quite believe Mistress Kevser had been blessed by a visitation by either of the Good Brothers; they would be too clever to believe any man would marry Mistress Kevser for the sake of a pouch of gold. Yet, Hürü was determined to hang a red pouch on one of her rosebushes that spring: the Brothers must already know she was a girl truly distressed with a pain she couldn't name.

On the eve of the festival of Hidir-Ilyas, she sat down at her writing tablet, hoping to name the demon who troubled her, the true name for the disposition of mind that prevented her from knowing who she was, or, for that matter, the disposition that kept her from loving her own fate. She couldn't just beg that happiness be granted her; she'd have to do some introspection first.

She wrote for hours. She wrote a thousand drafts of beautiful wishes and destroyed each before she was through with the salutations or the compliments. As midnight approached, in haste and in panic, not bothering with the niceties of spelling and punctuation, she wrote in a terrible hand the first wish that came to her mind, which, by this time, was addled beyond repair.

> give me a Teachr who knos the Beginning
> the Middl and The end

Without taking another look at her wish, she stumbled down the stairs and into the first courtyard where the roses slept in their beds. By the light of her oil lamp, she couldn't perceive which bush to hang her red pouch on with the message stuffed inside. Certainly, on the most beautiful one, the rose that bloomed China-red, a proud rose that had been bred for the Faghfurs of China. But she couldn't find the bush in the bad light, in her excitement, and the fear that someone might wake and discover her secret wish, which would have the effect of annulling it. She was obliged to hang her pouch on

the first rose cane that was awake and pricked her hand. No sooner
was this done than she heard the Frankish clock chime the midnight
hour; she ran inside, lest the Brothers arrive and not stay long
enough to read her wish since she, like some snoop, would still be
hanging around. The Good Brothers could meet anytime between
midnight and sunrise, anywhere in the world at all, and grant anyone
the wish that person's heart most desired.

Now, she must stay up and remove the pouch before the first
rays of sun touched the creation with colors. She fell to praying with
all her heart that it might be Hürü's bush where the designated
meeting took place. But, try as she might, she couldn't see the
rosebush in her mind's eye because she didn't know which one she'd
chosen; soon, her poor head nodded and she fell into a deep sleep.
When she woke with a start, still hunched on her prayer rug and stiff
as a winter bear, the sun had already risen, just a little over the hills
of üsküdar. Oh, no! thought Hürü; now I've done almost everything
wrong!

Turned out, she'd tied the pouch on a rosebush that wasn't
doing at all well! Even now, in the cool of the day, its tender shoots
were being sucked by wet and lascivious clusters of aphids. No one
in his right mind would find pleasure in this poor little bush! She
threw herself beside her pitiful specimen, grinding her forehead in
the damp earth.

◆

Back up the stairs, around the first landing, a hand clutched her
by the neck.

"Coming back from meeting someone?" a voice said. It was
Mahmut Jan's voice. He must have been skulking behind the curtains
again, apprehensive as always that someday the Sultan's mutes
would penetrate the house, slip a greased noose around his princely
neck and strangle him until he was dead. Provided, that is, that the
Sultan knew of Mahmut Jan's secret ambitions. Mahmut Jan didn't
sleep well. He must've thought Hürü was the assassin.

"N-n-no," Hürü gasped. "I was just inspect-inspect- inspect . . .
My Lord, I was looking at the roses."

"Even before you washed your hands and face?" demanded her
brother. "Before you said your prayers? Have you any idea what
happens to girls who make assignations?"

"N-n-no," Hürü said.

Mahmut Jan unsheathed his dagger. His hand still on her throat, he placed its hard, cold point on her breast.

"They get their hearts removed," Mahmut Jan said, "and tossed to the dogs. Where were you then?"

"I was just . . ." Hürü wept, revealing the little silken pouch, "was just . . ."

"Speak up! What is it?"

"Just a w-w-wish," Hürü pleaded. "It's nothing, my Lord."

Before she could caution him not to read her wish, lest it be denied for its being revealed, the pouch had already been opened and the contents read.

"You misspelled *teacher*, *knows*, and *middle*," Mahmut Jan said. "So you're writing to Prodigious Persons now, are you? You stupid girl!"

"Now it will n-n-never come true," said Hürü who felt both violated and relieved of the charges against her modesty.

"You watch it!" he said, his thumb pressing once more on her jugular before he unhanded her. "Women, because their minds are idle, are more depraved than the most depraved man. What women don't have in sense, they make up in deceit."

"Who?" Hürü said. "Me?"

"That's right," Mahmut Jan said. "When the Prophet stood at the gate of Paradise, lo!, most of its inmates were the poor. And when he stood at the gate of Hell, who were most of Hell's inmates?"

"Women," Hürü said, hanging her head.

"That's right," Mahmut Jan said. "Now remember your lesson!"

Chapter 4

THE FIRST THRESHOLD

Hürü Faces the Double-headed
Monster called Lust

For some time now, the Physician and his wife had been seeking the Sultan's permission to travel to Mecca, a request denied every year on account of sickly courtiers. For some reason, that year the health of the courtiers could be left in the hands of God because, at last, the Physician was granted leave to make the difficult journey and make himself a blessed pilgrim. But why did Turhan Bey and Lady Gülbahar wish to risk their lives, health, wealth—such as it was—on the road to Mecca, where it was reputed to be exceptionally hot, and where people not used to the food or water were stricken with terrible cases of the gallops and other unknown diseases? Well, who knows why, really. Going on a pilgrimage was something that was done, provided one had the means, the stamina and the courage. Some pilgrims actually survived the ordeal and, on their return, received the sort of veneration that went with the title of Hadji. Besides, becoming a Hadji provided the pilgrim with a foothold in Paradise, which was populated, as witnessed by the Prophet, by those hounded by poverty during their earthly lives. Going on a pilgrimage, then, for someone not quite so uncomfortable in this life, was a surrogate means of tasting temporary poverty, hardship and humility.

Some guests were sipping refreshing drinks in the grape arbor when the Palace page brought the *ferman* announcing that the Physician and his wife were at last free to travel. Turhan Bey kissed the Sultan's edict and touched it on his forehead (the page was watching intently to see if all protocol was being properly observed). Turhan Bey offered the page a quarter piece of gold, which wasn't accepted until the Physician doubled the remuneration for bearing glad tidings.

"I'll go, too," Mahmut Jan said. "Why not? There's nothing here to keep me. I'll take the semester off, and we'll go by way of Konya."

"Me, too," Hürü said. "I'll go, too."

"No, you won't," her brother said. "You'd be a terrible nuisance on the road and a liability too."

"Your brother's right," Turhan Bey said. "The desert's supposed to be rife with bandits. Apparently, light-complected girls are much prized among these men, who, being dark as sin, either take women by force or else sell them into slavery."

"But I'm not that sort of g-g-girl," Hürü said. And, after casting an apprehensive glance at Mistress Kevser, who'd be sure to get her later, offered an opinion of her own. "There's nothing m-m-much to k-k-keep me here, either."

"You have your studies," her mother said. "Besides, you're pretty enough. And we love you."

Desert-bred Bedouins, the sort of men city-dwelling Arabs were deathly afraid of, profited from crimes against pilgrims, merchants, those travelling in the company of fair women, girls, boys, or those just wandering around in search of wisdom. These Bedouins went free to exercise their worst instincts, the lower halves of their faces wrapped in blue kerchiefs so they might not be recognized as perpetrators and suffer reprisals. Not only did Arab sovereigns have no power to curb these villains, but travel was considered by Arabs as something of a crime itself, ventured only under duress—as observed in many an Arabian exemplary tale. Advice against travel often took the form of a cautionary deathbed speech delivered by some well-heeled father whose amassed capital might tempt his sons to seek wisdom and experience by hitting the road. The stories of a culture, Turhan Bey thought, reflected its values as, for example, tales of Turkish origin in which heroes went questing willingly and far, not only because a nomadic culture makes its living on the road but because having been molded in hardship, the culture comes to cherish the hardship itself.

"One hopes," Lady Gülbahar said, "we won't have to test your theory on the way to Mecca."

The reasons for not taking her along were explained several times more to Hürü. She was too young and not yet worthy of outranking her elders and betters, such as Mistress Kevser who hadn't even stirred out of the neighborhood let alone the City. Besides, Hürü could neither ride nor take care of herself, as could her mother. As a maiden, Lady Gülbahar had excelled in wielding arms and had outdone young men in equestrian games. There was still much manliness left in Lady Gülbahar in her fortieth spring. She had all her teeth in her head yet, and a personal presence that was both imposing and well seasoned. Why, Lady Gülbahar might even end up having to protect her husband against marauders, if it came to an altercation that required strength. As to Mahmut Jan coming along, her brother's presence would aid the pilgrims as well as broaden Mahmut Jan's views. Travel was just the ticket for a young man whose studies had gone somewhat stale on him at the School of Theology and Islamic Jurisprudence.

"My stud-stud-stud . . . they're pretty st-st-stale, too."

"Yet I do worry about leaving you behind, Sweet Idiot," the Physician said. "You know nothing about running a household which, in a sense, is our fault. We've required nothing of you but scholarship."

"Have no fear on that account, Turhan Bey," Mistress Kevser said in her brazen voice. "I will run your household with the same iron-clad hand as you yourself."

"Well, I hope my hand is not quite so iron," Turhan Bey said, reflecting. "But what happens, Mistress Kevser, if, heaven forbid, an occasion arises when you have to deal with the outside world?"

Before Mistress Kevser could brag on her own behalf, how capable she was and how learned, another volunteer sprang up to wrest the helm from the tutoress's pudgy hands.

"What's friendship," asked one of the guests rhetorically, "that won't serve a friend in need?" Properly bearded and trousered, he was the Imam of the Grand Mosque, certainly the most distinguished personage among Turhan Bey's acquaintances. "Please, Turhan Bey, command your obedient servant to undertake the governance of your household. Your servant will do his utmost to provide for your household's needs in your absence."

Although speaking in the third person, the Imam meant himself.

Clerics often practiced this method of self-effacement. The Physician, however, was pleased with the Imam's offer, seeing he could hardly leave his daughter in hands more humane and ethical than the cleric's, who'd risen to the rank of Imam, who was in charge of the Grand Mosque, and who enjoyed the privilege of spiritually guiding the Sultan himself. The Imam was certainly a meritorious fellow and one with well-deserved influence around town. Besides, the Imam had given Mahmut Jan his basic religious instruction when he was but a wee boy.

"I just knew it!" Hürü cried. "My wi-wi-wish won't come true."

"What wish, Sweet Idiot?"

"Oh, nothing," Hürü said, disappointed with life. "I asked for a bet-bet-bet . . . a good teacher."

So, by the end of May, Hürü's parents and brother, with enough retainers to ease the way for the pilgrims, put everything in readiness to depart for Mecca, a trip that would take six months if travelled speedily and without mishap. Turhan Bey left their wills and testaments—just in case the trip proved unpropitious—in the Imam's safekeeping. The governance of the house and his daughter were also confided to the cleric, with absolute authority over disposing and procuring, punishing and rewarding at his discretion. Although tearful, her parents departed with relatively easy hearts, a mule team of provisions, and a son who could hardly wait to get going on an adventure that seemed to him, despite its religious aim, exciting, vigorous and passionate. The trip offered Mahmut Jan a means to his political dreams which lay en route to the province of Karaman.

To Hürü, after her parents' departure, the house seemed robbed of its peace and harmony, the joy and kindness she'd come to take for granted. Strangely, it was she who suffered from terrible homesickness, more poignant than the pilgrims' who might be diverted by new sights and sounds, excitement and challenge. Now, the serene household was transformed into the site of unmitigated gluttony. Mistress Kevser, who took great pleasure in having the servants whip each other for every little offense, let the housecleaning go to pot and, as lint and cockroaches overtook the place, diverted all industry into the kitchen where many fatty, syrupy and spicy dishes were prepared in addition to what still arrived from the Palace. The mendicants, who'd become accustomed to getting fed regularly, were mercilessly beaten and chased away without a mouthful. On top of that, the next time the Imam showed up, Mistress Kevser lodged a complaint against certain city beggars by name who'd been caught pilfering food from the absent Physician's pantry.

Before Hürü could stammer out the truth, the Imam was gone like a shot so he might have the hands of those certain beggars lopped off. Hürü cursed her slow tongue and even slower wits. She couldn't believe the moral laxness in the servants who, though they'd been such a fine crew before, now seemed content with this miscarriage of justice. They kept their mouths shut, Hürü supposed, for the sake of the rich food for which they must've always had a hankering; as for the chaos, the beatings and lies, they must've had a taste for that, too. Hürü felt like a prisoner in her own house.

The Imam took to arriving every evening so he too could partake in the gluttony. He wouldn't eat with Mistress Kevser, seeing that such conviviality wasn't seemly (perhaps because Mistress Kevser's countenance turned the Imam's stomach), but demanded to be served by the daughter of the household all alone in a room overlooking the Golden Horn. Hürü, who was not accomplished in the arts of serving and pleasing, did her simple best to discourage the requirements of the Imam. But he indulged her every shortcoming and showered on her the kind of praise that bordered on flattery. She couldn't fathom the Imam's deference.

Unbeknownst to Hürü, the Imam was dying of passion. Poor child, she had no inkling that the Imam had developed a keen yen for her whom he beheld every day uncovered and whose corrupting innocence compelled a wicked passion in the aging cleric who saw around him, everywhere, unholy motives and black sins. To a man like the Imam, it was Hürü's fault that she inspired in him such a powerful temptation. So much so, even Mistress Kevser noticed he didn't touch the delectables set before him and wore black rings around his eyes. She didn't have to press him much to learn the cause of his apparent enervation. In his line of work, he'd acquired some experience in discerning character. He must have guessed in Mistress Kevser an accomplice.

"I'm burning, Mistress Kevser," he confessed. "I'm dying of passion for that fetching student of yours. But she won't even look in my direction. I am a man in his prime, amply endowed with what pleases women. What does she want? Tell me what I might do to please her insouciant heart."

"Who knows what pleases that clod of a girl!" Mistress Kevser

said testily. "But each to his own taste. To me, she's nothing but a
burden. I'd guide you to her room right this minute where you might
take her by force. But the servants have ears. And their tongues will
wag once the master returns, if he ever does. Still, I might just obtain
her for you; that is, if the price is right."

"Just ask," the Imam said.

"A pouch of red-gold," the Mistress said. "Old gold. I don't want
any new currency debased with God knows what metal."

"Done!" said the Imam, who was dying of Hürü as if she were
some dread disease.

That's how come Mistress Kevser devised the ambush at the
baths. Now, in the Physician's home there was a fine bathhouse
where the inhabitants bathed privately. Turhan Bey had noticed that
mischief always brewed in public baths and that often people who
went there hale and hearty soon after came down with some sickness
or other. So, Hürü had never seen the inside of the famous public
baths of the City, where entertainments took place, where men and
women bathed on separate days, gossiping and singing, eating and
drinking, reclining on the hearthstones and on sofas, bathed by
experts, kneaded and pummelled, massaged with rare oils, their
unwanted hair plucked and depilated, and out of which they came
clean and white as newly laid eggs.

Mistress Kevser, all smiles and affection for once, informed Hürü
that the Chief Sultana had rented the baths for a day so she could
throw the party of the year, replete with musicians from distant
climes, singers of unparalleled talent, and storytellers whose art
could spellbind an audience. Wouldn't Hürü, who'd been invited out
of the court's respect for her father, like to go? If Hürü didn't go,
neither could Mistress Kevser who was dying to partake of the
pleasure, the company, the music. Hürü couldn't imagine what Mistress Kevser wanted with music, she who had a tin ear and the voice
of a crow. But she was tempted to experience the fine art of bathing.
Sure, her father wouldn't like it, remembering how adamant he was
about the baths, but she was curious to see, just for once, what the
baths were like. The presence of famous musicians and storytellers
was an enticement she couldn't resist.

In fact, it was Mistress Kevser herself who'd privately rented the
baths; no guests had been invited, no singers, no storytellers of any
repute. Just an aging man waited at the bath, naked as a plucked
bird, sweating out his humors on the hearthstone.

When they arrived at the baths, both with bundles of clean apparel under their arms, Hürü was amazed at the grace and ornamentation of the entrance hall, the rooms for undressing. But she heard no music, no laughter, and saw no servants or slaves scurrying around with food and drink. Mistress Kevser told her to stop gaping and undress. And the schoolmistress did likewise, exposing the big bags of lard that hung down from her everywhere. When Hürü had nothing on but a towel covering her tender nakedness, the woman excused herself, saying she had to first heed a call of nature.

"You go in," Mistress Kevser said. "I'll be right along."

In the huge chambers under the dome supported by beautifully tiled pillars, Hürü saw no one. Thinking they might have come too early, she approached the hearthstone and, when her eyes became accustomed to the dim light, she perceived on the marble the Imam lying there all exposed, some odd-shaped parts dangling from his body. She froze.

"Come in, delight of my heart," the Imam said. "And sit on the hearthstone so I may lave your alabaster skin with my own hands."

Hürü wondered what was meant by "laving"; she suspected it was something she might not like. She ought to do something to gain time, at least until Mistress Kevser showed up and explained to her the meaning of an Imam all naked and ready to lave.

"With your p-p-permission, Mr. Imam, Sir," Hürü said, "let m-m-me l-l-l . . . wash you first, Imam Sir, Mr. Imam."

"One doesn't call an Imam mister," the Imam said laughing, delighted by her twisted tongue. "*Imam* is already a title an intelligent and perceptive cleric earns. But you call me Muhterem, my given name, so I may hear it on your sweet tongue. And then I will lie down before you so you may lave me for all eternity—nay, so that we may lave each other tenderly on this day when we become as one."

"You first," Hürü said, "Muh-Muh-Muh . . . Mr. Imam, Sir."

Laughing and indulging the object of his desire, the Imam reclined on the hearthstone so Hürü might begin with his back. Merciful God! Hürü thought. How is it that you've made men so ugly? So repulsive? And with so much black hair on their butts? With such enlarged pores and so much stinky sweat? And what's that organ that hangs?

Gaining control over her trembling and revulsion, she filled the brazen washbowl with hot water only and poured it all over the Imam's head.

"Ouch!" cried the Imam. "Mix some cool water with the hot, my love." But Hürü mixed only a little cold water, keeping the Imam's bath too hot for anyone to retain his wits for long. Bowl after bowl, quickly and with all her might, she laved him in the awful heat so he might be dazed and fall prostrate from exhaustion. Soon as she noticed him turn a kind of purplish red, she applied the huge cake of soap on his razor-stubble hair, now thumping, now banging the man's heavy head, now with the soap, now with the bronze bowl, until she was sure he'd either completely passed out or else was somewhat dead.

Without inquiring any further into the Imam's state of health, she hurried out of there, put on her clothes and, in the absence of Mistress Kevser whose bundle was gone, she hoped she could remember the way home.

"So!" said her shameless teacher when Hürü returned all flushed and still trembling. "Did you have a good time?"

"N-n-no," Hürü said, hoping the Imam was too dead to tell on her.

So, imagine Hürü's surprise when the Imam turned up in the evening, looking dark as a thunderhead, his mouth a dried prune, but quite distastefully present in the world.

"I've written your father a letter," he informed Hürü, "telling him all. He should receive the letter when he arrives at Baghdad."

Hürü wondered how the Imam had explained his own behavior. And what did he say to complain about her? Your daughter bathed me too much? But she was glad he seemed so cold to her now, that he no longer wished to be attended by her, saying she was a wretch and a clod, quite undeserving of a man's finer sentiments. Well, if he couldn't take the heat, let him keep out of the baths! Not being the object of some Imam's affections suited Hürü fine. She could easily put up with Mistress Kevser's tortures until her parents returned home.

Chapter 5

BROTHER-BATTLE

Mahmut Jan will not share Destiny with a mere girl

Meantime, on the road to Mecca, the pilgrims detoured to Baghdad, which city, it was said, had to be seen to be believed. The easier half of the journey had been done, and Turhan Bey thought it advisable they should acquaint themselves with the famous metropolis now—just in case—and take in the sights, a show or two, talk to the natives and learn what they did, what they thought. Of course the pilgrims could not but compare Baghdad to the City; and everywhere, in every way, Baghdad scored second best. Istanbul was just better endowed by nature, sweeter, cleaner, the greens greener, the blues bluer, the architecture more graceful and various, the waters of the Bosphorus clear and invigorated with salt.

The great River Tigris that flowed through Baghdad, in the travellers' estimate, was just too murky. The fish in the Tigris were ugly and fuscous as mudpuppies; should a morsel of food be thrown in the river, the river teemed and boiled with fish vying with each other hellishly. The bridges over the water seemed to dominate the street life; the denizens idled on the bridges, watching pleasure boats, commercial barges and fishing vessels, trafficking, chatting, listening to hawkers and musicians, kicking beggars, indulging madmen, eating, spitting and fulfilling more private bodily functions. The pilgrims saw a big Arab squat on the bridge, spread his robe around him, cut up a melon and eat it, enjoying himself thoroughly; just as they were about to comment on the Arab's contentment, the man rose to go. The pilgrims were shocked by the pile he left on the bridge.

"Dear God!" the Physician exclaimed. "I don't suppose they wear any underdrawers."

The Physician decided the city of Baghdad was like an ancient whore whereas Istanbul, although once widowed, was still a wholesome matron a man could take to his heart as well as to his marriage bed. Baghdad was just too old and too used; the paint on her face peeling everywhere, toothless, sagging, the suggestive words in her mouth so foul they turned off a man instead of inspiring him with longing. Turhan Bey shivered to see the *jinks*, dancing boys made up as girls, gyrate on the street to the sounds of drums and cymbals.

"We are still a young people," he told his wife. "A vigorous people. We're staunch and skeptical. Most importantly, we guard our privacy and dignity."

Here, the music was sadder, the religion showier, the politics dirtier, the poor poorer, the rich richer, the food greasier, the animals mangier, the corrupt more corrupt, the sick sicker and, worst of all, the streets narrower.

"Does that mean, then," Lady Gulbahar wondered, "that what's good about Baghdad is even better?"

The Physician couldn't say; he hadn't yet seen what was good about Baghdad. They returned to the caravanserai where the Physician observed that the inns in Baghdad were, literally, lousier. As he groused over the meal he was served, a boy brought him a letter.

"Imagine that!" exclaimed the Physician. "A letter all the way here!" He had his son, who spoke Arabic more fluently, ask the innkeeper by what method the letter had arrived. He was amazed to hear it had been delivered by teams of homing pigeons.

"The postal service is better," he told his wife, enormously pleased by the reliability of air mail.

The contents of the letter, however, didn't please him at all; in fact, he sighed and said that it was true bad news travelled fast and found its destination. Good news, chances were, would invariably fall in the hands of those for whom it was not intended. Then, they all read and reread the Imam's letter, stunned and scarcely comprehending the meaning of such accusations.

"Simple," Mahmut Jan said. "My sister's taken this opportunity to paint the town red. She won't heed the Imam's admonitions but goes to the baths and lets sailors in the house."

"Hürü's just a child!" Lady Gülbahar said, weeping.

"You never know what women are like," her stepson said, "until you leave them to their own devices."

"Not Hürü! Not my daughter!" the Physician exclaimed. "But how can the Imam's letter be explained?"

"Why should he accuse her falsely?" interjected Mahmut Jan, the logician and the budding practitioner of jurisprudence.

"What's a father to do?" the Physician said, wringing his hands.

"Simple," Mahmut Jan suggested. "I return home posthaste and discover the truth of the matter."

"I won't have my daughter slandered and suspected!" Lady Gülbahar exploded.

"No one has sentenced her," Mahmut Jan said, "not yet! We all know what justice demands from wayward daughters."

"Not her life!" Lady Gülbahar exploded again through her tears. "Not my own true baby!"

Eventually, a sad consensus was reached. The parents should continue on the way to Mecca; but Mahmut Jan should return to Istanbul and fetch Hürü so they might all meet again in Baghdad at this very inn. Then, and only then, could Hürü be given the third degree. Mahmut Jan should never, never, under any circumstance, attempt to take the law in his own hands. He must not divulge anything to Hürü, lest, if the accusation prove false, her sensibilities be damaged. He must tell Hürü only that her parents had become so lonesome for her, they could not stand her absence. This decided, the party separated at the city gates to go on their opposite journeys, the son to find out the truth in earthly concerns, the parents the truth in the spiritual.

Well, Mahmut Jan travelled fast as his spurs could inspire the fresh horses he obtained along the way; he rode hard, and he rode furious, catching only forty winks now and then; he rode like a messenger carrying to the Sultan a head on which there was a reward. He was back on the Asian shore of Istanbul in a mere fortnight! Dead tired, pissed as all hell, dirty and uncomfortable, he sat on his horse and beheld for some time the sun roll behind the slender minarets that rose into the European skyline of the City of Two Continents. He listened to the calls to evening prayer which travelled across the sound of the Bosphorus lapping his horse's hooves, and he wept with an emotion he couldn't name.

As Mahmut Jan had himself rowed across the Bosphorus, he decided he shouldn't just walk straight into the house. He ought to first subject his sister to a test. So he took lodgings at an inn near his own neighborhood and bought himself the clothes of a ruffian in order to disguise himself. As soon as night fell and the Imam quit the house, he went and knocked on the door. And acting the part of a drunken sailor, he rapped and hollered, demanding of the servant that he be conducted to the daughter of the house. The servant wouldn't let him in, telling him to scram; and much more besides. But he insisted so loudly and drunkenly that the servant cautioned him to shut up before he roused the whole neighborhood and got himself the severe beating he deserved. Finally Hürü, who herself had just suffered a thrashing from Mistress Kevser for having been rude to the Imam, was called to the door. Mahmut Jan could hear his sister sniffle behind the heavy portals. Well, maybe she has a cold, he thought.

"Open up!" he said in the rudest accents he could muster. "And I promise to give it to you! I'll give it to you like you never had it before!"

"Go away," Hürü said from behind the door, although she wondered what it was the man was selling. "We don't w-w-want any."

He insisted; she refused. She wouldn't even open the peephole. The contest of wills went on until he gave up and went away. But he wasn't through. The next night, thinking maybe the fellow he impersonated the night before seemed too lowlife for her taste, he disguised himself as an amorous merchant and arrived more discreetly. Once his sister came to the door, he gave her some cock-and-bull story about having met her parents in Baghdad, who'd taken such a liking to him that they'd offered in marriage their only daughter. He had come to court her before he committed himself to a life of happiness for which, undoubtedly, she too longed. Would she please let him in?

"No," Hürü said. "My p-p-parents aren't here."

"I know, Sweet Idiot!" he said, biting his tongue for the slip. "That's why I'm here. We could make some time together until the old folks return."

Hürü wondered why strangers had taken to knocking on the door of late. Besides, how did this merchant know to call her stupid in the familiar and tender way?

"I don't want to make t-t-time," she said. "What t-t-time I have is troub-troub-troub . . . bad enough."

So he went away again, having proven nothing but that his sister had taken to neither fellow. The third night, he arrived as a travelling musician and promised her many new songs if she let him in. She weakened momentarily and requested that he play a sample out on the street. He complied and played on the saz a song he'd learned in Baghdad. As he sang, he laid on the passion thick.

"Very s-s-sad," Hürü said from behind the door. "But p-p-pretty. Come back when my p-p-parents return."

"I'm your brother, you silly goose!" Mahmut Jan said. "Don't you even recognize my style of playing?"

"My brother's on pilgrim-pilgrim . . ." Hürü said. "He isn't here."

"But I am Lord Mahmut Jan!" he said. "Don't you know my voice?"

"Go away," Hürü said. "And don't c-c-come back."

"Open the peephole so I may stick in my ring finger," Mahmut Jan said. "If you don't recognize my signet ring, you may have my finger cut off."

"Oh, all right," Hürü said.

It was Mahmut Jan's signet ring. The door opened and Hürü's arms were wound around her brother's neck; as he tried to wrest his shoulder away from her hot tears, he was touched by the girl's affection for him while he himself had been thinking about her some evil black thoughts. Once he bathed, put on clean clothes and ate what Hürü prepared for him with her own hands, Mahmut Jan informed her that she was to accompany him to Baghdad where their parents would join them. The folks were sick with longing for Hürü.

"Going as far as Baghdad will make you half a pilgrim," he said, "so you'll be half-blessed in God's eyes."

"Whee!" Hürü said, jumping for joy. "I'm going on half a pilgrimage!"

And, without stuttering or blushing one bit, she repeated her news as she ran through the house, hugging each servant, and, dizzied by her incredible good fortune, she was even moved to blow a hand-kiss to Mistress Kevser. The latter was relieved enough that the girl seemed to have forgotten about the fiasco at the baths, assured, once more, that the girl couldn't hold two conflicting thoughts in her mind at the same time. When Hürü settled down at last, her brother made for them their travel plans; they'd leave before sunrise, she only taking one change of clothes, and they'd ride hard until they arrived at Konya. There, they'd take a few days' rest.

"I just l-l-love you," Hürü said. "I love you to p-p-pieces."

"Well, control yourself, then," Mahmut Jan said, frowning. "It isn't seemly to gush."

"Would that my Lord forgive me," Hürü said, "I have a confess-confess . . . I have something to tell you. I didn't know it was you the first night. The s-s-second night, I sus- I sus- I sus . . ."

"You suspected something," Mahmut Jan said, "because I let 'Sweet Idiot' slip from my tongue."

"Yes," Hürü said. "Tonight, I knew it was you, preten-preten-preten . . . making like a musician. And if you came again tomorrow night as someone, I was going to have the s-s-servants give you a good basti-basti . . . a severe beating."

"You'd have a legitimate Prince of Karaman bastinadoed?" Mahmut Jan said. "Knowing, all the time, his true identity?"

"Would you vex a prin-prin-princess of the same?" she replied.

"You've grown since we left, haven't you?" Mahmut Jan said, inspecting her querulously. "One just hopes it's for the better."

Hürü didn't ride as badly as she expected. After a bit of basic instruction from Mahmut Jan, she was up and away. Horses just took to her as if they sniffed something in her of a horse sense. Perhaps riding came naturally to all Turkoman people. Who knew. But what countryside! The freedom of it all took Hürü's breath away. She'd never been so happy in her life. She forgot even to mention the scene with the Imam at the baths. Who could dwell on shameful incidents when life was so wonderful? She loved cooking and eating camp food, stopping at little inns, talking to peasants with open faces and hospitable ways. She could travel all her life, never stopping anywhere for long but sleeping under the big sky as the stars just dripped on her, the mercy of God sustained her, blessed her with the whole creation.

She couldn't believe the vastness of the Konya plain where, in the height of summer, the wheat waved and billowed in the wind like a spun-gold ocean. She expected, any minute, a magic galleon to appear in the fields, on which she'd sail the oceans of ripe wheat for all of eternity. The peasants who worked in the fields, browned men, women big with child, children redcheeked as fresh apples, soon as they spied the two horsemen on the horizon, came by the roadside with water jugs, cheeses and fruits so the travellers might refresh themselves. And they asked questions a child might about a place called Istanbul where the streets were paved with gold. Was it really true? And what was the name of the present Sultan? Was he a good man, then? And could anyone walk into the big tent and put to him a question? Hürü felt very, very smart.

When they had but half a day's journey left to the holy city of Konya, the half brother and sister camped for the night in a piney wood in the middle of which was a charming lagoon secreted from casual travellers. Hürü had never slept as soundly as she did on the forest bed of pine needles which smelled sweet and felt warm on her skin. But Mahmut Jan spent the most hellish night of his life, considering and reconsidering, debating, accusing, clearing, changing his mind, accusing again, deliberating, rebutting, condemning, sentencing. And when Hürü woke up with a great big smile on her face, he'd already prepared the rope.

He took her by the arm and led her to the ancient pine tree that had dipped one big toe in the water; without saying anything, he proceeded to tie Hürü to that tree.

"But . . . but," Hürü said.

"God forgive you," he said, "for I can't."

"But . . . but," Hürü said.

"For the life of me, I can't decide if you're innocent," he said; "if you are, then help will surely materialize. I don't plan to join the folks in Baghdad at all. I have business to attend to in Konya. You know how important that business is, how I must fulfill my destiny."

"But . . . but," Hürü said.

"God help you," Mahmut Jan said, "and keep you."

And tying her horse's reins to the saddle of his own horse, he sprang up, dug his spurs in the animal's sides and, in a cloud of dust, he was off—and out of the picture.

"But I didn't even get break-break-break . . ." Hürü explained to the ancient tree against which she was pressed and tied. "I didn't even get to eat, old man."

Chapter 6

*F*IRST *G*LIMPSE
OF THE *W*ORLD *N*AVEL

The Good Brother,
the Helpful Shepherd, the Cruel Prince

*G*oing without breakfast," the tree said, "certainly ruins the morning. We must see what we can do about getting some."

Hürü whipped her head around and saw she was tied fast to a venerable gentleman with intense green eyes, swathed in green robes, a huge green turban on his head. Even his beard and skin seemed tinged with green.

"Excu-excu-excu . . . look here, Sir," she said. "I don't want to offend you, but weren't you a tree a moment ago?"

"I may have seemed a tree to the young man who tied you to me," the green gentleman said. "But you knew at once I wasn't a tree, didn't you? You called me an old man, which, obviously, is what I am."

"But I often s-s-speak to things," Hürü said. "I always have. Things don't mind if I stam-stam-stam . . . if I don't speak so good."

"People's hearts," the green old man said, "can be heard much more clearly than their words. Things listen to people's hearts."

"My brother," she said, "he seemed fine last n-n-night."

"So he did," the old man said. "But we can't stand tied together like this, can we?"

"No," Hürü said. "We haven't even been intro-intro- intro . . . we don't even know each other."

"But we do," the green gentleman said. "I know who you are. And you know who I am."

"So tell me," Hürü said. "Who am I? I'd really like to know."

"You are one who's been noticed," the old man said, "and found desirable. We have designs on you."

"Oh, no!" Hürü said. "No, you don't! Not again! I've had it with dirty old men."

"Our design is not the Imam's," the green old man said. "You've been deemed a desirable Friend."

"How do you know about the Imam?" Hürü said, astounded. "I've told no one!"

"I don't know what made me mention the Imam," the personage said, "seeing I don't know any Imams. All I know is that we're tied together, and you, being the younger and more flexible, ought to do something about it. Can you bend at the knees and twist a little?"

"Sure," Hürü said.

And the knots all fell loose. Like her tongue. She wasn't even aware she'd stopped stuttering in the presence of the green old man.

"About breakfast," the green old man said. "See that brindle cow approach? Her udders are heavy with milk."

"Now what am I to milk her into?" Hürü said. "Into my skirt? Even if I knew how to milk a cow, I need a container. Have you something I might use?"

But when she turned around to chide the silly old man further, she saw that she was only speaking to herself. There was no old man in the piney woods, just herself and a brindle cow approaching. She began to stutter again.

"P-p-pardon me, mad-mad-madam," she said to the cow. "But I'm fam-fam-fam . . . I'm awful hungry."

The cow mooed sweetly and stopped beside Hürü, her beautiful eyes regarding Hürü as if they'd always known each other. She didn't seem adverse to being suckled at all, even though this calf of a girl was so gauche going about it.

"Oh, that was good," Hürü said, wiping her mouth. "Maybe you could h-h-hang around until I think of something."

The cow settled down to chew the cud. Hürü looked around to see what else was around that might sustain her. There were wild raspberry bushes along the edge of the lagoon, but the birds had already harvested them. Perhaps she should move on to where people were settled; yet, she feared that without her brother, folks might treat her differently. She was dressed in inappropriately rich clothes that might give people ideas.

"There must be a way, sweet l-l-lady," she said, petting the charming white mark on the cow's forehead. "But what?"

That's when the shepherd showed up, a slight young man who kept looking left and right and shouting: "Hullo-a! Hullo-a!"

"Ah, there you are!" he said, seeing the brindle cow take her ease beside Hürü. "Let's go, lady!"

"She's a good l-l-lady," Hürü said. "I had a little of her m-m-milk. Do you mind?"

"Her milk's sweet and rich," the shepherd said. "May it give you good health. But she's some lady, that one, always running away. She has a mind of her own, Lady Gülbahar does."

"What?" Hürü said. "Is that the c-c-cow's name?"

"Yup," the shepherd said, "that's who she is."

"But that's my m-m-mother's name."

"Could be," he said.

The shepherd shifted from foot to foot. He was a shy fellow who didn't even look Hürü in the eye; he perhaps knew as little about the etiquette of the situation as did Hürü. His dour face and natural politeness inspired Hürü with an idea.

"What do you s-s-s-ay we exchange appar-appar-appar . . . our duds?" she said. "You take my caf-caf-caftan and my riding trous-trous- trous . . . my pants. And I'll wear your v-v-vest, your shirt and whatever you c-c-call those bag-bag-baggy things."

"My *shalvar*?" said the shepherd, astounded. "But it's dirty, worn and too scratchy for the likes of you."

"That's all right," Hürü said. "I can t-t-take it."

"But you're wearing rich stuff," the shepherd said. "Gold embroidery, is it? And is that what they call silk?"

"Yes," Hürü said.

"But a man shouldn't take advantage of someone's youth," the shepherd said. "It's not right. You really want to give it all up for these old rags?"

"Yes," Hürü said.

"Turn your back, then," he said. "A man doesn't want himself watched undressing, does he now?"

"I'll turn my back," Hürü said. "You do the same."

When they were done with the complicated business of exchanging clothes without offending each other's sense of propriety, Hürü thought the shepherd looked like a prince in her clothes.

"You sure you're not really a gentle-gentle-gentle . . . ?" she said.

"A real oaf, I am," the shepherd said, fingering the fine materials he had on. "A hayseed dressed in some fancy finery. Bet you this stuff's what they wear in Paradise."

"How do I look?" Hürü said.

"Awful," he admitted. "An eyesore."

"What's that thing dang-dang-dangling from your hand?" Hürü said. "I meant to ask you before."

"That's what's called a sheep's bladder," he said. "You make cheese in it."

"That so?" Hürü said. "Let's see it."

Looking the bladder over, another idea came to Hürü.

"Can I have it?" she said. "I really n-n-need it."

"Cost you your earrings," the shepherd said, getting to be quite the barterer by the minute.

"Oh, take them," she said. "So heavy, they never gave me anything but head-head-head . . . a pain in the head. Wear them in good health."

"What do you think I am, now!" the shepherd said, hurt. "They aren't for me but for a girl I know. These real stones?"

"Rube-rube-rubies," she said. "And take these boots to her."

"Real gold studs in them boots?"

Hürü nodded.

"Imagine!" he said. "Just imagine my girl!"

"Pretty?" Hürü said. "Your girl."

"Ohhh!" he said.

Hürü wound her long red tresses into a twist on top of her head. "Now help me get this blad-blad-blad . . . this sheep thing on top of my hair."

"This real hair?" the shepherd said.

"Now, what do you think?" Hürü said.

"Never seen color like that, not on folks' heads. Spun-carrots."

"Yes," Hürü said sadly. "Unfor-unfor-unfor . . . it's too bad."

The bladder in place, the improbably colored hair was now completely covered by the repulsive membrane which hugged her head like a second skin, looking more like a terrible scruffy and mangy scalp which showed no signs of any hair ever growing back.

"How do I l-l-look now?"

"Worse yet," the shepherd said. "Folks will chase you and make fun of you, thinking you have some awful mange on your head. Nobody'll want to look at you even. They'll prod you with a stick, like they do to them lepers."

"That's good," Hürü said.

"Your business," the shepherd said.

They thanked each other for being one another's stroke of good fortune, shook hands, while Hürü kissed the cow's snout once more. Then they separated to go their opposite ways: the shepherd and Lady Gülbahar back to their summer grazing grounds, and Hürü back on the road to Baghdad.

Hürü had taken but a few steps on the road when she saw a whirlwind approach like a *jinni* materializing in the dust. In fact, she knew it was a *jinni*, considering how those creatures were supposed to hang around crossroads, waiting to pounce on unwary travellers. She ran back into the woods, furiously stuttering anti-*jinn* formulas— *Hadid!* *Hadid!* and *Dastur ya mubarak!*—in Arabic because *jinn* weren't linguists enough to learn a second language. One mentioned iron because *jinn* hated that metal so much even the name gave them the willies. And one begged "Permission, ye blessed!" hoping flattery would do the job. Doing her verbal utmost, Hürü ran back, deep into the woods and scrambled to the firry top of the tree that had become an old man, who had turned back into a tree.

The *jinni*, it turned out, was only a game animal and a wild horseman giving it chase; the rider, soon as he had a good aim in the little clearing by the lagoon, let loose an arrow which whizzed by Hürü's tree like God's wrath. The charming animal with soft brown fur mottled on the back slipped on its knees as if falling to prayer; its almond-shaped black eyes glanced up to the heavens for a moment, then, without uttering a cry, it expired. It must be a gazelle, Hürü thought, or else a hart, poor thing. How quickly a creature dies!

The hunter dismounted, crying "Ahh!", and sprang down next to the dead animal. With what seemed like awesome strength, he pulled his arrow out of the animal's throat. "Ahh!" he said again. He threw down his bow and jewel-encrusted quiver beside his victim, groaned, scratched his armpits, stretched, and, of all the trees in the woods, he chose to lean his back on the trunk of the tree in which Hürü was hiding. Soon, she heard him snore.

Drat, Hürü thought, I'm stuck up this tree! Who knows how long this beastly person will sleep. She thought she might climb down the other side of the trunk without waking him. But what if she shook loose a cone and hit the sleeper on the bean? Better wait, she told herself. The person just slept on and on. The sun made its way up to the zenith. If he keeps this up, night will fall, and I'm not yet on the road, Hürü thought. What rotten luck!

She noticed she was scratching like a beggar. Her back was on fire, her thighs, her buttocks. She realized, in alarm, that the shepherd's clothes must've been full of vermin who were feasting on her fair skin. Trying very hard not to disturb the tree, she ripped the clothes off her back, thinking she'd wash the lot soon as the hunter was gone, dry them, and then be on her way. Then her head began to crawl. The more she thought about it, the more it crawled. She tore the stinky bladder off her hair which came tumbling down her shoulders. There she was up a tree, naked as the angels who don't have to wear clothes, not having, as they don't, any shameful parts. But Hürü had plenty of shame to conceal. Hope I don't start sneezing, she thought, and wake the snorer below. I'm not doing well at all! And I thought I was so smart, dreaming up the exchange of clothes.

Just as hunger bells began to peal again in her belly, the stranger below, giving off a loud but arrested snore, awoke as suddenly as he had fallen asleep. Groaning and yawning luxuriantly, he rose, and fell on his face before the lagoon to drink deeply. Hürü, who'd tasted the lagoon water and spat it out because it was so salty, peeked out of the branches that hung over the water to see how the stranger would deal with mouthfuls of brine. Apparently, he didn't like the taste either. The man had stopped drinking, but he just stayed where he'd dropped to his knees to drink, without any movement at all, as if waiting for the ripples he'd caused to becalm themselves. He seemed to be watching the ripples grow out of their circles. Maybe he just died there! Hürü thought; the poor ruffian has just expired. Merciful God took away his soul!

But she was mistaken. The man rose vigorously and turned his face up, scanning the trees. Hürü pulled herself deep into the fir.

"Who's there?" he shouted alarmingly. "Show yourself!"

Oh my God! Hürü thought; he knows I'm here! He must've seen my naked reflection! And, with what might be extrahuman speed, she put the lousy clothes back on. The branches shook because the man was already climbing the tree. She'd barely got the bladder back over her head when his head appeared in the lower branch.

"Who's there?" he bellowed again.

"Just us b-b-birds," Hürü said.

"Come down, bird!" the man said. "Or I'll spit you on my sword and roast you for lunch!"

Soon as she slipped down to the lower branch, his hand gripped her throat.

"What were you doing up there, bald boy?" he said.

"I . . . I . . ." Hürü said.

He released his grip a little, but his thumb still pressed on her jugular vein. It was a terror reminiscent of another.

"Speak up then!"

"Just a b-b-boy," she said. "A bald boy."

"Ugh!" the man said, removing his hand from Hürü's throat to rub it on his clothes. "How did you get to be so repulsive?"

"Just b-b-born that way, I guess," she said.

"Mercy!" he said. "Will you take a look at that furfuraceous scalp! What's your name, boy?"

"Bald Boy," Hürü said. "That's my n-n-name."

"That's no name!" the man said. "That's the boy in a fairy tale. You know the one I mean."

"No," Hürü said. "But tell it."

"If you think I'm someone who'll sit up in a tree, telling some boy without a proper name a fairy tale," he thundered, "then think again, Bald Boy! I have a province to govern, a throne to seize, and thousands and thousands of men to kill."

"Oh, my!" Hürü said. "Right now?"

"In due time, Bald Boy," he said, laughing. "In due time. Now, get down, you worthless sneak, so you may pray before I chop off your ugly head."

"But . . . but . . ." Hürü said.

"You're fond of your ugly head, are you?" he said, roaring with laughter. "I tell you, you'd be better off without it. You want your head spared, do you?"

"Yes, please," Hürü said.

He laughed as if he'd die from some colossal joke; Hürü just couldn't see the humor. When they got down the tree and stood sizing each other up, she took a good look at her tormentor. He was not a tender youth, nor was he a man who'd worn away too many years. He must be what people called a man in his prime. A huge man dressed in a leather tunic, leather breeches and boots, he seemed to keep his apparel simple if she discounted the jewel-encrusted quiver and the bejeweled hilt that showed on top of the fancy scabbard that hung at his side. His complexion was what Hürü's father called choleric. Yet, his mouth was red and sensitive under his neatly upturned moustache. No beard on his chin which a foe might seize; his hair, Hürü suspected, under the small white turban, was probably shaven clean. But the remarkable thing about him was his eyes. Gray and luminous, but fierce as a hawk's which don't focus quite like a human being's, they had that crazed look of a bird of prey.

"I am *mean*, Bald Boy!" he bragged.

"You're a little cross-cross-cross . . . you're a bit wall-eyed, that's what," Hürü said, thinking if she were to die, she might as well die telling him he wasn't quite so perfect himself.

"That's true," he said. "A little imperfection that haunted all my ancestors worth their salt. But do you know how many people have bit the dust for mentioning that little defect?"

"Thousands?" Hürü suggested.

"None," he said, laughing again. "Because, so far, none dared. Come now, Bald Boy, let us go to Konya," he said. "Spring up behind me. But don't rub that head of yours on my back!"

"But . . . but . . ." Hürü said. "I'm on the road to Baghdad."

"Forget Baghdad now," he said. "I'll take you there when I conquer Baghdad. For now, I want you for my page and licensed fool. Oh, God Almighty, how you'll turn everyone's stomach!"

"No, thank you."

"You refuse?" he said, his hand moving to the hilt of his sword.

Hürü sprang up on the pillion. But she'd seen the bleeding gashes in the sides of the black stallion. She caressed the animal's rump as if she could make up for what he'd suffered from his master.

"Who are you?" she asked. "And why are you so c-c-cruel?"

"I'm cruel because my name's Selim," he said. "Prince Selim of the House of Osman, the governor of Konya, and heir-unapparent to the throne."

"But you want to app-app-appear?" she said.

"That's right, droll boy!" he laughed. "And I will!"

"But . . . but . . ." Hürü said. "Aren't you going to take that poor beast you k-k-killed?"

"Some peasant will luck out," he said. "Or else, the wolves will have themselves a feast. I don't kill because I need meat."

Chapter 7

MAN'S WORLD

Disguised as a boy,
Hürü finds a place in Prince Selim's life

*A*ll in all, the life of the fool in Prince Selim's court, which was more like a garrison, wasn't too bad. No ladies around, of course, just travelling whores or those who, under duress, were made into whores. A man's world. Life around Selim was eventful and stimulating; it exploded with recklessness, florid gaiety, brutal gusto.

Hürü couldn't understand how the Prince could be two such different men at the same time: in him the instinctual barbarian coexisted with the cultivated scholar. He devoted himself to literature and grammar with the singlemindedness of a seminarian; he'd written a book of odes in Persian (the language of a people he hated as being effeminate and whose eventual and total demise he assiduously planned); he liberally patronized learned men and dervishes at the Mevlana Institute of Konya, engaging in their conversations with becoming hostility. But, if he felt like it, he'd lop off the learned man's head at whose feet he'd gleaned knowledge only the night before. Everybody, but everybody, was expendable. They lived perilously. Perhaps it was the constant undercurrent of danger, Hürü thought, that made life around Selim so interesting, each moment so full of itself.

Hürü slept on a mat just outside the Prince's bedchamber, just in case he couldn't sleep, or he was bored and wanted to do some laughing at her expense. Hürü didn't have to think up comedy material; just being herself amused the Prince. Her appearance as the most unfortunate of men, she guessed, must tickle his funny bone in which ran a thick marrow of cruelty. She was an endangered Bald Boy for sure; any minute, he might grow tired of her scabby head, her foul smell, and the way she scratched all the time. She'd already had a brush.

One night, as Selim paced his room restlessly, Hürü had the misfortune to laugh.

"What's so funny, Bald Boy?" Selim roared. "You find my pacing comic perhaps?"

Hürü quickly excused herself and told the Prince she'd just happened to think of a joke with which a Bektashi dervish had been amusing the Mevlevi dervishes at the Dergah that afternoon. Further, she observed, it was interesting that one order of dervishes praised God by clowning while the other did so by whirling around in ecstatic dance.

Well, the Prince must hear this joke! He ordered her to go at once and bring the funny dervish to his bedchamber. She found the comedian at the local wineshop where he was entertaining the drunks. On the way over, having heard how it happened that the Prince desired a command performance, the Bektashi dervish made Hürü an offer. Whatever reward the Prince saw fit to give the Bektashi for his joke, one third of the reward would go to Hürü.

"After all, it was you who brought my joke to the Prince's attention," said the Bektashi. "Otherwise, I'd have entertained the drunks all night. How about it, Bald Boy?"

Hürü agreed, thinking it might be nice to have a few coins jingling in her pocket; Selim gave her nothing for all the amusement she provided. Perhaps sharing in the Bektashi dervish's reward might start the seeds of an escape fund. She thanked the dervish for thinking of her.

Brought to the chamber, the funny man performed admirably, for he was a true professional. Selim did not laugh. He didn't even move a muscle in his somber face. He just stared at the poor joker with those crazed eyes of his, his brow gathering thunderheads by the minute.

"You done?" Selim finally shouted at the dervish. "Your reward is three hard blows for making up stupid jokes when you seem smart enough to do something useful with your life."

He dealt the Bektashi such a blow, the holy joker went flying into the Prince's pisspot. Selim waited for the dervish to extricate himself and rise to the occasion of the second blow; this time he sent the befouled Bektashi tumbling backwards.

"Wait, my Prince!" cried the Bektashi dervish, who could no longer rise anyway. "The third blow is due your Bald Boy, on account of an agreement he made with me."

Once informed of the condition of the agreement, Selim laughed until he fell over backwards. Then, pulling himself together, Selim dealt Hürü the blow that was coming to her, so hard she flew out of the open window and into some prickly bushes. Selim was so pleased with his antics, he gave the dervish a pouch of gold with which the holy joker disappeared far from Konya, and without giving Hürü her share. Hürü couldn't walk for two days; nor did she laugh again for a long, long time.

Another fearful moment arrived, although not unforeseen by Hürü, when Selim ordered her to go see his physician, a local Jew who'd won the Prince's trust in medical matters. The physician would surely recognize the bladder as something that just doesn't grow on people's heads. She malingered for several days. But Selim reminded her forcefully by boxing her ears until he knocked her off her feet.

"Hmm," said the physician. "Yours must be the only terminal case of dandruff in the world—but wait! It comes off. What's this thing you're wearing on your head? By Moses, Jesus and Mohammed, it's a rancid bladder."

Her hair came tumbling down over the clever Jew's hands.

"Have m-m-mercy on me, Jew Physician, Sir," Hürü said. "I am undone!"

"You certainly are," he said. "Well, let's hear it, then."

Hürü told her story in brief: her parents' trip to Mecca, her brother's inexplicable behavior, her meeting with the green sage, the shepherd, and the Prince. She begged the physician to keep her secret.

"So your father's a physician, too," the Jew said. "And what might be his name?"

"Turhan of Karaman," Hürü said. "And he's a g-g-good man, Jew Physician, Sir."

"You mean old Licorice Turhan?" the Jew said. "We went to school together right here in Konya. We called him Licorice Turhan

at medical school because he was sweet, dark, and rich. Imagine that!
So you're Turhan Bey's daughter, huh? In that case, you're in double
jeopardy, girl. Prince Selim won't like it that you fooled him by
impersonating a boy. He won't like it that you are from the rival
House of Karaman."

"I know," Hürü said.

"On my Hippocratic oath," he said, "I won't give you away. But
you'd better make yourself scarce soon as you can. I have my own
head to worry about. Tell you what we'll do. We'll shave off all your
hair and then bandage up your head. In a few days time, take the
bandages off and show the Prince you're cured of your terrible
scrofula."

Hürü fell on her knees and kissed the physician's hands. On top
of being so kind to her, he gave her a couple of gold pieces so she
might make her way out of Karaman, the ancient seat of her forefathers.

"I wish your father had become the sovereign of the Realm," he
told her. "Because the Princes of Karaman were tolerant, cultured
and humble men. They were all imbued with the liberalism that
blesses our town. On the other hand, the House of Osman is a home
of no pity. It's not that I don't prosper under Selim too. But one never
knows when Selim might decide there's one too many Jews in the
world."

Prince Selim was a bit soured at first that his fool had recovered
from the head plague. Seeing the stubble on her clean white scalp,
he scuffed her hard on the neck.

"You look a worse sissy without your disease!" Selim scolded.
"Do you call that thin stick a neck? Let's see what can be done to
make you more like a man!"

He bestowed on her a set of page's uniforms. Yes, she was to
be enrolled immediately at the provincial court school of pages,
bending the rule that free-born Moslems could not be educated to
rise in the hierarchy. The Prince had his scribe forge papers that she
was a bastard of unknown origin, enslaved in the woods by the
Prince himself.

"I feel sorry for you," Selim said. "And I don't know why. Perhaps
because you're such a know-nothing."

Hürü wondered what would happen when her fool-appeal was
rectified at school. Maybe she ought to sneak out of town immediately. Yet, the hope of learning something useful was a temptation she

couldn't resist. Some of the teachers at the school, top men in the arts and sciences, came from the Mevlana Institute, from Istanbul, from the land of the Franks. Prince Selim wasn't stingy when it came to paying teachers.

She was the tallest boy in class, the other beginners being eight- and ten-year-olds who'd been newly gathered from many parts of Europe; she was made the head boy at once with the responsibility of tanning the hides of the little ones when they cried from homesickness, for their mothers, their hurts or flagging courage. She was to help them with their Turkish, Arabic, Persian, correct their grammar when they slipped; she was to be merciless when they spoke a single word in their native tongues. The little boys were there to forget all else besides their loyalty to their Prince. They were rewarded for the smallest service to their master and punished exorbitantly for the smallest fault.

Hürü didn't like one bit inflicting pain on the poor little beggars; she went easy whenever the instructors weren't looking or when none of the boys closer to her own age were around to observe her indulgence.

The older boys, who'd gone through the system themselves, had been converted so thoroughly that they wanted every new boy to suffer the same course of training. But they gave Hürü a wide berth because it was known that this head boy went to sleep at night by Prince Selim's chamber and not in the barracks with the rest.

Hürü received top grades on her written work, seeing her advantages over the other beginners in the complexities of language, grammar, the Arabic alphabet and syntax, Persian literature with its difficult poetry and its chivalric romances. She loved Turkish history, which stuck in her mind even if she read an account just once. But she had to labor over her Islamic history, which seemed ever so dreadfully dull. She was excused from religious instruction since she was, on that account, miles ahead of everyone else in school. Since she didn't know girls weren't supposed to understand mathematics and geometry, and no one, not knowing the truth about her, clued her in, she excelled in those subjects. Students who were observed, by discerning masters, to show promise in a special field received more concentrated training in that field. Hürü's preoccupation with music was discovered, which entitled her to instruction in Turkish music, both martial and classical; as her instrument, she was assigned the *mizmar*, a kind of wooden flute.

Her stuttering and stammering, however, were a terrible handicap that earned her severe beatings; so much so that Selim, who was all in favor of corporal punishment, was alarmed when he found her in a coma outside his door. He consulted a Sufi teacher down at the Mevlana Institute as to what could be done for the incorrigible stutterer. The Sufi suggested that the page be rewarded for *not* stuttering; it was far better to build on desirable behavior than to punish weakness.

Hence, the instructors were to discover what reward the page liked and treat him to that reward whenever he got through a sentence without getting stuck.

Hürü was amazed that she was allowed so many extra music lessons; instead of getting beaten, she could toot on her flute all she wanted. She was even excused from her head boy duties. Suddenly, it seemed, a blocked world of heavenly sound opened. She mastered the *mizmar* so quickly, she was soon put on the school band that gave the Prince regular concerts as well as saluting him musically an hour before dawn and an hour-and-a-half after the sun had set. She was certainly a favored boy; she didn't know why, but she no longer was as fearful of speaking up, either.

Her muscles developed; although she wasn't quite as strong as a real boy about her own size, she was surprised to see how much actual physical stress she could take. While wrestling, some lummox of a Slav boy tore her lip so brutally she couldn't blow on her *mizmar* for several weeks. In armed combat, she did better. But she never received more than a passing grade in physical education, for which she expected Selim to thrash her. But the thrashing never came. Not even a scolding.

Since every page also received some vocational training as well, Hürü was assigned to the gardens of the Mevlana Institute to learn from a dervish horticulturist the secrets of plant life. There, she was put in charge of a row of cabbages, the coarse roses of the vegetable garden.

After some time at the Institute, Hürü began to receive the glimmers of more subtle influences. About love, for example; about the image of a life infused with creativity, freedom and constant rebirth. But the sort of love the Sufis spoke of remained elusive. It dawned on her that whatever love was, it couldn't be perceived from a distance; one must submit one's everyday self completely, even physically, in order to make the spiritual leap. One must devote oneself to an object of desire, love it and through constant vigorous action become *one* with the object of desire.

But *what* was an appropriate object of desire? She inquired of the sufi Master of Horticulture, under whose tutelage she picked, one by one, cabbage worms off the row of her coarse roses. The cabbages in the next row, tended by the Master, didn't have a single worm disfiguring their leafy heads.

"No one can tell you that," the Master said. "Look in your heart."

"But I have," Hürü said. "Many times. There's nothing solid there to see. Can't you suggest something?"

"Cabbages," the Master said.

"Cabbages for my heart's desire?" she said, astonished. "Don't be silly!"

She reflected on cabbages for several minutes.

"What happens if I do become *one* with cabbages?" she asked.

"You might not have to pick off so many worms," the Master said.

Oh, they taught through indirection. Any fool could see that. Instead of prayers and religious rituals, they transformed spontaneous feelings into the Truth of *sam'a*: singing, music and ecstatic dancing. Another place in the Islamic world, the Mevlevi dervishes might be crucified or flayed alive, accused of using the tools of Satan himself; in Konya, where their subtle influence soothed even Selim's heart into tolerance, they were protected against orthodox cries of revulsion and shock. And Hürü, as she toiled over her cabbages, could listen to heavenly music that lifted the very domes under which the musicians of the Mevlevi Order played.

It was at the Institute gardens that Hürü laid eyes again on her brother, Mahmut Jan. She saw him hurry into the kitchens with a bundle of wood in the basket on his back. Although dressed in the humble clothes of a woodcutter, he seemed quite full of himself. She was relieved that he didn't know her. And she was relieved that, in giving service at the Institute, he might receive from the dervishes the happiness of how not to be afraid. She had a notion that her brother had abandoned her in the woods because of the fear of something. Or the hope for something.

"You know that young man?" she asked the Master toiling beside her.

"That person," the Master said, straightening his back, "feels like a soul in distress."

"So you know him."

"Not his name," the Master said. "I only hear his heart. His heart argues and disputes; it makes categories and refuses to know what is in its best interest to know."

"All that from his heartbeat?" Hürü cried.

"Not his heartbeat. His behavior. When I say heart, you musn't take it literally. As the young man passed by, he sensed you, but he didn't perceive you. He only saw a page taking unnecessary pains with some cabbages."

"Why should it be in his best interest to perceive me?" Hürü said.

"Your heart," the Master said, "leapt when you saw him pass. But he didn't perceive that your hand trembled on the spade."

With preceptors like that around, one might as well give up all pretense right now. Yet, it's hard to know what one pretends in order to hoodwink oneself. She wasn't, she despaired, suited to the other-worldly life of knowing oneself. That's why she was surprised when the Master of Horticulture offered her a fellowship at the Institute.

"Who, me?" she said. "But I'm not even who I seem to be."

"We know," the Master said. "Your being a female doesn't exclude you."

"Oh, my God!" Hürü cried. "So you know. What do I do now?"

"We're not in the business," the Master said, "of giving others away. But should you decide military life is not for you, you have a place among us."

Out of a thousand applicants, the dervishes might accept one student; they were famous for advising aspirants to take up other occupations. To be invited to be one was a great honor. But Hürü knew, from observing herself, that if she felt it was such an honor to be asked, then she was not ready to give up praise and reward. Praise and reward, as well as punishment and deterrence, were for ordinary folk. The Sufis could neither be intimidated by the stick nor bribed by honors. But she wanted to play the *mizmar* extremely well for the glory of Hürü and not because she was *at one* with the instrument. She intimated her feelings.

"This, too, shall pass," the Master said.

She was dying to inquire if the greatest musician of the time, a composer who created music for the flute ensemble at the Institute, could give her lessons without her being consecrated to the Brother-hood. But she felt she'd already received too many special blessings. Better not press her luck. She didn't ask and did not receive.

Winters on the Konya plateau were very harsh. It snowed so heavily, roads became impassable and life was cut off from the rest of the world. A dry cold put the chilblains on the hooves of the horses, on children's hands, on men's noses. Doing outdoor chores, Hürü's bare hands would freeze on metal objects, sometimes necessitating the sacrifice of a bit of skin. She sniffled constantly.

"Sneeze once more," Selim threatened her, "and I'll cut off your nose!"

"Ah-chou!" she went, despite the threat.

But he didn't cut off her nose. Although the infirmary was full of pages like Hürü, the snow was a blessing. Young wheat slept warm and safe under the thick white blanket; then, the spring thaw watered the earth deeply. The dervishes, on the other hand, never caught the sniffles, nor were they subject to plagues that descended on the townspeople and the soldiery. Their atonement with the climate, among other things, sometimes strained relations with the townspeople, causing folks to blaspheme against the dervishes. The folk in Konya, Hürü thought, no matter how much they praised themselves for their own liberal and tolerant ways, were not unlike people elsewhere who only wanted things for themselves. So things just happened to them: accidents, bad luck, infirmity. Nothing good or bad ever happened at the Institute. The Institute just was.

In Selim's study, sitting on the hard floor by the door, Hürü learned lessons of another sort: the practical workings of statecraft and warcraft. More war room than study, this was where Selim made his secret plans which he divulged to no one, and where he gathered information from strategists and tacticians, financiers and lawmen, historians and geographers, technicians and theorists. He deliberately set out to prepare himself to gain for the Empire all that his Sultan father either ignored or wasted.

At a time when the Ottomans were the only real power in the world, the present Sultan had set a course of inaction and status quo; the Janissaries caught flies in the barracks while the world went begging for conquest. Selim observed that his father concerned himself with trifles such as the furthering of the immigration of the Jews, who'd recently been driven out of Spain, into Ottoman dominions where the Jews might take over the baffling business of trading with infidel Christian brokers. Not only that; his Sultan father was unable to curb Turkoman nomads who roamed the marches of Anatolia in defiance of central authority, and who, every time the going got tough, took refuge with the Memluk ruler of Syria, or the heretic Shah of Persia, Ismail. Recently, pacification of the turbulent Turkomans had been achieved only through the shame of having to concede some border towns to the Memluks of Syria.

"The Old Man can't even bring Shah Ismail to battle," Selim said. Seems the Shah's strategy was to retreat deep into Persia, burning and razing his own domains, so that the Ottoman armies froze and starved.

The only course, it seemed to Selim, was to depose his father Sultan Bayezid—not depose him in favor of his two elder brothers, but himself, the youngest and the one blest with intelligence and talent. But the Sultan favored his middle son, Prince Ahmet, who served as the governor of Amasya. Word was that Prince Ahmet, too, had donned the Red Hat of the Persians and turned heretic Shi'ite. Those days, the color of one's hat told the world of one's religious affiliations. As if the hat had become one with the head, folks of Shi'ite persuasion were called Redheads.

"His father's son!" Selim groaned. "Worrying about whose religion is better when there's so much else at stake!"

Selim thought the time was ripe, seeing Bayezid was in poor health, to arrive surreptitiously in Istanbul and canvass the support of the Janissaries for his cause. The Janissaries were reported to be sullen, resentful of their long idleness and eager for new conquest. Selim's advisors thought the idea reckless and impetuous. The Prince might end up losing his head.

"A head not risked is not a head worth having!" Selim bellowed, "which maxim you fools illustrate amply. I should have the lot of you beheaded right away. What do you say to that, Bald Boy?"

"Don't do it," Hürü said.

"And why not?"

"The man who can't put off his whims," Hürü said, "becomes a slave to his whims."

"Listen to the clever boy!" Selim said. "And who taught you that little gem?"

"The dervishes," Hürü said, "who understand worldly life because they concentrate on the spirit."

"Remind me to close down that wasp's nest," Selim said, "and have the lot sold into slavery. Before I know it, they'll take over the mind of every man, woman and child."

Selim left for Istanbul soon as the roads were partially clear of snow: he must put his finger on the Janissaries' pulse before he made his bid. For Sclim, information and preparedness was all. He was a master of logistics, of the details of transport, quartering and feeding the troops. Armies that won were armies that moved with speed, and whose feeding and quartering were not left to mishaps of razed fields, burned granaries and destroyed towns. Heroism without luck is doomed to bleed on the battlefield, Selim said; but the lucky general is the one who makes his luck. And Selim was not afraid of imagining the worst.

During Selim's absence, an odd change overcame Hürü. Having always taken Selim's presence for granted, and being resentful and afraid of that presence besides, she couldn't understand why she was so stricken by his absence. She longed to hear his extraordinary voice, unbearably strong and clearly articulated; she longed to see his sword belt that went energetically all the way around his solid hips. Suddenly, Konya seemed empty, music a bunch of sounds, the copper domes of the Institute meaningless. Selim was not in Konya.

But what did sorrow, and the act of loving his own fate, for which he so deliberately prepared himself, mean to Selim? She'd like to wake him for herself, this sleeping Prince with the crazed and predatory gray eyes. He slept on the dark side of the paradox, tossed his head as if to say: No! He dreamed of terrible conquests. He slept on the dark side of the paradox: that which binds, frees.

"I don't get it," she said to the gardening Master. "I don't even *like* Sclim! I hate it when he treats people as if they were nothings. He assumes someone is an asshole even before the person's finished saying hello. Why do you suppose I'm so agitated about Selim?"

"Why, indeed?" the Master said.

"Sometimes, though, he lets himself be carried away by an idea, a scent in the air, the quatrains of a song. Yet, I don't understand him at all. There's a terrible inconsistency between his intellectual and emotional life. While his mind is clear as the sphere of angels, his heart is murky as hell. Why should it be so?"

"Why, indeed?" the Master said.

"Basically," Hürü went on, "Selim's a miser. For example, on a walk after a hearty meal, he'll stop by some townsman's house and demand to see what's in the man's larder. Then, he'll gobble up the poor man's store of victuals for the hell of it, the best bits, too. And he won't even reward the man for his hospitality."

"One doesn't reward hospitality," the Master said, "that one forces."

"That's right!" Hürü said. "Come to think of it, that might be the reason Selim has no amatory virtues. He can force copulation. So he treats his women as worthless adversaries."

"Are they worthy?" the Master asked.

"I don't know. But I haven't yet seen a free woman cross his threshold. Still, even slave girls and tarts deserve better treatment than what he gives them. He doesn't even uncover their faces, you know, just falls on them like a plank. He fits it in and bangs away like a . . ."

"Please!" the Master said. "Spare me the details."

"He makes me watch!" Hürü said. "Is that all there is to love?"

"The world's run by those who can't make love," the dervish said, "or those who do it badly. That's why the world's in trouble."

"Can't lovemaking be learned?"

"Of course!" the Master said. "But who takes the time? Making love is supposed to come naturally. No pun intended."

"You know, I don't understand myself, either," she said. "I've seen how it works. Some of these women, I mean the ones he takes by force. Well, after they've been had, they often fall desperately in love with him. They hang around Selim's haunts like mooncalves. They send messages, gifts, lovesick poems to him. Some are even formerly virtuous women, like the wives of honorable men. They seem to fall in love once they thoroughly understand there's no way Selim will ever reciprocate their feelings."

"He has the power," the Master observed, "to wound and destroy indiscriminately all women who fall into his hands."

"I hope he never comes back!" Hürü cried. "I hope his father gets him before he gets his father!"

"Our master, Mevlana Rumi," the Master said, "fell in love with a man called Shams. At the time, Rumi was at the peak of his social and religious position. His devoted followers, sons and friends felt betrayed when Rumi was diverted from leading them for the sake of Shams's love. In everyone's opinion, Shams was nothing but an imposter and charlatan who cast a pernicious spell upon the greatest mind of the age. But it was through his passion for this flimflam man that Rumi perfected his heart."

"Are you saying that even if the object of passion is unworthy," Hürü said, "it's the passion itself that counts?"

"I'm not as good as you at tagging morals," the Master said. "I was just observing that Rumi accepted not just *resembling* Shams but *becoming* Shams."

"I scc," Hürü said.

But she didn't see at all. On Selim's return, just looking at his face, she thought she would expire. Or, like a small fox in a trap that gnaws off a limb to get free, she'd gnaw out her heart if she could. Living here, out in the open as men did, no latticed windows, no veiled eyes, how was she to deal with the consciousness of her passion? She felt so agitated, so utterly alone, as she called for uneasy answers to unbearable questions. Seeing Selim, the resolutions of the past seemed to founder; all that spiritual activity, thought, vigilance, study, clear conscience at knowing what's what, thanking God. God? He's not here!

She asked politely how his mission had gone.

"Well, I wrapped it up," Selim said. "The Janissaries swore undivided allegiance and bound themselves to me as their future chief. But you can't trust the bastards. They're fickle as fashion—which is precisely why they're so powerful. They don't know a man except by the color and shape of his hat. For now, they don't like the Red Hat Prince Ahmet has donned; they prefer the military cone that sits atop my head."

"What's the next move?"

"Next move is Ahmet's. And he's sure to make the wrong cne, you can bet on it. You can count on religious fanatics to make the wrong move. He'll be protecting his Bishop while his King is mated."

"You contemplate doing in your father and brother so coolly."

"What?" Selim said, laughing. "Filial piety and brotherly love? That stuff's for common folk like yourself. You all go under the yoke of abstractions so that you might never have to do something you want. You choose to be content with what your fathers and brothers dish out. I'm the only free man in this whole fucking Empire."

If, despite his disagreeable nature, Selim were capable of inspiring such inexplicable love in Hürü's breast, then was he not entitled to know he inspired love? But playing woman games? Hürü didn't know how. What was flirtatious advance and modest retreat? No good. No good at all. She wasn't some slut hanging around Selim's headquarters.

But there she was, helping Selim bathe! She'd so often before scrubbed his back, resenting the breadth of it, applying the loofah so hard as to make the Prince caution her about instant reward of Paradise for Bald Boys who skin their lord and liege alive. Now her arms were noodles; her wrist syrup. How could she wash his back and not see the wholesome and huge manhood that ornamented his loins? She'd rather fall on her back and have him take her as he might, give it to her, as it were, to surrender so she might possess him, have him plow her cruelly so she might extract from him the tenderness of that single moment when he cried, Ahh! But she was fearful, shrinking, embarrassed. She dropped the heavy gold washbowl, Selim's own handiwork, on his princely head.

"Watch it, Bald Boy!" Selim scolded. "If you can't do a job properly, you'll be replaced by one who can."

"I . . . I . . ." Hürü said.

"Speak up, dumbbell!"

"Why don't you t-t-take a p-p-proper wife?" she said. "Swear to l-l-love her before God and be forever t-t-true?"

"What's all this infernal stuttering again?" he shouted, bringing his nose dangerously close to Hürü's. "I don't like a limp-wristed stutterer, especially not when I've bent so many rules to make him into a man."

"I'm not stut-stut-stuttering," Hürü said. "You just don't want to ans-ans-answer my question."

"Love?" Prince Selim said. "I'd like to catch the lamebrain who invented love so I may wring his neck for him. He could've made a man of himself but, instead, he fell in love."

"But you p-p-penned love poems yourself."

"That's formal love, idiot!" the Prince said. "Think love poems speak to the beloved? Most certainly not! Poems have always spoken to each other and always shall."

"Maybe," Hürü said, her head already tucked under her arm, "that's why your poems are so dull."

"Well, I'll be damned!" Selim said, dunking Hürü's head in the pool and letting her come up just as she drowned. "Heads better than yours think otherwise. They tell me I'm an accomplished poet."

"But they still like Prince Jem's poems better," she said, determined not to fear Selim, at least in this arena. "Even your eldest brother, Prince Korkut, has a couple of interesting things to say in his poems."

"That does it!" said Selim. "What makes you think you're indispensable?"

"No one else will tell you the truth," she said. "I love my Prince too much to let him deceive himself."

"Love, *looove* again!" he said. "Listen, fool, you benefit from me, that's what! Don't deceive yourself, boy. Call it self-interest, call it fear. Just call it by its right name. I'd have men fear me any day than have them think they *looove* me."

"Still," Hürü said, "why not marry yourself to some nice Turkoman princess, some intelligent and resourceful woman who might give you a legitimate son or daughter? Why not marry a woman who can teach your children? Then your son won't plot *your* demise."

"I've already done my duty," Selim said. "I've sired many sons. And I legitimized Süleyman. If the bastard has to kill me to get my Empire, so be it. But I might just get him first. He isn't indispensable. I must have other bastards around somewhere. I'll just legitimize another."

"What kind of a person is Süleyman?"

"I don't know," Selim said, "and I don't care."

"And his mother?"

"Couldn't see her in the dark," Selim said.

"See what I mean?" Hürü said. "He who goes to bed blind will beget crosseyed sons."

"May I write that down in my diary?" Selim said. "The wisdom of that moves me so, I might weep any moment."

"If you do have a diary," Hürü said, ignoring his irony, "which I doubt, what I said will be the only interesting entry in the whole damn thing."

The Prince laid a stiff one on Hürü's head.

"Bald Boy!" he said. "You're still a virgin. What do you know about women? And what's all this about *looove*? Come, let's have it. Out with it! Who's the lucky girl? Tell me, and I'll get her for you so we won't have you pine away. I don't suppose you can get her on your own. Not the way you look!"

"No girl," Hürü said. "Where, around this place, would I meet a decent girl?"

"Then I'll get you an indecent one," Selim said, "before you break out in pimples all over your fucking head. Tell me, what do you fancy? Blondes? Brunettes? Tall? Fat? I recommend a black one. Blacks are great! They just fall back and take it like a man. None of this infernal weeping or all that cloying after-fuck stuff. Besides, their cunts are small and not hairy like some blasted Greek cow's, nor dry and bony like some pale Slav's. It's ready when you are. But avoid Armenian women at all costs. Boy, they've got hair coming out of their teeth!"

Back at the Institute, though she didn't like using the good dervish Master as her sounding board, Hürü couldn't help talking to him about the man who obsessed her, whose very noxious existence tormented her, and to whom, in her dreams, she gave more than what was required. If only she could melt like that when she was awake! With him on her, riding her, fused with her! But she musn't make a sound or give a sign. She told all this plainly. The dervish Master seemed bored.

"Illusion prevents fusion," he told Hürü, exasperated at last.

"I want nothing from Selim," Hürü said.

"Indeed!" the Master said. "If I were you, I'd look critically in my heart: what is there in Selim that I want for myself?"

"I don't want to resemble Selim!" Hürü said, beginning to weep now. "Let alone *be* Selim. Besides, he wouldn't even give me a tumble. Not only don't I conform to certain sexual prerequisites of his, I'm not even beautiful. Nor black."

"I'd say you're a knockout," the Master said. "Since hair is a woman's jewel, should yours be allowed to grow, you'd be a real beauty. Although I'm not someone who's quite versed in the attractions of women."

"You're just being kind," Hürü said, dying to ask if the Master were versed in the attractions of men. And how in the world did they do it?

"Mind your own business," the Master said, guessing her thoughts.

"There's one thing I can do for Selim," Hürü said. "I can tell him hurtful truths. You've taught me to speak my mind."

"Beware of that compulsion," the Master said. "One feels powerful when one communicates something unexpected or rude to a person's face, taking him by surprise, as it were. You want to move him and to be disposed to yourself, especially because he has over you the power of life and death."

"You mean Selim might, one day, make good his threats?"

"No," the Master said. "But you might deceive yourself into an automatic habit. A compulsion to influence is no different than a compulsion to steal or tell lies. When choice is gone, all you have is a habit."

But, it turns out, Selim was already sufficiently disposed towards the Bald Boy. He took Hürü by the arm and led her to his workshop where, during idle winter months, he plied his craft. Every prince, as every soldier, must learn a craft with which to occupy his hands. Selim had chosen goldsmithry as his vocation. Or else, goldsmithry had chosen him. In his shop, beside golden utensils and filigreed ornaments, Selim made tiny chess pieces of gold, so fascinating that collectors and souvenir hunters, foreigners and goldfingers, seekers after the exquisite and the rare, as well as those who sought influence with Selim, sought and snapped up and sometimes even killed for them. The chess pieces were entirely Selim's own invention, so he didn't even have to sign his work. He'd invented a method of alloying his metal so cleverly that the opposing courts were of two different colors of gold, red and white. Worked out with Selim's devotion to detail, the chessmen, the two chesswomen wearing charming tiaras and the miniature courts transported the viewer into a magic world.

Hürü often contemplated the warlike stage upon which the courts stood, where they were regularly trapped, humiliated and killed, yet still returned another day. Selim's chessmen, and two women, were the inhabitants of an ideal universe where only the action was transitory, but the figures eternal. Whereas, in the real world, the figures were transitory but the action eternal. Here, after mercilessly slaughtering each other, the courts rested together on the chessboard and took afternoon tea, conversed, danced the quadrille or did whatever polite courts do during peacetime.

"I have something to show you," Selim said, taking a red velvet pouch out of a drawer. "But you must take an oath never to breathe a word of it to anyone, not even to your father—if you had one."

Hürü swore on the Koran; she was then shown what was in the red pouch. It was an amulet to be worn around the neck, made of pure gold, on which was embossed the profile of a woman.

"You made this?" Hürü asked. "Who's the lady?"

"Someone I had a brief glimpse of," Selim said, "once. Although I might have just guessed her reflection. If I knew who she is, be she a daughter of Adam or the issue of a demon, I'd consider loving her and winning her, even marrying her with the sort of pomp women adore."

"She must be a fairy princess," Hürü said. "Since she's impossible to attain, of course, you don't have to worry about falling in love, ever."

"You find her for me," Selim said, "and I shan't fail."

"How does a Bald Boy accomplish what a Prince can't?"

"That's your problem," Selim said. "I have enough at hand without hitting the road in search of a dream woman. I'm not about to lose my wits or appetite. You find her for me, and I'll make you the Shah of Persia when I take that realm."

"Your gratitude would cost me my head," Hürü said. "If I found her, the best course would be to make my way where you can't reach me."

"How well you know your Prince!" Selim laughed. "He who loves his life must never incur my gratitude."

"So you'll have to do without your dream girl!" Hürü said.

"She will appear," Selim said, "with or without your help."

His confidence gave her an unreasonable pang, something akin to cruelty. She wanted him to suffer too.

"Wouldn't recognize your lady even if I saw her!" she spat out. "Like your poetry, your lady, too, is formal. She looks exactly like everyone's idea of a beauty. What color were her hair and eyes?"

"How should I know?" the Prince said. "All I know of hues is how intense they are and how saturated. The lady's hair and eyes were of medium intensity but high saturation."

"Are you color blind?" Hürü asked, astounded. "You mean to tell me you've never seen the sky?"

"Sure, I have!" the Prince said. "Sometimes the sky is intense."

Hürü groaned. Never had she loved Selim more. He lived in a world of shadows, the light of white, the dark of black and the myriad grays. No wonder he was *indiscriminate*! Even people's faces, to Selim, must appear gray. He'd never beheld our miraculous creation as it bursts forth in an abundance of hues; his world was made of forms to which he assigned values, almost mathematically, in terms of intensity and saturation. She fell on her knees and kissed Selim's hand.

"My poor Prince," she sobbed. "Poor, poor Prince."

"Don't be a sap!" he said. "I get along quite well, thank you!"

But he was touched. He sat Hürü down in his workshop and told her the entire tale of the original Bald Boy. Turns out, Prince Selim was a marvelous storyteller, interspersing high drama into the narration, holding back, foreshadowing coming events, but always pouncing in for the kill—as most storytellers, like hunters, do with wit, pith and point. At the end of the story, Selim observed that Bald Boy was the spirit of the Turkish nations: a poor and pitiful creature, thin-necked, his head full of sores, illegitimate, uneducated, having

no claim to hearth and home. Bald Boy lived on his wits, his stamina
and the blood of a stout and valiant heart. He was more a changeling
than a bastard, whose action, with both strange and human qualities,
impish playfulness and pathetic humanity, changed the lives of those
he met, opening people's eyes to their own hearts. We beheld the
man in ourselves by perceiving what was not quite a man. Prince
Selim took a long, hard look at Hürü's face.

"Aren't you glad my nurse told me the story?" Selim said. "I
recognized you in the woods at once."

Hürü realized she'd been allowed to live because Selim wanted
to embrace the illegitimate, poor and scabrous creature in himself;
he set about to make that unfortunate boy legitimate, learned and an
invincible master of his own fate. Selim, born of a slave girl whose
name history books would never record, brought up by strangers,
knowing neither the warmth of sire nor dam, was the lost little boy
who'd always lived in fear of his life and on the enormity of his
hopes, which depended on his native wits, stamina and the blood of
his heart. And he went at the world brutally, steeling himself against
all ranges of emotion, scarcely aware of the world's miraculous
variation of color.

She hurried to the Institute to tell the Master her newly acquired understanding of Selim. Would the Master think her concep-
tion real or imagined? But, as she passed through the garrison gates
absentmindedly, the foot of a hanged man brushed her shoulder. She
hadn't even been aware that there'd been a public execution. Hürü
looked up. The blackened face with the swollen purple tongue lolling
out of it was none other than Mahmut Jan's. Her brother had
managed to martyr himself to his cause.

Hürü reeled inside herself with anger and grief. She felt, rather
than heard, a cacophony of voices, a drumming of blood. She made
an effort not to fall where she stood. Her blurred eyes tried to focus
on the hangman who sat by the gates with a basket into which he
expected the spectators to toss a few coins for a job well performed.

"Why was this man hanged?" she asked.

"Some guy who was inciting the townsfolk," the hangman said.
"An enemy of the state, he was."

"Did he die well then?"

"Oh, about average," the hangman said.

Hürü spat in the hangman's basket.

She backtracked to the headquarters. Just as she'd decided to

devote her life to Selim, Mahmut Jan had to go and get himself
hanged. Now, there was no choice. She, too, must rebel. She must do
violence, or else be a nuisance. Her head rushed ahead of herself,
making plans. She imagined herself with a dagger in hand. Or a
poisoned cup. But she knew at the same time that she couldn't go
against her nature any more than the leopard could change his spots.
By nature or, as the Master of Horticulture would say, by condi-
tioning, she was a healer. She'd been trained, on her father's knee, to
heal, fix, bring illumination. Never could she be a priestess of the
darker side. A demystifier was she; better to shed light into dirty
corners, to notice the corners were only dirty when somebody else
might say they were evil. Better to bring health; to nurture. Her
action would never have any madness in it—except, perhaps, a
compulsion for order, ethics, light.

The war room buzzed with excitement. The news was that
Prince Ahmet had committed himself to his inevitable bad move. The
foolish prince, fearful of Selim's influence on the Janissaries, had
raised the battle standard against his Sultan father and was moving
to seize Bursa, thereby sacrificing the Sultan's support.

"We march immediately," Selim told his henchmen, "and force
the Old Man to abdicate. The Janissaries will fall right behind us,
seeing how the Old Dotard can't even control his favorite son."

It was hardly the time to face Selim in the midst of all the
uproar. But Hürü couldn't see what else she could do. As she
dutifully harnessed Selim into his armor, she quite suddenly felt like
spitting on the floor. She spat on Selim's toe.

"Why do you spit, heedless boy?" Selim said. "Explain yourself!"

"I can no longer serve as your page and slave," Hürü said.
"Release me at once. I must go where I can breathe again."

"The air here is just too foul for you, is it?" Selim said. "I don't
get told when and how I dispose of my slaves. But, let's say,
theoretically speaking, I were to listen to reason. What's yours, Bald
Boy?"

"You hanged my brother," Hürü said. "I don't serve a prince who
has my blood on his hands. I'd rather die."

She confessed that Mahmut Jan had been her half-brother. She
wasn't the orphan boy she seemed, but now the last surviving issue
of the House of Karaman.

"I realize you must kill me for deceiving you," she said. "But you
assumed I was the bastard boy from some fairy tale. I couldn't ever

have been your slave. I was always an enemy prince who penetrated your house. Yet, I've never done anything to undermine you, Prince Selim, but accepted your friendship and patronage in the spirit intended. This I can no longer do. Kill me now. Unless, of course, you'd rather release me. Where you're concerned, Prince, I am no longer of any use."

Selim groaned hard.

"As God is my witness," he said, "I can neither release you, nor can I kill you. If you go, you must go at your own peril. Be sure that I will proclaim you absent without official leave. The military patrol I shall leave behind will pursue you, capture you and no doubt will put you to death."

Selim turned to go and meet his troops. He clicked his tongue for his gray wolf, released from the kennels on the occasion of war. The gray wolf, after casting Hürü a baleful look, caught up and ran ahead of the master. The she-wolf was the last image of Selim that stayed with Hürü, this half-tamed wild animal that would run in front of Selim's armies, the harbinger of the indiscriminate slaughter that would follow.

Hürü wondered why she'd failed to tell the Prince she was also a girl masquerading as a boy. Had she done so, things would've been even stickier. It seemed to her she'd already disappointed Selim enough for one day.

She decided to leave quietly, stealthily. To abscond. To vanish forever and ever. She must. The plan was simple. First, Hürü hid in a closet until all the military clanking, neighing and swearing died down; then, as night fell, she let herself into Selim's workshop. There, for some inexplicable reason, she pinched the gold amulet on which Selim had embossed the beautiful profile of a demoness. She didn't know how she could retrieve her *mizmar* from the band room without attracting someone's attention. She hoped the instrument would fall in the hands of a deserving boy with whom it might become one. Gathering the meager allowances she'd been salting away, as well as the two gold pieces from the Jew physician, she deserted.

The year was 1512, our time. In Hürü's reckoning, it was the 918th year of the Prophet's Flight. She was eighteen; she had the gold likeness of a woman concealed in her boot; she left without bidding her favorite Master farewell.

You knew about it all along, didn't you? she asked the Master in her mind's eye. By going under the hegemony of a strong man, I wanted to escape my own insignificant life. But how can anyone hope to partake of the greatness of someone else? What I want for myself is the same kind of unwavering devotion to my fate as Selim has to his. Not only does he not try to avoid it, he's deliberately preparing himself for this destiny that will unfold. That's right. I too must have a fate somewhere, waiting to be discovered.

Chapter 8

JOURNEY BY SEA

Willy-nilly, Hürü must help the
Alchemist as he searches for The Book

*H*ürü headed southeast. She must proceed to the Mediterranean on foot, then catch a ship to Beirut. From there, she'd travel on to Baghdad. Although her parents would be long gone from that city, heading towards Baghdad, her original destination, seemed the right course. And God be praised for all those lessons in geography! She decided to follow the imperial Roman highway the Byzantines called the Pilgrim's Road, now known as the Road to Baghdad; then south towards Tarsus. The natural route lay in the range of foothills that seemed impassable, but our fugitive knew exactly where in the Taurus mountain range there was a pass. Even in high summer, snow covered the peaks, and the rocky ranges rose sharply south of the Konya plateau. At times the route was barely discernible, its paving often completely buried or sunk.

Hürü could also read the stars, the winds and the mosses. She knew how to find food, water and shelter. At least her uniform would entitle her to some rural hospitality and respect on the way. But it was also a liability, in case they were out looking for a deserter whose description fitted hers. Knowing just where any military outposts were situated, Hürü avoided meeting any light cavalry brigades by swiftly circling around the large keeps where they camped and trained.

The last—and only time—she had been on her own, aid had

come to her from the Green Old Man who, she decided, must've been
Saint Hidir himself. Now she had no need of supernatural help—
though the company would be nice. Perhaps the green personage
observed her even now as she travelled south, cautiously, planning
against the mishaps that befall damsels in distress. But no longer was
she one of those afflicted damsels. Never again would she feel lonely
or helpless.

Hürü remembered when she tried to tell the Master of Horticulture about her meeting with Saint Hidir. The Master hadn't been
much impressed with the Green Old Man who'd seemed a tree trunk
one minute and a venerable old gent the next. "So what?" the
horticulturist inquired. "Have you seen Saint Hidir yourself, then?"
Hürü asked him. "Now, why would he bother to appear to me?" was
the Master's retort. She now understood that the dervish did not
seek supernatural aid; his true life's task was to increase his perception. True dervishes, whether wandering or sedentary, lived in accordance with Rumi's admonition: *If you desire to increase your
perception, then increase your necessity.*

Of course, Hürü wasn't perceiving the ineffable too much. All
her attention was riveted on the details of survival. Her hand rested
on her dagger always, even as she slept. She neither enjoyed the
countryside, as she had when travelling with Mahmut Jan, nor did
she stop to jaw with the peasants along the road. She was not only
a deserter but someone who knew all about the dangers of the state.

Crossing the famed Cilician Gates, a natural pass in the Taurus
Mountains, she arrived in Adana, the first large town on the road.
Soon as she hit the marketplace, she searched for a shady dealer and
found one in the person of the proprietor of a used clothes store. He
was willing to exchange her military garb for a less conspicuous
getup. Since he pretended he couldn't dispose of her uniform without
taking risk to his own welfare, she tried sweetening the deal by
throwing in her sword, a fine military-issue blade stamped with
Selim's beautiful signature. But the dealer wanted her boots as well,
boots of sturdy black leather and jingling spurs. In exchange he
offered her a pair of purple monstrosities, the kind that Armenians
had to wear so that people knew the feet inside the purple boots
belonged to an Armenian. But Hürü put her foot down. He couldn't
have them; not with what was hidden in the heel of her one black
boot! Finally, they came to terms when she agreed to take the yellow
turban of a Jew.

"Good choice!" winked the dealer. "No one would suspect a Jew of being a deserter, since he would know enough, in the first place, to keep out of the army."

"I happen to be," Hürü protested, "honorably retired."

"And I happen to be," the dealer said, "a monkey's uncle. Was I born yesterday, or what? No hair on your chin even, and you expect me to believe you're a retired soldier? In my line of business, you deal in men as well. So you keep a sharp nose, and you sniff them out. Young man, you smell like a suspicious character."

"You don't smell so good yourself!" Hürü said.

Berobed like an Arab, turbaned like a Jew, wearing the boots of a Turk, and with a military-issue dagger in her wide, orange Albanian's cummerbund, Hürü was an odd sight. The motley citizen of the Ottoman Empire. For comfort, she kept her small pouch of gold next to her heart.

When she reached Tarsus, funny looking as she was, the captain of a tramp vessel agreed to admit her on board for a few piasters. She had to travel strictly deck class, where the goats and the sheep, the crippled and the sick, the groaners and the vomiters, consumers of disgusting food and sounders of false alarms, the very dregs of humanity and animality had also booked passage. They were tolerable because the salt sea breezes filled her with a feeling akin to joy. Yet this was not the Bosphorus, nor the Golden Horn where she'd grown up, with salty light air that felt like the essence of universal Good. This was the southern Mediterranean, vast and open, the emptiness rocking the tramp vessel as if the boat were a nutshell. A fair west wind drove the ship toward ancient Antioch from whence the tramp would, provided it found the cargo soon, sail for Beirut.

Only a couple of days out, the horizon became filthy with unwelcome company. Among curses from the crew and shrieks of fear from the passengers, the tramp was boarded by pirate knights from Rhodes, who thoroughly robbed, raped and ravaged. After slaughtering the more unattractive passengers, the larger portion of those aboard, the pirate knights retained the better heeled ones for ransom and the fair ones for slavery. Hürü was among those dragged to the pirate ship, but not before, of course, she was relieved of her small pouch of currency and the military-issue dagger. After everybody's fate was meted out, the tramp was burned and sunk.

At first, the pirate knights didn't know what to do with Hürü. What should they do with a Jew boy? Then one of them thought up an attractive—temporary—solution. They stuck her into a contraption that looked like a bird cage and flung at her slops and spit. Since they didn't understand any of the civilized tongues Hürü spoke, they didn't appreciate the foul language she flung back. It seemed like she was in there for an eternity, but the sun had risen and set only a couple of times when the pirate ship set anchor at a small bay.

Amidst curses and blows she was dropped overboard, without, of course, being asked if she could swim. Fortunately for Hürü, her beautiful Amazon of a mother had taught her the breaststroke and the crawl, not to mention the butterfly. She came up for air.

"Sonso'bitches!" she told them off. "Where the hell am I?" She was answered with another pail of slop, flung at her open mouth. Then the pirates set sail again.

Hürü swam to the deserted beach and hauled herself onto the sand. Once again, here she was—penniless, ignorant of her whereabouts, hungry as the devil himself. Had she her dagger, she might at least fashion a spear and get herself a fish or two. She settled for some sea urchins which tasted rather like bloody eggs. Without any bread to make them palatable, not even a drop or two of lemon juice, the urchins made her sick. She spied a fig tree in the field beyond the beach. Scarcely was she halfway up the fig tree when a formidable matron materialized to let Hürü have it in the rudest sort of Greek. Since Hürü's Greek also consisted of foul language, she offered the matron the worst of her vocabulary. The matron felt obliged to get tough. With the aid of a sheepdog and a stick, Hürü was driven back to the beach. She sat down despondently.

"Now we know," she said, touching the heel of her boot where the golden lady was concealed, "that we're somewhere populated with one foul Greek woman and one disagreeable sheepdog."

She started walking south on the beach, travelling half a day without meeting a soul. By noon, she arrived at an inlet where the ribs of a wrecked ship rotted on the sand. She took refuge in the wreck, thinking she'd take a nap. But just as she closed her eyes, she glimpsed out of the corner of one eye a mounted figure who approached. She didn't move, hoping the rider wouldn't notice her in the wrecked ship. But the person rode on directly towards her.

When the rider came close, Hürü recognized him as a Maghrabi, some kind of North African arab, she guessed, maybe a Berber from the tribes that roam the Barbary Coast. Obviously a stranger to these parts, the Maghrabi sat on a mule hung with a pair of magnificently embroidered saddlebags, and was himself decked out stunningly, wearing much gold and silver on his clothes. Hürü wasn't sure exactly where Maghrabis usually hung out, but it certainly seemed odd meeting one in a place like this. The richly dressed figure alighted and approached Hürü, who sat staring at him in astonishment.

"Peace be on you, O Hürü, daughter of Turhan!" the man said in corrupt Arabic, murdering her father's name as well as hers.

"Peace be on you, O Strange Person!" Hürü said in her best classical Arabic.

The Maghrabi didn't bother to introduce himself, or approach her with polite indirection and the establishment of goodwill, etc., before he offered her a job.

"O, Hürü," he said, "I have a job for you."

"That's nice," Hürü said. "I sure can use the bread."

"You will get more than bread," he said. "Recite the *Fatiha* so I may attest to your true belief."

"Oh, all right," she said. "Here goes."

So, one had to be a true believer to get the job. The Maghrabi repeated the formula along with her, thereby indicating the truth of his own faith and binding Hürü in the common bond of Islam. Then, he took a length of silken cord out of his pocket and handed it to Hürü.

"Bind my hands behind me," the Maghrabi instructed, "as tight as you can. Then push me into the sea and wait. If you see my hands appear on the surface, free of the bonds, then cast this net over me and draw me out quickly. But if you see my feet come up first, know that I am a dead man. In that case, take the mule and the saddlebags and go to the market of the merchants. There you will find a Jew whose name is Solomon. Give Solomon the mule and the saddlebags; he will give you a hundred pieces of gold. Take the money, keep your mouth shut and go your way."

"What town am I supposed to go to?" Hürü said. "I don't even know where I am."

"The town is Famagusta," the Maghrabi said. "We're on the fair isle of Cyprus. Famagusta is a port farther south. Just follow the trail you saw me arrive on."

Hürü tied the man's hands behind him as instructed. All the time, this glutton for punishment shouts: "Tighter! Tighter!"

"Now take me out on those rocks and shove me in," the Maghrabi said. "There, the water is very deep."

Once in, the Maghrabi sank like a stone. Hürü waited, but he wouldn't come up. Just as she was taking off her boots to go after him, the poor bastard's feet appeared, bobbing up and down like two corks. Well, she'd have to give him up for dead. She took the mule, and the gorgeous saddlebags, and rode on the path the Maghrabi had indicated toward this town called Famagusta.

Once there, she found the marketplace as instructed, and soon she spied the yellow-turbaned Jew sitting on a chair at the door to his store. Seeing Hürü ride up on the mule with the gorgeous saddlebags, the Jew rose and, beating his breast, moaned and lamented.

"Verily," the Jew said finally, "the man has perished."

"So he has," Hürü said.

"Too covetous," the Jew said. "He was too covetous."

"What was he up to?" Hürü said. "Diving for sunken treasure?"

"Oyy!" the Jew said, beating his breast some more. "Oyy!"

"Imagine!" Hürü said. "Diving with your hands bound behind you! But, then, the whole business is astonishing."

Despite all his lamenting, the Jew took the mule and the saddlebags, quite businesslike, and handed Hürü the hundred gold pieces the dead man had promised, begging her to keep it hushed.

"You can be sure of that," she said. "I don't know a soul here." She bought herself the sort of provisions she liked: grapes, olives, cheese, little spinach pies, fresh loaves and a bottle of wine. Standing right by the stalls, she ate enough to appease her hunger; the rest of the provisions she put into a basket she'd bought, promising herself a fine picnic back on the inlet where the ship lay wrecked. The place was deserted enough to camp out; besides, she wanted to explore the meaning of all this unusual business in which she found herself involved. Why was she, of all people, chosen to take part in the stratagem? What secrecy surrounded the Maghrabi's covetousness? And how did he know her name, her origin, her sex? She couldn't resist the call of mystery.

No sooner had she returned and settled in, than lo and behold, approaches another Maghrabi, this one even more impressively dressed than the last one, and riding a much better mule. This must be the favorite haunt of the Maghrabis, Hürü thought; or else, there's mischief afoot. She'd heard Maghrabis were tricky people.

"Peace be on you, O Hürü, the daughter of Turhan!" the new Maghrabi said. "Did you, perchance, meet up with another Maghrabi yesterday?"

"Who wants to know?" Hürü said.

"I do," the man said. "Did you see him, then?"

Hürü didn't care much for this Maghrabi's mien; for one thing, he looked smarter than the first one and, somehow, more important. If she admitted to seeing the first Maghrabi, she'd also have to admit to standing around while the man drowned. Then, this disagreeable person might even accuse her of drowning a tribesman.

"Nope," she said.

"O, heedless girl!" the Maghrabi said. "That man was my brother. He thought he'd beat me to this place. Surely, you saw him. Didn't you bind his hands behind him and then throw him in the sea? Didn't he charge you to wait until he came up, either with hands first or feet; to cast the net over him if he came hands up; or, if his feet came up, to take the mule and go with it to the Jew Solomon who'd give you a hundred pieces of gold?"

"If you know all this," Hürü said, "then why do you plague me with your questions?"

"Because I want you to do the same for me," the Maghrabi said. "Exactly as you performed for my brother. If my fate is the same as his, then take the mule and the saddlebags, give it to the Jew, and you'll receive another hundred pieces of gold."

"Your funeral," Hürü said. "But may I try to dissuade you?"

"No," the Maghrabi said. "No power on earth can hold me back."

She bound the man's hands behind his back, tightening the silken cord, as the Maghrabi encouraged her, until his wrists bled. Then she pushed him into the sea as well. A while passed. His feet came up.

"This one's gone to Hell, too," Hürü said to herself. "Some racket! If I wait here, every day a Maghrabi will show up, dying to perish on the spot. Soon I will be quite wealthy. Doesn't seem right, though, prospering at the expense of these foolish people."

Nonetheless, she did take the mule back to the Jew who rose, beat his breast and lamented terribly before he took charge of the animal and the saddlebags.

"Now the other has died," said the Jew. "This is the reward for the covetous."

"Listen," Hürü said. "I'm not covetous. And I've already been paid amply. You don't have to pay me this time."

"No, no," the Jew said. "Take this hundred pieces for all your pains. But don't breathe a word of this to anyone."

She didn't know whether to return to the spot where Maghrabis came to destroy themselves under her care. What people said about the Maghrabis seemed to be true; they were a weird lot. Would she have to perform this disagreeable task until there wasn't a single Maghrabi left in the world? She decided to return one more time, just once more, to give the thing its due; after all, three was a magic number. And, sure enough, the third Maghrabi materialized, even grander than the first two, riding a white mule tall as a horse, hung with a pair of saddlebags which were encrusted with jewels as well as embroidery. Actually, this Maghrabi was more wide than tall; the slivers in his fat face that were his eyes burned like black malice. This must be the head-honcho Maghrabi, Hürü thought; he, too, probably knows my name.

"Peace be on you, O Hürü, daughter of Turhan," the mogul of the Maghrabis said. "Have any Maghrabis passed by this place?"

"Two," Hürü said.

"And where did they go?"

"In the drink," said Hürü, "from where their feet came up stiff."

"Too bad," the Maghrabi said unsympathetically.

"You probably can't wait to have the same happen to you."

"O, heedless girl!" the Maghrabi laughed. "Don't you know that every living being has its own destiny?"

"Then, let's get yours over with quickly," Hürü said.

Accordingly, she bound the man and thrust him into the water. And, lo! if he didn't put out his hands, crying, "Cast the net quick, heedless girl, before I drown!"

"This is a welcome change," Hürü said.

She threw the net over the struggling Maghrabi who, obviously, could not swim. Then she tied the rope at the end of the net to a rock and pulled with all her might at the net, terribly heavy with the fat Maghrabi, until she brought him up. He was out of breath but happy about the two little fishes he grasped in his hands, both fish the color of red coral.

"Get the two little boxes, one in each saddlebag," the man said. "And open the lids quickly."

"I'm surprised you Maghrabis will risk your lives for a couple of red mullets," Hürü said. "Where I come from, this fish, although it's delicate, isn't something for which people are willing to die. Fish-mongers sell them by the basketload."

"That so?" the Maghrabi said, putting his treasured fish in the boxes, one in each, before he quickly slammed the lids. Then, quite ceremoniously, he pressed Hürü to his hefty chest and, before she could prevent him, planted a wet kiss on her right cheek and, before she was through wiping that one, planted another on her left.

"God deliver you from all difficulties, Hürü girl!" he said. "Had you not drawn me out so diligently, I'd surely have given up the ghost, since I wasn't about to give up the two fish."

"But why," Hürü asked, "have you succeeded where the other two failed? Tell me the story of the fish, the dead Maghrabis, the Jew and you."

Seems the three Maghrabis and the Jew were all brothers. They had been brought up unconventionally because their father, a great diviner, had initiated them into the arts of solving mysteries and sleuthing for concealed knowledge at a tender age. The old man had acquired many a *jinni* and *marid* who served his every wish. When the old diviner died, leaving his four sons an abundance of marvelous possessions, the four divided the treasures and talismans among them equitably and peacefully, until time came to divvy up the books. Among the rare and wonderful tomes, it seems there was one entitled *The Stories of the Ancients*, also known as *One Thousand and One Nights*, which all four sons coveted. Each son had memorized parts of it when the book was still in their father's possession. But none knew the entire contents. Of course, each of the sons wanted to possess the book so that he might know it in its entirety. Such a terrible dissension ensued that they all went to consult the diviner whose name was Most Profound. Now, Most Profound, who'd been their father's master, told them to bring the coveted book and put it in his charge.

"'You are all sons of my spiritual son,' said Most Profound. 'So I cannot wrong any one of you by deciding which of you gets the book. The one who inherits it will be the one who opens the Treasure of the Tallest of the Tall and brings me the celestial planisphere, the kohl-pot, the seal-ring and the sword.'"

According to the diviner, Most Profound, all four objects had remarkable qualities. He demanded all four marvels in exchange for the book which was now in the diviner's possession.

"That was dumb!" Hürü commented. "Couldn't you four boys just share the book!"

"I guess we couldn't," the Maghrabi said.

Whoever applied kohl to his eyes from the kohl-pot would

perceive all the treasures of the earth. The seal-ring had a *marid* in its service, and whoever possessed it was invincible against any sultan or king; should he so wish, he could possess the earth in all its length and breadth. As to the sword, just drawing it and shaking it against an enemy would rout his whole army, and if the bearer cried "Slay this army!", a flash off the sword would destroy the entire number. The celestial planisphere, though, was the most marvelous of all. Anyone who possessed the planisphere could behold all countries, east and west: to see the inhabitants of a certain quarter of the world, he could just look in the planisphere without rising from where he sat. Moreover, if the possessor resented a certain city, he could bounce rays off the planisphere and burn the city to a crisp.

"Ugh!" said Hürü, shivering. "That's some doomsday device! If in fact these objects exist, I know a man called Selim who could make use of the last three."

"You mean Sultan Selim?" the Maghrabi said, shaking his head. "Some men accomplish what others can't even with the aid of magic objects. Sultan Selim doesn't need these instruments."

"So!" Hürü said. "Selim's become the Sultan, after all."

"Woe to us," the Maghrabi said, "he has!"

"But you have the wonderful instruments," Hürü said, her heart sinking. "Won't you use them against Selim?"

"Not yet, I won't!" the Maghrabi said. "That's where you come in."

Now, the Treasure of the Tallest of the Tall was guarded by the sons of a demon emperor, Red King, who'd secreted themselves in the inlet where Maghrabis were known to drown. The water was protected against intruders by the virtue of a strong talisman. But Most Profound had made calculations and divined that the Treasure of the Tallest of the Tall could only be opened under the auspices of a virgin from Istanbul, a girl called Hürü, the daughter of Turhan. She would be at a certain inlet off the coast of Cyprus on a certain day. The disputing sons were then informed by what method to descend into the water, the whole catastrophe in other words, until one of them was successful in grappling underwater with the two sons of the Red King and caught them both.

"They slayed my first brother," the Maghrabi said; "they also slayed my second brother. But they couldn't slay me. So I seized them both."

"Where are these demons you seized?"

"You saw them!" the Maghrabi said, amazed at her thickness. "I imprisoned them in those two little boxes."

"The two little mullets?" cried Hürü whose turn it was to be amazed. "But they're just about as harmful as two roses."

"Ah," the Maghrabi said. "Those aren't fish! They're *ifrits* in the form of two little fishes."

"And I'm a monkey's aunt," scoffed Hürü.

"O, but Hürü girl!" the Maghrabi exclaimed. "The treasure cannot be opened except through your good fortune. Will you go with me to the town of Kyrenia where I live and work? It's a pretty town on the north shore where we can wait in comfort until the time is auspicious. If you do, I will grant you whatever your heart desires. I will become your brother by a covenant before God, I swear it. And you will return to the bosom of your family safe and sound."

"I wasn't thinking of going home just yet," Hürü said. "I aim to get to Baghdad. And, thanks to your dead brothers, I have enough to get me there."

"But Baghdad doesn't have a treasure in your name," the Maghrabi said. "Here's a pouch with a thousand gold pieces in it. Take it. It's yours for accompanying me to Kyrenia."

"I seem to have a knack for making money," Hürü said. "But I'm not making much headway to my destination."

So, Hürü and the Maghrabi, who finally admitted to the name of Abd-es-Samad, mounted the big white mule. Hürü riding the animal's pointy butt, they set out for the seaside town called Kyrenia. They rode from noon until the time of prayers. Hürü, who was sore from the mule's hipbones, started squirming against Abd-es-Samad's back. She was stultified by the armpit odor that rose from him in fetid clouds and the heat of his fat buttocks that swelled out of the saddle onto her lap. The air in the inner regions of the island was so close that even without the Maghrabi's oppressive heat, one would still fall faint from heat exhaustion.

"Aren't you lucky you're riding, in this heat?" Abd-es-Samad said.

"Yes," Hürü said. "But had you drowned like your good brothers, I'd be riding in the saddle."

"Tsk, tsk," Abd-es-Samad said. "You want to stop?"

"Let's," she said. "I'm hungry as two mules. So what did you bring along to eat?"

They alighted. And Abd-es-Samad removed the beautiful saddlebags.

"Well," he said, "what would you like?"

"How about some bread and cheese?"

"Come now!" Abd-es-Samad said. "Ask for something fancy."

"What do you have?"

"You like oven roasted chickens, crisp and brown?" he said.

"Sure," Hürü said.

"Do you like rice the way Persians steam it?"

"Certainly," she said.

He named her at least twenty different dishes that Maghrabis consider fit for kings. Hürü thought the madman was probably trying to stir up her appetite in vain so he could laugh when he produced some jerky and stale dates.

"Will that menu suffice?" Abd-es-Samad said, a paragon of hospitality.

"Yes, yes," Hürü said. "Serve, already!"

So Abd-es-Samad plunged his hand in the saddlebag and took out a dish of gold in which were two browned chickens steaming; he put in his hand a second time and pulled out a dish of hot shish kebab; he didn't stop putting in his hand and pulling out another dish he'd named until she had before her a feast of twenty dishes, entirely and perfectly prepared.

"You really are a magician!" Hürü exclaimed. "I almost believe it!"

"It's not me," Abd-es-Samad said modestly. "The magic is in the saddlebags. They're enchanted."

But Hürü ate of the food anyway. It tasted substantial; in fact, the dishes were somewhat greasy and heavy, if not downright responsible for killing kings everywhere. When they were through, Abd-es-Samad put the gold plates in the saddlebags where, Hürü assumed, the servant of the saddlebags would clean the dishes. Packing up, Abd-es-Samad invited Hürü to ride in the saddle this time; he'd ride the butt himself. He was some polite host, this Abd-es-Samad.

"In this heat," Hürü said, "the poor mule's going to die from the weight of both of us. Especially since you're so fat."

"Just guess how far we've travelled," Abd-es-Samad said, looking as if he had another trick up his sleeve. "Just guess."

"Four or five hours' journey," Hürü said. "What's to guess?"

"Guess again!" Abd-es-Samad said, beside himself with gloating. "We have already travelled the equivalent of five days' journey. Each hour of travel on this mule is equal to that of a whole day. Know, Hürü, that this mule doesn't mind heat or unbearable weight, having made worse trips through Hell. It's not really a mule but a..."

"I know, I know," Hürü said. "It's a *jinni* or an *ifrit*, or somebody of their ilk."

"That's right!" Abd-es-Samad said, his slit-eyes twinkling. "The mule's been travelling slowly on your account so you won't be dizzied from the speed. I could've made him go much faster."

"Thank you," Hürü said. "But can't you do anything in the normal way, Abd-es-Samad?"

"Why should I?" he said, amazed at such a suggestion.

"You might not get so fat," she said, "if you did something for yourself once in a while."

"Since when is being fat a crime?" he wanted to know, rolling his triple chin. "Everybody'd get fat if he had half a chance."

"Where I come from, we try to stay thin," she said. "And we rise from the table when we're still a bit hungry."

"Remind me not to go where you come from."

They travelled on another day, quarreling over what was fit to eat, stopping for naps from which it was difficult to rouse Abd-es-Samad, and arrived at Kyrenia in what was sixteen days of actual time.

"Abd-es-Samad!" Hürü said. "Do you realize that you're throwing your life away? Where does all that speeded-up time go?"

"That's a problem I haven't yet solved," he admitted shamefacedly. "I'm working on it, but until then, I avoid travelling any more than I have to."

The mule stopped in front of a great house. Abd-es-Samad knocked on the door and was answered at once by an attractive young woman. She wiggled her hips at Hürü, thinking Hürü was a boy whose reason would flee from her wiggles.

"Oh, Rahmeh, my beautiful daughter," said Abd-es-Samad, "prepare the pavilion for us, there's a good girl."

"On my head and eye, O my father," said she, casting another devastating glance at poor Hürü.

"You live here?" Hürü said. "How come you live among infidels?"

"The neighbors leave me alone," Abd-es-Samad said. "Were I to live where I grew up, the neighbors would always be snooping around, preventing me from doing my experiments. It's your own people who'll do their utmost to keep you back, just like themselves,

ignorant and poor. But the poor devils around here never expect to
live as I do. They say to themselves, well, he's a rich foreigner. And
they leave me alone."

Removing the saddlebags from the mule, he whacked the animal
on the rump.

"Depart!" he said to the mule. "God bless you!"

And the ground parted where the mule stood; the mule descended and the ground closed up again as if nothing had been there.

"Poor beast!" Hürü cried. "What a dirty trick, Abd-es-Samad!"

"Don't worry about it," Abd-es-Samad said. "I've told you and
told you..."

"It's a *jinni*," she said. "I know. But he resembles a mule so
much, I keep forgetting."

"Come into the pavilion," Abd-es-Samad said. "Welcome to our
humble abode."

He said it swelling with pride because there was nothing humble
about Abd-es-Samad's abode. He searched Hürü's face for signs of
amazement, but Hürü wouldn't satisfy him.

"Aren't you ashamed of yourself?" she asked. "How can you live
in such luxury when your neighbors live in hovels?"

"You're no fun," he said pouting. "You always say the wrong
thing."

"I'm sorry," Hürü said. "I didn't realize I automatically criticize
you every time you do something amazing. A certain dervish Master
I know..."

"Don't talk to me about any dervishes!" Abd-es-Samad cried. "I
won't have talk about dervishes in my house!"

"Consider the subject closed," Hürü said. "But could you get
something clean for me to wear? Please don't order something
embarrassing. So I won't have to refuse."

"Girl's or boy's?"

"How about something suitable for a young man about town?"

Abd-es-Samad pulled out a wrapper of silk satin from a drawer,
opened it and clapped his hands. In the wrapper appeared a new pair
of galligaskins, a doublet, jerkin, a linen shirt and underwear, a
thrummed hat, a short blue velvet cape; along with the clothes came
a bodkin, a rapier and an arquebus.

"How very nice!" Hürü said, clapping her hands. "But isn't this
the garb of a Venetian?"

"So what?" Abd-es-Samad said. "You have the figure for it.

Besides, when in Venetian territory, wear what they wear and you'll wear your clothes in better health."

"I see you didn't order me any boots," she said.

"Didn't think you'd part with the ones you're wearing. Who's the golden lady? Your mother?"

"Now, that's amazing!" Hürü said. "Do you have vision that goes through leather?"

"No," he said, "just the foresight to examine your boots while you slept."

"I really do love good clothes," Hürü said. "Thank you."

"Thank the wrapper," he said. "Let's eat."

"Let's hope your daughter's a better cook than your saddle-bags."

"Why should she cook?" he said. "The whole house runs on powers."

"The *jinni* of this, the *ifrit* of that," Hürü said. "But don't these beings get tired of serving you day and night?"

"Just between us," Abd-es-Samad said, "the *jinn* are dumb as rocks. Having no imagination, they can never think of something to do on their own. So they're always hanging around humans, poking their noses in business that doesn't concern them. Or else, they skulk in the lowest realm of the heavens, hoping to overhear the angels converse."

"But what good's that?"

"They get to learn things that way," Abd-es-Samad said, "since the *jinn* are very poor conversationalists themselves. Left to their own conversations, they bore each other silly. But they're useful. If you capture a *jinni* who's overheard something important and make him spit it out, you become privy to the talk of the angels. The angels know everything, but you can't get at them, see? There's nothing you can tempt them with, since angels are made entirely of pure reason. On the whole, angels are no fun. Like your dervish friends."

Abd-es-Samad clapped his hands and his daughter came in with the saddlebags. Not again! Hürü thought. But Abd-es-Samad was already pulling viands, sweetmeats and, obviously to please Hürü, great big bunches of grapes, bananas and some tropical fruit that looked armored.

"Pineapple!" Abd-es-Samad said with great pride. "Advance and eat, dear person. And don't be displeased with us."

Hürü now examined Abd-es-Samad's daughter, Rahmeh, whose

name meant Compassion. And she knew she was in the presence of
a truly beautiful woman. Moon face, arched eyebrows, pale white
skin framed by hair in the darkest hues of the night, coral lips, pearly
teeth, pomegranate breasts, pinched-in waist, billowing buttocks.
Maybe Rahmeh was the creature who'd appeared to Selim. But no!
This woman was too indolent, too flirtatious; besides, somewhere
behind her languid black eyes lurked something akin to ill will.

"How did an ugly cuss like you," Hürü asked Abd-es-Samad, "sire
a beautiful daughter like this?"

"She's not really my daughter. But she..."

"A *jinniye*!" Hürü said. "I should've guessed."

"Well?" Abd-es-Samad said. "I released her from the eternal
workhouse where she was sentenced to scrub the floors. On the
whole, she's been a good daughter."

The beauty winked at Hürü. The *jinniye* must be very dumb,
Hürü thought, if she can't figure out I'm a girl. Then, another thought
occurred to her; she resolved to lock the door to whatever chamber
she slept in that night. She wasn't about to indulge in forbidden
activities with some no-account *jinniye*. She hoped locks kept *jinniyes*
out.

"Don't worry on her account," Abd-es-Samad said. "Give her a
certain cue, she behaves in a predetermined way. Just because
you're wearing pants, she has to flirt with you. She has no choice.
You see, a *jinn* or *jinniye* is really an automatic device. Although they
have superhuman powers, their intelligence isn't creative."

"Poor Rahmeh."

"You don't understand," Abd-es-Samad said. "She's perfectly
satisfied. She's been told she's the daughter of the house so she
behaves accordingly. It makes no difference to her whether she's
scrubbing floors or just lolling around, just so she's performing a
function at the discretion of an authority. She'd curl up and die if I
told her to."

"So poor *jinn* behave evilly because they have no choice?" Hürü
asked.

"Hasn't your dervish friend told you," he said, "that it's stupid
to judge others according to your own standards? Never mind! Let's
not discuss it. The hairs on the back of my neck are already standing
straight up."

Although he hated Sufi influences, Abd-es-Samad entertained
Hürü for twenty days. But he was very agitated every time Hürü

wanted to go out on her own, take a walk, see the town and its inhabitants. He was afraid the Venetian masters of the island might chance upon her, detain her and, when her answers didn't add up, throw her in the dungeons.

"I'm not your possession," she told him.

She stood on the beach from where the distant mountains of her homeland could be seen across the water, faint and smoky. If she said she was not homesick, she would be lying. She wondered if she would ever live there again, this so close and yet so distant land, among her iron-willed people.

On this island, she saw a whole people enslaved by foreigners. Though the Cypriots seemed resentful of their Venetian masters—if the rotten egg she took in the face was a reliable sign—they engaged in little besides childish outburst to change their fate. Industrious, talented in trading, clever with their hands, nimble in their speech, they stomped their grapes dutifully and worked in the copper mines. But their Venetian masters treated them like dirt, took the fruits of their labors, wouldn't even let them perform their religious rites. So, the Cypriots held devotional meetings in secrecy, grumbled among themselves, indulged in useless shows of rebellion, throwing rotten eggs and pails of slop out the window on the beplumed hat of a strutting Venetian, spitting, making obscene gestures which, of course, landed the perpetrators in the dungeons.

"Why is it the inhabitants don't recognize they're all Phoenicians?" Hürü asked Abd-es-Samad. "There are more of their nation on the island. They could get rid of the Venetians, just like that."

"I don't involve myself with politics," Abd-es-Samad said. "But what is it that you call nations? Aren't we all descended from Adam and Eve?"

"Well, I'm a Turkoman," Hürü said. "We Turkomans don't go under foreign yoke. We never have and we never will."

"So you know who you are," Abd-es-Samad said tauntingly. "Well, good for you!"

"You don't care about anybody but yourself," Hürü said. "What would you know about collective action?"

"It's because I know about it that I avoid it," Abd-es-Samad said. "I'm interested in unlocking the mysteries of the universe. It matters not a whit to me whether the knowledge I unlock benefits, or harms mankind—let alone a bunch of slovenly Maghrabis!"

"Who are you, really," Hürü asked, "the Maghrabis?"

"Maghrabis are people who dress a certain way," Abd-es-Samad said. "Being people, they must obviously cover themselves with some sort of garb. Otherwise, they'd fry out there in the hot North African sun."

"And why is one of your brothers a Jew?"

"And," says Abd-es-Samad, "why not?"

Abd-es-Samad just wouldn't give up. He must have power over so many forces. Yet, Abd-es-Samad was true to himself—although he held no high-minded principles, no personal habits that might be considered desirable, no physical attractions that might recommend him. He was true to himself because he insisted on living in order to live off the fat of his powers. Abd-es-Samad made no pretenses. Hürü had begun to think Abd-es-Samad was attractive in a repulsive sort of way.

But why did Abd-es-Samad hate the Sufi masters? Maybe hate was too strong a word. Maybe Abd-es-Samad was competing with the Sufis and, no matter how much evidence he amassed, he came in second. The Sufis, too, were engaged in unlocking mysteries: for example, the greatest mystery of all—the human heart. Yet, they weren't interested in exploiting an unlocked mystery for personal gain. The unlocked heart, for them, was of no other use besides the perfection of itself.

Chapter 9

THE FIRST BOON

Hürü lifts the Stone Lyre
from the Magic Treasury

O n the twentieth day of her guest-
hood, Hürü was informed the
time was ripe for opening the Treasure of the Tallest of the Tall. They
rode out of town with two demon slaves following on their demon
legs. And when they arrived at the seaside, the supernatural mules
started to sort of hover above the water—and headed north—toward the smoky coastline of her homeland. The two demons behind
them, apparently of the diving kind, followed the party underwater.

"But," Hürü said, "we're headed for my homeland!"

"Indeed," Abd-es-Samad said.

They travelled for an hour, the mules' feet skimming the water.
The so-called flight over the Mediterranean, Hürü now knew, must be
equivalent to a whole day's journey. By the time they reached the
coast, the mules were going at a dizzying speed. Just as Hürü was
ready to throw up and befoul her charming Venetian finery, they
slowed down to a mulish gait. But the landscape and the colors still
streamed in Hürü's eyes. Once she adjusted, she saw they'd stopped
at the piney woods by the clear lagoon where she'd first been
abandoned, where she'd met Hidir, the shepherd and the Prince who
set about to change Hürü.

"But I've been here before!" she cried. "I'm back on square one."

"Sometimes we have to go back in order to move forward," Abd-es-Samad said.

Beside the clear lagoon, one of the demon slaves pitched a tent; the other brought forth a comfortable sofa on which he scattered fat cushions. The first demon then brought the two little boxes in which the little coral fish were imprisoned; the other approached with the saddlebags. Then they stood before their master, hands folded, awaiting further orders.

"You must have all the comforts of home, mustn't you?" Hürü said to her fat friend. "Even when you're on the most important mission of your life."

"Let's eat," Abd-es-Samad said. "There's no virtue in suffering discomfort."

After wining and dining himself royally on the provisions of the magic chef of the saddlebags, Abd-es-Samad took the two little boxes in hand and recited a charm over them.

"At thy service, O Alchemist of the Age!" said a little voice in one of the boxes.

"Have mercy!" said another wee voice from the other. The little voices kept praying for help, for compassion, swore blue oaths as well as unspeakable obscenities, but Abd-es-Samad wouldn't desist. He went on relentlessly reciting his charms, tormenting the owners of the little voices, until the two boxes burst into smithereens; as the fragments whizzed about through the air, there appeared two creatures with their hands bound behind them.

"Quarter! O Alchemist of the Age!" said one. "What dost thou desire unto us?"

"My desire is to burn you into two crisps if you don't open for me the Treasure of the Tallest of the Tall."

"Hold thy fire, I pray thee!" said the first creature. "We promise thee obedience."

"That's a good demon," Abd-es-Samad said.

"We will deliver thee the Treasure," the second said, "on condition that the virgin called Hürü, the daughter of Turhan, be present to open it. For the Treasure cannot be opened save by her."

"Here she is!" Abd-es-Samad said. "Did you imagine I'd come without her, you imbecile? She beholds you as you make an idiot of yourself, trying to squirm out of your promise."

"Mercy!" said the first creature, crestfallen.

"We were told she'd be a virgin damsel, O Alchemist of the Age!"

the second said. "Yet, she looks to us like an infidel gentleman."

"See what morons they really are?" Abd-es-Samad said to Hürü as he made a gesture which set both creatures shaking and trembling as if struck by a lightning bolt.

"Quarter!" said one. "Wouldst thou destroy us, O Alchemist of the Age?"

"At thy service," said the other," I prithee!"

With all their "thys" and "thees," Hürü thought, these creatures must have been out of circulation for a long time. But they both looked quite young. Perhaps age didn't tell on demons.

Abd-es-Samad took a glass tube out of his sleeve and some tablets of red carnelian which he placed in the tube; then he brought forth a vessel, put in it some charcoal and blew in it a fire with a single puff. The charcoal was kindled at once.

"Now, my dear Hürü," he said, "I will first instruct you before I recite the charm. Once I throw the necessary ingredient in the tube and recite the charm, I cannot speak. Or else the charm will be frustrated."

"Shoot," Hürü said.

"When I recite the charm, I will be in a mighty trance. The water in the lagoon will dry up; there will appear a door of gold, the size of a city gate, on which are two metal knockers. Descend to the door and knock lightly. Wait a while. Then, knock a second time with more force. No one will answer. So give three sharp raps without intermission and with great force. You will hear someone say: 'Who knocks at the door to the Treasures and knows not how to solve mysteries?' You reply: 'I am Hürü, the daughter of Turhan.' The speaker then will open the door for you.

"He will appear to you at once with a sword in his hand. 'If you are Hürü,' he will say to you, 'then stretch forth your neck so I may smite off your head.' Don't be afraid. Just stretch out your neck. As he brings the sword down on your neck, he will fall before you. He has no soul. His sword cannot hurt you. But if you resist him, the apparition will acquire the strength to slay you, for he will draw power from your fear.

"If you've performed your task obediently, you will see another door. Knock on it. The door will open and a horseman will charge, his spear tilted at you. 'What brought you to this place where neither *jinni* nor man enters?' he will demand as he shakes his spear. Don't answer him but open your shirt fearlessly and present him your chest for him to smite. When he strikes your breastbone, he will fall off his horse lifeless. You will see that he, too, has no soul. But if you oppose him, he will pierce your heart.

"Then, knock on the third door. An archer will immediately take aim at you. Don't run away. Just stand there fearlessly. His arrow will not pierce you. But he, like the other two, will fall down soulless once he releases his arrow. If you try to evade him, he will pierce you through.

"Out of the fourth door, a fierce lion will rush at you, gnashing his teeth. Don't flee from him. Present him your hand which he will bite only to fall before you in a heap. His bite won't hurt unless you try avoiding it; if you do, he will maul and devour you.

"At the fifth door, you will meet a black slave. 'Who are you?' the slave will ask. Reply, 'I am Hürü.' And the black slave will say, 'If you are Hürü, then enter the sixth door.'

"Advance at once to the sixth door and there say: 'Oh, Jesus, tell Moses to open the door.' The door will open. You enter. There, two vile serpents will dart at you. Stretch out a hand for each serpent to bite. As before, these apparitions, too, will curl up before you. But if you shrink, their poison will prove deadly.

"The last door, the seventh, has behind it the most infernal illusion yet. Simply Satanic! The semblance that will approach you shall be none other than your own father, the good father, the good Physician called Turhan. 'Welcome, my darling daughter,' he will say; 'approach so I may embrace you, my Sweet Idiot.' But you must reply: 'Keep your hands off me, foul old man!' Don't let him embrace you under any condition. Instead, say to him, 'Start stripping off your clothes, old man; when you're down to nothing, dance before me like the fiend you really are!' He will say: 'I reared you and loved you, my daughter. Have you no shame? No sense of propriety? How is it that you would have your father strip off his clothing to humiliate himself before you?' But pay him no attention. Tell him: 'If you don't start pulling off your clothes at once and dance before me naked, I will kill you for sure!' Draw your rapier to show him it's not an idle threat. And say 'Pull off!'

"Well, he will do his utmost to beguile you, begging and humbling himself, mentioning a hundred things that are dear to you, ideas that you cherish. Yet, show him no mercy. Each time he strips off a piece of apparel, demand that he pull off the rest. Don't stop threatening him until he's down to his birthday suit. Then, make him dance until he's exhausted and falls down before you lifeless. He, too, has no soul. If you show him mercy, he will show you none."

"What if I can't make my father dance?" Hürü said. "What then?"

"He's not really your father, fool!" Abd-es-Samad said. "He's an apparition just like the rest. You must understand this. If you fail, he will give you the most severe beating you've received and from which you won't recover."

"Not at all?" Hürü said. "You mean he will kill me?"

"Might," Abd-es-Samad said. "Or else cripple you for life. But if you make the image of your father strip and dance naked, the mysterious contrivance will all have become dissolved, the talismans annulled, and you will be safe. Then you will enter the treasury.

"In the chamber, you will see mountains of gold and gems piled everywhere. Pay no attention to the stuff. Gold and precious gems aren't what we're after. At the end of the chamber, you will notice a canopied bed. Pull the curtains. You will see the arch-magician called Tallest of the Tall lying on a couch of gold. This gigantic figure is the arch-magician's mummy. On his chest there will be something round, shining like the moon; that is the celestial planisphere. The mummy of the magician is also equipped with the wondrous sword hanging from his belt; on his finger is the seal-ring; around his neck, attached to a chain, is the kohl-pot. He has no need of these things. Remove and bring the four reposited objects back here, without lingering over the treasures. Now, have you got it?"

"I think so," Hürü said.

"Recite what I said, so I know you've memorized everything."

Abd-es-Samad made Hürü recite until she had it down pat. Then, he continued speaking his charms until he charmed himself into a mighty trance that had him on the ground, thrashing about like a madman. The demon slaves and demon mules were out cold too. Only Hürü was insensible to the charms. And Lo! the clear lagoon dried up just as Abd-es-Samad had said; and in the dry bed appeared the door to the Treasure. Looking at Abd-es-Samad once more, Hürü saw he was still reciting through the hot foam on his lips, thoroughly entranced out of his mind. He never gives up, Hürü thought.

She descended to the door and knocked on it. Now she was on her own to endure the horror Abd-es-Samad had predicted.

"Who knocks at the doors of the Treasury and knows not how to solve mysteries?" a voice asked from within.

"I am Hürü," she answered, "the daughter of Turhan." The door opened and the person came forth, drawing his sword.

"Stretch forth your neck," the person commanded, "so I may cut off your head."

So she stretched her neck. The person smote her neck, which didn't hurt at all, and the hostile fellow fell down before her.

Chalk one up for me, said Hürü to herself.

Abd-es-Samad had been right; the other doors proved no more difficult than the first; the apparitions, although startling, were no more harmful than the inhabitants of her dreams. Hürü proceeded intrepidly until she arrived at the last door behind which she knew lurked the image of her own father whom she hadn't seen for such a long time, and for whom she longed.

"Welcome, my darling daughter," Turhan Bey said, as tears of rejoicing fell down his dear cheeks, "where have you been, Sweet Idiot? Approach, so I may embrace you."

"You keep your hands off me, foul old man!" Hürü said, her heart longing to fall into his arms like a child, wishing to be cuddled, pampered, made to feel safer than safe. "Start stripping off your duds! And when you're stark naked, dance like the foul fiend you really are!"

"I reared and loved you," Turhan Bey said. "I stayed by you when you were afraid in your little bed, rubbed your tummy when it ached; I took joy in everything you said and felt your pain when you injured yourself. Is this the way to repay me? Have you no shame? No sense of what's right and proper? You cannot mean to have your dear father strip and dance naked before you, as if he were some nautch girl."

Hürü wanted so much to agree with him, to apologize and withdraw her irrational command, let happen what may. But she remembered Abd-es-Samad's remonstrations that this wasn't really Turhan Bey but some infernal contraption to make her lose heart.

"Quit blithering," she said, "and pull off your clothes. Or else, suffer instant death! See this rapier? I'm not holding it for show."

"So you raise your hand against your own father!" Turhan Bey said sadly, pulling off his coat. "Your heart must be made of stone."

I can't do it, Hürü thought; yet, I must! How can I raise my hand against the semblance of a man who never raised his against me, even when I most deserved punishment? What kind of monster have I become? Abd-es-Samad must've divined the heartless terrorist asleep in me who rages indiscriminately against the most sacred bonds.

As soon as Turhan Bey stripped off one piece of apparel, Hürü forced him to remove the next, telling him to hurry up and not give her any gibberish about the duties of a proper daughter.

"At least, let me keep my underdrawers," Turhan Bey begged. "I implore you by all that's sacred. Would you gaze on your father's shame?"

"How should you be my father, you accursed semblance?" she said. "My father lives in Istanbul. And he's not in the least interested in guarding some stinking treasure."

But she felt uncertain: the semblance gave a very convincing performance; so, it wasn't clear as to what was art and what life. She'd already humiliated Turhan Bey enough as it was. What harm would there be in letting him keep on his drawers? She was abashed. She didn't want to see her father's manhood dangle, undulate and wobble before her as he danced. All these years, she hadn't even considered that her father, too, must have a mantool. How else would she have arrived in this world?

"Didn't you hear me, old man?" she heard herself say. "I said, strip off everything! How many times must you be told?"

"God will get you for this!" Turhan Bey said, stepping out of his drawers.

"Now dance!" Hürü commanded. "Put your heart in the dancing, too. I don't want a token performance. Do the belly dance. That's right! C'mon faster, faster! Shimmy a little. That's right. See, you can do it!"

Turhan Bey's manhood didn't seem as horrendous as she'd imagined. It was just a bunch of dingles and wattles between his legs that looked a bit ineffectual in a mass of graying curly hair. The apparatus moved sadly to the rhythm of his appallingly bad dance.

"You never learned to dance, did you?" she said. "Faster, I said! Get on with it, old man. I haven't got all day, waiting on you to split in twain your black heart."

Turhan Bey endeavored to move himself with the speed his heartless daughter required; finally, exhausted, he crumpled lifeless at Hürü's feet. Once the motion ceased, Hürü could see this wasn't her father at all: it was just a body as empty as the begging, the admonishments, the fear of God, the familial love he so cleverly invoked. The apparition had tried to make Hürü behave in obedience to a promise she'd made as a child: Daddy, you're the only man I'll ever love; I will never be anything but your little girl; touch my heart and hope to die.

She entered the chamber where heaps of gold and mounds of precious gems were stored. Ignoring the riches, she drew the canopy that concealed the Tallest of the Tall, where the arch-magician slept his petrified sleep, the four objects of absolute power sitting uselessly upon him. She advanced, loosened the sword, took the seal-ring off his finger, the kohl-pot off the chain; lastly, she removed the devastatingly bright celestial planisphere from his chest. And, oh, listen! A heavenly music filled the vault. Scarcely believing her ears, Hürü searched for the source of the music. It was a lyre of stone that played all by itself, as if unseen fingers plucked its strings. She listened, transported, until the stone lyre stopped playing as suddenly as it had begun.

"I will have the lyre, if you don't mind," Hürü said to the mummy. "You're so petrified, you can't hear it play. The stone lyre is the reward I give myself for suffering through the last test."

And, although it wasn't instructed, she took the lyre in addition to the four objects of absolute power. She wasn't struck down for taking the lyre unbidden, as she thought she might be; instead, she heard voices which applauded her robbery.

"May you enjoy, O Hürü, that which you obtained," the voices sang in contrapuntal harmony; "may you instruct and delight."

The voices didn't cease until she went out of the treasury into the fresh air. Once she stepped on the bank, the lagoon materialized back into its bed, erasing her tracks and reclaiming piles of gold and gems that were not meant, obviously, to do mankind any good. Outside, Abd-es-Samad was just recovering from his trance, clouds of fumigation still thick around him. He seemed surprised to see Hürü all in one piece.

"But it wasn't written," he exclaimed, "that you'd succeed the first time! You were to be beaten to an inch of your life. Yet, here you are with the four objects! It was written that you were to succumb to the last apparition!"

"I guess," Hürü said, "whoever wrote it didn't know I'd be spending some time at Selim's boot camp, learning to take orders that go against the grain."

"But it was written we were to repeat the whole process again next year, the same time, the same place. How did you resist your father?"

"He almost had me there!" Hürü said. "But, look what I got for my trouble!"

"What's this?" Abd-es-Samad said, fingering the lyre which remained mute even as his fat, greasy fingers plucked the strings. "Is this thing really what I think it is? I had no idea that the Stone-Born Lyre existed in the Treasury."

"Goes to show," Hürü said, "not even Abd-es-Samad knows everything!"

"But the Stone-Born Lyre appeared only two times before!" cried Abd-es-Samad. "Once, back in time immemorial, it was in the hands of a man-god whose singing soothed even the savage beasts, but incited housewives into savagery. Tore him to bits, they did, those mad mothers! That's how Orpheus bit the dust. The second time around, the Lyre awoke in the hands of a blind bard, centuries ago, whose voice became immortal. Homer. Know him?"

"Don't know any Homer," Hürü said, "but I've got the Lyre."

"I must have the Stone-Born Lyre!" Abd-es-Samad bellowed, turning purple from covetousness. "You are still but a child, Hürü. What do you know of a man's longing for immortality? You'll end up losing the Lyre. You just wait and see. Easy come, easy go. Whereas I know how to hold onto things. So, let me have the Lyre, Hürü girl, and I will give you something more delightful than a mute instrument. I'll trade you the magic-chef of the saddlebags. How's that?"

"You know what I think of your greasy cuisine."

"Then what do you say to all the gold and the gems in the Treasury? You will be enormously rich!"

"Cut it out!" Hürü said. "You know my name's written on this Lyre."

Abd-es-Samad worked himself up to such a tantrum that, in his fury, he burned the two wretched and fishy sons of the Red King down to two blackened cinders. He looked around for other destruction to wreak as his demon mules and demon slaves cowered and whimpered in the weeds.

"You're being childish, Abd-es-Samad," Hürü said. "You promised those two devils mercy if they complied. They did. Yet, you burned them just because you're having a tantrum."

"Ah," Abd-es-Samad said. "Who keeps promises made to demons?"

"I would," Hürü said. "That's why it's not in your power to take the Stone Lyre away from me."

"That's true," Abd-es-Samad said petulantly. "I can't take the Stone-Born Lyre unless you give it freely. Keep the lousy lyre. I don't have an ear for music anyway."

"But you can't resist the temptation," Hürü said, "of owning something special. You're too covetous, as your Jew brother said. And I fear these four objects you wanted so badly will eventually ruin you."

"I'm not listening to sermons," he said, "from some mere girl. Save your breath."

"Now," Hürü said, "let's go back to your house. There, I will teach myself to play this lyre while waiting for a ship that sails for Beirut."

"Who's inviting you to my house?" Abd-es-Samad said, still resentful despite the four fantastic objects Hürü had brought up for him. "You're back in your precious country now. So, hie yourself to your parents' home."

"I'm inviting myself," Hürü said. "Tell your demons to transport us back. Or else I will tell them why they don't have to obey you at all. Then where would you be? You'd have to get yourself around on your own two fat feet. Look, Abd-es-Samad, I braved the image of my own father. Believe me, I shall have no trouble braving you."

"Some people!" he said. "Give them an inch."

But, back home, Abd-es-Samad was too preoccupied with his objects to get even with Hürü. He just sat in his study, debating whether to turn in the four wonderful objects to his father's teacher or keep them for himself. Maybe he'd let the book called *The Stories of the Ancients*, or *One Thousand and One Nights*, go hang itself. Of course, he'd rather have the objects and the book as well. So mighty was his dilemma, the talismans sat gathering dust while Abd-es-Samad paced around like a madman.

Hürü began finger exercises on the lyre. The lyre responded. She knew only a little something about string instruments, but the lyre seemed to be a teacher itself. Abd-es-Samad was too engrossed with his possessions to be aware of the golden tones, but Rahmeh, his *jinniye* daughter, sat at Hürü's feet, thinking she adored Hürü, entranced by the music the lyre made. Hürü just couldn't shake off Rahmeh, who followed her everywhere, swooning, screaming, tearing her hair in ecstasy. So intense were the *jinniye's* feelings, Hürü was afraid the creature would tear her to pieces from an excess of idolatry. She asked Abd-es-Samad to order his daughter to stay away, but either the Maghrabi was losing control over his demonic child or else the magic of music was stronger than the magic of bondage. Rahmeh grovelled and begged to be allowed her presence. Perhaps the female demon wasn't as soulless as Abd-es-Samad thought. When the *jinniye* fingered the lyre shyly, the lyre remained mute.

"You see," Hürü explained to the poor devil, "my name must be written on the lyre."

Despite her entrancement with the lyre, she knew she couldn't remain on Cyprus and face her fate. Her fate would never become manifest if she settled for the life of a virtuoso musician. She must have more. She must move on. So Hürü made travel plans.

Just as the news reached Hürü that the ship on which she'd purchased a first-class ticket was ready to sail, another sort of news pierced Abd-es-Samad through both ears. He rushed into the room where Hürü was packing her few things.

"Your Selim has just taken Persia," he informed her. "He finally cornered Shah Ismail and forced him to give battle in the valley of Chalderan. Shah Ismail fled, leaving his famous throne on the battlefield. Selim followed him deep into Persia, razed the countryside, the cities, massacred the people. Blood runs so heavily down the streets, Selim has earned himself the name of Selim the Grim."

"Ohh!" Hürü said, one hand covering her face, the other on the lyre. "He has fulfilled his fate. He has the blood of Moslems on his hands! Now Selim won't ever enter Paradise."

The image of Selim, which had been receding in her mind, re-emerged now with heartbreaking vitality. She'd abandoned Selim to his worst nature, the she-wolf that ran ahead of him to carnage, while she, Hürü, indulged in senseless adventure, aiding the likes of this greasy Abd-es-Samad and learning to play an instrument whose action was as fugitive as time. Suddenly, she felt wearied of herself. How much better it would be if she didn't have time to exist in Selim's time! An idea came to her head.

"What year's this?" she asked Abd-es-Samad, drying her tears. "I mean, in actual time."

"Let's see," he said, consulting his tables. "In good time, it's the 920th year of the Prophet's Flight. In infidel time, I reckon it to be the 1514th year of the birth of Christ."

"How awful!" she exclaimed. "I wasted two years of my precious life in your company. Seemed like a couple of months, too! Where does time go?"

"Nowhere," Abd-es-Samad said.

"But can you turn time back?"

"What a fool you are!" he cried. "Women just don't understand time! See, time both flows away and also remains in particulate form. It isn't so difficult to visualize. Just think of an hourglass where time is sand that flows away and also abides in small, discrete and reusable particles. People liken time to a river. All right. But time's particulate matter also has the capacity to dilate and contract; so, it can move in different speeds and directions simultaneously. Time is an immaterial throb; it is also material. Understand?"

"No," Hürü said. "But do go on."

"In the paradox," Abd-es-Samad observed, "there's much energy to be harnessed. If anybody can harness time, it's yours truly. I've sent animals around in dilated time. Some I've retrieved. Other beasts have remained stuck in time which recontracted on itself."

"Well," Hürü said, "I'll risk it anyway. Send me, Abd-es-Samad! Send me to Baghdad at the time of Harun-er-Rashid. He's reputed to be the last of the just and compassionate monarchs. I want to see for myself how a man like Harun-er-Rashid conducts himself."

"Save yourself the trouble," Abd-es-Samad said. "Go play your lyre like a good girl. Besides, I can't promise to send you back with any sort of accuracy. You might find yourself stuck in a very disagreeable time."

"Can't be worse than this time," Hürü said. "Send me! If you want to avoid trouble with me."

"You're probably right," Abd-es-Samad said, sighing. "But you do understand, don't you, that you're going at your own risk? Release me of any sin. I don't want to burn in hell for having caused the negligent destruction of a human being."

"How touching!" Hürü said. "I didn't know you had any scruples about interfering with life, considering the way you treat animals and poor devils."

"I've told you and told you," he said, "but it makes no impression. Devils and animals are just machines! But you think, just because my appearance displeases you, I must be a wicked man. I'm not."

"Go ahead," she said, "treat me as if I'm just another machine. I don't mind."

"Nope!" Abd-es-Samad said. "Swear that you hereby absolve me of any harm I might cause you by mistake. Otherwise, you shan't get off the ground."

"I hereby absolve you of any harm you might cause me by mistake."

"Hold onto your hat," Abd-es-Samad said, "and your Stone-Born Lyre. And so, goodbye!"

Time opened and dilated, sucking Hürü away. Just before she lost consciousness of experiential time, the last thing she heard was Abd-es-Samad asking her to bring back from Baghdad something good to eat.

Part Two

INITIATION

*Wonder Journey back to
Eighth Century Baghdad and
The Book of A Thousand
and One Nights*

Chapter 10

THE CANDYMAKER'S TALE

Hürü wakes up in Sweet's candy vat and sings for her Freedom

*H*ürü woke up in a vat of hot gumdrop mixture. From the taste and the smell, she judged it to be rose-essence flavored *lokum*. At once, she wiped the sticky sweet off her eyes and peered over the rim of the vat. She was in a sweet shop where the person in charge seemed either to have fainted, or been killed, by Hürü's materialization in the confection.

"Hey, somebody, help me out," she called weakly, wrestling with the hot, sweet goo that sucked at her clothes; fortunately, although in the soft-ball stage, the concoction had somewhat cooled. But it was jelling fast.

"Hey, somebody!" she cried again.

Somebody opened his eyes from where he was stretched out cold.

"Iron!" he cried. "Iron, ye blessed!"

"Only a human here," Hürü said. "So get up, please, and help me out. I'm being candied to death."

"You ruined the confection, rotten boy!" the sweetmaker said, struggling to rise. "What's the idea of hurtling into a perfectly good vat of *lokum*? I was preparing it for the Caliph's birthday reception too! Now I have nothing to show for all my pains."

"Just scoop me out," Hürü said. "The Caliph will never know his candy was ever visited by a person."

"I wouldn't be so sure," the sweetmaker said, "if you're as much in bad taste in person as you are in your pranks."

Presenting his broad back, he helped her out anyway. She hoisted herself up, clutching his shoulders. With a considerable amount of rose-flavored jelly still enveloping her, she looked like a candied Venetian dandy. Were she back on the fair island of Cyprus, the inhabitants would've gladly provided the feathers. The sweetmaker complained and grumbled that this was no way to treat the most accomplished confectionist in Baghdad; he wanted to know which of his rivals had put Hürü up to such a nasty business. So she was, after all, in Baghdad! The sweetmaker's pure and clear Arabic delighted Hürü's ear. She must be in Baghdad before the time the language had become vulgarized. Even a sweetmaker spoke it with the authority of the Koranic texts.

"Sorry," Hürü said. "The man who hurtled me here must've been thinking of some rose-flavored *lokum*."

"And you're an infidel to boot!" cried the candy man. "The confection is spoiled for sure. I couldn't serve the Faithful something so impure."

"Just in infidel's garb, man," Hürü said. "Under my costume beats a heart of pure fidelity. I'm the one who should complain. Your sweet completely ruined my fine Venetian getup. And just look at my Lyre! It may never play again."

"Who asked you," said the confectioner, "to fall in? Excuse me while I call the cops. Let's see how you like getting your butt basted. That'll show you to scare a man half to death!"

"Wait!" Hürü cried. "Don't go for the police yet."

"So give me one good reason why not," said the candy man, running his finger on the candied Lyre and then, for some reason, licking the stuff off. Suddenly, the man's expression changed. Not only was he full of smiles, he seemed quite eager to lick the Lyre clean. "Delicious," he kept saying in between the virile tonguings he gave the Lyre. "Do you mind?"

"Suit yourself," Hürü said, quite surprised that the man changed his tune so suddenly. Must be the Lyre, sweetening the man's thoughts. But she thought it was wise to play for time anyway. "And when you're through with it, I'll try tuning my Lyre. Then I'll sing you a heroic song that runs to at least a couple of thousand couplets. It'll take me several days just to sing it—and many more, of course, to compose the *mathnawi* called 'The Song of Jaudar.'"

"This I gotta hear!" the sweetmaker said. "Just make that stone thing play a single note, I'm ready to forgive and forget."

"Now you're talking," Hürü said.

"Of course," the man went on, smacking his lips as he went at the Lyre, "my taste for music is stronger than most folks' for candy."

"If that's the case," Hürü said, "you must be a helluva music lover."

"That I am, alas," the man said, sighing and returning the Lyre, candied no more. "I'd better close the shop. The Caliph's slaves won't leave us alone, clamoring at the door for their sweets. Those people at the Palace! They have some heavy habit."

The candy man closed shop so that the singing wouldn't be interrupted. He tacked on the door a sign that read: Recovering from the Plague. With all the trouble this man was going to, Hürü hoped she wouldn't disappoint such a faithful audience. But the Lyre didn't seem indisposed from being dunked in rose-flavored jell-candy. In fact, it had never played better. After striking an improvisational arpeggio to find her musical theme, Hürü began to sing of a young man called Jaudar from Cairo. Jaudar's talent, or his tragic flaw, was that of being too good a son. She was amazed at herself, hearing the Arabic meter and couplets, not to mention the prescribed rhyming scheme, fall so easily from her lips—the same ones which, some time ago, couldn't even properly pronounce a simple text. It was as if she'd learned to versify in her sleep. And in a foreign tongue, too! Or else, necessity made her sing.

She sang of Jaudar who was lovable and lucky. But dumb. She sang about him for several days. And the candy man, impressed out of his skull, kept treating her to the choicest morsels of meat as well as sweets, mopping her brow with clean towels when the singing and the composition made her break out in a sweat, putting her to bed when her eyes closed from exhaustion.

The story she gave about Jaudar had its basis in Hürü's own experience with the three Maghrabis and their Jewish brother. But her hero was the one involved with the complicated and dangerous enterprise of snatching treasured objects. Yet, since Jaudar had his tragic flaw, the story had to end badly for him. For several days she sang of Jaudar's sufferings, of his luck that always got him screwed, of the way he couldn't win from losing. Once she had set Jaudar in motion, his nature predicated the action as if by a force of its own. She knew now how Jaudar would end up, given his compulsion to be

loved by everyone. Each stroke of good fortune had to be counter-
poised with an evil. For Jaudar's deathbed speech, he'd have to wind
up forgiving those who killed him. On the twelfth night, Hürü finished
up with Jaudar's funeral. "The Song of Jaudar" was done.

"What a sad *mathnawi!*" the candy man said, mopping his own
tears. "And too true!"

The good man wept profusely for the fate of Jaudar. He pressed
Hürü to his breast and wetted her head with his tears. Hürü, too, was
surprised and pleased with the integrity of her inventions, although
the story was part lie. The sweetmaker had no trouble believing the
lie. He felt Jaudar's life so completely, he supposed "The Song of
Jaudar" was one and the same with Hürü's own. The story of all
artists, she supposed, was always being suspected of singing thinly
disguised autobiography. This, of course, was true, in a way, for she'd
become the person she'd impersonated. A chord of Jaudar still
vibrated in her heart.

"Stay with me, dear Jaudar," the candy man said. "And I'll treat
you like a son. I'll even teach you the art of making candy. You sing
well, but minstrels don't live half as well as a confectionist does.
That's right! Folks will always throw away money on something
sweet. But after they listen to your songs, boy, even if they dig them,
they sneak away without tossing a penny in your hat."

That's how Hürü came to exchange her Venetian dandy's garb
for an Arab street boy's robes and stayed under the name of Jaudar,
a name so simply assumed for her by her benefactor. Under his
tutelage, she began learning the mysteries of treacle and cream,
nougat and caramel, crystallizing and pulverizing, candy coating and
taffy filling, syrups and sherbets, and about confiture and scents so
fascinating that people's tastebuds went wild. Nobody could stop at
just one piece. That's how formidable were this candy man's sweets!

He was a fair complexioned man in his early forties, this sweetmaker, and still something of a ladykiller although he took no
advantage of his potent manly attractions. His name was Bedr-ed-Din
Hasan. And quite a mouthful to say, too! Since his disposition was so
suited to his trade, Hürü asked if she might call him Sweet. He
agreed. And Sweet he was.

Every single day the Caliph's slaves stopped at Sweet's shop to
obtain the daily satisfactions of the Palace's immense sweet tooth.
The orders Sweet filled were so large, the purchases had to be loaded
on several camels. The brisk candy trade meant Sweet had to work

from the time the first birds twittered until the hoot-owls went to bed. Hürü's willingness to work was certainly appreciated by Sweet. He promised her that one of these days they'd take off a whole day and go see the Caliph in person when the Caliph held open court. But the day never came. They were far too busy to even scratch their noses.

Hürü was pleased to find out that the Caliph of the time was none other than the King of the Age and the Commander of the Faithful: Harun-er-Rashid himself. She told Sweet about her burning desire to meet the greatest ruler of all time.

"The trouble with kings is the same the world over," Sweet said. "Since they are responsible to no man, they soon forget their responsibility to God."

"Sweet, what would you know about kings?" Hürü laughed. "You're better off not knowing any king in person. You're a lucky man. After all, you've devoted your life to sweetness."

"Ah, I know more than you'd think," Sweet said. "You'd never believe what I know, though, seeing me slave over a hot stove. You'd think I was always a working-class man. Once I was very close to the throne. Indeed, too close."

"How close?"

"If I told you my story," Sweet said, "you'd never believe it anyway. Nobody ever has. So, I've quit telling it."

"Try me," Hürü said, pouring hot caramel into a pan. "I, too, have seen some incredible things. I might just be the person who believes you."

Sweet, it turns out, was born in Basra. But his father (called Nur-ed-Din) was one of the twin sons of the Prime Minister to the Sultan of Egypt and had begun his life in Cairo. The twins were brought up there in great luxury, and when the old Prime Minister died, the boys (Nur-ed-Din and Shems-ed-Din), both excellent young men, were made co-Prime Ministers of Egypt. They performed the duties of their joint position so admirably that not even hairsplitters could find fault with their administration. But the twins were still bachelors. One evening, while discussing pleasant subjects as well as matters of state, they decided to look for wives and get married. They planned on the same day. What's more, if their wives presented them with a son and a daughter respectively, they'd affiance the boy and the girl in the crib and join them in marriage when the children came of age. Pleased with their stratagem to become even closer to one another, the twin brothers broke out another bottle.

"'So,' said Nur-ed-Din, 'What wedding gift should my son give your daughter?'

"'I think,' Shems-ed-Din said, 'your son should give my daughter three thousand dinars, three gardens and three farms. Hey, it wouldn't be right if the young man tried to settle for less.'

"'Get lost!' exclaimed Nur-ed-Din. 'That's asking way too much. Remember, we're twins. And what's more, we're running the show here together. You shouldn't be asking for any wedding gift at all. Left hand asking the right hand for a gift. So maybe you want to show off. All right, we can work something out. Something nominal. You're smart enough to know that a son is worth more than a daughter. Hey, my son will be the one to carry around our family name. Not your worthless daughter!'

"'So what's wrong with my daughter!' cried Shems-ed-Din, jumping up from his seat, his face redder than the wine in the cup. 'If you think your son's better than my daughter, think again! What's more, a sexist like you has no business sharing the highest office in this land. I've always known you had very little sense. I let you tag along all these years out of pity, seeing how you never could've made it on your own. Hey, I wouldn't let my daughter marry your stupid son for all the tea in China!'

"'Who's asking her anyway?' Nur-ed-Din said, hopping mad. 'Her father happens to be a ninny who's studying to become an idiot.'"

Remember, both of them were unmarried as yet, and certainly not blessed with any children. Still, they quarrelled bitterly and swore they'd never let their children see each other, far less marry. Nur-ed-Din, Sweet's father-to-be, felt he could no longer breathe the same air as his twin, corrupted as the Cairene air was with said twin's foul breath. And his so-called twin didn't even appreciate his official help, though he'd always carried on about how two heads were better than one. Well, let the stinker try in his own fat! So Nur-ed-Din quit Cairo in a huff and set out to find himself another life far from Shems-ed-Din and his worthless, future daughter.

That's how come Nur-ed-Din ended up in Basra where, through his natural talents, he won the trust and affection of the current Prime Minister to the Sultan of Basra. Pretty soon, he married the old P.M.'s daughter and eventually succeeded his father-in-law in office. The happy issue of the marriage between the old Vizier's daughter and Nur-ed-Din happened to be Sweet. Sweet grew up in Basra with much affection bestowed upon him by doting parents, maternal relatives, even the Sultan of Basra himself.

"I was thought to be a very fetching boy," Sweet admitted modestly. "Things came to me easily. My father was a wise and compassionate man, and my mother a handsome and affectionate woman. But all this changed rapidly when my father died. At the time, I was only fifteen."

On his deathbed, Sweet's father informed his son of what had transpired between him and his brother, Shems-ed-Din, who still lived in Cairo. He gave Sweet a document, complete with names and dates, sealed with the old man's official seal.

"'Bedr-ed-Din Hasan, my son,' wept the dying Prime Minister, 'keep this document safe. It's proof of your origin, your rank and your ancestry. If things go badly for you in Basra when I die, travel to Egypt and ask for your uncle, Shems-ed-Din. Go to him and tell him I died in exile, all the while longing for him and my homeland.'"

Perhaps his father hoped, Sweet thought, the broken covenant would somehow be fulfilled; perhaps he foresaw that things in Basra might go sour for Sweet. And sure enough, Sweet quickly fell into disgrace with the Sultan. Sweet's crime against the throne was that he mourned for his father too long, thereby neglecting to go to court to entertain the Sultan, who longed for Sweet's constant company. The King of Basra, turns out, was a flaming queen.

"That's when I realized that being overly attractive can also be a curse," Sweet said. "The Sultan was enraged that I seemed to shun his love."

"Did the Sultan want you that way?" Hūrū asked, shocked.

"I believe so," Sweet said. "Why else did he act like a lover spurned?"

Fortunately for Sweet, a courtier who respected the dead Vizier's memory informed Sweet that the Sultan planned to confiscate all the houses, the wealth and land that now belonged to Sweet by provision of the laws of inheritance; Sweet himself was to be arrested, brought before the Sultan and sentenced. There wasn't a moment to lose. Sweet must flee Basra at once. As the troops kicked in the front door, Sweet escaped through the back, the skirts of his coat thrown over his head. After much dodging and many close calls, he hid in the cemetery by his father's tomb. There, exhausted from all the running, he fell asleep.

"That's when inexplicable events began taking place," Sweet said. "I woke up in Cairo."

"How'd you do that?" Hūrū said.

"For reasons of their own," Sweet said, "a *jinniye* and an *ifrit* flew me there. When I woke up, a lovely *jinniye* and her companion *ifrit*, the ugliest creature I've ever seen—the kind that dive into latrines—were sitting and staring at me."

The two supernatural creatures informed Sweet that the loveliest maiden in Cairo, the daughter of the Vizier Shems-ed-Din, was being given in marriage that night to a hunchback. The marriage was being inflicted on the fair girl by order of the Sultan because her father had refused her hand to the Sultan, saying that the girl had been promised to her cousin even before she was born. The Sultan, incensed by the refusal, had ordered the girl to marry his fool who was a hunchback. The *ifrit* and the *jinniye* seemed unaware that Sweet was the cousin to whom the damsel had been promised. Sweet, however, saw the augury at once. The two supernatural creatures admitted they also had a dispute between themselves as to who was the fairer of the two: the damsel in distress or Sweet. They'd flown Sweet to Cairo to settle the question. So, Sweet would just have to come along to the wedding party, which was now in progress. They'd see for themselves how the young man's beauty stacked up against that of the young woman's.

Before they all crashed the gate of the wedding, the *ifrit* coached Sweet on how to embarrass the hunchback, and the *jinniye* on how to win the affection of the wedding guests. Sure enough, the more the hunchback was insulted, the more the wedding guests applauded Sweet, and the more determined grew the hunchback to reap the treasure the Sultan had bestowed on his deformed person. But the two supernatural beings wanted the two youths to get into bed together so that they might compare them all the better. So, the *ifrit*, the kind that dives in latrines, fixed the hunchback by frightening him out of his wits and standing him on his head in the hole of the latrine adjoining the bridal chamber. That was how Sweet enjoyed the nuptial night with his fair cousin while, in the latrine hole, the bridegroom stood on his head all night long.

Despite the demons' invisible eyes on them, the couple made much joy, kissing and cooing, speaking vows, singing songs, reciting poetry into the wee hours. Then, they fell to impassioned lovemaking until they both fell fast asleep, exhausted from the heavenly exercise. The promise their fathers had made, so quickly broken, had somehow become fulfilled. But, Sweet supposed, human beings' destinies meant nothing to demonic beings.

"I woke up next morning," Sweet said, "not next to my fair cousin and wife before God, but outside the gates to a strange city. To top it all, I was in my nightshirt, stone cold, hungry, penniless."

One could not, Sweet said, depend on demonic intervention to operate on one's behalf; the demon could as easily carry one away impersonally, negligently, just for the hell of it. Out in the cold, Sweet soon found out from passers-by, who all stopped to extoll his physical attractions, that he was outside the gates of Baghdad. But, when Sweet told the folks who so admired his beauty that he came from Basra, was married in Cairo and woke up in Baghdad—all within twenty-four hours—they laughed at him, while some even wanted to drag him to the local madhouse.

Fortunately, a confectionist, who was among the spectators, took Sweet under his roof and taught him the art of making sweets. Since the old confectionist had made Sweet his heir, Sweet still ran the same shop, bearing his mysterious fate with what he hoped was a stiff upper lip. He'd never taken another wife and had lost hope of ever reuniting with his fair cousin and his wife of one night. And though many a damsel and widow of Baghdad pestered him plenty, even if it were union for a mere hour, he found he had no taste for aggressive wretches.

"You could go back to Cairo," Hürü suggested, "and see for yourself what happened. That's what I'd do if I were you."

"Ah, but something strange befell me," Sweet said, sighing. "I have a broken heart inflicted on me by a fair boy to whom I was inexplicably drawn."

"So!" Hürü said. "You prefer boys, after all!"

"I don't think it's that," Sweet said earnestly. "But love at first sight it certainly was."

Sweet told about the strange meeting with the boy called Ajib. Seems the youth was travelling through Baghdad with his family on their way to Basra. Seeing the city with its beauties, the River Tigris so celebrated by the poets, the family decided to pitch their tents in a square so they might take in the sights, go in the famous bath-houses, divert themselves for a couple of days. The boy Ajib, accompanied by his eunuch and other slaves, just happened to pass by Sweet's shop. Sweet was arrested by the boy's beauty, his elegant manners, the regal way he carried himself. He had just finished preparing a tray of marzipans.

"'Oh, my young master!' Sweet cried out of his shop although he wasn't in the habit of hawking his goods. 'Won't you come in and taste my marzipan, so I might refresh my heart by watching you eat my sweets?'"

As he extended his invitation, so bad in form, Sweet couldn't keep the tears from pouring out of his eyes, stricken as he was with an emotion he couldn't name. The elegant boy, who carried in his hand a camelwhip, seemed fascinated by Sweet's invitation.

"'Let's go in,' he said to his eunuch, 'and have some of this poor man's sweets. I feel sympathy for this candyman.'

"'By God, young master,' said the eunuch, 'it's not proper. But, if you insist, I'll drive the other slaves away, so none may know you entered a sweetshop like some common person.'

"'Truly, sir,' Sweet said to the eunuch, 'my heart loves the boy.'

"'Let's hear none of that!' the eunuch said crossly.

"'You, too, come in, Black Sir,' Sweet said. 'Although your face is like soot, angels will wait on you in Paradise as they do on those whose faces are lily white.'"

The eunuch was so pleased by Sweet's invitation into Paradise, he allowed the boy to enter. And Sweet put before them the marzipans he'd molded into the shape of tiny hearts; he ladled out two bowls of pomegranate compote; he poured them sherbet infused with musk. The slave and the youth ate and drank with much appreciation of Sweet's skill.

"'Sit down and eat with us, candy man,' the boy said. 'Perhaps God will unite us with our father whom we've never seen. We're on a pilgrimage to find our lost father.'

"'My young master, you're so tender in years,' Sweet said; 'yet you already know the anguish of losing someone dear.'"

The boy sighed and burst into tears. Seeing this lovable boy weep so pitifully, Sweet couldn't hold back his tears either, even the eunuch joined the lachrymose scene, and they all had themselves a helluva good cry. After drying their tears, the youth and the cunuch rose and took their leave. Soon as they quit the shop, Sweet suddenly felt inconsolable, as if his soul had departed too. Quickly, he closed his shop and pursued the two customers, not knowing why he did such an unseemly thing. Following hot and heavy, he caught up with the boy and the eunuch.

"'What do you want, candy man?' the eunuch said, greatly distressed.

"'When you two departed,' Sweet said, 'I felt as if my soul, too, left me. I'll accompany you to your tents and then return to my shop.'

"'Scat!' the eunuch cried. 'Shameless man! My young master, see what you brought on us? The candy man isn't satisfied that we condescended to eat his sweets. Now he must follow us from place to place.'

"'You can't drive him off a public thoroughfare,' young Ajib said to his eunuch, his color rising as he lashed his whip on the pavement, 'but if he follows us to the square where the tents are pitched, we'll give him the hiding he deserves.'"

Sweet didn't know what was happening to him; yet, he still hung his head and followed the angry pair. Once the boy and the eunuch drew near the tents, the boy looked behind him to see Sweet persist. Who knew? Maybe Ajib was afraid his family would discover he'd entered a common shop; perhaps the boy thought he saw a gleam of deceit in Sweet's eyes. Perhaps the ardor of the handsome older man revolted the boy. For whatever reason, Ajib seemed terribly incensed. So much so, he picked up a large stone and aimed it perfectly between Sweet's two eyes which took delight in the boy's form and grace. The stone struck Sweet's forehead like a missile; he fell down as one dead. And when he regained his sense, the tents were all gone. Sweet cut a length of linen off his turban and bandaged his forehead, blaming himself for the unfortunate incident.

"I wronged the boy," Sweet told Hürü, beating his fist on his breast with the shame of it all. "I closed my shop and followed him when I shouldn't have. He must've thought I was a pervert."

"You certainly gave a good impression of one," Hürü said. "But whatever did you see in that insufferable young prig?"

"I don't know," Sweet said. "I wish I did. That's why I can't leave for anywhere just now. I'm waiting for young Ajib's caravan to pass by on the way back to Cairo. I must explain myself to him."

"Good luck!" Hürü said. "He's probably the Sultan of Basra by now."

That night, after completing her chores, Hürü treated herself to the magic lyre. She composed her first song of amorous longing. An aging candy man falls in love with the sweet image of youth. He treats his beloved to a dish of marzipans fashioned into hearts. As the marzipan melts in the boy's mouth, the candy man's heart melts in inexplicable tenderness. He must always follow the boy. But the boy is older than the stone with which he smites the older man between the eyes. The candy man's love kills the candy man. Hürü called the song "Death in Baghdad."

"Death appears to the candy man," Sweet commented, weeping deeply again, "in the form of a beautiful boy. How sad! How true!"

And to return the favor of hearing his strange and embarrassing love immortalized in song, Sweet concocted a new confection he named Jaudar. Made of date paste around a core of almond, the confection was molded in the shape of a turtle.

"You go slow, dear Jaudar," Sweet explained, "but you get there." And, as time went on, the confection gained as much popularity in town as the song called "Death in Baghdad."

Chapter 11

THREE LADIES OF BAGHDAD

Hürü sings to save a royal head or two

*H*ürü couldn't forget she was living neither in her own place nor her own time. Despite her happiness in making music with the Stone-Born Lyre and making sweets with a good man, something dreadfully unreal hung over her existence. She lived in exile. She was obliged to sing in a tongue not her own. She lived disguised as a man in the world of men. And she was that Barbarian who'd come to loot another culture.

When she woke up that morning, she still lived in Baghdad. Sweet snored reassuringly in the bunk below. Her tongue hurt. She'd bitten it so hard in her sleep, salt blood filled her mouth. What else can I do? she asked herself: I have no other choice but to sing woodenly in Arabic. What a disastrous language! Guttural, agglutinate, elastic, ambiguous. Arabic must've been invented by a person whose mouth was full of lamb fat and sticky syrup. Yet the thick, gluey, ambiguous sounds that filled her mouth had their own harsh beauty. Arabic destroyed the natural impulse to speak with directness and clarity, but out of this disaster came a formidable succession of sound.

Now, Turkish—her mother tongue—was altogether different. So sweet, so direct and clear. Yet, no one who wasn't born to that language ever learned Turkish well enough to hear its poetry strike clarity that broke your heart. In Turkish, poetry never had to be forced. It arrived on its own, simply and calmly, in the syllables uttered by the peasant in the field, the warrior on the horse, the woman in labor, the child in the crib, the aged grandmother on her deathbed. So why abandon the natural grace of Turkish for the borrowed difficulty of Arabic?

Perhaps, Hürü thought, it's the fascination of the impossible that compels me to hobble along in Arabic. Perhaps because the *Koran* is the touchstone for all inspired speech. Or maybe even that I, like my countrymen, do not honor my native tongue.

How seductive it was to distinguish oneself, under a cloak of mimicry, in a culture whose traditions had been long established! The real difficulty was forging something out of pure freedom: the freedom of having no established cliches. She could've gone for unlimited invention. Yet, she'd bound herself to the thick cliches of the Arabic forms. Was it to break the molds and free the tongue? Perhaps that which binds, frees.

At last Sweet woke to the joy of the morning in Baghdad. Hürü felt so safe in the comfort of having Sweet know both her work and her heart, she could not wait to unmask herself. She could no longer go around letting Sweet think she was a Cairene called Jaudar. She thought she'd first confess to being a Turk. If that sat well, then she'd confess to her real sex.

"Sweet," she said, "guess what I really am."

"A prince," Sweet said, "a poet and a punk."

"Maybe," Hürü said. "But I also happen to be a Turk."

Sweet gasped and grasped his heart as if to protect that besieged organ.

"A Turk!" he finally spat out contemptuously.

"You seem taken aback," Hürü said. "What difference does my origin make now that we're such good friends?"

"Turks are incapable of any real friendship," Sweet said. "I hate to say it, but it's true. I don't pretend we Arabs don't have our faults. We certainly do. But they're minor compared to the flaws of the Turk. Everyone in the world knows what I say is true. By God, it's written that nine-tenths of all the cruelty in the world is in the heart of the Turk."

"Oh?" Hürü said. "Now tell me the name of the fool who wrote that."

"I don't know," Sweet said. "But he was a wise man who knew the hearts of many nations. According to him, nine-tenths of all the intrigue in the world belongs to the Copts, nine-tenths of all perfidy to the Jews, nine-tenths of all stupidity to the Maghrabis."

"And what nine-tenths do the Arabs get?" Hūrū said, trying to joke.

"Bravery," Sweet said, without batting an eyelash.

"Arabs themselves," Hūrū said sadly, "admit to nine-tenths of all the world's envy. But where does this nine-tenths foolishness get you? Nowhere. Just shuts down your mind. But, I guess, you don't have to be a Maghrabi to be stupid."

"Who are you calling stupid, boy?" Sweet said belligerently, going for a very large ladle that he held up as if he'd conk Hūrū on the head.

"Not you, certainly," Hūrū said. "Just your ideas."

"'Just your ideas,'" Sweet imitated her, as if suddenly he loathed her accent, and accompanied the imitation with a limp-wristed gesture. "When the cops get here, we'll see how kindly they take to your lip. Cops hate wimpy homos like you. They hate the way you mince your words. So do I!"

"I'm not a homo," Hūrū said, "and you know it."

"Nonetheless," Sweet said, "you did invent that cruel song about me. I did wonder how a scrawny nobody like you knew about Death who appears in the form of a beautiful youth. You almost convinced me, boy. You almost convinced me to die of love in Baghdad. Is that a nice thing to do?"

"Sweet!" Hūrū cried. "That's just a song!"

"Don't call me Sweet, boy!" Sweet shouted. "My name is Bedr-ed-Din Hasan, a man of rank and ancestry—unlike you. Who are you anyway? Just some trash who blew in from God knows where with God knows what evil intentions. No, I don't see how I can harbor you under my roof any longer. I couldn't bear to touch your hand."

"I cannot believe it! Your heart cannot be so superficial!"

"Who's asking for your opinion anyway?" Sweet quarrelled. "I let you in out of pity, now I find out I've been thoroughly used. You're a user, whatever your name is—complete and unabashed!"

"And you," Hūrū threw back, "you're just like your father and uncle, those half-baked twins. That's what you are. You're a ninny studying to become an idiot!"

"Get out!" Sweet bellowed. "Get out of my shop. And get out of Baghdad! I cannot bear to breathe the stink of your breath!"

That's how Hūrū, having lost her friend over nothing, found herself out on the street. Beware of good men, she thought, for they will not forgive. And perhaps Sweet was justified in his aversion for the Turks: maybe her hand could not be touched without a shudder. The blood her people shed, in the name of conquest, might be on her hands too. But why should she have to feel guilty for the sins of her people? Still, she felt bad enough to bawl. Right out on the street, leaning against a porter's basket abandoned in front of Sweet's shop, she began to weep in earnest. She wept and wept, because it felt good to weep.

"Hey, boy!" she heard a woman's voice say. "Boy, don't cry. Be a good boy and bring along your basket. Just follow me."

In front of Hürü stood a lovely woman who wore a gold-lace veil so thin, her black, thickly fringed eyes could be clearly seen. Hürü picked up the basket and slipped the Stone Lyre down in the bottom. She followed the lady who rustled ahead briskly in her silken garb. They stopped in front of a Christian's shop where the lady bought a jug of olives and two vessels of wine which she placed in the basket strapped on Hürü's back.

"Take it up and follow me," the lady commanded.

Next, the lady stopped at a fruit stand. She bought Syrian apples, Persian melons, peaches from Oman, dates from Aleppo, cucumbers that came from the banks of the Nile, seedless grapes from Smyrna. She also bought dry and fresh flowers: sweet scented myrtle, sprigs of henna and camomile, anemones, violets, pomegranate flowers and eglantine. She placed these in the basket, too.

"Take it up, boy!"

Then they stopped at the butcher's where the lady went hogwild, buying up half a lamb which she had the butcher wrap and drop in the basket. Hürü's back started to give, but the lady wasn't done. At the dry fruit stand she bought a little of every kind of dry fruit; at the confectioners, a rival of Sweet's, she had the man pile up a tray of desserts.

"Lady!" Hürü ventured. "You should've told me right off that you meant to buy up the whole marketplace. I'd have begged, borrowed or stolen a mule. I can't take too much more!"

The lady smiled but paid no attention to Hürü's discomfort. After all, street boys were put on this earth to bear elegant ladies' burdens. She now stopped at the perfumers to buy ten different kinds of scent: rose, orange-blossom, violet, willow, tuberose, musk, frankincense, aloe and jasmine. She bought tall wax candles; she bought silver-gilt sprinkling vessels; and she bought hashish.

"Take it up," she ordered.

Hürü followed the lady. But she couldn't feel her shoulders: the basket straps cut into her chest and her knees buckled as she veered from left to right. Still, the lady forged on, briskly rustling.

Finally, the big spender stopped in front of a handsome mansion. The doors were made of ebony overlaid with gilt designs, like the house of a prince. The lady knocked gently on the portals which were opened by a tall, even lovelier woman, fair complexioned and high bosomed, who moved with the ease of an athlete.

"Come in," said the lady at the door. "Did you get everything?"

"I hope I didn't forget anything," the cateress said.

Hürü groaned while the two ladies seemed amused by her plight.

"You enter, too, porter boy," said the beautiful blonde at the door.

The two ladies took Hürü by both hands, Hürü still buckling under the weight, and led her to a large salon which was extremely ornamented with carved wooden pillars, fountains, settees and drapes. At the end of the salon was an alabaster couch over which was a red satin canopy. On this couch reclined a mature woman at the height of her womanliness, a formidable beauty whose raven-black hair was streaked with a hank of pure white that distinguished her heart shaped face. Now, this must be the noblest daughter of Arabia! Hürü thought.

The lady, undoubtedly the mistress of the grand house, rose and advanced to the middle of the salon where Hürü and the two ladies stood; she knit her brows and patted Hürü on the turban.

"Good boy," the great lady said. "Why do you stand still, you two? Take the burden down off this poor porter boy."

"Thanks, lady," Hürü said.

The other two ladies removed the basket and unloaded the contents on a table. Finally, the lyre came into view and was, thank God, still in one piece.

"Here," the great lady said; "take these two pieces of gold for your trouble and depart."

But Hürü hesitated. Not only was this house the grandest she'd ever seen, even compared to Abd-es-Samad's, but her curiosity was aroused by these beautiful women who seemed to live without aid and company of men. She gazed at the wine, fruits, sweet-scented flowers which foretold the preparation for a feast, hesitating to depart without putting the ladies to a single question.

"What's the matter, boy?" the cateress asked tauntingly. "Two gold pieces not enough for you? Sister, give this boy another piece."

"By God!" Hürü said. "I've already been overpaid. I was just wondering about the three of you. Here you are, preparing a sumptuous feast, but I can see no man among you to entertain you with his conversation. It's said that the pleasure of women isn't complete without men. So, it occurred to me that a man who's sensitive, discreet and acute might not be an unwelcome addition to your celebration."

"Are you that man, boy?" the great lady said.

"Why not?" Hürü said. "I have terrific good sense and have done some travelling. I've read books and studied histories. Besides, I play the lyre passing well."

"We avoid men," the mistress said, "because we, too, have read books and perused histories. It is said that she who entrusts her secrets to a man is the woman whose secrets are known abroad."

"Let him stay anyway," said the tallest of the three, the blonde Amazon at the door. "He looks like a good kid."

"We know who has a soft spot for young boys," the cateress said pointedly to the blonde Amazon, "but remember, the calf will become a bull sooner than you think."

"Now, now!" said the mistress.

"You saw what kind of money I spent on this stuff," the cateress said to Hürü, "didn't you? Our custom here is to divide the expenses three ways, and each pays her share. So, if you can't pay yours, boy, there's the door. You certainly won't stare at our beautiful faces for free, nor swill our wine and wolf down our food."

"Friendship that isn't backed up with material means," the mistress of the house said, coining a phrase, "isn't worth beans."

"Good God!" Hürü exclaimed. "You women are materialists, aren't you! Where I come from, we esteem companionship above all the gold in the mines of King Solomon."

"Then go back there," suggested the cateress.

"Really, sisters!" said the tall blonde. "I'll pay for him out of my own pocket. So, let him stay."

"I'm willing," Hürü said, "to sing for my supper."

"Who needs your song?" said the fireball cateress. "All three of us sing and play LIKE ANGELS."

"I suppose he can stay," said the mistress of the house, "after all, he's a mere lad. That settles it. But you can't expect to take it easy lad, while the rest of us prepare the repast. You have to work even if you carry between your legs your manly pride. Share and share alike, that's the house rule."

"I have nothing against women's work," Hürü said.

They all rose, tightened their girdles and set to work. As the cateress, whose name was Amine, cooked the meat, Tall Safiye prepared the table by the pool. The mistress of the house told Hürü to strain the wine while she herself arranged the fruits and the flowers. Amine was a formidable cook despite the elegance and delicacy of her form, wielding the cleaver masterfully as she trimmed the lamb, embedded in the meat slivers of garlic, stuffed it with spicy rice, currants and pinenuts. These are some tough ladies, Hürü thought; they've turned a woman's place into an entire world.

When everything was made ready, they sat down. Feisty Amine took the jar of wine and filled a cup, then, down the hatch. She then filled another cup and passed it to her sisters who each took a sip and passed the cup to Hürü. The wine continued to circulate among them until the sisters were ready to sing and dance. All three were indeed accomplished musicians. The mistress of the house, whose name was Lady Zubaida, played the Persian harp which she called *junk* (the corruption of the Persian word *chang*, which Hürü knew from her studies); Feisty Amine played the *oud*, the Arabian lute that's made of pistachio wood; and the Blonde Amazon, Tall Safiye, played the *kanun*, an instrument with an entrancing sound quality, which Safiye laid on her knees and plucked with the two plectra attached to her forefingers. The trio would not suffer Hürü's strings.

"You call that a musical instrument?" Feisty Amine wanted to know. "The miserable thing's made of stone with stone strings. I can't imagine that it'd have any range at all. What do you do with it, boy? Beat your head against it?"

Indeed, the Stone Lyre looked pitiful next to the three sisters' instruments, which were inlaid and decorated lovingly by craftsmen who knew how to make something look as good as it sounds. And it was also true that Hürü had never before rehearsed with a string quartet. So, she relaxed and enjoyed the sisters' playing and singing, the fragrance that rose from the fresh flowers and incense; soon, she was so looped that she started hugging and kissing her benefactresses. While one slapped Hürü's face for being a forward boy, the other teased and pulled her, the third beat her ears with sweet-scented flowers. As the wine, the scents and music went to their heads, the sisters unbuttoned themselves; they toyed with Hürü as if she were, in fact, a young lad. The hour of the night advanced.

"Porter boy," Feisty Amine said, "show us the breadth of your shoulders now."

Hürü was terrified that Feisty Amine meant to have Hürü expose her upper torso. No matter how drunk she was, she wasn't about to strip naked. How would she explain the presence of the two small breasts that hid under her coarse shirt?

"I have a birthmark on my chest," Hürü said, "I'm ashamed to show. So, I can't remove my shirt to show you the breadth of my shoulders."

"Where have you been all your life, boy?" Lady Zubaida said, laughing. "When someone says, show us the breadth of your shoulders, it's a figure of speech. It means: depart, scram, make tracks."

"But I have no place to scram to," Hürü said. "Put me up for the night."

"Let him stay," interceded Tall Safiye. "He's so innocent, he's downright droll. Besides, I love the way he cooes like a turtle dove when he speaks. Let the sweet rogue stay."

"Lad," said Lady Zubaida, "you can stay the night on one condition. You must not ask for any explanation of events that might rouse your curiosity."

"Mum's the word," Hürü said.

"Get up and read the inscription over the doorway," Lady Zubaida commanded. "Most male visitors fail to notice it."

So, Hürü rose and read the inscription, written in gold letters over the archway. "Speak not of that which doth not concern thee, lest thou hear that which will not please thee," the inscription said.

"I promise," Hürü said, "I won't question anything."

Then, Amine rose and brought in the meat which was roasted to a turn; after they ate a little, Safiye the Blonde lighted the candles and burnt some aloe wood. Lady Zubaida rolled up a joint which she passed around the table. And while they were nibbling on some sweetmeats, they heard a loud knock on the door.

"Who can it be at this hour?" Lady Zubaida said. "Safiye, dear one, go see to the door."

Tall and Blonde Safiye went nimbly to answer the knocking. She came back with three men in tow, all dressed in the garb of merchants, one a big black man, the other a frail old man, the third a man in his prime who bore himself with dignity and seemed to be the other merchants' boss.

"Who might these men be, Safiye?" asked Lady Zubaida in astonishment. "Now we have in the house four men too many!"

"I took pity on this old man," Blonde Safiye said, "and couldn't very well turn away the rest."

"I apologize for this intrusion," the old man said, advancing, "and beg you not to be alarmed, bountiful mistress of the house. We are three merchants from Tiberias who've been in Baghdad for ten days, buying and selling. Tonight, a town merchant invited us to an entertainment, but he drank himself to oblivion; so we took our leave without our merchant friend who was not in any condition to guide us back to our inn. Out in the dark in a strange city, we missed our way. We were afraid we might be set upon, mugged, robbed. Hearing the music and revelry in your house, we thought you might be good enough to let us spend the night. God will recognize you for your generosity to three strangers who have lost their way."

"Come in then," Lady Zubaida said, "seeing that we've already broken the house rule when we admitted this lad."

The three merchants sat down, gazing about them in astonishment and at the fair ladies who were still somewhat too unbuttoned from all the carousing. But they said nothing. Feisty Amine brought more food and wine.

"We will have some of your delightful food," the bossy merchant said. "But no wine for us, thank you."

"You disapprove of wine, then?" Lady Zubaida asked. "Please! Spare us that old chestnut that wine makes hypocrisy grow in the heart as water promotes the growth of corn."

"We won't mention it," said the bossy merchant. "We are not prigs who spend our lives disapproving of others. We have been known to consume wine, in moderation, of course. Right now, though, we three are pilgrims, and pilgrims must keep their wits about them."

When she heard the three merchants were pilgrims, Blonde Safiye spread before them an embroidered cloth and placed on it a china jug. She poured some orange blossom water in the jug, added lumps of ice and sugar. The abstinent merchants thanked her for her kindness, sipping their beverage and keeping their wits about them.

"Arise, Safiye, my sister," Lady Zubaida said, "so we may fulfill our debt."

"Must we?" the tall and blonde Amazon said. "Even tonight?"

"Even tonight," Lady Zubaida said, "and every night."

"C'mon, boy," said Feisty Amine, "don't sit there like a lump! Get up and assist us!"

Amine pulled aside a curtain behind which two Afghan-hound bitches woke up startled from their naps. The silken hounds wore big iron collars which were tied to chains. They whined pitifully.

"Bring us one of the hounds," Lady Zubaida commanded Hürü.

Lady Zubaida then rose from her alabaster couch, rolled up her sleeves and removed a whip which hung on one of the walls. She spread her legs apart in readiness. Hürü dragged one of the Afghanhound bitches, who resisted, by the chain until the animal stood trembling before the mistress of the house. The lady began to whip the hound, not paying any attention to the howls, the screams, the blood that oozed on the animal's silky coat; she lashed at the beast until she was too tired to lash any more and threw aside the whip. Then, inexplicably, Lady Zubaida pressed the thoroughly beaten Afghan hound to her breast, wiped the tears of pain that had welled up in the animal's eyes, kissed the bitch who still whimpered, cradled her poor sore head.

"Take the bitch back," Lady Zubaida ordered Hürü, "and bring the other one."

She then beat the second hound senseless after which she bestowed much affection on the animal, consoling the bitch for the pain she herself had so cruelly inflicted. Hürü saw the bossy merchant rise in his seat as if to ask a question, but the older and wiser merchant brought his forefinger to his lips, making a sign of silence. Hürü, of course, had already taken an oath to keep her mouth shut, although she was burning with questions.

Her duty done, Lady Zubaida withdrew to her alabaster couch and collapsed there on the cushions.

"Now, it's your turn, Amine, my unfortunate sister," Lady Zubaida said. "Perform your duty."

Tall and Blonde Safiye took up her *kanun* and, leading Feisty Amine by the hand, walked up on the dais. Feisty Amine stood up there as if on a stage where actors perform, looking as if she'd shed her belligerence in favor of melancholia. Blonde Safiye then sat on the steps and, running her fingers longingly on the *kanun*, proceeded to sing a ballad which spoke of love as if it were a dread disease: sleep had been ravished, reason has fled; the upright woman has been seduced by the hostile glance of a man; she forgives him for shedding her blood with the poisoned dagger of his eyelashes, for she's the cause of her own murder; her mind is the mirror that reflects and directs his sun-like countenance into her own vitals which are scorched and burned.

When the song was done, Feisty Amine pulled and tore at her own garments. She didn't stop tearing away until every stitch was off her and she stood in the nude with only her chestnut brown hair sweeping down her fair back and buttocks. Her breasts, with their tender pink aureoles, stood firm and high. Modesty isn't one of the house rules, Hürü thought, wondering how the three merchants were able to deal with so much naked, and lovely, flesh. The quarrelsome beauty raised her shimmering chestnut brown hair, exposing the deep and unsightly scars on her slim buttocks. As Hürü stared in amazement at the charming back so savagely marred, Tall Safiye laid aside her *kanun* and brought the scarred victim another set of garments.

By this time, at Hürü's end of the salon, the excitement among the three merchants had risen to a feverish pitch. Not only were they unaccustomed to entering houses where beautiful women did as they pleased, they weren't used to having their manly presence discounted in this fashion. They felt, in all likelihood, that they, being men, should bring reason and order to the proceedings.

"What are those lash marks on that beautiful woman?" the bossy merchant asked the old one. "I can't rest until I find out the meaning of these strange performances. Why the hell did the two bitches get their hides tanned? And why did the lady first punish them and then beg forgiveness?"

"My lord," said the old merchant. "Haven't you noticed the inscription over the arch? Clearly, we are under compulsion not to ask what doesn't concern us, lest we hear something displeasing."

"My lord can ask whatever he pleases," said the black merchant.

"We are," the old merchant said, "after all, guests here, my lord."

But Safiye took up the *kanun* again, struck the chords and sang of hopeless love: if she spoke of love, what could she say? if consumed by desire, how could she escape? if she sent a messenger, how could he interpret her condition? if she were patient, what would remain to her but grief and mourning? Oh, absent beloved, who constantly dwells in her heart, has he kept faith? Has he changed? Has he forgotten his suffering lover who wastes away? On

the Day of Judgment, she's going to have God intercede on her behalf
and have him tried through and through.

Hearing these verses, Amine gave a repeat performance, stripping down to bare essentials, rending apart the new set of clothes
she'd just finished putting on. Tall Safiye, once more, brought her
brand-new clothes.

"I can't take this one more time!" exploded the bossy merchant.
"By God, am I not a man?"

"My lord," the old man said, "I wish we'd never entered this
house."

"We are four men here," said the black merchant and, looking
at Hūrū, added, "well, three-and-a-half men. We will, therefore, ask
these women the meaning of all this. If they don't answer willingly,
then they will by force, as God is my witness!"

"This is not right," the old merchant said. "Let them be for now,
my lord. The night is almost over and soon we can be on our way.
Tomorrow, my lord, you can send for the three women and question
them at your leisure."

"I can't wait until tomorrow," the Big Cheese said petulantly. "I
must be answered right now. But who shall put the question to
them?"

"The boy," said the Big Black. "I nominate the boy."

"Not I!" cried Hūrū. "Before you three arrived, I made an oath to
keep my mouth shut."

"Well, then," said the Big Cheese to the Black, "you are elected,
Mesrur. Go to it, man!"

By this time, the mistress of the house noticed the commotion
at the other end of the salon.

"You men over there!" Lady Zubaida chided, "why do you buzz
like a hive of drones?"

"Mistress of the house, beautiful lady," said the Black whose
name was Mesrur, advancing forward, "by God, we beg of you to
enlighten us as to the mystery of the two bitches you beat to an inch
of their lives and then wept at their pain and kissed their snouts.
Then, tell us why the charming lady strips down when she hears
songs about love, exposing the terrible scars on her lovely back. Why
was she beaten so severely? And by whom? Tell us, for we're all
dying to know."

"Is this true?" Lady Zubaida said. "Are all you men dying to
know, along with this black?"

"Yes, certainly," said the Big Cheese.

"Of course," cried Hürü.

The old man said nothing.

"In that case," Lady Zubaida said, tucking her sleeves in her belt, "you'll all get what's coming to you."

Lady Zubaida rose and struck the brazen gong beside the alabaster couch; immediately the door opened on what at first had seemed to be a closet, out of which rushed perhaps fifty warrior-maidens of all races and descriptions, all but naked, half-clad in the skins of wild animals, uttering battle cries to chill the heart of a seasoned general. The wild women bore swords, spears and maces, while their glistening limbs displayed musculature developed by hard exercise.

"What!" exclaimed the Big Cheese. "You dare keep a private army?"

"What!" exclaimed Lady Zubaida. "You dare ask questions?"

Before Hürü knew what was happening, she too had been bound and blindfolded along with the other three. Besides, someone kept beating on her noggin with the flat of a sword.

"Virtuous Mistress," said a voice which must belong to the captain of the warrior maidens, "which of these worthless heads do you wish severed first?"

"Wait!" cried Hürü. "I didn't get to sing my song yet!"

"You've already been told, boy," Amine's voice said. "No one here needs to hear you sing."

"You need it bad, you feisty bitch!" Hürü cried. "You don't know what's in your best interest to know. You're so opinionated, you can't apprehend anything but your own awful songs. Then you swoon and rend your clothes like some madwoman. I challenge you; I'm the better musician. I don't just repeat what I've always heard; I make up my own songs as I go along. Match that, Amine! And I mean to sing my song before I die!"

"I beg of you on my knees, Sister Zubaida," Hürü heard Blonde Safiye say, apparently entreating her now on Hürü's behalf, "let the lad sing his last song."

"He's just playing for time," Lady Zubaida said, ripping the blindfold off Hürü's face. "But if your song doesn't please me, boy, I mean to behead you all, beginning with that Swell Head there who puts on precious airs."

Help me now! Hürü begged silently of the Stone Lyre; I will do my utmost not to embarrass your magic nature, O Lyre who's known hands purer and more blessed than mine! Let the hands of your past masters now guide my fingers that woodenly pluck your magic strings!

"I will now sing," Hūrū said, composing herself as best she could, "a lullaby of my own composition. I call it, 'Awake, Demon Prince.'"

She sang a lullaby to an enchanted prince, half of whose nature slept a demon's sleep; for he despised the tears he himself had caused. That part of him which also wept, which had the capacity to weep, slept an awful sleep. It was the demon woman inside him whom he could not name by her true name and invoke forth. If he could but waken the demon woman inside him, he, too, would free his human soul to support the doubleness of love, its mixture of cruelty and tenderness, its aggressiveness and passivity, its possessiveness and heavenly surrender. But the prince slept his half-sleep, stirring with a pain of which he was only half aware.

The listeners kept silent, stunned by the perception that rendered them free for a moment as they switched from one set of views on conventional love to an entirely new outlook. The sadness of it all! Our convention-laden lives! Like demons, whose natures are mechanically habituated, we too taste freedom for a moment, that slight moment as we abandon one view without having to settle on another. Then, the powerful magic of transformation dissipates as we open our mouths to justify our enslavement.

"Certainly a long, complicated song," said Amine, who was the first to recover. "But is it true?"

"Ahh!" said Lady Zubaida, the mistress of the occasion as well as the house, beating her bosom. "My heart knows it is true."

"May we go now?" said the black merchant.

"It isn't established if the song has saved us," the old merchant said. "One hopes it has, for one is accustomed to life."

"Untie them all," Lady Zubaida ordered the warrior maidens. "But escort them to the door to make sure they depart in peace. Wait! The lad may stay."

"No, thank you," Hūrū said.

"What troubles you, boy?" Lady Zubaida said. "Your song tells me that you've come to know the woman in your heart, even though you're a mere youth with no hair on his chin. Do you fear women still?"

"I'm not quite ready to join a sisterhood," Hürü said. "There are men whom I must yet know."

The women all laughed, considering the drollness of what seemed a boy's honest consideration to give up his own sex in favor of the opposite.

"Come again, if you feel like it," Lady Zubaida said, stroking Hürü's chin. "But don't bring these men—that's a good lad."

Once the former hostages were out on the streets where the houses of Baghdad were starkly visible in the first light of dawn, the old merchant fell on his knees to thank God for the sake of the realm, thanking Him who's in His Heavens for allowing what's right with the world to remain right. The Black joined in the prayer, but the Big Cheese remained aloof.

"You're the Caliph, aren't you?" Hürü said to him. "I bet my life that you're Harun-er-Rashid himself."

"That's right, boy," said the Big Cheese.

"So why do you risk your life," asked Hürü, "going around in disguise? Quite conceivably, those women could've done you in."

"Why do you risk your own life, boy?" said the Caliph-in-disguise. "Are you bored with it already?"

"Not on your life!" Hürü said. "I'm enjoying mine tremendously. And I thank you for not interfering with it."

"We seem to owe you Our life," said the Caliph. "We wouldn't think of interfering with yours, unless you wish to be Our cup-companion at the Palace, enjoying the privileges and pleasures of that office. You play a mean lyre, boy!"

"Are you trying to hire me?" Hürü said.

"You're not too quick on the uptake, are you?" Harun-er-Rashid said, laughing. "But We like that. We prefer simple men."

"How much?" Hürü said, feeling anything but simple.

"What say you to a thousand dinars, monthly?" the Caliph said. "We will quarter you in apartments attached to Our own."

"Done!" Hürü said, pumping the Caliph's hand where it hung by his side. "It's a deal."

"The boy has cheek!" said Black Mesrur, rolling his eyes.

"His cheek is what saved us," said the old man whose name, as Hürü knew from reading history, was Jafar, the great Barmaki, who put wisdom behind the throne. She also knew, from the same source, the good Jafar Barmaki's end. That was the trouble with meeting up with historical personages; you had access to information for which they'd give their eyeteeth but which, if you told them, they'd never believe.

Chapter 12

LADY ZUBAIDA'S TALE

She travels into the future.
Her story, alas, gets her stuck in History.

*I*nstead of retiring for a bit of shut-eye, as Hürü had hoped, the Caliph immediately, and surrounded by a gaggle of valets, exchanged his merchant's attire for royal garments of red. Hürü remembered, from reading history, Harun-er-Rashid's custom of wearing red to manifest his anger. He meant to spill blood. Whenever the Caliph saw red, his subjects trembled, took cover, rode hard out of the city gates.

Now, the Caliph sat upon his throne, no more the endangered merchant of the night past; scowling, he dismissed his courtiers and the pending business of the morning.

"Bring before me," he commanded his Vizier Jafar and the Executioner Black Mesrur, "the three women and the two bitches at once! Take with you troops sufficient to the task."

So! the Caliph meant to pay back the three ladies in their own coin. Probably there was a law against women living independently, protected by private troops (even if the troops consisted of wild and woolly warrior-maidens). If there weren't such a law, the Caliph could quickly invent one. Hürü tried to think of a stratagem through which to save the three beautiful sisters whose harmony and safety she had intruded on and whose secret order she had unwittingly destroyed. At least this command audience was to be a private one, which might prevent the ladies' secret from being broadcast about in the streets of Baghdad. And if the Caliph had all three executed, then it didn't much matter to the three ladies if their secrets were known. But Hürü hoped it wouldn't come to that.

Indeed, the three ladies, hustled into the audience chamber along with the two Afghan hounds, didn't seem as grand now. Not only must the ladies be suffering from hangovers larger than Hürü's (considering how liberally they enjoyed wine), they hadn't even been allowed to don their street clothes. Snatched from slumber, dishevelled and ill-used, the three ladies appeared no more independent than newly captured slaves. The two bitches, however, weren't as subdued as they were the night before; barking joyously and fawning on the Caliph, they wagged their tails in a state of delirium. The bitches seemed to thoroughly enjoy the sight of their mistresses kneeling in front of the Caliph, hands folded, heads hung low.

"So!" the Caliph bellowed. "You imagine yourselves the equal of men, do you? Had someone told me that three women lived under their own authority in Baghdad, I wouldn't have believed the rumor. But keeping armed troops on the premises and vexing your Caliph when he visits your house are activities so absurd and implausible that I command you to explain your ridiculous world. Who are you? And why do you persist in defying authority?"

The eldest, Lady Zubaida, advanced and touched her forehead on the floor. She made as if she'd kiss the hem of the Caliph's red robe, but he motioned her to keep her distance. He wasn't taking any chances with this one.

"Oh, Commander of the Faithful," Lady Zubaida said, humiliating herself before the Caliph, "forgive our transgression against you. We didn't know you and the gentlemen in your company."

"Cut the soft-soap!" cried the Caliph. "Get to the point."

"These two Afghan-hound bitches," Lady Zubaida said, "are my two half-sisters. The truth of what I say might seem absurd and implausible, but so is the order under which we three ladies endure in Baghdad. The other two ladies aren't my blood sisters but sisters to my soul.

"My father, who was a clever and lucky merchant, left me and my two half-sisters great wealth. My half-sisters, being older, married soon after our father's death, each taking with her a hundred thousand pieces of gold as her dowry. Married life seemed to suit them for a while, but soon their husbands became restless. Pooling together the two dowries, the husbands gathered an immense stock of merchandise; then, taking along their wives, set out on a commercial journey. They were all gone for four years, during which time I received not a word of their whereabouts, nor of the success or failure of the enterprise. One day, my two half-sisters reappeared on their own, tired, hungry, wearing beggar's clothes. Their husbands, who'd lost everything through mismanagement and bad luck, had abandoned them in a strange land and departed for parts unknown.

"At first, I didn't even recognize them at the door, so miserable were my sisters, so worn, so downtrodden, full of vermin and sores. As maidens, they'd been accustomed to much pampering and ease; neither would've picked up a handkerchief she dropped, let alone learn how to look after her own well-being. I sent them to the baths, gave them new clothes, called in physicians to cure their ailments and lodged them under my own roof, thinking, since I was the youngest, the most inexperienced and entirely on my own, that it was providence who'd sent them to me. My sisters would watch over me, bring solace to my lonely existence, advice to my green ears. At the time, I was embroiled in an enterprise that posed some danger. Having my sisters with me seemed to lessen the burden and the cares.

"In their absence, my fortunes had prospered. My share of the hundred thousand pieces of gold had increased threefold, and I was, in my own right, a very wealthy young woman. My associates were a cartel of Jews who dealt in arms, and though I provided the capital, I remained the silent partner—a provision necessitated by my gender. We provided weaponry for peoples who lived under less benevolent princes, who in turn, though they couldn't feed the populace, also came up with cash for hardware. Since there were nice profits to be made, I backed the enterprise of arming both the peoples and the princes. As anyone can see, it was a delicate and dangerous operation."

"What!" cried Harun-er-Rashid. "You supplied foreigners with arms under Our very nose and We were none the wiser?"

"I'm out of that business now," said Lady Zubaida. "Forgive me, O Commander of the Faithful, but had I not supplied the weaponry, you know someone else would. Was it not far better for our country that weaponry made in Baghdad flooded the market rather than, say, that made in Isphahan?"

"Go on," the Caliph said. "Let's see what other dirty deals you managed to make."

"Well," Lady Zubaida said, "it was good to have my two sisters back with me to share my good fortune as well as business troubles. For a whole year they remained with me, but I could see they grew more restless with each passing day. Having known the pleasures of the bedchamber once, they must marry again. They could no longer abstain, they wailed, from the joys of copulation.

"'But you found no happiness in marriage before,' I reminded them. 'A good husband is an item that cannot be readily found. The failure of your marriages instructed *me*. How is it that you two haven't learned?'

"They wouldn't listen and married again without my consent. Yet, I gave them generous dowries, given from the heart, and with no strings attached. That's how they rushed into marriage again after having already experienced that state's sad futility. Wouldn't you know it— soon they were both defrauded out of their assets by the new husbands, too. Both lost their husbands, one to wanton women, the other to compulsive gambling. And so, once more my sisters arrived on my doorstep, this time so bereft, they wore floursacks to cover their nakedness.

"'You are the youngest, Zubaida,' said my eldest sister, direly embarrassed by her inability to hang onto husbands, 'yet the most mature. Take us back, Zubaida; we promise never to mention the subject of marriage again.'

"What can one do with foolish sisters but press them to one's bosom? And they did seem contrite, resolved never to look at another man. For an entire year, we enjoyed each other's company, living together as true sisters, sharing good news along with the bad.

"After a year, it became necessary to fit out a vessel for a commercial voyage. For some time, now, I had heard that aborigines who lived beyond chartered oceans were reputed to trade ingots of gold for mere beads and trifles from our marketplaces. Accordingly, I stocked a large sailing vessel with all manner of gew-gaws and necessary provisions for a long trip, resolved to make the journey myself to assure the success of the enterprise. The voyage promised much distress and danger, not one to be ventured on without seriously considering the implications. So, I briefed my two sisters, presenting all the angles, and inquired if they wished to remain in Baghdad, in relative safety, or if they would accompany me on this highly dangerous adventure.

"They decided to chance their lives and well-being on the voyage with me, saying they couldn't bear to part from their young-

est and most mature sister who'd surely thoroughly weighed the
pros and cons. Just listening to the ins-and-outs of business made
their heads ache enough to split.

"'You know best, Zubaida,' said my middle sister. 'Where you go,
we go.'

"But, I suppose, I didn't have the same blind trust in the venture
as did my sisters; so, before we set out, I divided my fortune into
two equal portions. One portion I took with me, the other I concealed, thinking if some unforeseen accident befell us, and we still
remained alive, at least we'd have a hefty nest-egg with which to start
over again. So we all risked ourselves on the vast oceans, setting sail
for parts unknown beyond the Sea of Darkness.

"The sailing proved fair for some time. But, once we were a
couple of days beyond the mighty Straits of Gibraltar, a big storm
steered us off course. The captain didn't know which way to turn the
ship, for we'd entered an ocean he could not even name, let alone
chart a course on. Even the configurations of the stars puzzled him
and the pilot, till we knew not whether we sailed the oceans of this
earth or another. It was as if we'd entered a zone out of our time and
not of our own space. For an entire six months we sailed in this way,
well-nigh blind, sighting nothing.

"In the meantime, my sisters bickered and nattered. They'd
come along trusting me; now that they'd lost that absolute trust, they
were bitter. They felt that hitching their fates to me had proved more
unfortunate than marrying the worst of husbands. They'd rather
have some fellow beat and rob them than sail off course on a ship
bound for God knew what hell.

"I began to appreciate the erstwhile husbands' difficulties with
these sisters, who certainly could prove a loathsome twosome,
making life hell for a couple of men whose enterprises fell short of
their expectations. I came to sympathize with the poor bastards!
Have you noticed how a voyage will bring out someone's true nature?
Sometimes I think young people who plan to marry should first take
together a long and difficult voyage; if they still love each other
afterwards, only then should they take the plunge.

"Anyway, the winds drove us on until on the horizon there
appeared a continent. We followed the coastline for several days,
looking for some terrain recognizable to the captain. But he was
confounded. At last, what appeared to be a great city loomed before
us in the distance.

"'What's this city?' I asked the captain.

"'Search me,' said he. 'You already know I've never navigated on this ocean nor been under so much distress. But, since we've come so far in relative safety, we might as well dock at this strange harbor. Who knows, you might just find some trade, selling and bartering and buying up curious goods we could take back. Even if the business prospects prove to be poor, we can still rest for a couple of days, take in fresh provisions and find out where in the hell we are.'"

✦

"Even as we glided into the harbor, we knew something strange was up. For one thing, we'd never heard about or dreamed of structures so tall; man-made towers that ascended hundreds of stories into the sky. We sailed by a small islet on which stood the figure of a giantess holding up a torch in one hand and a stone tablet in the other, wearing a serene expression and a diadem shaped like a star. Seeing the giantess on the islet and the towering structures on the mainland, we thought we must be sailing toward a race of giants. We were quivering in our boots, and would have turned back but, at the same time, we burned with curiosity.

"The harbor was very quiet, empty of people. Many vessels we'd never seen before, vessels without sails or oars, and some huge tubs made entirely of metal, and smaller craft and pleasure boats crowded in the bay—no traffic was visible to our eyes. We docked without seeing a soul. The captain went on shore first, shouldering the responsibility for whatever faced us in this place where destiny had blown us. He returned quicker than we expected.

"'Come down to the city!' he shouted up to us. 'And look upon and wonder what God has done to his creatures! And pray that you too may never so incur God's wrath!'

"We climbed down in silence into this wondrously mute city. Believe me! When I say we found all the inhabitants converted into black stones, or some kind of coal, I'm telling the truth. In amazement, we wandered through the bazaars and shops of the city and discovered all the buildings and structures, all the vehicles, all the merchandise, all remained intact, untouched. Much gold and silver could be viewed behind immense panes of glass that God's wrath had not shattered. We couldn't help but rejoice, though saddened by the fate of the inhabitants, that the circumstance afforded us so much gain. We separated in the streets, each attracted by different objects and wonders in the shops and the buildings. Never was there a city so laden with material goods and so destitute of a public that might enjoy the riches.

"As for myself, I was attracted by the city's tallest buildings, hoping to get a bird's-eye view of this unique place. You won't believe this, Commander of the Faithful, but doors would open by one's mere presence at the entrance, making a hiss; then, they would close behind one. It was as if an invisible *jinni* served as the doorman. Inside the building, the great salons, chambers, audience rooms all blazed with light that did not come from a source of fire; though each light gave forth the brilliance of a thousand candles, touching the globes would not burn the hand. There was such an excess of light that the place was lit up continuously day and night. Everywhere, there were comfortable sofas, deeply stuffed seats, rugs of plain colors that covered every bit of the floors. I thought to myself, the inhabitants must've loved comfort.

"Floor after floor, I saw squadrons of men and women dressed in beautiful stuffs, wools and silks beyond price, dyed into shades of color unknown to our dyers. And all who wore those rich materials had turned into coal. Viceroys and chamberlains, generals and tycoons, princes and princesses, attendants and scribes, squires and journeymen, cooks and chambermaids, even little children—all stood petrified as they made their speeches, ate a delicacy, scolded someone, hands on machines, hands on each other, blowing their noses, or blowing a kiss, each frozen in his gesture for all eternity. What had they done? Were these really people who'd been punished by being turned to coal? Or was it so much coal getting punished by being turned into the shapes of people?

"Stupified, I entered what must be the harem of the citadel. Men and women had mixed freely on all other floors, but in this salon there were only princesses who'd been turned into coal while receiving beauty treatment from white eunuchs and female attendants. Some sat under clear domes with their hair rolled up on tiny rolling-pins with hot air still blowing inside from an invisible source. Some women still held books in their blackened hands; others leaned back into basins into which hot and cold water ran continuously. And although the clothes these princesses wore were too plain for the women in your harem, Commander of the Faithful, I could see everything was costly in an understated way. It wasn't so much a show of ornaments on their persons as is the fashion among us, but

the extravagant aura of the place, the privilege of being with each
other at a certain place, to have certain things done—if you see what
I mean.

"As though all this were not strange enough, I found myself
walking out of this salon, in a little room that ascended. It was a very,
very small room, decorated with costly wood and damask, and
accidentally my elbow touched a button on the wall. Suddenly, the
doors closed with a hiss. I discovered myself imprisoned and I had
the strange sensation as though the whole room were moving! My
stomach lurched. I said my prayers hurriedly, preparing to meet my
death, when the door to the room opened again on its own, and I
rushed out to the safety of a solid floor.

"Before me was some sort of machine that clicked and buzzed
all by itself, with spools and reels winding and unwinding, lights
flashing on and off, and dials with arrows moving back and forth. The
machine's attendants sat before it, blackened hands on the controls,
and not one of them moving. The machine took up an entire floor,
humming with a mysterious power, and I suddenly had the feeling
that it controlled that whole tower, lifting the small rooms up and
down, opening and closing doors, cooling and heating to keep the
place an even and comfortable temperature. And I thought further, it
might even have done the converted people's thinking for them, for
I had the distinct impression that somehow the machine was too
powerful not to be sacred.

"I wandered through apartment after apartment, seeing many
wonders and never meeting a live soul; but when I wished to quit the
building, dazed and confounded, I couldn't find my way out. By this
time, I was also desperately hungry. But even if I did find some food,
would it be safe to eat?

"In the hallway, I noticed a blackened gentleman in front of a tall
metal box which was lit from the inside; this former man had been
petrified in the act of dropping a coin in a slot. I observed that there
were packaged goods behind the little windows of the box, and the
contents looked like food. Taking the coin from the charcoaled man's
hand, I dropped it in the intended slot. The metal box came alive
and, with a buzzing and whirring, a small package dropped into a
receptacle below. I tore open the strange metallic paper; inside were
two small dark brown mounds made of a substance unknown to us.
Taking my life in my hands, I bit off a little piece. It was a delicious
confection made of coconut paste, the brown substance merely

coating the center which, in itself, was delectable. I waited awhile, and when nothing happened, I knew their food was safe.

"But their shopkeepers, instead of people, were those metal boxes that lined the halls. In them I found other kinds of food. From the pockets of the blackened people, I obtained more of their coins, and though some of them I lost into the boxes, believe me when I say I ate hot chicken cooked up in a flash by the box. I ate hot meat patties inside small sesame-seed rolls, and drank a dark, sweet and bubbly refreshment. The food wasn't exactly delicious to my palate, but what can one expect of food that's not one's own? I did like an iced custard that was frozen on a stick, but couldn't understand how the custard hadn't melted side by side with the hot chicken.

"Finally, I laid myself down on a comfortable sofa, repeated some passages from the *Koran* and hoped to compose myself for a little nap. But sleep just wouldn't come, dog tired as I was. My mind kept wondering about small details. How come the place wasn't dusty? Where were the latrines? Did the inhabitants get born and die always cooped up in the same building? Where were the animals? Did they, too, share in the humans' fate?

"Seeing I couldn't sleep, I rose, determined to reach the top floor, even though it was now dark outside and the hour past midnight by my reckoning. Out of immense windows that reached from floor to ceiling, the city could be seen blazing with artificial light. It was as if the stars in the heavens were all captive in this city. More than anything, the inhabitants must've loved light and cleanliness.

"Finally, dead tired from climbing all those stairs, I reached the top, pushed open a heavy portal and, out on a terrace above the city, I took a breath of fresh air—so much so, the headache that pounded in my head began to recede as I breathed in and out. That's when I heard somebody recite, in a soft and melodious voice, but in a strange accent, the first chapter of the *Koran*.

"Just imagine my amazement! Looking about, I spied an open door, leading to an apartment on the terrace, behind which there was candlelight. Incredulous that light as we know it also existed in this world, I entered through the door and found myself in a small oratory lit by actual candles. And, on a prayer-carpet spread on the floor, sat a young man who, although black in skin color, had not been converted into coal. He was just a black person, handsome in a delicate way, who was applying himself so thoroughly to his recitations that he hadn't even heard me arrive. I wondered how he'd escaped the fate of the others.

"'Hullo!' I said. 'Peace be on you, young man.'

"He raised his eyes which were tender and profoundly dark, fringed by long curly lashes, and in those eyes I saw a serenity one sometimes sees in the eyes of older folk who've made peace with death, not fearful anymore but full of acceptance of death. Yet in actual years, the young man seemed somewhat younger than myself. We gazed at each other for a long time—as if we'd always known each other. Although he seemed to recognize me, as I did him, he never said a word.

"'Tell me, I beg of you, what happened here?' I said. 'I know you won't withhold the truth from me, for I heard you recite from the Book of Truth.'

"He smiled an enchantingly shy smile, but instead of answering my question, he made a brief confession of faith in the accents of someone not used to speaking our language.

"'There is no deity but Allah,' he confirmed, 'and Mohammed is Allah's Apostle.'

"'I know that,' I said, laying my hand on his beautiful black fingers. 'Tell me why you alone remain in this city of the dead?'

"'There is no deity but Allah,' he repeated, 'and Mohammed is Allah's Apostle.'

"I realized that all he knew of our language was what he'd memorized of the Book. The ways of God are marvelous: a sacred text need not be understood for its words to work their miracle. And a miracle was wrought in my cold and virginal heart which had calculated the price of everything but had known the value of nothing. Suddenly, I knew I could not live without this black youth, though he could not respond but only repeat our sacred texts.

"'Will you go with me to the city of Baghdad?' I asked him, pressing both his hands on my bosom. 'Come with me where life abounds. Oh, come where you can increase both your knowledge and perception. If you come with me, I will be your handmaiden—though I am mistress of a great commercial empire and have authority over scores of men. I sailed on a ship laden with merchandise, but destiny drove me here. For I was fated to find you, dear man, and my own life. I found my heart in this strange city of charred inhabitants where you alone survived.'

"He seemed to understand for he assented, nodding his head.

We embraced. I feared he might think me too forward, but I couldn't help myself; I touched and caressed him, kissed his hands, his forehead, his eyelids, his cheeks, his chin. And I found his sweet mouth. Oh, God help me! I'd never known joy so akin to pain.

"I slept that night at his feet, scarcely conscious of the strange world around us; in the morning we rose, and he showed me how to descend in the little room that moved up and down. There were more of those little rooms. Noticing my interest in objects that were light in weight but great in value, he guided me from treasury to treasury where I collected riches that struck my fancy. Laden with goods from this abandoned world, we went down from the citadel into the street.

"But, instead of walking to the harbor, as I aimed to do, the youth loaded the goods into one of the wheeled carriages that lined and choked the streets. Made of metal and painted exorbitant colors, these were curious vehicles. My wonderful guide seated himself in the vehicle and, turning a key, brought it to life. The thing shuddered and sputtered, passed an odious wind. I thought I'd die of fear if I boarded it, but the youth laughed and pulled me in the seat beside him. He closed the doors and guided the vehicle, turning a small wheel that looked like a ship's helm. No horses, no camels, no bullocks, no elephants! This vehicle seemed to be powered by an extremely disagreeable noise.

"That was how we made our way to the ship. We found the captain, my sisters, the crew and the slaves had all been searching for me, fearful that I might be forever lost in this city which was too large to investigate thoroughly in an entire year, let alone a single day. They all exclaimed on the strange virtue of the vehicle that brought us to the docks; though all had noticed thousands of carriages like this one abandoned everywhere, none had discovered how to make one work. I told them how I met the young man I'd brought with me, and they too marvelled at his survival, for in all their wanderings about that great, silent city none had met another live soul.

"'As soon as we set sail out of here,' I said to the captain, 'I mean to have you, under maritime authority, marry me to this youth.'

"'But he's black as a slave!' cried my eldest sister. 'Did we get blown all the way here just so you might disgrace your family name?'

"'He's not a slave!' I cried. 'He alone survived because he bound himself only to God. Binding the soul to God frees man from bondage to men. Isn't the fact of his survival enough to prove he's a free man?'

"'Words! Words!' my middle sister said. 'All I see is a youth whose face is black as soot. Nothing you can say can change the color of his skin.'

"I let my sisters grumble on their own time. As my intended linked his fingers docilely with mine, the captain and I fell to speculating about the mysterious catastrophe that had befallen the city. The captain thought the inhabitants must've been fire worshippers. He'd seen a wondrous little box which showed pictures that moved, and through the moving picture was recorded the wrath of their god. Their god must've been an infernal fire that sprang up more brilliantly than a million hells, grew from a stem of inferno into a swirling ball of fire that spread and spread until the heavens burned, and it rained devastating fire.

"'But how do you explain the fact that the buildings and materials weren't consumed in the fire, as were the people? It makes no sense,' I said. 'The nature of fire is indiscriminate consumption.'

"'This wasn't fire as we know it,' the captain said; 'I'm sure of that. It was fire that burned from within. That's why I think it must've been some sort of god.'

"'We shall never solve the mystery,' I concluded, smiling at my sweet beloved, 'unless we manage to teach my fiancé the living language.'

"'Sooner we get out of here,' the captain said, 'the better.'

"In spite of my happiness with my young man, I wasn't too far gone to neglect the merchandise I'd acquired. I had the gew-gaws unloaded on the dock, replacing them with the artifacts of this destroyed culture. The wonders we obtained were too innumerable to name right now; suffice it to say that we prepared to bring materials to Baghdad that would entirely change our lives. As soon as the winds were favorable, we set sail, and I married my young lover.

"The honeymoon was sweeter than I'd imagined. My young husband not only pleased himself but took me along on his pleasure tours. My sisters seemed reconciled to my choice; they even troubled themselves to teach my husband a few pleasantries, the names of things, and so on. We soon found out my husband's given name had been Sam, but later he'd chosen for himself the name of Latif. And pleasant he was like his chosen name. Many of his race had been converted to Islam in name only, but Latif was a true believer. He didn't have enough words to explain everything, but I understood

the inhabitants had not been fire worshippers, in the true sense as
such. Latif made the sign of the cross, but frowned as he made a
gesture to indicate that the faith had been lukewarm. We understood
the inhabitants had been Christians who went astray.

"I felt sorrow for these people who'd been so intelligent, so
inventive, so developed in their comforts and work-saving devices;
they seemed to have understood nature and unlocked the mysteries
of the universe. Yet, they hadn't foreseen the catastrophe that
awaited in the form of a fire that burns only the living. Or perhaps
they had foreseen the danger, but their inventions, like some demons, had gone out of hand. I looked forward to a time when I could
fully converse with my delightful husband, learn from him the philosophies and sciences that had survived in his mind as his soul had
survived in his body.

"But it was not to be. My sisters, having bribed some slaves to
aid them in their perfidy, had us lifted out of our sleep while we lay
entwined in each other's arms, and thrown overboard into that ocean
of perils. Latif couldn't swim. Despite my efforts to save my husband,
the undertow pulled him from me. Latif was recorded among the
company of Allah's martyrs while I was counted among those whose
life was yet to be preserved. I wept salt tears into the salt ocean.

"I treaded water for two full days and nights, exhausted and
numb from the cold; then providence supplied me with a floating
piece of timber on which I raised myself. The waves cast me on the
beach of an island. There, I fell asleep as one dead.

"In the morning, I stripped off my wet clothing to dry in the sun;
as my clothes dried, I made a circuit of the island, which was
extremely small, so rocky that it hardly supported any plant life.
There I was, naked, with only my drying clothes between me and the
elements, without any visible form of sustenance, and no sign of help
in the open sea or the blue sky.

"Then I beheld a small snake approaching me, hotly pursued by
a large serpent whose mouth was so unhinged that it was clear it
meant to gobble up the small, delicate snake. The little creature was
so exhausted in its winding flight that its tongue hung out pitifully as
it tried to escape its fate. For some reason, the small snake's plight
aroused compassion in my heart, although I ordinarily shrink from
creatures that slither and coil. Without further reflection, I lifted a
big rock and brought it crashing down on the large serpent's head.
The odious bully died instantly. Saved by my intercession, the small

snake fanned out a pair of gossamer wings and soared aloft into the sky, leaving me in wonderment.

"Although killing the serpent hadn't been such a strenuous exercise, I felt drained all over again and lay down to a merciful sleep. Who knows how long I slept. I awoke to the pleasure of something gently rubbing the soles of my feet. A delicate noblewoman sat at my feet, rubbing them as if she were a servant or a slavegirl. I immediately sat up, ashamed that a lady should perform such a menial service for me.

"'Who are you?' I exclaimed. 'And what do you want?'

"'How soon you've forgotten me!' she said, laughing coyly. 'I'm the one whose life you so kindly saved. At the time I was a small snake, but you see me now as I am, a *jinniye* of rank. The ugly serpent was a dreadful *ifrit* who'd resolved to destroy me. He nearly had me there, and none other than you came to my aid. So, I thought I'd do you a good turn.'

"'How nice!' I said.

"'Rubbing your feet is not all I've done for you,' said the graceful *jinniye*. 'Once you delivered me, I flew to the ship from which your sisters had you and your husband cast overboard. First, I turned them into Afghan-hound bitches and flew them to your house in Baghdad; then, I sank the ship.'

"'You shouldn't have done that!' I cried. 'That ship contained valuable cargo!'

"'You penetrated into the future,' the *jinniye* said, frowning, 'through a chink in the present. But Powers that be cannot allow you to keep the future's artifacts. Those things that are not yours cannot be kept. Don't you see? It's dangerous enough that people plunder the past, but they may not plunder the future. I'm sorry your young man had to die.'

"I wept for my beautiful Latif again and my tears were now truly for him instead of for my loss. The *jinniye* tried to console me, but I was a woman destroyed: ship sunk, sisters turned to bitches, husband drowned. Was this the *jinniye*'s way of repaying me for my kindness?

"'Look on the bright side,' she advised. 'At least your sisters have received the punishment they so bitchily deserved. And you've certainly stashed away in your house a nice nest-egg with which you can start all over again. You're too smart a woman not to prosper even better than before. Put your clothes on. I propose to fly you home at once. Won't that be nice?'

"'At this point,' I said, 'it really doesn't matter.'

"'Look here,' the *jinniye* said, 'you are a real survivor. Don't disappoint me now! You're certain to become the most powerful woman of your time. But there's a condition you must fulfill.'

"'Now what?' I said.

"'By the rules of the enchantment,' she said, 'you must swear to inflict three hundred lashes on each bitch-sister every night, or else I will come and transform you into the third bitch.'

"'Why must you impose such a terrible condition on my life and welfare?' I asked. 'Isn't it enough that you turned my sisters into dogs?'

"'I am sorry,' the *jinniye* said, 'but it's not in my power to change the conditions of the enchantment.'

"Well, the little snake of a *jinniye* had to be believed, for she flew me, as promised, to Baghdad and left me on the roof of my house. And so to avoid turning into a bitch myself, every night I lash three hundred stripes on each sister, grieving all the time for the pain I must inflict."

"Well, well!" said the Caliph. "So, these aren't bitches but women! I don't know if I believe your story or not, but I'll not deny it was both entertaining and inventive, certainly one for the books. As to the bitches, one of the dogs does remind me of a certain aunt of mine— although that's no reason to believe that in those animals dwell two actual women."

"My story is true," Lady Zubaida said, "whether you believe it or not."

"Besides," went on the Caliph, "while I've heard many times about some lucky people who've managed to press *jinn* into service, I've heard of many more people who were interfered with or destroyed by supernatural commerce. What I cannot believe is your story about having been blown into the future. That just isn't possible. Even the *jinn* cannot fathom what the future holds in store because no one can know what doesn't exist yet. If you had a single artifact to show me, the slightest little thing, I might believe your story."

"I'm sorry," Lady Zubaida said. "I don't have a thing to show."

"In any case," said the Caliph, softening, "I've learned much about how a woman like yourself might feel about the world of men."

Hūrū, on her part, saw no reason not to believe Lady Zubaida's account of her encounter with the future. If the past could be apprehended in person, then why not the future?

"Time," Hürü said, trying to remember what Abd-es-Samad had taught her on the subject, "both flows and curves upon itself. It wastes itself and yet redeems itself. It's not one or the other but both simultaneously."

"How can one thing be two things at once?" the Caliph exclaimed. "And, if so, how would you know?"

"Because I'm from the future myself," Hürü said foolishly. "But not from the future Lady Zubaida describes. In my time, we hadn't yet made such material progress. And where I came from, people were mostly Moslems, both good and bad. The Christian world quaked in its boots, hearing in our battle drums the end of all Christendom. But, somehow, they must've prevailed over us, considering Lady Zubaida's report, only to burn themselves out from the inside in the end."

"Where's this future from which you come?" said the Caliph, thinking to humor Hürü.

"Constantinople," Hürü said. "We call the city Istanbul."

"I've always said," the Caliph observed, "that one didn't need to be a diviner to know the Arabs would take Constantinople sooner or later. One doesn't have to come from the future to predict that!"

"Not Arabs," Hürü said. "Turks were granted Constantinople."

"Now that's amusing!" the Caliph said. "Turks are a bunch of nobodies who don't know how to blow their noses."

"In time," Hürü said, "they learn."

"And how does history remember me?" Harun-er-Rashid inquired, amused enough to chuckle. "Tell me the truth, now."

"Most benign ruler," Hürü said, "Yours was the last golden age for the Arabs; so they recorded you as a better man than you were."

"I knew there was something fishy about you, boy!" the Caliph said. "You're mad! And if you're not mad, you'd better be able to prove that you're from the future. Tell me one thing about my life that I don't yet know."

An idea occurred to Hürü.

"Well," she said, "history books record that you took a lawful wife whose name was Lady Zubaida. I bet you a gold piece that this Lady Zubaida is the one who becomes your wife. Although personally I think it's a shame to tie down an independent woman, as the sovereign, you probably can't afford to let her go. And you can't have Black Mesrur cut off her head, seeing you're too fascinated to finish her off. Yet, she's too powerful a merchant prince for you not to interfere with that power, if you get my meaning."

"I do," said the Caliph, tossing Hürü a gold coin. "You win the bet. But how do I know you don't foresee the future out of cunning rather than knowledge? You may be dealing in what's called self-fulfilling prophecy."

"You'll never know," Hürü said, "for sure."

But the Caliph was no longer interested in Hürü's news from the future. His attention turned to the mature woman who'd been forced to confront her heart and survive the confrontation.

"What do you say, Lady Zubaida?" said the Caliph, whose mind was made up. "Will you ally yourself with your sovereign under the protection of the law and the grace of God?"

"My lord," Lady Zubaida said, "I'm not a princess. I am a businesswoman who's accustomed to her own counsel."

"As I see it," the Caliph said, "in our time, a woman has to be twice as smart to be the equal of her man. Your first husband was just a boy, a pious parrot of virtue. He was someone whom you could've dominated until the end of his days and who, in time, would've turned against you. You may very well be smarter than I, but I'm a powerful man. Will you risk it with me?"

"My lord," said the lady, a delicate flush rising from her throat to her strong face.

"Ah, you blush!" said the Caliph. "I believe I've won. Call in the judge and the *imam*, Jafar! I will wed this woman!"

Hürü was amazed how quickly the marriage contract was drawn up; she noticed, too, how eager the Caliph was to make sure he was made heir to all Lady Zubaida's holdings in case of her death. But she didn't hear a word about Lady Zubaida inheriting the Abbasid Kingdom, should the Caliph bite the dust first. Nor anything about a wedding gift to the Lady. Presumably, marrying a Caliph was gift enough. Dung! thought Hürü. A woman should never trust a man, especially not a prince! It seemed to Hürü that the most reliable weapon a woman owned was her deeply ingrained suspicion; without that justified suspiciousness, one was condemned to go about barefoot, pregnant and jilted.

Hürü knew, from her perusals of history, that the Caliph would never remain true to Lady Zubaida; he'd even succeed in turning this extraordinary woman into a shrewish, jealous wife. History expounded on the instances in which the Caliph had outwitted this formidable woman, never dwelling on the times when the Lady won the day. Hürü wished she'd held her stupid tongue. But she hadn't. Was there something in her, she wondered, that always compelled her to show off?

Chapter 13

LADY AMINE'S TALE

*How a reformed slave of Love
finds herself back on Square One*

*A*t the wedding feast, Hürü was called on to commemorate in song the Caliph's marriage to Lady Zubaida. Hürü, who'd never tried her hand at nuptial songs and didn't even understand the nature of the epithalamium, left it up to the Lyre. The Stone Lyre, not at its most inspired pitch, nevertheless produced something about that celebrated membrane, the hymen. Or that's what Hürü thought she was being made to sing about: the tissue that was such an issue. Hardly an appropriate subject for Lady Zubaida, whose seal had been broken on the high seas, and certainly an unfortunate reminder to the Caliph that he had bought his goods secondhand. But there was nothing to be done about it. She was the Lyre's toy, and had to say amen to the bad along with the good. So she sang what the Lyre dictated.

> Raise high the roof-beams, carpenters,
> *Hymen!*
> The groom comes like the God of War,
> *Hymen!*
> Towering like the Lesbian Poet, he comes,
> *Hymen!*

The applause was politely lukewarm. No one, including Hürü herself, had caught the reference to the Lesbian Poet. Everybody would've preferred something more luscious than roofs, carpenters, a groom who came tall as some war god.

"Don't sing anything else," the Caliph advised Hürü, "not until you take a lesson or two."

"I'm not in the least surprised," said the Caliph's mother, "the lad couldn't sing properly. Did you see him just wolf down his food? I mean, he just wolfed it down! In my husband's time, musicians ate in the kitchen, so one didn't have to watch them stuff themselves."

The court musicians took up where Hürü left off, having, as they did, a stock of songs sure to please. The conversation at the table— that is, the Caliph's conversation—passed on to more burning questions, for example, what to do about the Afghan-hound bitches until an enchantress could be found to disenchant them. Certainly, it wouldn't do for the Caliph to have two bitches for sisters-in-law.

"For the time being," the Caliph decided, "our fool will take care of the two bitches."

It took Hürü a few seconds to understand that it was she he meant. She'd thought she was at last the royal lyre-player, but here she was being demoted to the fool again.

"Oh no you don't!" Hürü said. "Just because I sang one inappropriate song, why should I have to be the dog-catcher? I promise, Commander of the Faithful, I'll do better in the future. Please, Sir, don't put me in charge of the dogs."

"Why not, Fool?" said the Caliph, frowning.

"Because I'll grow to love them both," Hürü said. "Whether they're Lady Zubaida's disagreeable half-sisters or not, they look like a pair of innocent hounds to me. I used to have a dog, not even purebred like these two, and I know what dogs can do to a person's heart."

"Dogs are abominable," the Caliph said. "Our friends the Persians won't suffer a dog to touch them, since they have to take ritual baths to cleanse the contamination. Damn inconvenient, if you ask the Persians, to have a dog around."

"Nevertheless," Hürü said, "I'm not a Persian. I'd let the dogs touch me everywhere, including my heart. Then I couldn't bear to see them whipped three hundred lashes every night. Let Mesrur take care of the bitches; his heart has been hardened through the virtues of his profession."

Lord High Executioner, Black Mesrur, put a hand on his sword, but the Caliph stayed his hand.

"The lad has a babbling mouth," the Caliph said, "by virtue of *his* profession of tomfoolery. Take no umbrage, Mesrur; there's a good man."

"Before things get out of hand," Lady Zubaida said, "I should mention that the *jinniye* gave me a lock of her hair. I wear the demon-lock in the locket around my neck. Here it is. The *jinniye* said that whenever I desired her presence, I should burn a few strands, and she would appear to me even if she were beyond Mount Kaf."

"Burn a few strands then," the Caliph said enthusiastically, "and let's see what a jinniye is like."

The hair was placed in an incense burner and lit. To everyone's surprise, a gentlewoman among the guests rose. She looked just like a person.

"I am she whom you summon," said the gentlewoman. "Soon as I heard of the nuptials between the Caliph and the Lady who's my protege, I dropped by to keep an eye on things. If your desire is to have these two bitches restored, O Commander of the Faithful, I will certainly fulfill your wish. But I warn you, O Caliph, it's far better to have two bitches for sisters-in-law than two who can talk."

"I can deal with them," said Harun-er-Rashid. "I'm the Caliph."

"Here goes then," said the *jinniye* gentlewoman.

She walked over to the two Afghan hounds who were busy licking clean a golden plate on which they'd been served their meat. Instantly, two women found themselves on all fours, stark naked, licking a gold plate clean. The two humanized bitches desperately tried to cover their nakedness and shame. But everyone present had a chance to observe that what's attractive in purebred Afghan hounds is not necessarily so in women.

"You two," the Caliph said to the former bitches, "on this day of my marriage to your good sister, I give the pair of you in wedlock to my slave and Lord High Executioner, Black Mesrur. He's the man who knows how to requite you both."

"But he's black!" said the eldest sister in horror.

"And he's a eunuch!" said the middle one, shivering.

"That's right!" the Caliph said, laughing as if he'd die. "What do you think, wife?"

"Devilishly clever!" Lady Zubaida said, toasting her husband, her lord, her master, her mainstay, the support of her roof. Ah, the high-beam that raises the roof! Hürü got the Lyre's meaning at last.

As the attention of all the wedding guests was riveted on the two former bitch sisters' marriage to Black Mesrur, which was performed instantly and without formality, nobody noticed the *jinniye*'s disappearance. By the time the *jinniye* was remembered, she was long gone. And that's how Lady Zubaida's two sisters found themselves a husband, black and wattles empty, for the third time around.

The Caliph's curiosity turned to the feisty little lady called Amine, whose story hadn't yet been heard.

"Well, now, Lady Amine," the Caliph said, "entertain us, if you will, with your history. Tell us who put those brutal whip marks on your shapely wazoo!"

Lady Amine rose, made her obeisance to the Caliph and settled on her knees to tell the Caliph the story he now demanded. As she talked, her deep dark-brown eyes sparkled, now with defiance, now with sorrow. Hürü noticed, for the first time, the lines of care already marring the ivory-white of her skin around the mouth and the forehead. In the bright lights of the Caliph's dining-hall, Amine's soft curves were more visibly those of a young woman aging before her time.

"O Commander of the Faithful," Amine began, "know that the history of my life takes no turn to the extraordinary. I am but an ordinary Slave of Love. Oh, I suppose I'm smart enough to have done something other than fall in love. But I didn't.

"I grew up in a house where everything was in abundance; there was never a reason for me to strain or stretch out my arms. What I wanted was always immediately handed to me: amusement, safety, decisions, travel, jewelry, beautiful clothes. My father was, by trade, a jeweler. And both my parents were born into the Jewish faith, although so little was made of faith in our home that no one could tell us apart from the gentiles. My father even entertained himself away from the house in the company of other women, behaving more like an Arab gentleman than a true Jew who swears to remain faithful to his only wedded wife. And my mother was a fretful woman, cautious and watchful. Yet, no sooner had my father died, than my mother mismanaged her portion of the inheritance so quickly that I swear she revenged herself on him by losing the fortune he left her. She'd be destitute this day, were it not for my sisters, who married well to husbands capable of increasing their fortunes.

"Since we had no brother, my sisters and I were given educations befitting upper-class girls, as well as names in Arabic. Consider the inappropriateness of my name for a Jewish girl. Amine, as we all know, was the name of the Prophet Mohammed's mother—a good enough name, but hardly Jewish. I grew up not knowing what to believe. So it's not surprising that, instead of concerning myself with religion as many women do, I yielded to the scientific turn of mind to which I was inclined. Yet, I had none of the burning passion for science that singleminded scholars display.

"Sometimes I'd get myself into my father's library to look up books on a certain subject. The weight of the tomes, as I carried them to my room, would make me feel, well, sort of virtuous. For half an hour I'd find, say, astronomy quite fascinating. But then I'd see that I'd read several pages without understanding a thing while idly daydreaming of being loved overwhelmingly by a handsome and compelling man.

"Oh, I had a good head for figures. I still do. And I learned to solve mathematical problems, prodded by my father, who put great value on that science. But I never reached a point where I might invent a theorem of my own. Music, which often accompanies the facility for mathematics, also came as easily, and I am indeed a virtuoso player. Yet, I never could compose a song. Not the way the beardless youth who admonished me in your presence can. O Caliph, I'm too opinionated to hear what's in my interest to hear. The boy's right, damn his hide!

"In me there is still something of the little girl who can be led to the source but won't partake. Refusal was always my main source of power. That's the way I got even with my parents, too. A wonderful array of food would be brought before me on a tray, and I'd refuse to eat a morsel. Then I'd observe my parents watching me with concern as I lost weight. I think in the beginning I wanted to feel my power over them, but later, during my adolescence, I really couldn't eat a mouthful. Even a single pistachio nut would come right back up again as soon as I swallowed it. How I didn't die, I don't know, considering the living skeleton I turned into. All my parents could do was to have me force-fed by strapping slaves, and I suppose the bits of the food I didn't vomit nourished me.

"As soon as I turned sixteen, my father arranged my marriage to an older man, also a jeweler, who was older than my father himself. They consolidated their two businesses, with me as the living link. And a frail link I was. Not only could I still not eat the food provided by my husband, but I couldn't bear his husbandly demands. Fortunately, he was an old man who couldn't get up to eating me as often as he'd have liked. Only a year had passed when, within weeks of each other, both husband and father died. I grieved mightily for my father.

"Now suddenly I was a wealthy woman, with a double inheritance from my beloved father as well as my unregretted husband. And, in a sense, I was entirely on my own to do now as I pleased. But what in the world should I do? I couldn't think of anything that might be pleasant, exciting or absorbing. So I ordered myself ten suits of exquisite clothes, each set costing a thousand gold pieces, and I'd deck myself out like a queen each day just to sit around the house. A total failure of imagination. Then I slowly began to acquire a taste for food. At first, almost scientifically, I studied the nature of diets, the virtues of plants, cereals, dairy products and meats, experimenting with the healing and detrimental effects on my own person. These experiments put some meat on my bones, and I was pleased to see in the mirror that I was actually a rather attractive woman. Pleased with my bodily progress, I even performed physical exercises, dutifully sprinting around the garden walks like a nymph and stretching by the pool. Would that my father could see me now! He'd been so sedentary, he had slaves to carry him to the latrine.

"One day as I was breathing hard and glistening with perspiration after my exercises, which had to be performed compulsively lest I lose track of where I was, an old woman came to pay me a visit. She was a disgustingly ugly old woman, warts on her nose with thick black bristles growing out of the warts, one rotten tooth in her head and breath that would kill a camel at a single whiff. I thought she'd come to me for a handout—many persons in distress often did, considering I'd give them something just to get rid of them—so I pulled a pouch of coins from my girdle, trying not to look in the old woman's face, and handed it to her even before she spoke.

"'My kind mistress,' the old woman said, 'I didn't come here to beg for money but for your presence. I have an orphaned daughter whose nuptials are to be celebrated tonight. She's broken-hearted that there isn't a single lady of distinction among the list of guests. If you will reward my daughter with your presence, the poor thing will be beside herself with joy, for she has no mighty person, besides God, to befriend her in this hour, the most important hour in a girl's life. So, I beg you to ornament the celebration with your presence, and God will recompense you for your kindness.'

"Well, I thought, so there are girls who are worse off than I. At least I had a position in the world, granted me by virtue of the law of inheritance. What harm was there in doing a favor for someone less fortunate than I? I promised the old woman that when she came in the evening to fetch me, I'd be ready. I put on one of my ten magnificent suits and draped myself with enough jewelry to dazzle the female celebrants, for display of wealth seemed to be my purpose in this world, the nature of my existence. In my heart, I really didn't want to go to any wedding at all. I hated being stared at, the reason I shut myself in the house, to avoid the tedious and odious starers on the streets. I wished I hadn't made the promise to the old woman, and hoped she would fall and break her leg, so I could eat my yogurt and fruit instead in my own company. But the disgusting old hag returned at the appointed hour to guide me to her house.

"'Oh, my mistress,' she said, 'the women of the city have arrived. And when I boasted that you, too, were invited, they couldn't contain their excitement. Come, so they may receive you with the honor you deserve.'

"So, I put on my veil and cloak. Taking along my female slaves to shield me from the eyes of the curious, I followed the old woman until we arrived at a street in which a soft wind playfully raised my veils. But, instead of stopping in front of a poor hovel, the old woman knocked on the door of a palace. I stood marvelling at the gateway overarched with a marble vault, amazed at the elegance of the disgusting old woman's abode. We entered a richly carpeted hallway, illumined by lamps and candles, decorated with blue Persian tiles and carved arches. From there, we proceeded into a magnificent salon, furnished with sofas of silk, lighted by cut-glass lamps, draped with damask and velvet. From a canopied couch rose to greet me an elegant girl, quite young but in full possession of herself, and kissed me on both cheeks. If indeed she were an orphan, she wore her orphanhood in style.

"'Welcome to our humble abode, Lady Amine,' she said. 'Your company refreshes the heart.'

"We sat down together after I dismissed my slaves to the kitchens and the old witch made herself scarce. I wondered where the women of Baghdad kept themselves. Where was the excitement my name aroused? But before I could put my questions to her, the elegant damsel spoke.

"'Forgive me,' she said, 'for using this stratagem to lure you here. The idea was devised by the old woman, but it was my brother who bribed her to think up a way to gain an interview with you. Lady Amine, my poor brother is terribly inflamed with love for you.'

"'How did he manage to do that all by himself?' I asked, amazed at the temerity. 'I hardly ever go out.'

"'He was visiting a house adjoining your garden,' the damsel said, 'and he saw your sylphlike form straining in hard exercise. He fell desperately in love.'

"I thought to myself that the brother must be after my fortune; probably this showcase of a house was hocked up to its cut-glass chandeliers and debtors lined the street early in the morning. Probably I was the only prayer between the family and the poorhouse. I realized that I myself needed a prayer or two in order to escape the house, where I was, in a sense, held prisoner. My female slaves, who'd been herded elsewhere, could do little to extricate me from this mess and these people, if they so desired, could easily detain me against my will.

"'Don't be alarmed,' said the fair matchmaker. 'My brother desires to marry you under God and the law. There can be no disgrace in what's lawful and blessed.'

"'Well,' said I, 'let's see what this brother looks like.'

"She clapped her hands, and the brother, whose ear must've been at the key hole, entered the salon. Well, the young man who fell in love on the sly turned out to be a loving example of God's handiwork. Not only was he blessed with height, his shoulders were wide, his forehead high, his complexion light and his eyes burned with intelligence. I loved at once the way he strode so easily on his long legs, his weight on the inner part of his soles, so athletically economical in the expenditure of his energy. He must have been attracted by my athletic efforts. I couldn't have chosen a lover more to my taste; yet, for reasons of his own, he'd chosen me. My material fortune couldn't match this, even if I'd deliberately set about to find a husband. I'd attracted my heart's desire unwittingly.

"'This is my brother, Amin,'" said the cool noblewoman.

"'Will you wed me, Lady Amine?' Amin said without ceremony or ado. 'If you refuse, I will persist so long and so arduously, you will marry me in the end. If you still refuse, I will die and haunt you, and my spirit will possess thoroughly what you refused my flesh. Foul means or fair, I will have you. For there's no stopping me now that I've seen you up close.'

"His voice was so profound and velvety that I longed to touch my cheek against its smooth rich texture, its heavy undercurrent of iron mixed with persuasion. At this point, even if he hadn't wanted to wed me, I'd gladly have been his strumpet, without threats, without vows, without even love, either. Perhaps every woman wants to be broken under a man whose will is supreme?

"So, no sooner had we sat down together, than a judge and four witnesses entered, saluted and fell to drawing up the marriage contract. Vows spoken, my groom got rid of the judge, the witnesses, his gracious sister. Amin had no truck with conventions that might put off immediate gratification of his desires.

"'Now to bed,' said he. 'But before I give you so thoroughly all that you've missed in life, having first wed an old and feeble man and then abstained in widowhood, I want to impose a covenant on you. Otherwise, I will walk out of here without a backward glance. I will leave you burning between the legs. I will leave you with an emptiness that can never be filled again. Don't fool yourself, I see in your face telltale signs that you want me as I want you.'

"'Anything you say,' I answered, my loins aflame from his promise.

"'Swear then, on the Koran, that you will never, ever, even look at another man, let alone show any inclination toward any but myself.'

"'That's so easily done,' I said, placing my hand on his holy book, 'when I long for none but you.'

"'Forever?' he said.

"'Forever and ever,' I made my oath. Why not?

"Amin took me then. Although I was wild with passion, somehow that passion was not appeased. It was my fault, I know, since I knew nothing I might do to please myself, receive for myself what I most desired. At the very crisis of love, I seemed to retreat and be engulfed, instead of jointly engulfing him who was held inside me a willing prisoner. And each time I returned to the couch, resolved to take, I settled, at the last moment, for his contentment. Just as I felt death approaching, I lost heart and wouldn't die in the little death of love.

"I lived in the happiness of being owned by this husband whose possession set me apart from other women, those pitiful women who must put up with lukewarm husbands who can't even give a repeat performance the same night, those men who must be coaxed only to flag. My husband was voracious in all his appetites. He always must have more than enough. He leavened me, kneaded me, put me in the oven. When he felt me not baking, he took me out to leaven me again, to knead me, to pound me, to fire me again. He overwhelmed me so, I went numb. He moved in and out of a certain stale coldness. Yet, all day I burned for him, only to leave his couch in the morning without getting what I went for. I was able to conceal from my husband the truth by pretending that my joy in swinking matched his; so assured of himself was he that he was certain I, too, experienced the same delight.

"After a whole month of this, one day I begged him to let me go out, do a little shopping and put the house I'd so thoroughly abandoned into some sort of order, either selling the place or renting it before it fell into disrepair. He would consent only if I took the desperately ugly old house-hag with me as my chaperone. Besides, he informed me, he'd already put my affairs in order himself; there was no need to worry my pretty head over dull and dreadful business. If I still wanted to go shopping for trifles, well, I'd have to take the hag along.

"The hag accompanied me on my shopping spree with bells on her skirts. She was full of talk about a young merchant she knew who had gorgeous stuffs from all over the world, having a huge inventory on account of his wealth. We went directly to his shop, where the hag asked the merchant to show me nothing but the costliest stuff.

"'Isn't the merchant an elegant young man?' the hag kept on pestering me. 'Aren't his eyes blue as the heavens and his lips moister than glazed cherries?'

"'Look here, old woman!' I said. 'We're here to look at the merchandise, not the merchant.'

"'But look at the sweet way he bends his knee,' the hag insisted, 'when he shows you the material. Never have I seen such a gracious young man!'

"I made my selection quickly, so that we might get out of this shop where the old woman kept embarrassing me with her idle loose tongue. When I started to pay, however, the young merchant wouldn't accept payment.

"'The material is yours,' said he; 'your presence in my shop is payment enough.'

"'Return the material to the merchant,' I ordered the hag, 'if he refuses to accept payment.'

"'But I won't take the material back, by God!' cried the young merchant. 'There's no power on this earth to make me take back what I gave you as a present. No, by God, I will not take money from you, beautiful lady. All I will take in return is a little kiss.'

"'What damage can a little kiss cause?' whispered the hag. 'A kiss is nothing. It leaves behind no sign.'

"'The lady can have the entire contents of my shop,' the young merchant said, 'for the price of a little kiss. That's how much one kiss from her means to me.'

"'Tell him to forget it,' I said to the hag. 'He can either have the money or the material back. No kiss from me.'

"'What's in a little kiss?' the hag reasoned. 'Why are you so prim? Besides, this young merchant is making such a fuss that soon he's going to gather the whole marketplace around the shop. And word will reach your husband, no doubt distorted in passage, that you created a scene in the market like some ordinary wench. So, if you wish to quiet this troublemaker, unveil yourself, hold out your cheek, close your eyes and suffer this troublemaker's kiss. And let's be on our way.'

"'But I took an oath never to look at another man,' I protested.

"'You don't have to *look* at him,' the hag said. 'Just close your eyes, and your oath won't be broken. How could it be broken when you only have to let him kiss you?'

"So, to appease the young merchant, who was indeed gathering a crowd as he shouted demands for the kiss he was owed, I closed my eyes and lifted the edge of my veil, holding out my cheek to this shameless and insistent young man. The rascal put his mouth on my cheek all right! Instead of kissing the cheek, he bit it so violently, I fainted with the pain. When I came to, my head was in the lap of the hag, the shop closed, the troublesome merchant gone; so was the material.

"'It's just a bruise, thank God!' said the hag. 'It could've been worse. Someone could've seen you offer your cheek. Now, let's make haste and get home before your husband does. Once home, get in bed and pretend you're sick. I'll make a poultice and bring it up. It's a sure remedy to draw out the bruise.'

"I took the hag's advice and repaired to bed at once. After all, old women are clever both with poultices and stratagem. My husband, on his return home, hearing I'd taken ill, came up at once to see what ailed me.

"'I should never have allowed you to stir out of the house,' Amin said. 'See, you got sick at once. What hurts you, my darling?'

"'I'm not well,' I said.

"'Your blush,' he said, 'turned black-and-blue on one cheek. What happened to you?'

"'An ill-fated shopping trip,' I admitted. 'On the street, a camel loaded with firewood drove against me in the crowd, tore my veil and bruised my cheek. I tell you, the streets of Baghdad are too narrow."

"'By God!' cried my husband. 'The camel-driver will pay for this! Tomorrow, I will see the mayor and have every firewood-seller in the city strung up.'

"'Please, no!' I cried. 'Don't burden yourself with the curses of every firewood-seller in the city. Not on my account! The truth is, I was not wounded by anybody's firewood. I was riding an ass which took fright and threw me. A stick on the street poked me in the cheek.'

"'So!' he said. 'I'll see Grand Vizier Jafar Barmaki in the morning and have every ass-driver in town put to death.'

"'How can you have innocent people killed?' I said, weeping in anguish and fear. 'What happened to me was my own fate.'

"'Then, undoubtedly, you're the one who must be killed!'

"He seized me violently by the hair and dragged me out of bed, uttering bloodcurdling howls that brought seven black slaves running into the bedroom, their swords drawn. The slaves picked me up and threw me in the middle of the chamber. As I trembled helplessly, my husband ordered one slave to hold me down by the shoulders, another to sit on my head, a third to seize me by the knees and a fourth to pin down my feet. And the fifth then approached, naked sword whizzing.

"'My lord,' the slave asked, 'shall I strike off her head? Or shall I cut her into little pieces so we may feed her to the fish in the Tigris?'

"'Cut her up,' said the slave who sat on my head. 'Best punishment for a wife who disregards her promises to her lord and master.'

"'Strike her!' my husband ordered. 'I don't care how!'

"'Repeat your final prayers,' the executing slave said, 'and reflect on your crime. This, lady, is the end of your life.'

"'Good slave,' I said, 'release me while I make profession of my faith and make peace with my soul.'

"Once released, I fell before my husband, weeping as I spoke desperate entreaties. Then I recited for him two verses of a love poem; like every true gentleman, he too loved poetry, and I hoped I might soften his heart into compassion. So I kept prostrating and humbling myself, addressing him with tender words, thinking that he might be moved not to have me murdered, even if he ended up keeping all my property. But my husband was immovable.

"'Cleave her into two!' he commanded. 'She's of no value to us. Bury one half and toss the other half to the fish! All her life, she's been like two women. Let her spend eternity looking for her other half.'

"Just as I readied myself to commit my body to death, the old hag rushed in the room, making a great fracas, and threw herself at my husband's feet, kissing his boots and begging for my life.

"'Mercy, my son, for the sake of the milk you nursed from me,' she wept. 'Pardon your wife, for she committed no crime to deserve such a terrible punishment. You yourself carry half the blame. Why did you have to test her fidelity? Why did you have her set up with a rascal posing as a merchant? And why did I encourage and tempt her to dispense a kiss? I am afraid for myself, son. And I am afraid for you. If you spill the blood of an innocent, we may both come to terrible ends.'

"'She didn't resist,' my husband said. 'She went for the line of least resistance instead of remaining steadfast.'

"'A woman is a frail being, son,' the hag said. 'You can't expect from her the steadfastness of a man. Come, my lamb, let her live.'

"'For your sake, nurse,' he said, 'she will live. But I will put marks on her that will forever remind her of her perfidy. Her offense will be engraved on her body for the rest of her life.'

"My husband had his slaves strip me of my vest and pantaloons; taking a hardy stick cut from the quince-tree, he personally beat me on my back and buttocks until I became insensible from the blows. And when he was done marring me for life, he had his slaves dump me in my own house. All my former slaves were gone, having been resold at my husband's discretion, so that I had no one to see me through the months of illness brought on by the beating. He'd had the foresight to have every stick of furniture and each utensil auctioned off so that I wouldn't have even a basin in which to wash my face. Groaning and bleeding, I lay on the bare floor for days, without a single morsel of food passing my lips. Not even a kindly neighbor, or a single person for whom I'd previously done a good turn, came by with a bowl of soup or a wet rag for my burning forehead, I was so thoroughly disgraced and outcast. But, after that first week, Lady Zubaida, who'd heard the gossip and found in her heart sympathy for my plight, arrived to offer me a helping hand. Not only her hand—she had me installed in her own house and, under the direction of her physician, nursed me back to health.

"And with Lady Zubaida I've remained since. In her I recognized, for the first time, what an independent woman of means might be like. She endured success and failure like a man, without, however, losing any of her womanliness. Since, unlike her, I'd handed over my entire fortune to the first man who asked for it, I applied for and was granted the job of cateress for Lady Zubaida's household, earning a day's wage for a day's work. Finally, I'd found the occupation with which to balance my feckless life. I'd never liked going about the streets, shunned manual work and had a long war with food. Now, I shopped, haggled, wielded heavy utensils, kept the household accounts—as well as did the considerable bookkeeping for Lady Zubaida's business concerns—and prepared food like those famous cooks who are all men.

"And indeed, I had an army to feed! Those glorious warrior-maidens, who were former slaves freed by Lady Zubaida, had chosen to become her task force for which they received pay, quartering and honor. Ah, those women! They preferred to die rather than yield their mistress to the Caliph's troops—not before, however, they killed five men for each one of them. Lady Zubaida's residence was strewn with their beautiful bodies. Their souls must've been transported instantly to a warrior's Paradise. Yet, had your curiosity about our secret order not been so overpowering, O Caliph, those warrior-maidens would still be boisterously alive. How can I toast your health, O Caliph, when those courageous women lie dead?

"Some time after I began to live with Lady Zubaida, Safiye, the Sky-Wolf, joined our sisterhood. And a welcome addition she was! Safiye Sky-Wolf, O Caliph, whose talents in riding and swordplay were superior, became the commander of the household task force, training and honing the maidens. You might say she was Lady Zubaida's minister of state. In that household, we had no want of company, love and tenderness. To remind ourselves each and every day, Lady Zubaida had to whip her two bitch sisters, and I disrobed, submitting to the shame of exposing my scars. As every addict must, to stay the habit, I had openly to admit my addiction to love. I still long for that violent man; he comes to me in my dreams, inflames my imagination, only to wake me to my rejected flesh. Were he to touch me once, I'd instantly succumb again to being a Slave of Love.

"But there's safety in occupation. By becoming a gastronome, I overcame my girlish nausea. Not only have I put some agreeable flesh on my bones, I don't fear the success that comes on the heels of failure, although were my husband to take me back, I might become a wimp again."

✦

Lady Amine fell silent, looking down her delicate hands, the heels of which had a healthy layer of callous. The celebrants, too, remained silent for a few minutes, contemplating the young woman's story. We all know that our neighbors often suffer in secrecy, yet it shocks us to hear what a survivor has to say.

"Who, then," the Caliph demanded, "was this iniquitous wife-beater? I'd have a word or two with that fellow!"

"You wouldn't relish knowing who he is, O Caliph," said Lady Amine. "Best you don't know."

"But I must know," the Caliph insisted, "who among my subjects goes to such inhuman lengths! I want him brought before me and punished for stupidity."

"Punishment," Lady Amine said sadly, "would come too late, O Commander of the Faithful. A little fatherly concern might have helped before. Had you given your son the gift of love, O Caliph, I would not be humiliating myself before you, broadcasting the secret of my scars. The young man involved is none other than your son, Prince El-Amin."

"What!" cried the Caliph, swallowing hard. "I didn't know he got himself married! El-Amin marries but won't inform his father . . . and Caliph. This one's for the books!"

"Perhaps," Lady Zubaida offered again, "you have too many sons to keep track of, my lord."

"But this hurts," the Caliph complained to his new wife. "I suppose El-Amin thought I'd disapprove of a Jewess. Worse, he then beats her to an inch of her life and still says not a word. Find that rapscallion, Jafar, and fetch him here. Why isn't he present, in the first place, to celebrate my nuptials?"

"Perhaps," Lady Zubaida offered again, "because you never married his mother, my lord."

"Come," the Caliph invited his newly found daughter-in-law, "and sit beside me. You're as lovely a daughter-in-law as I'd wish—though you say you're not so good in bed. But, then, most women aren't. And most pretend otherwise. Every woman should copulate on the day she knows the human defects of her beloved, and not a day before. Oh, hunchbacks and monstrous cripples, I understand, give some women the only genuine climax they know. There are no dreams in copulation, you see, no illusions to diminish pure animal lust. Now that you know what a monster El-Amin is, daughter, there should be no illusion to prevent you from satisfying yourself."

Lady Amine looked perplexed, but sat beside her mighty father-in-law and then began to sob like one possessed. When El-Amin was dragged in, protesting, the young man seem enraged to see his alienated wife sitting beside and being consoled by his father. Yet, he made a proper obeisance and was allowed to kiss the Caliph's hand. He ain't much, Hürü thought; for one thing, he's too tall for Lady Amine, who's a tiny sparrow of a thing. Besides, El-Amin's complexion, in Hürü's estimate, was too sallow, his face somewhat too long. Horse-face, she thought, that's what!

"Is it true, Amin, that you married this charming woman?" the Caliph inquired with all the forbearance he could muster. "And then you beat the hell out of her?"

"I had the misfortune of marrying her," the petulant Prince admitted, "but the good fortune of getting rid of her. The woman's always looking to someone to tell her what to do. Not only can a common street merchant prevail over her oaths of fidelity, I hear she's now under the influence of a woman *sheik* who tells her how to conduct herself. How can a man trust a woman who doesn't know what she wants?"

"Amine has changed, Amin," the Caliph said. "She's suffered enough to have an idea or two of her own. Besides, I'm not interested in your complaints. I want you to do what's right. Reconcile with her at once!"

"I can't, O Caliph," the Prince said. "At the moment, I'm involved with another."

"Then uninvolve yourself!"

"But I've already married again," the Prince went on, whining a little. "And I've adopted my wife's son."

"By God!" thundered the Caliph. "First you marry a Jewess without my permission; second, you beat her senseless; third, you marry some woman left over from another man; fourth, you adopt the woman's bastard. Will it never end? Were you put on this earth just to vex and embarrass your father?"

Prince El-Amin stood before his father, his hands folded over his chest, looking sheepish but not a bit contrite.

"Hear this, then," the Caliph said. "You will take Lady Amine back and live with her in her house which shall be restored, out of the privy purse, to its former elegance. She will also receive a regular income befitting her station as a princess of the realm. Your allowance, on the other hand, shall be discontinued. Your wife will hand you pin-money as she sees fit. And I expect you, perplexing son of mine, to acquit yourself honorably."

That's how the Caliph's son El-Amin was condemned to live with his estranged wife Amine with whom he'd fallen out of love; he was exiled to live under his wife's roof and, to the degree allowed, her authority. Even though it's a caliph's job to marry everybody off, thereby solving numerous life crises, Hūrū couldn't imagine how the Caliph could so blithely sentence people to happiness.

"To bed, then!" the Caliph said, enormously pleased with himself. "We will hear Lady Safiye's story tomorrow. Now, my bride awaits!"

Hūrū, who hadn't slept for a couple of nights now, was overjoyed at the prospect of a pillow and a comfortable bed. How could the Caliph, no longer a student, stay up two nights like some seminarian and still expect to perform well in bed, she wondered. But that was his problem.

To her dismay, Hūrū found that she was expected to curl up on one of the benches outside the royal bedchamber, along with the other cup-companions who slept like beggars, just in case the Caliph couldn't sleep and wanted to keep everybody up, tippling. No apartment for her as the Caliph had promised! Ah, the promises of princes.

Hūrū thought bitterly, turning this way and that on the bench. Sleep would not come despite her exhaustion. No wonder Harun-er-Rashid's sons screwed up the Golden Age of the Arabs! An all-powerful father like that, the sons can't wait to monkey with his legacy! She tried to recall the issue of the Caliph's union with Lady Zubaida, but she couldn't remember his name. One would expect that a son born of a big, beautiful woman like Lady Zubaida, with her remarkable acumen besides, would be a good prince to guide the Arabs through tumultuous times. Who was he? Then, the history about the Godly Prince came to Hürü. Yes! The Godly Prince must've been Lady Zubaida's son! At the tender age of sixteen, the Godly Prince forsook the world and chose the Sufi Way.

The story Hürü remembered was told simply, without edifying exaggerations, by dervish teachers, as if the remarkable content were an everyday occurrence. Seems, one day, Harun-er-Rashid, attended by all the lords of the realm and the dignitaries of the state, met up with his ascetic son. Observing the Prince in a hair shirt, his head wrapped in a woollen scarf, the lofty personages were embarrassed for the Caliph's sake. "The lad makes his father a mockery among kings," they muttered to one another. "Is this a seemly way for a prince to behave?" "The Caliph really ought to see to it that the Prince behaves more appropriately!"

On hearing what his courtiers had to say, the Caliph said to the Prince, "Dear Son, you disgrace me in front of my retinue."

The Prince stared hard at his father but did not answer.

"What do you say for yourself?" the Caliph insisted.

"Only this, O Caliph:" the Prince said, "you disgrace me in front of the Saints."

So, the Godly Prince quit Baghdad and went to the city of Basra, where he toiled among common laborers. The remainder of the story, told by a Witness for whom the Prince worked as a stonemason, goes like this.

"'The lad,' the Witness related, 'would accept only a small sum for his labors. But I observed that every time he stopped for his meditations, the stones piled themselves of their own accord into a wall. That's how I knew this was no ordinary lad. Then I heard he had fallen sick. Wishing to look in on him, I found the blessed youth in a mean hut where he lay dying. He begged me to see to his burial and take to the Caliph whatever was found in his pocket. The next day, I buried him and found in his pocket an incredibly large ruby.

"'When I brought the ruby to Harun-er-Rashid, the Caliph understood at once that his son was dead.

"'Was the blessed lad really your son, O Commander of the Faithful?' I asked.

"'Alas, he was!' the Caliph responded. 'But the Prince avoided all that was in my power to give him. This ruby was pressed on him by his mother who, fearful that poverty might overtake him in strange lands, wanted to insure her son's life and survival.'

"'The Caliph then,' the Witness went on, 'travelled with me to Basra where I showed him the Prince's grave. There, the Caliph fell on his knees and wept as if his heart would break. He implored God and His Saints for forgiveness. And when the Caliph was done mourning, he requested that I become one of his Inner Circle of Friends.

"'O Caliph!' I begged, 'forgive me for my temerity. But I must refuse your offer of friendship. It's just that your son's example provides a warning I cannot forget.'"

Perhaps, Hürü conjectured, the Godly Prince was the issue of tonight's union. Perhaps the Prince was, at this very moment, busy getting himself conceived.

Chapter 14

LADY SAFIYE'S TALE

Why does a beautiful Amazon
always sell herself short?

Scarcely had the Caliph wiped his butter- and honey-smeared beard and dabbed the egg yolk off his pajama top, than he commanded Safiye, the Sky-Wolf, to entertain the royal couple with the story of her life. Hürü didn't fail to notice the way the new bride had quickly rearranged the breakfast tray brought them in bed so that the more choice morsels fell to her big and lusty husband. And Lady Zubaida's hand lingered just a moment too long on the Caliph's egg cup. Hürü guessed the Caliph must've done all right by his new wife, or better. Hürü was glad. Let Lady Zubaida get all she could while the getting and begetting was easy.

As the inner circle of courtiers drew closer to the royal bed, Safiye rose to her elegant height, bowed deeply, not without a hint of mischief playing at the corners of her luscious mouth, and swung her heavy blond braids behind her back. Hürü thought Safiye the most authentic beauty among the Three Ladies of Baghdad; but then perhaps Hürü's preference was rooted in Istanbul where people were fairer. Besides, it was this lady who'd shown an unwavering sympathy for Hürü since she'd arrived at their house as a porter boy. One was drawn to some persons at once, knowing the other would understand even those thoughts for which one hadn't yet found the words. In Safiye's long green eyes flickered that recognition of Hürü's being even now. As the lady prepared to address the Caliph and the distinguished company, she subtly acknowledged Hürü's presence by a glance.

"It is said, O Commander of the Faithful," Safiye, the Sky-Wolf, began, "that some are born into greatness while others are forced to surpass themselves. Know, O Caliph, that I was born high in the Caucasus Mountains, home to the Circassian race. Most people in the civilized world would consider my place of birth Nowhere. But, like my ancestors, I have a certain love of boasting which I indulge whenever I can do so with humor and flair. A gift of the gab, though perhaps self-deprecatory in nature, has allowed me to squeeze out of many a tight spot as well as get into trouble more serious than I'd imagined. Yet, trouble is for mankind as perfect serenity is for God. It seems, now that I look back, I've always sought out trouble and embraced it in its many guises.

"Consider what it is to be born a Circassian, my Lord. We are a race cursed and blessed by the comeliness of our youths, both male and female. We are sought in slavemarkets everywhere, fetching, on the block, such exorbitant prices that roughriders and slavedealers descend on us in hordes, raiding towns and campsites to snatch up our fairhaired and narrow-waisted crop of youths. At a very early age, we make friends with danger. On the Caucasus Mountains, the sheer precipice of the world where we live, we all learn to live endangered at the very edge of things. Risk, for us, is an intoxication more addictive than wine.

"Girls in particular, who haven't been endowed by nature with a prowess equal to boys, must make themselves less vulnerable. Before she can walk, a girl must learn to ride; before she can learn to ride, she must steal a horse. Stealing horses without being apprehended constitutes a virtue among us, for one must be able to steal and steal away. A girl must get up in the morning before her brother; she must mount her mare before he mounts his stallion; she must reach the camp of the enemies before he does; and she must bring her brother an enemy's stinking head. This rule is repeated again during courtship. An enamored Circassian damsel must outstrip her lover in terms of derring-do. That's why Circassian brides are so sought after by our warlike neighbors, the men of Turkoman tribes. Not only will a Circassian maiden stay out all night with a young man of her choice, she's a brave warrior who treats her man to a feast and a rollicking good time.

"We don't give up without a good fight, which is why a Circassian slave is still so rare an item. Otherwise there'd be a glut on the market, satisfying everyone's appetite for Circassian flesh, if we had let ourselves be captured easily. One hopes that someday the peoples of the world will all be bred to display our physical attributes so that we too can have a moment to breathe and do something more interesting than defend ourselves against marauders who can't see us as anything other than a commodity. Amen.

"When I'd just reached puberty, I lost my father to a raid. My mother, my towheaded little brother and I barely escaped, springing on the horses we breed to negotiate craggy mountains, while my luckless father held off the slavesnatchers. My father was an artisan, a curtain-maker by profession. I was apprenticed to this craft as soon as I could thread a needle. He'd work wonders on a curtain in a mere eight days, embroidering the material in colored silks, gold and silver thread. The curtains contained figures of birds, wild beasts, fruits, trees, landscapes with fountains, mountains, gardens where nightingales sang. He'd then glaze the curtain and sell it to foreign dealers who thought fifty gold pieces were nothing for a curtain of my father's make. I suppose they doubled, even trebled, the price on markets elsewhere. But the folks around us had no proper houses in which to hang even humble drapes, let alone fantasies created for princes and kings. As I said, we were too busy fending off slavesnatchers to settle down and apply ourselves to the task of amassing stationary wealth.

"Thanks to what I learned from my father, so long as I could pack my needle, I could always earn my livelihood. So it happened that, after my father's sacrifice of his life, the task of sustaining the family fell on my shoulders. My mother, who had no sense of color or design, helped out by collecting articles of clothing the neighbors cast off to sell to other neighbors who saw further use in those rags. She was the town resale-lady. At first, every year or so, I had a curtain finished. Then, as I mastered the craft, I trimmed down the time to months, and soon I, too, was down to eight days a curtain, just like my luckless father. In certain ways, I even improved on his designs. We began living comfortably enough for my mother to quit her resale business. My darling little brother grew up getting whatever his heart desired. The scamp had no thought in his head but to deck himself out in finery and flaunt his carefree life in the company of youngsters just as irrepressible as himself. Perhaps my mother and I went too easy on him. Yet, it seemed impossible to be tough with him. Not only was he a heartbreaking orphan, he was the most adorable boy anybody'd ever seen. The thought of his sweet dimples still tugs at my heart.

"At twenty, I was still a spinster plying her trade and exercising her cool discipline. Although I wouldn't tolerate it in myself, my brother's slovenly ways, his litter, the tumult that followed him everywhere, his rakishness brought variety to the days filled with needle and thread. Only fourteen, he'd be gone for days, God knows where, doing whatever struck his fancy. One day, my mother and I were summoned by the local chieftain who'd detained my brother for not paying up a gambling debt. The chieftain, who had authority over local mounted warriors, was so incensed that he threatened to take my brother's life.

"'How much does he owe you?' I said, my hand on the purse in my girdle. 'I will pay off his debt.'

"'Five hundred pieces of gold,' said the chieftain.

"That much! I was surprised that a grown man would gamble with a mere boy for such high stakes. I asked him if it were not indeed foolish to treat the colt as if he were already a stallion. But the chieftain wasn't interested in wisdom; it was his money he wanted. Or else! But that kind of money I didn't have.

"'Let me pay you on time,' I suggested. 'The debt can be paid up in three months, give or take a few days. This I promise.'

"'Promises won't do anymore!' said the chieftain, grabbing my brother by his blonde locks to expose his tender throat to the edge of the knife. 'Pay now, or say goodbye to this spoiled brat.'

"'Pray, give me half a day to raise the money,' I begged. 'If the debt isn't paid by sundown, my brother's blood is yours.'

"The chieftain agreed to grant me a reprieve of half a day. What to do? What to do? With my mother in my tow we rode to the warehouse where the slavedealers, mostly Jews, quibbled over wares brought them by raiders, examining and squeezing the merchandise, appraising and grading the value of each piece. My eye fell on a Jew who seemed to me a man more refined than the rest. He was an older gentleman, who sat a little apart from the haggling, reading a heavy tome. I suppose someone with a long white beard inspires trust in a young woman's heart, for we all have been kindly treated by our grandfathers.

"'Good sir,' I said to the venerable Jewish human-merchant, 'I'm here to sell you my freedom. But that freedom will cost you five hundred pieces of gold.'

"'That's a bit steep,' said he, looking up from his book, seemingly unsurprised by my strange offer. 'You are quite exquisite, but, then, I deal only in the exquisite. You probably haven't considered it, but there's tremendous overhead in this business. Often, half of the merchandise I purchase doesn't even reach its destination. Bandits, soldiers, local potentates, even, at times, ardent lovers take their share—without paying, I might add. Today, the hottest market is in Baghdad. But reaching that city takes three to four months, under good conditions. And then I have to underwrite all the transportation fees, quartering and feeding the slaves, as well as all the physicians' and spiritual healers' bills when the merchandise either loses health or heart. I tell you what. For you, I'm willing to part with four hundred pieces. That's four times what I normally pay for a fine specimen like yourself.'

"'Five hundred,' I said, 'and not a penny less.'

"'So,' said the merchant,· 'is there anything about you that warrants that sum? Do you have special talents? Just falling into bed isn't enough, you know. Any woman can do that.'

"'I am Safiye, the curtain-maker,' I said. 'My work is much sought after. Perhaps you've heard of me.'

"'Well, I'll be!' said the merchant. 'So you're Safiye, the curtain-maker! Your hands are made of twenty-four carat gold as pure as your name. Did you know that a pair of your curtains hangs in my house in Baghdad?'

"'No, I didn't,' I said, 'but I'm pleased you like my work. So, how about the five hundred gold pieces?'

"'Done!' he cried, slapping shut his book. 'Who do I pay? This is all a bit irregular, you know.'

"'Pay my mother,' I said. 'But before we conclude our business, I have a condition I must impose on you, Good Sir. Promise you will not sell me to the highest bidder but only to the person I choose.'

"'Highly irregular,' he said. 'The overhead . . .'

"'Take me or leave me,' I said. 'Other merchants here will jump at my offer, as you very well know.'

"After my mother was paid, she departed in a flood of tears, saying it was six of this and half-a-dozen of the other. The merchant questioned me on the strange business of selling myself into slavery. I told him about the necessity of saving my brother's life.

"'Tsk, tsk,' he commented. 'Saving another's life at the expense of your own is a treacherous thing. You might as well try saving the world from itself.'

"Although it was probably true that I couldn't save my brother from himself any longer, I trusted my own wits and talent to extricate myself from spending my life in bondage to another. If it took three to four months to reach Baghdad, by working every available moment, I could conceivably finish enough curtains to buy myself back. Once on the block, I would, naturally, choose myself as my purchaser and pay the merchant off on the spot. Of course, he'd lose his overhead. But he was used to that.

"During that long, arduous journey, working even as I rode, I finished fifteen curtains, paying for the materials from the small pouch in my girdle. Each time we stopped at some commercial city on the way, I sold the curtains that were done. At the inns where we stayed, women peddlers always arrived with dry goods for sale. It's strange. Slaves who have any money on them will spend it on some fancy article that gives them a feeling they're still human, someone with the means to own something luxurious and dear. So, the business for these peddlers at inns visited by slave caravans was brisk. I dealt with these often odious persons, making sure I got what my curtains were worth. Hardly any peddler could resist my work. By the time we reached Baghdad, unbeknownst to the Jewish merchant, I'd earned nine hundred pieces of gold, plus recouped what was in the little pouch in my girdle.

"The unforeseen, however, always dogs one's heels. A slave-dealer named Rashid-ed-Din was attracted to our convoy as soon as we made our stop at a caravanserai in Tabriz. And this man kept showing up every place we put up after that, watching our progress. To me, this Rashid-ed-Din looked like a snake. His fleshless triangular face had two beady blue eyes that stared unblinking, as if he'd mesmerize his victim. Oh, I hated him the moment he came to see me, insinuated into my quarters by a woman peddler, and offered twice the sum I usually received for a curtain. But I wouldn't sell. I didn't want that foul person to touch even an apple peeling I cast away, let alone a curtain into which I had ovingly worked my designs. Usually, I didn't much concern myself with who bought my work, but seeing Rashid-ed-Din was enough for me to know I never wanted him to own anything of mine. He was extremely put out. He swore he'd eventually acquire me totally, put me to work and, as it were, bend me to his pleasure.

"Certainly, the threat upset me. It's no good being followed by someone who's made himself your sworn enemy. I mentioned my dislike for Rashid-ed-Din to the Jewish merchant, begging him that under no condition was I to be sold to Rashid-ed-Din, neither for his personal use nor for resale. If I died on the road, not even my corpse could be sold to Rashid-ed-Din. I'd come back and haunt the Jew.

"'Have no fear on Rashid-ed-Din's account,' the good Jew said. 'I, too, have no love for that man. He's a double-faced fraud crusted over with disgusting personal habits, the sort of dealer who gives our trade a bad name. And so totally unscrupulous, he pretends to profess Islam, whereas I know for a fact he's a Christian—and a bad Christian, at that.'

"Once in Baghdad, we were herded to the baths, scrubbed clean, perfumed, our hair arranged by professionals, our bodies dressed in richly made clothes—part of the overhead the Jew kept talking about. And once rested and made presentable, we were taken to the slavemarket. There, the venerable merchant who transported us sat aside, and the broker took over. I was held to the last, being the most prized object. As I waited for my turn, I took a good look at the buyers. Most had come just to entertain themselves, ragamuffins and streetpeople, for the pleasure of seeing people being bought and sold. We were stared at like goodies in a sweetshop or jewels in a jeweler's case that can be hankered after even if the good things in life are out of reach. Standing there, I understood that we were more than articles for sale. We provided commonfolk with fantasy, as if one could have a pretty girl or boy by just looking. As for the wealthier clientele, their excitement came from being *seen* outbidding and buying because, as I know now, most wealthy buyers were already overstocked with more slaves than anyone could sleep with in a lifetime.

"As I gazed around me, in what must've been an arrogant stance, unwisely attracting the sort of men who just love to buy a proud slave they can break, my eye fell on a young man who elbowed his way up to the very front of the crowd. Obviously, he was there just for the hell of it, paying more attention to what buyers paid than to the attractions of those who were sold. Without knowing how or why, I took to this young man who couldn't be older than eighteen. His honey-colored skin glistened under the hot southern sun; his eyes seemed darker than olives, his mouth sweeter than the berries that spring up in the lush forests of my homeland. For a mad moment, I wished this youth would buy me. He looked as if he had the cash. The hardhanded denizens of Baghdad had stepped aside to let him pass; he must be the son of someone of substance.

"When my turn came, the broker displayed me this way and that; he told me to lick my lips so they'd glisten, groom my hair off my forehead suggestively—for this was a gesture that attracted men. I just stood still, watching the young man to see if my presence excited him as his did my own heart. The young heartbreaker showed no sign.

"'O Merchants of Baghdad,' the broker began his spiel. 'O Possessors of Wealth! Who will open the bidding for this damsel, the mistress of moonlike beauties, the gold-fingered curtain-maker called Safiye whose fame has reached far and wide? Behold this object of the seekers' wishes and the delight of desirers. Open the bidding. No bid is obnoxious; nor can the bidder be blamed and reproached.'

"'Let her be mine for five hundred pieces of gold,' said a merchant who fingered the material of my pantaloons.

"'And ten,' bid another.

"'And a hundred more,' called out that odious Rashid-ed-Din who'd suddenly turned up from God knows where.

"'And ten,' bid the first merchant.

"'A thousand pieces!' cried the hateful Rashid-ed-Din.

"Hearing the bid for a thousand, the tongues of the other buyers were tied. And so was mine. The odious man had already outbid what I had in my girdle. The broker walked to the good Jew for a consultation which I could hear from where I stood.

"'I am under oath,' the venerable Jew said, 'to sell her to none but the one she desires. So consult the damsel.'

"'O mistress of moonlike beauties,' the broker said out loud so the crowd could hear, 'the dealer called Rashid-ed-Din desires to purchase you for a thousand pieces. What do you say?'

"'Rashid-ed-Din is the king among hypocrites,' I announced, playing to the crowd. 'He's *soooo* faithless . . .'

"'*How* faithless is he?' the crowd responded, cackling.

"'. . . not even the Christians will own him,' I said, incurring much laughter at Rashid-ed-Din's expense. 'He'd buy himself the finest of flesh, yet he's *soooo* old . . .'

"'*How* old is he?' the crowd responded.

"'. . . not even pulleys could get it up for him,' I said to the crowd which was howling now with laughter. 'Why, his beard is whiter than the venerable Jew dealer's. Having Rashid-ed-Din kiss one would be *soooo* disgusting . . .'

"'How disgusting would it be?'

"'. . . a slave would rather have her mouth stuffed with cotton wads.'

"'By God, you're right, girl!' said the broker. 'Dirty old men like him have no business with a valuable piece like yourself. O Merchants of Baghdad, is there one among you who will spend a thousand pieces of gold on this beauty?'

"From among the rapt crowd, another man advanced.

"'I will take her for a thousand,' said he.

"I saw at once this man had dyed his beard with henna, and could not help but give the crowd a little more fun at his expense.

"'This man is so droll a spectacle . . .' I crooned.

"'How droll a spectacle is he?' The crowd was right there with me.

"'. . . that he deserves his neck beaten with shoes, so fascinated is he with the high color in my cheeks and the length of my legs as I stand here, untampered by cosmetics and dyes. Yet he conceals his real beard under one borrowed from the dyer. Is he a puppet, or what?'

"'By God, you're right!' said the broker. 'The man has dyed his beard.'

"The buyer with the hennaed beard immediately disappeared into the crowd, no doubt much chagrined with the laughter that rose from the spectators. But another fellow sprang forth.

"'I'm ready to pay a thousand for the damsel with the sharp tongue,' said he. 'Cash and carry.'

"'Will you be sold to this gentleman,' the broker said to me, 'whose beard grows past his belt?'

"'This man,' I said, 'reminds me of one whose beard grew to useless lengths. Besides, it is like the nights of winter: long, dark and cold.'

"'To whom, then, my clever and beautiful mistress,' the broker said, 'will you be sold? Point him out.'

"'That beardless one,' I said, indicating the sweet youth my eye caught. "and to no one else.'

"'My young master, Ali Shir,' the broker addressed the youth,

whom he seemed to know, 'this damsel wishes herself to you. Will
you have her? She's a bargain at a thousand. You buy her and you've
bought right. Not only does she put the moon to shame, she has a
memory stored with elegant verses. If you have fighting to do, she'll
hold your enemies at the point of her sword. If it's riding to be done,
she'll gallop to Cairo and back before you finish blinking your eye.
And her hands are better than any silver or gold, for she makes
exquisitely embroidered curtains in a mere eight days. Each curtain
fetches at least fifty pieces of gold. The man who buys this damsel
is indeed a fortunate man. Include her among your treasures, Ali Shir;
she will double the worth of all the gifts God has so unsparingly
bestowed on you. What do you say, Ali Shir? Will you buy her for a
thousand?'

"The charmer just hung his head and said nothing. He doesn't
care for me, I thought; he's too polite to say so. Maybe he fancies
someone else. The thought sank my heart. I didn't care, any longer,
to purchase myself out of my predicament. Somehow I must *make*
this aloof youth commit himself to me. But how?

"'Call the Jew and the young man for a private talk,' I said to
the broker. 'Maybe we can hammer out this deal.'

"'As you've heard, Ali Shir,' the venerable Jew said to the young
man, 'she won't be sold to any but you. What is your pleasure?'

"Young Ali Shir still hung his head and said nothing.

"'Ali Shir,' I said. 'I took to you the moment I saw you. Why won't
you take me to your abode and heart?'

"'Must a man be forced to buy you?' he asked, lifting his head
to look me in the eye. 'I've never been exposed to such high-pressure
salesmanship. Besides, your price is too high.'

"'Then, buy me for nine hundred gold pieces,' I said.

"'Can't do,' Ali Shir said.

"'Eight hundred then.'

"'How about seven?'

"'No.'

"Well, I abated the price for him down to a mere hundred pieces.
He still shook his head.

"'I don't have a hundred complete,' Ali Shir said.

"'How shy are you of the sum?' I said.

"'By God, I don't have a hundred,' he said, 'and nothing short
of a hundred either. The truth is, I don't even have a single coin, red
or white, gold or silver. Can't you understand, lady? I'm mortified.

You've managed to shame me in front of the citizenry. So, now, find yourself another customer.'

"Finally, Ali Shir's situation penetrated my thick head. I'd failed to observe how I'd embarrassed him, pressing myself on him, when he didn't want to admit he turned me down because he couldn't afford me. My heart leapt with joy. If Ali Shir was only stone broke—his financial embarrassment was something I could remedy.

"'I'd like a private interview with Ali Shir,' I announced to the Jew and the broker. 'Allow us a few minutes in that booth over there.'

"Once installed with Ali Shir, I handed him the bigger of my money bags, which contained the nine hundred pieces set aside for my freedom, and instructed him not to promise the broker and the Jew another penny, neither on time, nor in trade. Ali Shir managed to buy me for nine hundred pieces of gold without any further haggling. I suspect the Jew was ready to conclude the deal, which had taken so long that the crowd had already dispersed.

"With Ali Shir leading the way, I followed him to his house. The house had seen better days. Inside, the place was bare. Not a stick of furniture nor a dented pot could be seen in Ali Shir's habitat. No wonder he'd gone to the slavemarket just to entertain himself.

"'Where's your bed, Ali Shir?' I asked. 'And where is your stewpot?'

"'All I have left in this world,' he said, abashed, 'are the clothes I stand in. And now, unfortunately, you.'

"'But what happened, Ali Shir? You don't look like someone who's used to poverty.'

"'I'm not,' Ali Shir said, hanging his head. 'But I'm told it takes forty days to get used to anything. Yet, God knows, I'd rather not get used to unpleasant situations.'

"He then told me the story of his tender life. Ali Shir's father had been a Persian merchant who wasn't blessed with children until the ripe age of sixty. Then Ali Shir appeared to delight the old Persian's heart, granting him a boon and reprieve from sterile old age. And, duly, Ali Shir was doted on, pampered, adored for the comeliness of his person, the sweetness of his nature. On his deathbed, the Persian made long speeches and quoted much poetry and wisdom, for anxiety for his son besieged the dying man's heart. He regretted he'd have to depart without seeing his son reach manhood, for Ali Shir was inexperienced in the cruel ways of the world.

"But the old Persian gave advice while he could, deathbed talk being more memorable than everyday advice by virtue of the destination of the speaker. The dying Persian advised his son not to be overfamiliar with anyone, to rely on no man but himself, not to chatter away idly but to apply himself to learning. He must not associate with any wicked man, for an evil man was like the blacksmith's fire which won't burn the onlooker but whose smoke will cloud his eyes. He reminded Ali Shir never to forget that he was a foreigner in a foreign land, that Arabs might feign friendship but would never really take a Persian to their hearts. Ali Shir himself, however, must make sure he behaved well towards all men, no matter what religion, color or trade; he must perform good deeds because mere good intentions are no accomplishment; goodness must manifest itself in action.

"'Certainly, I'll be good,' Ali Shir reassured his dying father. 'Why not?'

"The dying father admonished Ali Shir to be on guard concerning his sizeable inheritance. As long as he was prosperous, people would value his friendship, but should he lose that wealth, he'd be surprised how quickly he collected enemies. As a wealthy individual, Ali Shir must always show compassion for his inferiors; he must not oppress those whom he had the power to oppress; and, most important of all, he must be careful and abstain from wine. For wine took away thought and reduced man to the state of childhood. And children couldn't be the masters of their fate.

"Advising done, the old Persian quit this earthly life. Ali Shir mourned properly for the departure of his father as befits a person of distinction. He had his father interred with great pomp and circumstance and, in order not to leave his father's soul in the hands of Sunnite clergy, he even invited a Shi'ite *ayatollah* all the way from Persia to give his father a proper send-off. He fed the poor for months in his deceased father's name. Scarcely was he done mourning his father, his mother succumbed to grief over the loss of her husband. She, too, was properly lamented, buried and missed.

"Ali Shir felt just too sad and lonesome in the great big house. He was, by nature, fond of company, of flattery, of indulging himself. He made friends with those who, he now understood, must've been sons of whores. In Ali Shir, these companions incited an appetite for licentious conduct. Not only did Ali Shir drink wine by the jugful; he repaired day and night to houses of ill repute, to gardens of pleasure and to dens of iniquity. His father, he reasoned, hadn't been able to take his wealth to the grave; so why shouldn't the son enjoy it while he had a chance? He paid for entertainments and carousals that lasted for weeks and months at a time. He showered presents on fancy women and procurers, on wags and wits. For quite some time, the city of Baghdad had a devil of a good time at Ali Shir's expense.

"Only the night before, he'd come to his senses when the last penny in the coffers was gone. Nor did anything remain of his inherited assets, the furniture in the house, the utensils, the clothes in the closet. He fell into a reflective grief in the bare house, fasting on the hard floor all night until he heard the crowing of the first cocks. Then he said to himself, Well, I'll drop by a friend's house and get some breakfast at least. But the friend on whose door he knocked had his servant tell Ali Shir the master wasn't home. He knocked on the door of everyone he knew in Baghdad. The answer was the same. By this time, hunger tortured him like a merciless master.

"'That's when I chanced on the crowd,' Ali Shir said to me. 'And you had to bedevil me, insisting I buy you. Why did you have to persist? There I was, without breakfast in my belly and badgered to acquire an expensive slave. I've never been so ashamed, so mortified in my life! What am I to do with you, fair lady? I can't even feed my own foolish face. And, even if I had a bed, I'm too weak from hunger to take you there.'

"'Don't worry your pretty head,' I said, 'over concerns about money. I have some money laid aside. Here, take these three pieces of gold. With the first piece, buy us a good dinner; with the second, buy a mattress and cooking utensils; with the third, a piece of silk, as much as will suffice for a curtain, and buy gold, silver and silk embroidery thread of seven different colors.'

"That's how Ali Shir and I set up light housekeeping and were able to consummate the passion I acquired. In the morning, I settled down to the business of embroidering the most beautiful curtain yet, depicting a pair of lovers sporting amorously in the Garden of Eden. As I worked like a *jinniye* on assignment, Ali Shir paced restlessly, full of questions about how a man could stay cooped up in the house all day, with nothing to do. He accused me of not loving him anymore when I didn't fall on the mattress whenever he thought of entertaining himself.

"'I'm crazy about you, Ali Shir,' I said. 'Just let me finish this row of tulips.'

"A craft demands from the maker time away from the world.

That's the nature of making. The craftsman must be willing to transform large segments of his life into an object. That willingness is what distinguishes a professional from one who dabbles. When the work goes well, the maker forgets even to eat. I explained all this very carefully to Ali Shir. He seemed to understand. But still, he'd beg that we go out to eat, or, at least, send out for Chinese food. When were we going to have some fun?

"'You could learn to do something, Ali Shir,' I suggested. 'You could at least ply a trade. You're still very young.'

"'I'm not a peasant,' Ali Shir said, shivering at the thought of toiling at some dull occupation. 'I'm a thinker.'

"'So, what do you think about, Ali Shir?'

"'Oh,' he said, 'this and that. Actually, I haven't quite settled on what subject to think about. One of these days, I'm likely to think up a great thought.'

"I offered to teach him my craft, considering how collaborating on a project strengthens the physical and emotional bonds between people who live together. Ali Shir was repulsed by the idea.

"'Ugh!' he said. 'You'd have me embroider like a woman?'

"Well, I suppose, what's acceptable in one culture is repugnant in another. I thought of my father who embroidered like an angel, yet still rode and swashbuckled with the best of men. Circassian men don't worry much about their manliness, seeing the division of labor between men and women isn't so absolutely set. But I wasn't willing to vex my beloved with talk about whose culture was better; I just kept on working. Within ten days or so, the curtain was done. I glazed it and gave it to my young master.

"'Repair to the market, Ali Shir,' I said, 'and make sure you don't get less than fifty pieces for this curtain. It's the finest I ever made. Don't sell it, under any circumstance, to a man called Rashid-ed-Din, the Christian who masquerades as one of the Faithful. He's made himself my mortal enemy. He must never, never know where I live and to whom I belong. Spend one piece of gold on materials and bring home the rest.'

"When Ali Shir finally turned up, he was pickled to the gills and certainly in a good mood. He'd sold the curtain at the desirable price and acquired the materials for another curtain. But he couldn't help celebrating at a tavern he passed en route. Later, as he repaired home, he couldn't resist a suit of clothes that hung in an apparel shop.

"'I gave myself a present,' he explained, 'for the ten days of boredom I suffered, watching you stitch. I didn't think you'd mind.'

"He'd spent twenty-five pieces of gold on a suit fit to wear to court. Considering we never went to parties and celebrations, I couldn't imagine where he thought he was going to wear it. But I didn't say anything. I kissed his sweet mouth and bid him wear his new suit in good health.

"For a whole year, I worked away diligently, and Ali Shir sold the fruits of my labors. We made out all right. We were able to afford items of luxury that so pleased Ali Shir. He even enjoyed appointing the house with new furniture, decorating the place himself with a blend of finesse and whimsy. As we settled down to heavier housekeeping, we learned from one another. I learned to take life a bit easier. And Ali Shir to take it a bit more seriously. In his attempts at interior decoration, he'd even occasionally bring home something useful, such as the best bake-oven ever made in Baghdad. He really tried. But he felt the merchants in the market made light of him, since he had no shop of his own but sold his slave's work out of the house. His heart was broken every time some merchant dropped a leaden innuendo concerning the luck of some Persians in finding women who'd earn their livelihood for them.

"'Everybody admires you, Safiye,' he complained. 'Even those who are our friends put up with me because it's your company they want. You're so beautiful and talented. It's as if you weren't a slave at all. I, too, want to be someone people admire. One of these days, I'm going to surprise everyone. I have the stirrings in me of a great thought.'

"'But I love you,' I said, 'and admire you.'

"'That's very nice,' he said, 'but not enough. A man must be admired among his peers.'

"One day, he arrived from the market in a state of agitation, looking behind him apprehensively as he asked me to fetch a mug of water. An odd presentiment impressed itself on my heart.

"'Tell me the truth, Ali Shir,' I said. 'Did you, perchance, sell the curtain to someone you shouldn't have? Who bought it? The usual merchant? Or Rashid-ed-Din?'

"'The usual,' said he, looking the picture of someone who lied.

"'And where,' I inquired, 'are you taking that mug of water?'

"'Men's quarters below,' Ali Shir said, 'to give a drink to a thirsty broker who followed me home.'

"Soon as Ali Shir went downstairs, I tiptoed down and pressed my ear against the keyhole. Ali Shir's voice rose angrily.

"'What!' cried Ali Shir. 'Isn't it enough that I invited you in the men's quarters? What are you doing skulking in the hallway, you dog?'

"'Don't be angry, my young master, Ali Shir,' the berated man said. 'What difference is there between the men's quarters and the hallway?'

"The odious, whiny voice belonged to none other than Rashid-ed-Din. I'd know the nauseating quality of that voice even were there fifteen doors between me and the ugliness of that tongue. I tried to control myself and not rush out there to kill the man on the spot. So, selling out to Rashid-ed-Din was the great idea stirring in Ali Shir's head! Then, I heard Ali Shir trying to repulse the shameless slave-dealer.

"'You've had your water,' Ali Shir said, 'now, depart.'

"'Ali Shir, my kind young master,' said Rashid-ed-Din. 'God bless you for giving water to a thirsty man. But how about something to eat? I'm famished. Anything will do, just anything in the house. I don't care if it's a crust of bread, even a head of onion.'

"'There isn't a thing in the house,' Ali Shir said. 'Just rise and go. Don't give me any argument, either.'

"'What will the merchants in the market say?' Rashid-ed-Din said slyly. 'When I tell them you refused me hospitality, they'll talk about you, Ali Shir. They'll say Ali Shir's a mean and inhospitable man. To save yourself the infamy, here, take these hundred pieces of gold and bring us something to eat from the market—even if it's a loaf of bread we might break together to establish between us the bond of friendship. And, Ali Shir, please do keep the change.'

"Ali Shir must've been tempted with the prospect of turning a neat profit. His first precaution was to lock the door against which I had my ear pressed on the keyhole; then he left for the market where, for a few pieces of silver, he was willing to bring the Christian dog something to eat—just to get his hands on the larger portion of the odious slavedealer's gold. He left me in the house with that nefarious person with only a locked door between us. I just seethed with anger. Had the idiot not locked me in, I'd have taken a kitchen knife and descended on Rashid-ed-Din, taken him by surprise, and taken his life. After I had killed him, come what may. I wasn't afraid of death or prison just then. But I was locked in as was Rashid-ed-Din locked out, the key in Ali Shir's pocket.

"Ali Shir returned, probably bearing some cheap food, and the two of them went in the men's quarters where the mad dog of a Christian might stuff himself. I just couldn't believe Ali Shir would entertain my sworn enemy under our roof when I'd admonished him so many times to beware of this snake. I had to content myself with sitting on my hands for a while; then I heard the front door open and close. Out of the window, I saw Rashid-ed-Din depart. Sighing a sigh of relief, I contemplated the scolding I'd give Ali Shir. But Ali Shir wouldn't come up and unlock the door. I rapped on the door, crying out to him. No sound. The house was deathly still between my cries and knockings. Damn! I thought. Ali Shir must've drunk too much of the mad-dog's wine and must be dead to the world.

"Then I heard clattering and shouts at the front door. Peeking out the window, I saw, to my great dismay, that not only had Rashid-ed-Din returned, he'd brought with him the other two merchants I'd insulted at the slavemarket, the puppet with the dyed beard and the little bead of a man with the immensely long facial hair.

"Still, no sound from Ali Shir. Next thing I knew, the bastards forced open the locked door and began chasing me all over our private apartment. I cursed myself for not having had the forethought to acquire some deadly weapon with which I could fend off all three. Then it occurred to me, I could take them out with ordinary household utensils too. With that thought, I fled to the kitchen, my chasers hot in pursuit. There, I first brained Rashid-ed-Din with a frying pan and then poked the eye of the dyed-beard puppet with a rolling pin. As I was busy chopping off the beard of the third with the kitchen knife, Rashid-ed-Din, who apparently wasn't as dead as I hoped, rushed me from behind and slipped a thick rope around my arms and torso. Damaged though they were, the other two sat on me while Rashid-ed-Din tied me up tightly.

"'What a hellcat!' the puppet with the dyed beard said, holding his bleeding eye.

"'She massacred my beard,' complained the hairy head. I just spat on them.

"Bound and blindfolded, unsheathed knives poking me all around, I was carted away, perhaps into irretrievable bondage. At Rashid-ed-Din's house, I was thrown among his other slaves and concubines into a miserable commonroom with barred windows.

"'See, impudent wench!' he cried, snickering perfidiously. 'I got you free of charge, practically speaking. Your boyfriend thought he had his dainty fingers on my gold, but I had the presence of mind to take it back while I lifted the key to the locked door. All the time, the dimwit slept like an angel, dreaming opium dreams from the hefty dose I introduced into his wine. Won't he be surprised—if he ever wakes up? Now, I've got you, and I mean to keep you. Let's see you lampoon distinguished merchants at the slavemarket now!'

"'God will get you for this, wicked dog!' I cried. 'And God will reunite me with beloved Ali Shir. You just wait, old pisspot!'

"'First, I will convert you,' said he, 'and then, I'll ride you for all you're worth. You wait and see.'

"'Pox on you and your religion!' I said, spitting in his eye.

"He was so angered, he called his big black eunuchs and had me tied and beaten with a cat-o'-nine-tails. I called for aid but was not aided. God is my sufficiency now, I thought, and stopped groaning for I'd passed out. When I came to, drenched with buckets of cold water, I heard Rashid-ed-Din order that I be put to work in the scullery but not be allowed to eat. I fasted that night. In the morning, I was savagely basted again and thrown back into the kitchen. That's the way it went for some time; in the kitchen all day, no food, and, in the morning, terrible punishment. The cook took pity on me and slipped me leftovers when the other slaves weren't looking. She was an elderly woman who jeopardized her own safety, for it appeared that Rashid-ed-Din meant to starve me to death. I warned the cook that she would get in trouble when I didn't die as expected, but she persisted in giving me just enough to survive from day to day. Although I didn't die, I became a shadow of my former self, too weak, God help me, to plan my escape.

"Once Rashid-ed-Din went on a buying trip, it was this cook who put on her veil and went in search of Ali Shir. She returned after being gone all day, for she'd had trouble finding him. The neighbors had told her that after my inexplicable disappearance, Ali Shir had lost his wits and taken to the streets, tearing his clothes, weeping, beating his bosom, reciting the saddest of verses. Children followed him around the streets, crying Madman! Madman! The cook found him at last, curled up and asleep in an alley. Waking him, she told him news of me. To his credit, Ali Shir recovered from his lunacy at once, kissed the cook's hands and wondered what might be done to spirit me away from under the eunuchs' watchful eyes. And the cook, bless her heart, devised for Ali Shir a stratagem.

"'Tonight, at midnight,' the cook told me, 'Ali Shir will arrive and sit on the stone bench outside the front door. He will whistle your favorite song. When you hear him, whistle back and let yourself down with this rope. And both of you, make haste and steal away. And may God aid you both.'

"I waited by the casement until midnight. At midnight, I opened the window and secured the rope by which I'd descend. But no sound from Ali Shir. No whistle. No footsteps. The night was pitch black; no moon or stars appeared to light the oppressive street. Then, I perceived the shadow of a man standing by the stone bench. I whistled at the shadow who whistled back. So, there was Ali Shir, late as usual! First, I let down a couple of saddlebags which I'd filled with some of Rashid-ed-Din's costlier possessions around the house, both to spite the old dog and also to ensure our escape from Baghdad. Once Ali Shir removed the goods, I pulled the rope up and, this time, slipped down myself. To my surprise, Ali Shir didn't even embrace me and say a few hurried words of love, but slung me over his shoulders and began running like a streak. I was amazed by the sudden commodity of strength granted Ali Shir.

"'The cook said your health had been impaired, Ali Shir,' I said as he ran; 'yet, now, you're stronger than a horse.'

"Ali Shir said nothing but continued sprinting with me on his shoulders, the saddlebags tucked under his arms. In the dark, I felt his face. By God! His beard was bristly and foul as a latrine broom!

"'You're not Ali Shir!' I cried. 'Who the hell are you?'

"'Shut up, wench!' said the fellow. 'Or I'll cut your throat! If you must know, I'm Jawan the Kurd of the Ahmad-ed-Denef Gang. So shut up already!'

"'Put me down, wretch!' I commanded. 'Or else my Ali Shir will overtake us and kill you with one blow. He was due on the bench in front of the accursed Rashid-ed-Din's. He'll show up any minute and be after you in a flash!'

"'You mean the fellow who was fast asleep on the bench?' Jawan the Kurd said tauntingly. 'He was so dead to the world, I even stole the turban on his head. His pockets were empty as promises.'

"Ali Shir must've fallen asleep waiting for the midnight hour; I'd mistaken a cutthroat for my beloved.

"'Oh, dear God!' I wept as I brought hard blows on the thief's head. 'Where are you, dear God?'

"'What a propitious night this was!' said the thief, whose skull must've been made entirely of stone. 'I came after some petty work, but I made off with a fortune that dropped right into my lap. Just imagine the delight of the guys when they see you! We haven't had a woman for quite some time and were afraid we'd all perish from nut-fever. And there are forty of us, too! You got your work cut out for you, wench!'

."'Let go!' I cried, slapping his face and kicking him with all my might.

"That angered the thief so, he set me down and with a blow of his hobbled boot knocked me senseless. When I woke up to a huge headache, I was in a cave of some sort, being watched over by the ugliest old woman I'd ever seen. Her thin gray hair stuck to her head in clumps of grease. The smell of her was so strong, flies dipped in and out of her person, a cloud of black buzzing attending her every gesture.

"'Good morning, Grandma,' I said, sweetly as I could. 'May God's peace be with you. Who do I have the pleasure of addressing?'

"'Don't give me that!' she snapped. 'They don't call me the Accursed Kurdess for nothing! I'm Jawan the Kurd's mother, if you must know.'

"'Ah, to me, you don't look accursed at all,' I said. 'You remind me of my own grandmother. If your hair were to be washed and dressed you'd look as fine a gentlewoman as any. Maybe we could go out of this damp, dark cave into the sunshine where I might wash and dress your nice long hair.'

"'Come to think of it,' said the foul old woman, scratching her greasy rat's nest, 'I haven't been to the baths in ages. That's what I get for following those forty hogs from place to place. I don't know why God, in his wisdom, had to create lice.'

"'I will wash and delouse your head, Grandma,' I said. 'And afterwards, I'll give you the latest hairdo that's all the rage in Baghdad.'

"'Remember this, though,' said the fouless, pulling out a stiletto from her voluminous pantaloons. 'My friend here knows all the lethal junctions in your body.'

"Outside, my eyes met the body of a man, completely naked and rotting in the sun. The stench was so unbelievable that most of the buzzing black cloud that accompanied the old woman veered to the corpse.

"'Who's this?' I said. 'And why wasn't he given a decent burial?'

"'Some Turkish trooper,' the foul Kurdess said. 'Who has the time to bury Turks? Let him rot, I say! Jawan, bless his hide, found the Turk asleep in front of the cave, his horse tethered to a tree. So, Jawan slaughtered the worthless heathen Turk right away, stripped off his uniform. Together, we hid his arms and clothes in the cave. Yonder is the Turk's horse, grazing.'

"'All manner of good luck befell Jawan last night,' I commented ingratiatingly. 'First, I fell into his lap; then, he found himself a sleeping Turk.'

"'That's right!' the Kurdess said, fairly swelling with pride. 'Ahmad-ed-Denef was much pleased with Jawan's haul.'

"'Where's the gang now?' I asked. 'They must be up to some ingenious enterprise.'

"'They rode west,' the Kurdess said. 'They mean to ambush a caravan of pilgrims. Guess who spied the pilgrims' approach?'

"'Jawan!' I said. 'He has some sharp eyes!'

"The Kurdess seemed very pleased to have in her possession a female to whom much stored-up bragging could be done; she gave me the high points of Jawan's robberies, murders, rapes. According to the fond mother, the Ahmad-ed-Denef Gang always got away in the nick of time, thanks to Jawan. The Forty Thieves hoarded their loot in an enchanted treasury, the door to which wouldn't open unless a certain shibboleth was spoken: Open Sesame. There wasn't a king or sultan who could brag of such riches; for one thing, kings and sultans dispensed what came into their treasuries, whereas the Forty Thieves never touched a penny laid away. I inquired why the Gang didn't retire, considering they'd already amassed more than enough for generations of little thieves to come.

"'It's a matter of professional pride,' the hag said. 'What kind of thieves would they be if they didn't live off the fat of the land? No, going straight wouldn't be any fun.'

"One should be grateful for small miracles. Jawan, in his professional pride, might've cut Ali Shir's throat as well as snitch his turban. Perhaps my inexplicable descent into his arms prevented Jawan from finishing the job.

"Leading the grand dam of the thieves by the hand to a small stream a little way from the cave, I first washed her awful hair, dried it on my own blouse, and, with a comb I happened to have in my girdle, began dressing her hair under the sun. The warmth, the fooling with her hair as I cracked her lice between my fingernails, the soothing strokes of the comb tranquilized the hag so much, she soon began to yawn heavily. All the time, I spoke soothingly until I was quite sure she was fast asleep. I considered bashing her head in with a large rock, viper that she was, but I didn't want to carry the Kurdess on my conscience the rest of my life. No one knows if she or he has the makings of an assassin until the opportunity to strike presents itself. I didn't take it. Striking someone who's asleep isn't the same as taking out an opponent in combat. The Ahmad-ed-Denef Gang took pride in insolence, seizing, forcing, murdering those who fell into their hands; but they were really fearful little men banded together who bolstered their frail existence with outrageous dastardy. How could this miserable old woman be blamed for bragging about her pitiful son? After all, what good is a son about whom a mother can't brag? Besides, I'd made away with Rashid-ed-Din's valuable possessions; I was in no position to sit in judgment on a gang of Forty Thieves.

"So I let the sleeping hag lie. Quickly, I went into the cave, where I donned the Turk's uniform, and took up his arms. Then, retrieving the saddlebags full of Rashid-ed-Din's riches, I went and saddled the dead Turk's horse. As I mounted, the clattering and neighing of the horse woke the Accursed Kurdess. Angered, stiletto jabbing the air, she ran after me cursing, but I blew her a hand-kiss and urged the horse. We were off.

"I was terrified that we would pass through some city or town where the dead Turk's family and friends might recognize the horse and seek revenge, thinking I was responsible for the trooper's demise. I decided to avoid inhabited places until I was well out of Arabia. Instead, I'd venture across the desert eastwards and then up north to my homeland high up in the Caucasians. At this point, I didn't mind if I never laid eyes again on Ali Shir.

"The journey across the desert was terribly hard both for me and the horse. The horse turned out to be a wonderful animal—the sort of small, shaggy brown horse Turks breed which are amazingly durable and more intelligent than cunning. Besides, the horse seemed to know a certain route. He and I shared the herbs of the earth and drank of the same water in the oases, the locations of which the horse seemed to know. Pretty soon, I let the horse have his way, seeing he'd been taught to follow a certain trail his dead master must've taken many times. And at night, while I slept, the horse kept watch over me, nuzzling my hair and hands. In all my life I'd never known a horse more solicitous of his rider's well-being. I wished, in return, I could offer him something really good to eat. But all that was available were the same tasteless herbs. We travelled on, desert tract after desert tract. We should've long since reached Persia; yet, I could see nothing to remind me of the Persian terrain I'd once crossed with the slave caravan. I thought, mistakenly—since I knew no geography to speak of—that Persia was mountainous, dotted with verdant valleys and ribboned with clear streams. I didn't know, then, that Persia is also, and mostly, arid desert. I just didn't know what to think. Perhaps I'd made a mistake in letting the horse have his way. He'd gotten us lost.

"Then I saw, in the distance, a mountain chain so dark it looked black; when we rode up close to it, I could see the living rock was black as soot. Amazed by the color and the utter nakedness of these mountains, I let the horse carry me across the range, taking trails that nomads must've carved out in thousands of years of wandering.

"On the other side, a fair plateau came into view, large and wide as God's mind. Winter with its cold sword had departed from this fair land, and Spring had come wearing flowers. The plateau vibrated with a thousand-and-one breeds of flowers. I thought if God had a prayer carpet, this must be it! Jumping down off my shaggy brown horse, I kissed the ground. The horse nuzzled my hair and settled into a bed of sweet clover.

"'Henceforth, your name's Deli Kachar,' I told the horse. He seemed pleased with the name, taken from the language he'd probably heard as a colt. The name meant Crazy Fugitive in Turkish, a tongue we Circassians learn of necessity, for our neighbors can be very warlike, coming, as they do, in forceful hordes. Though they don't stay long, it's a good idea to get along with them in their language while they stay.

"After Deli Kachar and I rested and ate some fresh almonds still green and succulent, we both took baths in a stream that flowed clear on a bed of pebbles. This happiness! I thought. God, in his wisdom, has created the deserts where he fries Arabs, but He's also made this verdant plateau where He's put a more blessed folk. Forgive me, O Caliph, but at the time, considering my misfortunes in Arabia, I had little in my heart to recommend Arabs and the tribes who lived under their hegemony.

"But, just in case the folk who lived on the blessed terrain were not as sweet as their homeland, I tucked my hair completely into the dead Turk's astrakhan hat, hoping to pass for a man and not be hindered by those who think women have been put on this earth to be molested.

"And so it happened that in the distance I saw a city, a fair city without walls that shone freely in the early morning light. Even as we approached the outer limits, birds warbled in orchards, and the young wheat billowed in gentle breezes. In a large playing field, either a festival or a tournament was being held. Civilians as well as troopers seemed to have gathered to behold some spectacle. Now I've had it! I thought. Considering that the troops wore uniforms just like mine, I must be in the lands of Turan, the region known as Turkistan. Deli Kachar had brought me to his home!

"Still wondering why all the folks had gathered outside the city, since I'd been seen approaching, I decided to brave it out, whatever the reception. I thanked myself that I'd gone to the trouble of learning Turkish and could come up with a story that rang true. I'd tell the denizens that I was a Turkish nobleman of a family settled in the Caucasians, thereby excusing my accent, and I'd left my home-land because my family opposed my marriage to a maiden of humble birth.

"As I rode closer, the mounted troops hastened forward to meet me. The soldiers dismounted and kissed the ground before Deli Kachar. Their officers and generals ranked themselves, all saluting with raised sabers. They've mistaken me for someone else! I thought. Or else, the dead Turk must've been a more important person than he seemed rotting under the hot Arabian sun. Or, perhaps, Deli Kachar was a more pedigreed horse than his shaggy brown ap-pearance would suppose.

"'God aid you all,' I said in greeting. 'But what's the meaning of this unusual reception?'

"'Long live our Khan, the King of all the World!' exclaimed the most decorated soldier of all, bowing deep enough to touch his forehead on the ground. 'May your reign be felicitous, my Khan!'

"'Long live the Khan!' a shout rose from the troops.

"'Long live the Khan!' echoed the civilians in the distance.

"That I was a Khan certainly surprised me. Reigning was not an occupation I'd have chosen for myself. As they say, the head that wears the crown is a head worn under the arm. The fortune that raises a person to such heights can also render that person quite dead.

"'Who among you is your Chamberlain?' I said. 'I'd have him explain me a thing or two.'

"'At your service, my Khan!' said a capable-looking gent.

"The Chamberlain was a man in his prime and seemed to have weathered the previous Khan in fine shape. He kneeled and put his head on Deli Kachar's stirrup. Well, at least, this fellow must know something about governance, I thought; maybe he can even be persuaded to take over from me.

"'What's the story, Chamberlain?' I said. 'Only this morning I was a freeborn cavalryman who did just as he pleased. Now you tell me I'm your Khan, mounting on my head more cares than I fancy.'

"'The gods have bestowed their favor on you, my Khan,' the Chamberlain said, 'and made you Khan over the people of Karaman. You were the one chosen to rule us from the fair city of Karaman-kand.'

"'The gods,' I said, 'never let me in on their plan. Why must I rule over the people of Karaman?'

"'Have you so soon forgotten our customs, O my Khan?' the Chamberlain said, seemingly surprised by my forgetfulness and a-bashed at having to explain. 'But perhaps you've been away too long from our fair land. Time and distance sometimes erodes the memory. Know that, O my Khan, when the reigning Khan dies, our custom is for the troops and the inhabitants of Karamankand to gather outside the town for three days. On the third morning, the first person who arrives from the direction of the Black-Soot Mountains, which is the ancestral home of the Karaman and the residence of the Sacred She-Wolf, is appointed to rule over us as our Khan. We know that the Sacred She-Wolf has allowed you to pass through the mountains unhindered, thereby blessing you with her special gift. Praise be the She-Wolf for having sent us a son of the Turks and an attractive person at that! For had She sent a deformed heathen of some sort who came in your stead, we'd still be obliged to make him our Khan. We are all exceedingly pleased that we've been sent a man we can love as well as obey.'

"Well, well! If Khan I was, then I'd better behave like a Khan. I dispersed the gold and silver loot from Rashid-ed-Din's treasury among the troops, who sent up another loud cheer. That's how I became the Khan of the Karaman, and Deli Kachar the king among horses and a legend in his own time. As I said, he was some smart horse. It must've been Deli Kachar who had a covenant with this

Sacred She-Wolf, whatever deity she might be to these gullible people.

"As for me, I won't bore you, O Caliph, with the day-to-day details of governing a kingdom. Let me say that my palace was no larger than the smallest of your hunting lodges, Commander of the Faithful, and certainly not as luxurious. The people still called the palace the Big Tent, although the building was made of stone; in the center of the building was raised a high beam symbolic of the center pole of a warrior's tent, to which they attached much sentiment. The ways and the governance of the Karaman Turks weren't as complicated as in your domain, although my subjects called me the Khan of the Age and the King of the World. Those people must be excused their innocent pride, for though they had only recently settled down to the niceties of sedentary life, they still lived by nomadic perceptions. They thought it remarkable to no longer be obliged to travel from grazing ground to grazing ground, following the ancestral trail of deep dark wells and clear-running streams, always on the move, unable to develop ideas and artifacts. But they'd finally learned, under the tutelage of the Sacred She-Wolf, the arts of blacksmithy and agriculture. They thought the whole world would someday be theirs under their sky-blue banner, embroidered with the gray head of the She-Wolf. They called it the Flag of the Sky-Wolf, their foremost deity.

"I must say, embroidery was quite advanced in this kingdom, these people having seen, somewhere along the way, the art of Chinese stitchery. Among their arts, which were few and primitive, the most remarkable was rug-weaving. Not only were the colors glowing and fast, the craftspeople, both men and women, had abstracted from nature a subtle geometry.

"Their religion, too, partook of a childlike wonder inspired by natural forces: the wind, the sky, running water, mountains, trees, the barons among the wild animals that roamed the terrain. Nowhere have I known a people who loved wilderness with such passion. Their songs celebrated atonement with wild and dangerous elements in nature that might strike terror and loathing in the hearts of the denizens of Baghdad. In Baghdad, we love nature cultivated by men: gardens, fountains, the cool of the night, the more sweet-tempered of the animals, not things in the raw.

"In Karaman, sons remained nameless until the youths distinguished themselves in valorous deeds. Then, names of brutes were bestowed on the heroes: Ox, Wolf, Lion, Ram, Hawk. Or if the youth didn't come up to snuff, he might get saddled with Rooster, Goat, Mole, Butterfly, Bug, adding an adjective to round off the appellation, such as Plucked Rooster or Black Bug.

"Once the grandees of the land raised me up by the armpits, as was their custom, and seated me on the throne, I was terrified that I might now be expected to prove my virility on a well-stocked harem. I was delighted that the practice of keeping a stable of women was unknown among the Karaman. They married only once. Since the custom of arranged marriages didn't exist here, lovers married the ones who loved them. As I said, since they had little idea about civilized ways, the notion of marriage as an economic alliance hadn't yet occurred to them. And being unmarried didn't constitute shame. Not only was I safe from being forced to marry, producing an heir was not a duty of the reigning Khan, considering they chose their Khan through a prearrangement with Destiny.

"On my ascension to the throne, I remitted taxes for an entire year, an act that endeared me to the hearts of the citizens, though some of the hard helmets grumbled. After doing some thinking, I proclaimed that the kingdom would hence be ruled through legislation that won majority in governing sessions open to every citizen. This system wasn't entirely foreign to these people who'd always been free to speak out; the novelty of the new regime was that my voice carried no greater weight than that of the Chamberlain. Thus, the council of chamberlains would act in accordance with the wishes of the populace and not, as the case had often been, in reverse. The citizenry was delighted with the prospect of participating in sessions where their will would carry in open balloting.

"Among the Arabs, it is said that it's far better to bear the tyranny of a tyrant a hundred years than the tyranny of the people a single day. But the wisdom of a truism in Baghdad isn't necessarily true or wise in Karaman. Governance by will of the people seemed suited to these folk, since their family structure already allowed even youngsters a say in any decision that involved all the members of the family. They were used to listening to each other.

"In the meantime, I spent a great deal of time meditating, praying and fasting in the fashion of one who submits to God, beside Whom there is no deity. Part of my motive was to forestall any luckless daughter of some chieftain from falling in love with me. If I made a name for myself as an ascetic, I might not present a desirable prospect for some foolish girl. I don't know why I didn't reveal my true gender, seeing how these people saw nothing shameful in womanhood. They might've said: So what? Hence, you will be our Khanum. But the fear of my gender had been too ingrained in my heart by now for me to give up the manhood I'd stumbled on accidentally.

"My devotions having been observed, I was asked the meaning of my ablutions, the exercise of prayer, the name of my God. When I spoke about the virtues of Islam and revealed the ninety-nine beautiful names of God, they longed to learn more. That's how I became my subjects' spiritual teacher, a role that suited me better than a tyrant's. In time, my subjects embraced Islam out of their own choice. It was a conversion of love, not force. Although learned Islamic scholars would disagree and blame me, I saw no damnation in my subjects' former devotion to the forces of nature; in fact, I sought to preserve their ancestral worship. I converted them without intending to, almost through accident. Perhaps it was this reluctance that made them eager and willing to outgrow their former gods, professing, in unison now: There is no God but Allah.

"Had I been a dyed-in-the-wool missionary, the people of Karaman would've probably rejected Islam and run me out of town. Or, those who had converted would've oppressed and mistreated those who had not. But the more reluctant I was to teach, the more they clamored to learn. Like children who learn better what they aren't forced to learn, they wrested from me the tenets of Islam.

"Not only did the citizens consider the Palace their home, arriving unannounced, expecting breakfast cooked by the Khan, and good conversation as well, the Khan was also expected to give the subjects a feast every month which they called 'Plunder-Feast.' This meant that, after festive eating, the Khan's guests (that is everyone in the domain) carried away with them whatever of the Khan's possessions caught their fancy. No family ever acquired more than one item, though there was no law against taking more. Greed was not honored. The monthly feast was held at the hippodrome where tents were pitched, rugs laid down, and the people ate hearty, made merry and took away with them the royal gifts they had selected. A handy method by which the Khan's goods were redistributed among the citizenry. The euphemism for these gifts was 'rent for teeth' since there's onus in the word plunder. In other words,the Khan had to pay rent for the use of his subjects' teeth on the food he provided. It was thought the people were performing the Khan a service by wearing away their teeth on his feasts. And, in an odd way, it was a service. As they ate and talked, the Khan learned what his subjects thought. The ways of different peoples are wonderful. If I could, I'd spend my life travelling from land to land, studying the ways of one people which illuminate the ways of another.

"It was during my second year as Khan that at such a Plunder-Feast my eye fell on the accursed slave merchant Rashid-ed-Din, my odious enemy. He'd dyed his beard with henna and was wearing the garb of a weaver. But despite the flaming beard on his chin and the humble clothes on his back, I recognized his beady blue eyes and his hateful stare. So, he'd come on his own two feet to receive justice! He'd probably come to check out the prospect of slaving among the Karaman, who were still innocent of dealing in humans. The Karaman knew about prisoners of war, but they hadn't yet learned that one person can be owned by another. War captives were either exchanged for captured Karaman tribespeople, redistributed to other climes where they might not again engage in hostile acts against the Karaman or freed en masse in order to give thanks to the prevailing gods. The Karaman never sacrificed humans, nor did they take captives, unless it was unavoidable. They preferred fighting to the death themselves if the tide of battle went against them, so they imagined their enemies would also rather die than be taken alive. They preferred fates that were clean. Yet, here was Rashid-ed-Din ready to teach the Karaman unclean activities.

"As one group that was already fed were vacating their seats for new arrivals, this Rashid-ed-Din, beady eyes glued on the free grub, elbowed his way right next to a whole lamb roasted on the spit. After he gorged himself on the meat, pulling the flesh with his yellowing tusks, he cast a greedy eye at a tray of steaming rice cooked with sweet cherries. The rice was out of his reach. So he leaned over several diners and pulled the tray in front of himself.

"'Hey, fella!' said one of the guests, 'eat from the dishes in front of you.'

"'Where are your manners, stranger?' asked another guest. 'In this land, a guest does not reach.'

"'You pay for this food?' asked Rashid-ed-Din disrespectfully. 'Well, then. I'll eat whatever I please. Save your etiquette lesson!'

"'So eat!' said the first guest. 'But I hope the food doesn't do you any good.'

"A hashish-head who sat next to Rashid-ed-Din applauded the ill-manners of the shameless slavedealer.

"'Let the man eat of the rice,' said the hashish-head. 'I, too, was hankering after that dish. You were all hogging the tray while we, at this end of the table, went without.'

"'Keep your grubby fingers out of my rice!' cried Rashid-ed-Din, slapping the hashish-head's hand. 'Eat food suitable to persons of your own class!'

"'Persons of my own class?' the hashish-head said. 'What do you mean, stranger? There's no school of swallowing hashish. So I have no classmates.'

"'Rank, I mean rank, pothead!' Rashid-ed-Din exploded. 'I mean you're a beggar, that's what I mean.'

"'He's not a beggar, either,' said the commander of the cavalry, a big man called Blowing Bull. 'He's the son of our former Khan.'

"'You are a topsy-turvy people!' Rashid-ed-Din exclaimed. 'You make beggars of your princes and you make princes'—casting me his evil eye— 'of beggars.'

"'I became the prince of hashish-eaters all by myself,' the hashish-head said. 'Give credit where credit's due.'

"Enough was enough. Just as Rashid-ed-Din stuffed another fistful into his gaping face, I turned to the two soldiers who stood on either side of the throne.

"'Quick!' I said. 'Seize that stranger who's stuffing his face with sweet rice! Don't let him swallow what's in his mouth. If you must, put your fingers down his gullet.'

"The soldiers seized Rashid-ed-Din, made him spit out the rice and brought him before the throne. The insolent wretch stood there easy as you please, as if he were the Khan and I the slavedealer. But seeing the wretch seized, the citizenry lost appetite; they wiped their mouths and stared at me in shock. For at Plunder-Feasts no act of violence was permitted, either from the people or from the Khan.

"'Whee-oh, man!' said the hash-filled prince. 'I sure am glad that stranger kept me from the rice! The Khan doesn't like his rice reached for and pawed at!'

"'Shush!' said Rangy-Flower, a woman who was the chief of a division of archers. 'Go back to your dope!'

"'Unfortunate wretch!' I said to Rashid-ed-Din with the most awesome voice I had under my belt. 'You with the beady-blue eyes of deceit and the henna-dyed latrine brush of a beard, state your name and your business in Karamankand.'

"'O King of the World and the Noble Khan of the Karaman,' dissembled the accursed slaver, 'my name is Ali the Weaver. Hearing the fame of the weavers in your realm, I came here so I might learn from your weavers.'

"'You lie!' I cried. 'It is known that your name is Rashid-ed-Din, and your trade is, in fact, dealing in slaves. We also know you came here in search of someone.'

"'Pray, O Khan, inform your servant how you knew his identity,' Rashid-ed-Din said.

"Many things are known to the Khans of Karaman,' I said. 'We know you are a crypto-Christian who passes himself off as a Moslem. And we know you don't have an honest bone in your body.'

"'Forgive your worthless servant Rashid-ed-Din,' begged the wretch, falling on his face and trying to kiss the soles of my boots, which I prevented by kicking away his ugly mug. 'I have erred, mighty Khan,' he went on. 'But now let me excuse myself by speaking the truth. Yes, it's true my name is Rashid-ed-Din, and I deal in slaves. And it's also true I am a Christian. Christianity was recognized as a true religion by the Prophet Mohammed. So, clearly I am a true believer.'

"'If your religion is true,' the Chief Chamberlain said, 'then how come you conceal your faith?'

"'For business reasons, my good Chamberlain,' Rashid-ed-Din said. 'Do you think Moslems would pay a Christian dealer if they could get away with not paying? Never! I wouldn't only lose my money and my wares, but I'd be eligible for public beatings whenever a Moslem brought a complaint against me. That's why I don't breathe a word about the Word.'

"'How terrible for you,' the Chief Chamberlain said. 'But tell us your true name.'

"For a second, Rashid-ed-Din seemed stumped, searching for his real name under layers and layers of deceit.

"'I know!' he said finally. 'It's Barsoom. I never cared for the name. Certainly not a name for a businessman of substance.'

"'I agree with you,' the Chief Chamberlain said, laughing. 'Your real name sounds like a fat man farting. Tell us, Bar-*sooom*! Is buying and selling humans a profitable business?'

"'You bet you!' said Barsoom, alias Rashid-ed-Din, alias Ali. 'I deal only in northern slaves. Merchants down south can't get enough white flesh.'

"'So you admit to being a slavedealer?' the Chief Chamberlain said. 'And have you come to Karaman to acquire people?'

"'Heaven forbid!' Barsoom said. 'The Karaman are too rough to make pleasing slaves. What I seek is a slavegirl who made off with my life savings. I mean to find the thievish wench and tear her limb from limb.'

"'As you can see for yourself,' the Chief Chamberlain said, 'there are no slaves in this company. For your information, we don't like persons who come to our land under false pretenses. Our Khan, in his wisdom, saw right through you, Barsoom.'

"The guests were impressed that I knew a man's life history just by watching him eat. There's a saying among the Turks: you know a man's mettle by the way he eats his yogurt. The saying having proved true once more, the guests turned their adoring faces to me, sighing satisfied sighs.

"'Barsoom plies the most accursed of trades,' I informed the public as well as the grandees and chamberlains. 'He makes his living by buying and selling people who were born as free as yourselves. Peaceable people are snatched from their homes and pressed into slavery at this fellow's instigation.'

"'If Christians, too, are people of the Book,' the Chief Chamberlain reasoned, 'then, my Khan, how is it possible for this man to live unimpeded under the eye of All-Powerful God?'

"'A very good question!' I said. 'Perhaps God has sent us the wretch so he may receive his comeuppance, with us as God's instrument.'

"Now that this wretched Barsoom had admitted to his falsity, and to dealing in humans, which revolted the people of Karaman-kand, the problem was what to do with the unregenerate miscreant. A heated debate ensued, necessitated by the lack of any precedent for Barsoom's offence. No impartial punishment existed to fit the crime. With the intrepid archeress, Rangy Flower, taking up Barsoom's defense, it looked like the citizens would settle for deporting Barsoom, a favorite Karaman method for dealing with almost any crime. The citizenry turned this sentence into a festivity as they equipped the offender with a goat's horns and goat skin and booted him into the wilderness. Rangy Flower argued that although Barsoom came into the country concealing his identity, the man had yet committed no offense besides displaying poor table manners. Expulsion was enough. Let him go elsewhere and eat like an animal.

"But loathing in my heart for Barsoom was so instinctive, so ingrained by now as to have become visceral. So I urged my subjects not to fear handing Barsoom the stiffest sentence. It was either Barsoom or me, O Caliph. I could not live in a world where Barsoom was also present and actively seeking to destroy me. It was possible the villain might have recognized me, despite the robe of authority on my shoulders, the scepter in my one hand, the globe in the other, as I sat presiding over the deliberations. What then? Cautioning the citizenry that once Barsoom blabbed to his cohorts in slavedealing and crime about the easy pickings in Karaman, the land might become a regular site of illegal traffic, I was so eloquent in evoking the dangers of letting Barsoom escape with his life that, although a group of bleeding-hearts held out, a sterner majority stilled their scruples. After much discussion about applying a severe beating on Barsoom, the people finally spoke for the death sentence, the only punishment I'd settle for. Barsoom, alias Rashid-ed-Din, was given a choice between being drawn by forty horses or being quartered by forty axes. Barsoom chose to get himself drawn.

"Duly, the treacherous slavedealer died like the swine he was in life. But the people of Karamankand vowed never to touch another morsel of rice sweetened with cherries, that dish being the reason why a stranger, albeit pernicious, had lost his life. In a way, I understood my subjects' unhappiness. Barsoom, alias Rashid-ed-Din, was more like a caricature of a single humor—in his case, treachery —than a real man. That I unmasked this character, making a public execution of his nasty secret, displeased even the tough majority who had passed the sentence, as if the punishment had been esthetically as well as morally false. The people were displeased with what they had done and this displeasure, naturally, was easily translated to their Khan. I hoped, in time, my subjects might come to forgive and forget. But the incident became the turning point of the people's honeymoon with their new Khan.

"At the Plunder-Feast the month after, I noticed how the guests avoided the seat next to the rice sweetened with cherries. Not only that, they talked loud enough for their Khan's ears.

"'Hey, Blowing Bull,' said one to the other, 'listen to me.'

"'What is it, Immaculate Ram?'

"'Avoid the sweet rice, Blowing Bull; there's a good man!'

"'You do the same, Immaculate Ram,' said the Bull, 'and your tongue will remain wagging in your head.'

"No mistake about it, the folks were disgruntled. Now that they'd voted to accomplish Barsoom's death, they resorted to black humor, implying that the wretched manners of a foreigner had cost him his life, and that the absolute wrath of a ruler, no matter how bland he seems, can come from something as insignificant as a bowl of rice. It seemed to me that the time had come for me to move on. But before I could think of a way to extricate myself from this kingdom, guess who comes into the hippodrome to whack his teeth on free food but Jawan the Kurd! Now, what brings him here? I thought with dismay. He, too, was probably looking for me with the hope of getting even.

"The thief couldn't find a vacant seat at first, but his eye fell on the empty place right where the tray of rice with cherries steamed untouched. Jawan sat and reached for the rice.

"'You out of your mind, brother?' Immaculate Ram said. 'What do you think you're doing?'

"'I'm reaching for some rice, that's what,' the rude Kurd said. 'What's it to you, busybody?'

"'Brother,' Rangy Flower interrupted, 'if you eat of the rice, you'll get yourself drawn or quartered. Take your pick.'

"'Shut your mouth, woman!' said the thief. 'Women don't speak unless spoken to. Did you hear me speak to you? Well, then! Go home where you belong instead of eating like a shameless hussy, face out in the open in front of your betters.'

"As the guests wondered aloud who were Rangy Flower's betters, considering she was as good as they come, Jawan the Kurd plunged his hand, which had turned into a claw from his habit of snatching things, into the rice dish. Greedily, he compressed the fluffy rice into a ball the size of an orange and heaved it into his cavernous mouth. The ball of rice descended down his throat making a glurping noise like a latrine hole. The bottom of the tray showed where he'd gathered the rice.

"'Thank God, I'm not a dish of rice set before you, stranger!' joked the Chief Chamberlain. 'You exhausted the dish with a single mouthful!'

"'Let the condemned man eat!' cried the hashish-head, moving away from the vicinity of Jawan. 'When I look at the wretch, I already see him torn apart.'

"Just as Jawan the Kurd made another ball of rice, I had the two sentinels seize him. The sentinels twisted Jawan's arms so roughly, the ball of rice flew in the Chief Chamberlain's face. As the Chief Chamberlain sat, rice dripping down his nose, the people seemed unsure if laughter was appropriate. The sentinels brought Jawan, whose first nature was thievery, to stand before the throne.

"'See?' said the Bull to the Ram. 'What did I tell you?'

"'The man was warned,' the Ram said to the Bull.

"'We should rename this dish,' Rangy flower suggested archly, 'Slaughter Rice.'

"'Why are you here?' I asked the Kurd. 'State your name and your occupation.'

"'My name is Osman, O Khan,' said the thief. 'I came to your land in search of something I lost. Losing things doesn't come naturally to me. So, I intend to find what I lost and put it where the moon don't shine. By occupation, I'm a gardener.'

"'More likely,' I thundered at him, 'you harvest what you haven't sown! To me, your face bespeaks a seasoned thief and cutthroat. It attests to belonging to one Kurd name Jawan, adjutant to the blood-thirsty gangster Ahmad-ed-Denef and his gang of Forty Thieves. Am I not right? Your face also proclaims that your mother is a witch so iniquitous that people call her the Accursed Kurdess.'

"'My face says all that?' replied Jawan the Kurd. 'Forgive me, O Khan, but I'd better steal myself another face.'

"'Insolence will only make matters worse for you!' I shouted. 'As to your motive in coming to this land, you spoke only a half-truth. You did lose something. But that something never belonged to you. You cannot steal a person as if she were an object and then expect her to stay put. Tell me the truth, muckabout swine, or I'll have you executed without a trial.'

"'If you know my name, occupation and motives, O Khan,' said the thief, 'why do you plague me with so many questions? You're right, it's a wench I seek. She duped my poor mother and ran away. And I, in justified anger, beat my mother so savagely, the old woman died under my hands. I search for the wench so that I may avenge my mother's death.'

"'O People of Karamankand!' I said. 'The thief and cutthroat bears witness against himself. First, he kills his own mother in anger and haste, then he blames a maiden who escaped his murdering hands. Moreover, this Kurd is responsible for the deaths of thou-

sands, including one Turkish trooper whom the Kurd slaughtered as
the trooper slept in front of the thieves' den. That luckless trooper
was none other than the owner of the wonderful horse called Deli
Kachar who brought me to your land. Even now, that trooper lies
exposed in the heat of Arabia because this son of a whore wouldn't
give the man a decent burial.'

"'I don't understand,' the Chief Chamberlain said, 'why bad men
have made it a habit to turn up here. For some reason, they arrive
to glut themselves on sweet rice. What do you say for yourself, thief?'

"'That the dead don't tell lies,' the hashish-head interrupted.
'That's what the thief says for himself. I can already hear him croak.'

"'Have we been put on this earth,' asked Rangy Flower, 'to pass
judgment on the world's unsavory characters?'

"'I say the Khan ought to do his own dirty work,' Blowing Bull
said. 'I ain't casting another vote!'

"'Yeah!' said Immaculate Ram. 'Let the Khan do his own bidding
and forbidding, his own sentencing and his own beheading. I have
my own job to do. Do I ask the Khan to do my fighting for me?'

"'Why does the Khan talk so much?' Rangy Flower said, echoing
the sentiments of the guests at the Plunder-Feast. 'If he's so righ-
teous, let the Khan speak out his own judgments.'

"'That's right, sweetheart,' agreed a young fop with henna-dyed
fingernails. 'I couldn't have put it better myself. If the Khan is a man,
let him behave like one.'

"'Am I to understand then,' I asked, 'that the people of Karamankand don't relish sharing the nastier aspects of self-governance? Just
say so. And I'll gladly do the bidding and forbidding and rule over
you as I see fit.'

"'The People feel, O my Khan,' said the Chief Chamberlain,
rising from his seat, 'that they don't want to be the instrument of
your personal grievances. If you have complaints, you should complain publicly. But we don't want you to make us judge and sentence
men with whom we have no quarrel.'

"'But this man, and the one before him, are both criminals who
admitted to their crimes,' I said. 'Both have incriminated themselves.'

"'Yet you took them by surprise, O Khan,' the Chief Chamberlain
said, 'so they didn't know their right to remain silent. Had they kept
their mouths shut, we'd have been none the wiser. You've exposed,
O Khan, the true natures of these fellows. But isn't your all-seeing

eye a means of entrapment? After all, no one saw them commit crimes here, though, admittedly, their table manners are shocking.'

"The ways of the Karaman were curious. They slaughtered slit-eyed Tartars and beer-bloated Slavs on the battlefield without batting an eyelash. But they were squeamish hairsplitters in the arena of justice, feeling that enemy warriors came to battle knowing the score, whereas miscreants blundered on the Plunder-Feast not expecting to stumble into their deaths. Like children, the Karaman, too, demanded strict adherence to the rules. They were revolted by the gray areas of jurisprudence.   •

"'Do I get to speak on my own behalf?' asked the Kurd, emboldened by the difficulties in public relations encountered by the sovereign.

"'So speak,' the hashish-head said, giving permission.

"'Well, then,' the thief said. 'Your Khan must be a great seer, by God! He's so perceptive of my unlucky life that I swear before you people that I shall never lift my hand against another, or take what doesn't belong to me. If I do, I will personally cut off both my hands.'

"'I can see how you might cut off your first hand,' quibbled the hashish-head, 'but I don't see how you'll manage cutting the second.'

"'A figure of speech,' the thief said. 'I mean to steal no more. I mean to keep my hands. Had I a mother in this world, I'd swear never to beat her again.'

"'If you believe that habits can be broken by mere words,' I said, 'then believe that I won't take your word for anything, Jawan the Kurd. I mean to break your habit for you. I hereby sentence you, by the authority vested in me, to have both your hands and both your feet sawed off for you so you're crippled for life.'

"'How's he to make his living?' wondered Immaculate Ram. 'Or get from place to place?'

"'More moot point,' the hashish-head said, 'how's he to fling rice balls in his mouth?'

"'Jawan the Kurd will be kept and fed at public expense,' I said, 'so he may be a permanent example to us all.'

"'Better maintain him out of the privy purse,' Rangy Flower suggested. 'Keeping him at public expense is a gross misuse of taxes.'

"'Hey, lookie here!' Jawan the Kurd cried. 'How can you all talk about me like this while I stand before you with my hands and feet attached to me still? Yipe! What a bloodthirsty bunch! And what's going to happen to my hands and feet?

"'You may keep your hands and feet,' I said.

"'On?' said Jawan. 'Or off?'

"'Off,' I said.

"'Ick!' urped an adolescent girl, holding her mouth.

"Once Jawan the Kurd was dealt his justice, I could feel the coldness of my subjects to my very marrow. Perhaps the time to abdicate gracefully had long passed. As a ruler, I'd failed miserably; despite my efforts to share the responsibility of public business with my subjects, I'd ruined their trust that business would be transacted fairly by publicly revenging myself on personal enemies. Somehow, I'd been unable to resolve the conflict in my own heart and marry the private to public. Born a female with charms that made me an object of acquisition, I'd bungled the task of being the subject of my own destiny. Here in Karamankand, I'd first been drafted into office and become the object of slavish devotion; now, I was the object of much rebellious derision. I couldn't bear this kind of failure. But why not? The answer eluded me.

"The next Plunder-Feast after Jawan's sentence was carried out was hardly well attended, to say the least. For one thing, that footless and handless man was well in evidence, being fed by the two sentinels. One look at him made even the hardier citizens lose appetite. Jawan, not being stupid, was well aware how his presence had turned out to be a sentence I had passed on myself; he flaunted his misfortune all the more.

"But it was at this joyless feast that an unexpected pleasure met my sore eyes. A young stranger seated himself in the vacant seat next to the tray of sweet rice. I recognized Ali Shir at once. Seeing his fetching person reach daintily and, with two fingers dip in the rice, the guests stopped eating to watch him with consternation.

"'Oh-oh!' said the hashish-head. 'Here we go again!'

"'Young man,' begged outspoken Rangy, 'for the sake of your sweet life, don't eat that sweet rice.'

"'That's right, sweetheart,' joined in the fop with the henna-dyed fingernails. 'He who eats of the rice has either his life or his limbs shortened for him.'

"'Don't do it, little brother,' implored Blowing Bull. 'That rice is certain death.'

"'Take my word for it,' said Jawan the Kurd, waving his handless stumps.

"'That may be a blessing in disguise,' Ali Shir said. 'I am weary of this life. I've tried to forfeit it without any success. Death won't claim me, no matter how much I court it. Death shuns me as if I were undeserving of the bliss of eternal sleep.'

"And, heedlessly, Ali Shir fell upon the rice. I thought to have him brought to me at once, but then let him finish eating. Perhaps the poor thing hadn't eaten in days. He ate until he was sated and then leaned back.

"'Now what?' said Immaculate Ram.

"'He's still among the living,' the pot-head said, 'though the rice is practically gone.'

"'Perhaps the Khan fancies this youth,' the fop with the henna-dyed fingernails said. 'Who can blame the Khan? The youth is a beauty.'

"'Young man,' I said, 'you who've eaten of the forbidden rice, I'd have a word with you. Will you approach the throne?'

"'Goodbye to you all then,' said Ali Shir, burning to martyr himself. 'No blame can be attached to anyone. I was forewarned.'

"'Ah,' said Blowing Bull, 'if the Khan had it in for the youth, he wouldn't have let him eat all the rice he wanted.'

"'Maybe this is a new grain,' Rangy Flower suggested, 'in the Khan's old rice.'

"Ali Shir bowed to the ground before the throne and waited respectfully while I returned his salutation by placing a hand on his shoulder.

"'State your reason for coming to Karamankand,' I said, 'also, your name and your occupation.'

"'My name is Ali Shir, O Khan,' he said. 'My ancestral home is Persia though I was born in Baghdad. The only occupation I've plied successfully so far is doing nothing. The names given to my profession are Ne'er-do-well, Know-Nothing, and Prodigal Son. As to my reason for coming here, I'm in search of a slavegirl I lost. She was dearer to me than my eyes. Yet, I didn't know how devoted I was to her until she was taken from me. That's the sort of idiot I am. Show me no mercy, O Khan! Perhaps you will help me achieve the martyrdom for which I long.'

"At this point, Ali Shir was so overcome with his woes that he wept until he fell down in a swoon; once aromatic water was sprinkled on his face, he recovered only to sob some more.

"'Don't grieve, Ali Shir,' I said. 'I have a feeling that good fortune is in store for you. Here in Karamankand I believe you will take hold of yourself and shed those self-deprecatory names you apply to yourself so mercilessly. No more the ne'er-do-well, the loser, the prodigal son; you don't even have to die of love for a lost slavegirl. You are not the only person in the world who suffers, Ali Shir, though you may have never noticed other folks' sorrows since you're too busy kicking around Ali Shir.'

"Ali Shir looked at me in wonder but without, I might add, recognition. And I'd always thought the eyes of true love saw through disguises! No matter. I ordered that Ali Shir be taken to the baths, given a robe of honor and brought back to the hippodrome where I'd decide what was to be his fate.

"'Well, at least,' Rangy Flower commented, 'the Khan treated the youth courteously. That's a plus.'

"'Didn't I tell you the Khan means the youth no harm?' Blowing Bull said with satisfaction.

"'The youth is cute!' simpered the fop with the henna-dyed fingernails. 'Appearances will get you everywhere, including the Khan's bed.'

"'I never saw the Khan look at you twice,' Immaculate Ram told the swishy fop.

"'Nor at me,' the hashish-head said, 'although I'm twice as pretty as anyone here and a prince to boot.'

"Everyone had a thoroughly ripping time, each commenting on the situation to his heart's content. Ali Shir finally returned from the baths, smelling as sweet as he looked. The robe of honor had certainly enhanced his figure and improved his mood. I agreed with the people: Ali Shir was adorable. For a moment I regretted what I was to do—but my mind was made up.

"'People of Karamankand,' I said, 'lend me your ears. Today I feel your hearts warm a little toward me, whereas for some time I thought I'd die from the chill. Perhaps a ruler shouldn't desire his subjects' love, and be content, instead, with their fear. But much remains for me to learn before I can teach and lead you. In Karamankand I was obliged to study a hard lesson. It seems that I want to rule like a tyrant, yet wishing all the time for your absolute love; I want to be your friend, wishing all the time to bid and forbid. As of now, I know of no way to reconcile the contradiction in my heart. This, then, is my last bidding. I wish to go back to Baghdad from whence I arrived, to study my heart and learn from sages who do not flinch from knowing themselves. My proposal to you, O People of

Karamankand, is to grant me a leave of absence. During that time, my wish is to appoint young Ali Shir as my Viceroy, to exercise his authority over you until I return and, God willing, take over the helm again as a better man.'

"'This, my Khan,' the Chief Chamberlain said, 'is indeed an unusual request. Granting a Khan a leave of absence is an unprecedented affair. Perhaps the request should be put to vote.'

"'By all means,' said Blowing Bull. 'I'm all in favor of letting the Khan go.'

"'But are we willing,' Rangy Flower reasoned, 'to put up with a Viceroy we don't know from Adam?'

"'We didn't know the Khan either,' Blowing Bull said, 'when he blew in from the Black-Soot Mountains. And yet, the Khan turned out to be a decent human being, faults and all.'

"'Why can't we choose a Viceroy from among ourselves?' inquired an older woman known as Barren Aunt.

"'Because, dear Barren Aunt,' said Immaculate Ram, 'we know each others' faults only too well. There's an element of hope in a ruler who comes from the outside.'

"'Hope that's dashed and dashed again,' said the hashish-head.

"'We know, Barren Aunt,' Immaculate Ram went on, 'you carry a big chip on your shoulder, because you never had kids. And you all know that I'm too damn bellicose. Then everybody knows the hashish-head forgets his princely dreams in the pleasurable weed.'

"'We're all incurable romantics,' said the fop with henna-dyed fingernails. 'Always looking for a hero to worship.'

"'Hard to know what our ancestors were thinking of,' the Chief Chamberlain added, 'but our rulers have always been outsiders. In a way, it makes sense. A foreign king has no family or friends in Karamankand to favor and protect. He's equally disposed to every citizen.'

"'But he brings with him,' Rangy Flower observed, 'his own personal baggage, his grievances and vendettas.'

"'I say we grab our tooth-rentals,' Blowing Bull said, 'and get to the ballot box. Though I probably am the man for the job of Viceroy, I have no stomach for campaigning, making promises I can't keep.'

"'I'd make war any day,' Immaculate Ram agreed, 'rather than promises.'

"'We ought to elect a woman ruler,' Rangy Flower said. 'After all, it's women who make babies. A Khanum's desire would be to create instead of to destroy. Some of you fellows tear down just for the hell of it. I've seen you carry on in battle.'

"'Guess who,' teased the hashish-eater, 'has a secret ambition in her heart! If you want to be our Khanum, Rangy Flower, just say so!'

"'No, I don't,' Rangy Flower said. 'I'd consider it were I not married.'

"'Now, now, Rangy Flower!' her husband said. 'Don't bow out on my account. I won't have you blame me for holding you back. I've taken care of the babies all these years while you matched your archery against the best of Tartars.'

"'That's true, dear,' Rangy Flower said. 'That's what you get for marrying the biggest and the most beautiful woman in the realm.'

"'In my opinion,' Blowing Bull said, 'women are twice as savage.'

"'That's right!' Immaculate Ram agreed. 'It's not for nothing our ancestors used to say: Don't wrestle with the girl; don't race with the mare. You're sure to lose, that's what.'

"'Are we going to jaw here all day?' Rangy Flower demanded. 'Or what? I don't care a piss about the opinions of men. If you haven't been a woman, Sir, how can you know what a woman wants or what she's capable of?'

"Ali Shir stared around in amazement, watching his fate develop. I thought how ironic it was that Ali Shir had been preparing himself, without knowing it, to become a prince. He had no trade, no ideas of his own, no personal ambition. His subjects would mold him into the kind of Khan they liked. He was a perfect ruler for the earnest, young and charming nation of Karaman. And in a way, I would continue in Karaman through my beloved Ali Shir, assured that he'd never be a tyrant who'd oppress the people. He'd be a charming figurehead the people loved, cherished and protected. At least Ali Shir would forget his tough-luck story and quit trying to martyr himself to love. But I did regret not keeping Ali Shir for myself! I'd have him in my bedroom in a thrice, but I loved Ali Shir too much to make him into an object of passion—not again. I'd gone that route before and been brutalized for my possessiveness of my lover.

"It wasn't surprising that the majority of the people thought Ali Shir a fitting Viceroy. When I didn't return, as I didn't intend to, Ali Shir would be eased into the real job, provided he developed the knack he already had for pleasing and endearing people.

"I embraced Ali Shir with what appeared to be princely affection, passing on the scepter and globe, the robe of authority. Then, the grandees of Karaman, lifting him up by the armpits, raised him to the throne. Cheers arose for Ali Shir.

"'We have a gift for you, our Questing Khan,' Rangy Flower said to me. 'The people think you've earned yourself a name.'

"'And what's the name you've bestowed on me?' I asked. 'I hope I can wear it well.'

"'The name we give you,' said Rangy Flower, 'is Sky-Wolf. We hope it pleases you, for it's our most precious name.'

"'And here are a pair of saddlebags full of gold,' the Chief Chamberlain said. 'The people want you to have the stuff to ease your way. We want you to remember us as we are.'

"'Yeah!' cried Blowing Bull, blowing his nose, 'We hope you find a teacher who'll teach you to see your heart.'

"For a moment I fought the tears that welled up in my eyes. Ali Shir came to my aid with all the grace native to his person.

"'Happy is the man, Sky-Wolf,' Ali Shir said, squeezing my shoulder, 'who doesn't need to rule in order to be somebody. Be sure I will hold your place until you return. Go speedily, brother, and return to us with haste. I feel a bond for you that's stronger than the bond of office we were fated to share. Ever since I laid eyes on you, Sky-Wolf, I've been asking myself: don't I know that young man from somewhere?'

"'Your heart knows me,' I answered, 'though your eyes do not.'

"'Now that everything's hunky-dory,' the hashish-head said, 'let's all go home and swallow our hashish in peace.'

"'Speak for yourself, pot-pie!' Immaculate Ram retorted angrily. 'I have a slew of Slavs to slay before I can rest.'

"Ah, the way the Karamans avoid sickly sentiment is truly wonderful! That's how I left the domain to my lover Ali Shir without making my identity known. Yet I feel he knows me better now than when we shared the pillow. For now he knows me as the true friend I was for him all along.

"Once back in Baghdad, I made contact with Lady Zubaida, whose fame as an astute businesswoman had reached my ears. I wanted to learn from her how a woman wields the power to which she's either born or which is thrust upon her. She started out by making me her four-star general and the intimate of her heart.

"That, O Commander of the Faithful, is the substance of my history."

Chapter 15

THE SECOND BOON

*Hürü takes a woman to wife
and consummates a sacred marriage*

"And has my wife taught the knowledge you sought?" the Caliph in-
quired, looking pleased as punch that his new wife was considered a
great teacher of the age.

"Turns out," said Lady Safiye, alias Sky-Wolf, "self-knowledge is
a continuous field of study. Lady Zubaida listened to me, O Caliph,
as I repeated the story of my life in alternate versions. You see, as
much as I am Lady Safiye, I am also Rashid-ed-Din, alias Barsoom,
the turncoat Christian. I am also Jawan the Kurd, the thief whom I
deprived of hands and feet. I am treacherous and thievish. And I am
also Ali Shir, a ne'er-do-well with a gentle heart who longs to be
somebody."

"I don't see why you're so hard on yourself," the Caliph said.
"Considering you're just a woman, I'd say you acquitted yourself
admirably in that kingdom of fools. And you had the good sense to
turn over powers where they belonged. The sad thing is you chose
not to remain and be Ali Shir's queen. A woman needs a man to love,
guide and protect her. What do you want with a cold and lonely bed
when, by any man's standard, you're such a luscious piece? I say, if
Ali Shir isn't the man for you, marry a man you can respect. And
abandon this endless study of yourself."

The Caliph cast his eyes around the bedchamber to see which

of his grandees and viziers might be a suitable husband for Lady Safiye, the Sky-Wolf. His eye lit on the celebrated Jafar Barmaki, an older man—actually, an old man—who had behind him a lifetime of steering the most powerful monarchy in the civilized world.

"Jafar!" cried the Caliph. "Take this woman as your lawful wedded wife. I command you!"

"O my Caliph," Jafar Barmaki said, advancing apprehensively. "I already have a lawful wedded wife, as you well know."

"The Prophet allowed the Faithful four wedded wives," the Caliph said. "You still have three to go."

"But the Prophet, in his wisdom, put a stipulation on that law," said Jafar Barmaki. "A man who marries more than one woman must *treat* all four *equally*, in terms of economy, regard, love and number of tumbles in the hay. If he can't manage this, he may not marry more than once. Should one interpret this law in the spirit intended, it is immediately clear that the Prophet meant no man could marry more than once and still keep a clear conscience. He knew personally, extraordinary a man as he was, that it's impossible to treat several wives equally. Our Prophet Mohammed was unable not to favor his youngest wife, even though he wished to be fair.

"Now, O Caliph, consider the lovely Lady Safiye, her learning, her talents, her history as a king. A man she is, a true man! She's someone who's confronted—as a human being—her humanity. And then, O Commander of the Faithful, consider my wife who, though she was a beauty once, has now seen much use. Not only does my wife have no talents, she's hardly ever been out of the house. Her only occupation has been that of wife, mother and, now, grandmother. She and I have knocked around together so long, we've smoothed each other's harsher edges. I just couldn't stand breaking in a new wife. I love my old woman, O Caliph. I have for my old woman much regard.

"But, should I marry Lady Safiye Sky-Wolf, how could I give my old woman the same time in bed? I'd be at Lady Safiye as often as the old boy between my legs could rouse himself. There'd be no juice left over for my old woman. I, too, am a man, O Caliph, albeit old. No, I'm sorry. I just can't have Lady Safiye for my wife."

"What!" cried the Caliph. "You dare refuse this precious gift? Quick, Mesrur, draw your sword. I'll have this foolish old man's head!"

"If you insist, O Caliph," said Jafar Barmaki who was used to abandoning his better judgment in favor of his head, "I will certainly marry Lady Safiye Sky-Wolf."

"Oh, no, you don't!" cried our Hürü, who could no longer contain herself. "You can't marry off Lady Safiye without consulting her, O Caliph. You've just heard the story of her life. For one thing, we all know by now she likes her men young and beardless. Give her a break! Jafar Barmaki is older than all the sands in the desert and long in the beard as he's in tooth."

"Fool!" the Caliph said. "It's not what she likes that Lady Safiye needs! But for sake of argument, who would you choose for her?"

"Me!" Hürü cried. "I'd choose myself."

"You?" said the Caliph, roaring with laughter. "Why would any woman want you, miserable boy? Besides, Lady Safiye's old enough to be your mother."

"I'm twenty," Hürü said. "I might not look it, but it's true."

"Then, you're certainly a lad who'll never see his beard," the Caliph said. "What do you want anyway? A wife? Or a mother? I get it! You want somebody who'll wipe your nose for you."

"Have you never been twenty, O Caliph?" Hürü asked. "Hasn't your mouth ever watered for a lady in full possession of herself? Did you not want her more than all the simpering damsels put together?"

"If I did," the Caliph said, "I probably had her. I don't remember."

"Not all of us are born Caliphs," Hürü said. "Nor do we get to have women like Lady Safiye—unless, of course, we have a Caliph for a friend who'll help us get the Sky-Wolf."

"What do you say, Lady Safiye?" the Caliph finally asked the lady concerned. "Do you fancy the young puppy?"

Lady Safiye, instead of answering the Caliph, advanced toward Hürü and took her hands. She studied Hürü's face steadily.

"Your eyes," Lady Safiye said, "are long and hazel as lakes between mountains. I like you, redhead! But I want to remind you that I'm already thirty-five years old. When you're forty and get the itch that comes with the first intimations of mortality, I will be a woman of fifty-five."

"So?" Hürü said.

"Our world is one of change," Safiye Sky-Wolf said, "of shedding old skins. I will have you as long as I may have you, provided you understand this. To say I love you is not to say I love you forever. I see in you myself as I was at twenty. I, too, was an audacious youth who thought she could outsmart this world."

"Will you have me?" Hürü asked.

"I will," said the Sky-Wolf.

"That's settled," the Caliph said, yawning. "Where's the judge and clergy?"

"Waiting right outside the door," said Jafar Barmaki, enormously pleased.

"So," the Caliph said, teasing Hürü, "what will you give Lady Safiye as her wedding present?"

"I'm not quite the pauper you think," Hürü said. "No, thanks to you, I have in my belt twelve hundred pieces of gold. I'll have everyone know I earned this tidy sum by the sweat of my brow, putting up with stench-mouthed magicians and chasing after phantasmagoric monsters. All of it is the Sky-Wolf's, given from my heart, to do with as she pleases. And I'll even throw in my Lyre which is worth more, O Caliph, than all your kingdom."

"I accept the gold you earned," the Sky-Wolf said. "We won't need to touch it, seeing the Karaman gold I brought with me has been carefully invested, thanks to Lady Zubaida's business acumen and Lady Amine's bookkeeping. But I won't accept your Lyre, knowing, as I do, that the Lyre and you are an inseparable pair. I don't intend to be the sort of wife who'd come between her husband and his talent."

"And I give the happy couple," Lady Zubaida said, "my house in downtown Baghdad. May the place provide them a fecund domicile."

"Hey!" the Caliph said. "Wait a minute! I have half-share in that house. You can't make presents of what's half mine."

"O my Caliph," Lady Zubaida said, "my husband."

"Oh, all right," the Caliph said petulantly. "Let them have the house. If I'm not mistaken, it's full of corpses anyway. But make sure the new owners understand they bury the dead at their own expense, not mine. Did you get that, Jafar?"

"Yes, my Lord," Jafar Barmaki said, turning to the scribe. "Write down that whatever expense may be incurred in taking possession of the property described, the new owners accept sole responsibility and will pay the costs."

Once the happy couple had begged themselves released from court in order to take possession of the mansion as husband and wife, Hürü heaved a sigh of relief. She'd been afraid that, any minute, a certain discovery might be made, preventing her alliance with the Sky-Wolf. And if discovered, the Caliph might just decide that Hürü's head had been connected to her neck too long already.

The mansion, as predicted, was indeed strewn with the corpses of the women warriors. And the passage of two long and hot days hadn't much helped the scene of sad carnage. These had once been women of extraordinary splendor, dressed in their wild animal skins, straw, plumage, their skins glistening with health and the virtues of their several races.

"I say," Hürü asked, "shouldn't we bury our dead ourselves?"

"Of course," the Sky-Wolf said. "In the gardens."

"But is there a town ordinance against it?"

"Perhaps," the Sky-Wolf shrugged away the town. "But what people don't know won't hurt them."

"Guess not," Hürü said, laughing. "I imagine people would turn green, thinking the dead are seeping into their drinking wells."

"Worse stuff than the dead seeps into their wells," the Sky-Wolf said. "That's why they keep thinking there are *jinn* down there, pissing and shitting."

The pair spent their wedding day, and several days after that, digging graves; at night, they were too exhausted to do more than drop off to sleep in each other's arms. Hürü was surprised how soothing it was to be held in the Sky-Wolf's arms. She hadn't been embraced like that since her mother had departed for Mecca. Yet, she dreaded the moment when the truth must come out.

At last, all the warrior-maidens were laid to rest in the extensive gardens, with a rosebush marking each grave. Down at the flower market, each rose was carefully selected by Hürü. A dusky and durable maid? Then, the rose must be vigorous and dark.

Now, the newlyweds could bathe and rest themselves, turn their strength into more pleasant exercise. Hürü felt terribly fearful. But the moment couldn't be put off forever.

"I have good news," she said to the Sky-Wolf, "and bad. Which will you hear first?"

"The good news."

"My real name is Hürü," she said. "And what I told the Caliph is God's truth. I did come from another place, another time. There's no telling when I may be recalled. I might be snatched up into the future, just like that."

"You call that good news?" the Sky-Wolf said. "Let's hear the bad."

"I'm a girl," Hürü said, removing her shirt.

"So I see," the Sky-Wolf said.

"You mind?"

"I don't know," the Sky-Wolf said.

"Forgive me," Hūrū said, "but I thought marrying you was the only way to save you from the grubby hands of some man."

"Oh, my God!" the Sky-Wolf said. "But you're just a girl!"

"I married you under false pretenses," Hūrū said. "If you want, I'll divorce you at once."

"Let's not do something rash again," the Sky-Wolf said, squeezing her head between the heels of her hands. "Imagine! I married a girl!"

"You didn't know," Hūrū said.

"I must have! Why else did I jump at your offer? Oh, my stupid, stupid head! Once one turns thirty-five, one can no longer avoid becoming a woman. Sexual abstinence is an easy answer to a hard question. Fact is, one is no longer a girl."

"What's so great about being a girl?"

"The girl has potential," the Sky-Wolf said. "I chose self-awareness as the guide to light the way through dark moments, as a dervish chooses God. Don't think I have not fought doubts about my femininity, my attentiveness, my intellect. You wouldn't believe the size of the headaches I suffer periodically, such as the one I'm having now."

"I'm sorry," Hūrū said. "Can I get you something?"

"Nothing helps," the Sky-Wolf said. "Nothing, that is, besides discovering the truth."

"Lie down and let me rub your back. My mother always rubbed my back when I got headaches. But I don't get them anymore. Somehow, whatever it was, the anguish just stopped."

"That's nice," the Sky-Wolf said, not interested, but letting go a little under Hūrū's ministering hands.

"You're too tight."

"Who wouldn't be if she were me?" the Sky-Wolf said. "After all my talk about self-awareness, I up and marry the young girl in myself! And I'm thinking, all the while, that I'm ready to make peace with the male of the species. Yet, in reality, I've married a wife!"

"Me, too," Hūrū said. "But doesn't every woman need a wife?"

The Sky-Wolf sat up, her emerald eyes sparkling with excitement.

"Now, why didn't I think of that? Every woman does need a wife! It's true! But not every woman is so lucky as to marry one."

"Is your headache gone?"

"Yes!" the Sky-Wolf cried.

"Then," Hürü said, "you discovered the truth. Now, you want to hear another piece of news?"

"Not again!" the Sky-Wolf sighed.

"This news won't bother you," Hürü said, "because it's about the future. I'm the granddaughter of the last Khan of the Karaman Turks. This is true. The Karaman left their homeland in search of another. They settled in the heartland of Asia Minor. As a matter of fact, they're due to start on their long journey just about now. The Karaman formed the heart of the mighty Seljuk Empire."

"But did they make something of themselves? Did they distinguish themselves in the civilized world?"

"And how!" Hürü said. "For an entire century, they were the greatest might in the world, politically, intellectually and socially. Unfortunately, the culture decayed as fast as it flourished."

"Why?"

"I've heard two different explanations," Hürü said. "First, they took on too many waves of Crusaders—that is, fanatic Christian armies—since as new converts, they eagerly took upon themselves the protection of all Islam, shielding the Arabs against the Crusaders. Secondly, they borrowed the whole cloth of the Persian culture, which was already decadent."

"I wonder whatever happened to Ali Shir," the Sky-Wolf said. "Do you know?"

"Not directly," Hürü said. "But I can speculate. If you consider how the Karaman fell in love with all things Persian, he must've succeeded in charming his subjects."

"So, Ali Shir seduced a whole population. Imagine that!"

"If I may speculate a little further," Hürü said, "it's not inconceivable that I might, this very moment, be carrying in my veins a bit of Ali Shir's blood."

"That's just too wonderful a coincidence to be true!" the Sky-Wolf said. "But why would the Karaman leave their homeland? They had there the best of all possible worlds, it seemed to me."

"Maybe the move was motivated by your absence. When you didn't return, they picked up and went searching for you; tents and packmules, goats and sheep, children and grandmothers, they rode out into the greater world. There's enough reference to a Sky-Wolf in their folklore to sustain this. A Khan who vanishes becomes a legend. Don't you think?"

"Good God!" the Sky-Wolf said. "Is it possible that Ali Shir and I were the pair that lost the Karaman their paradise?"

"You said the way of our world is change," Hürü said, "and shedding old forms."

"Everything changes," the Sky-Wolf said; "everything stays the same. You figure it out."

"I'll let you know," Hürü said, "when I've got it figured. But don't expect an answer soon."

"It won't do," the Sky-Wolf said, "if you fail to keep Harun-er-Rashid entertained. Newly married or not, royal fools must show up. You better think of getting up early in the morning and getting yourself to court."

"Are you tired of talking? We've just begun."

"There's tomorrow night," the Sky-Wolf said, "and many nights after that. Some of us can no longer stay up all night."

"Yes, Mother," Hürü said.

"Now was that nice?" the Sky-Wolf said, pouting. "Come, arrogant girl, lie beside me here and behave yourself!"

Yet, it was the Sky-Wolf who didn't behave herself. She guided Hürü's hand to one breast, ripe and firm still, as it had seen no use from babies and little from men. Her nipple stood erect and hard under Hürü's touch.

"Kiss me," the Sky-Wolf whispered, "kiss me, quick."

And she ran her strong hands on Hürü's breasts which Hürü had always thought too small. But each stroke awoke in Hürü an inexplicable feeling that her tender nipples were attached to a dark and seething place below. She kissed Sky-Wolf's full lips rapturously, as if she'd swoon from the pleasure. Then she pulled away, ashamed of herself. What would her mother say? Hürü wasn't that sort of woman!

"Why not, love?" Sky-Wolf whispered. "How exquisite is the sensation of sweet lips on sweet lips! Let me lie on you, love, breast to breast, nipple to nipple."

"Don't talk so!" Hürü said, sitting up. "It's not right."

Yet, the Sky-Wolf was a most enticing woman. Clad in a lovely loose silk wrapper, her long blond hair shimmering on the pillow, she reclined with one leg raised over the other knee, one embroidered slipper dangling from her pretty foot with the tender-pink heel.

"Take off your trousers," Sky-Wolf said. "Have you much hair down there?"

"I won't tell you!" Hürü said, shocked.

"Touch mine," the Sky-Wolf said, pulling Hūrū's hand between her thighs. "Feel the smooth, sweet flesh. Rest your fingers in my notch, bury them in the plump lips, the silken hair. There, rest there, my sweet!"

Hūrū didn't reply, but felt deep into the Sky-Wolf, her fingers resting in the well-developed notch of her wife. The Sky-Wolf seemed inflamed by the fingers even though they were motionless.

"How wet it is!" Hūrū said.

"Isn't yours?"

"A little," Hūrū said. "Maybe."

"We want each other," the Sky-Wolf said. "Let me feel."

"Now, leave off," Hūrū said.

Sky-Wolf's breath came in short gasps; her eyes almost closed as Hūrū allowed her to remove the trousers. Now, naked excepting her boots, Hūrū felt herself ready to die under the Sky-Wolf's tenacious mouth on her breast. As if that weren't enough, the older woman commenced a fierce fingering in her notch.

"Lovely, isn't it? Open your thighs more, dearest, and let me feel all of that delicate virgin flower."

"O-ho!" Hūrū gasped.

"You're so lovely," the Sky-Wolf said, "and I want it so badly. It can't hurt you, for I have nothing with which to hurt."

"No, don't," Hūrū whispered, almost inaudibly.

The Sky-Wolf gently pushed her back and lifted up her legs. As Hūrū didn't resist, the Sky-Wolf passed her thighs over Hūrū's loins, joining herself flat on Hūrū's motte. Sky-Wolf began building a fire by rubbing fire against fire. She rode Hūrū like the horsewoman she was, not slackening; her lips drank Hūrū's mouth as she rode until they both were spent in a voluptuous frenzy. Then, both rested silently, regarding each other reflectively.

"What is it called?" Hūrū said.

"Must you know the name of everything?"

"Did we enjoy it?" Hūrū said. "I mean, is it as good as it is with a man?"

"But certainly," the Sky-Wolf said. "Now let me give you the same pleasure over, but more exquisitely. With my mouth, lips and tongue."

And Sky-Wolf was right. The bliss of coming under Sky-Wolf's mouth and tongue saturated Hūrū, carrying her beyond herself into a dark cavern that burst forth into huge purple flowers.

"Purple," Hürü said hoarsely. "The color of bliss is purple."

"Your cunt is lovely," the Sky-Wolf said. "It's so delicious smelling, I could eat you all night."

And they were up to it all night, taking turns, getting into each other's most secret places without fatigue, inflaming each other with dirty talk, inventing, reinventing, postponing shame as Hürü took to her apprenticeship with muscle and heart.

"You're a fantastic woman," Hürü said. "Also, shameless."

"You, too!" the Sky-Wolf said. "But how sweet we still smell! If one of us were a man, by this time the bed would smell like a fishmarket. And you, the novice, wouldn't even know what it was all about."

"Their spunk stinks?"

"It does."

"Have you done this with women before?" Hürü said. "Were there others before me?"

"Not really," the Sky-Wolf said. "As a child, I played with a servant girl only a few years older, playing what papa does to mama. An amazing discovery for a child of five that there existed a secret, and somehow dirty, pleasure. The older girl warned me I must never tell. We just lifted our skirts and went at it flat out, you know, with our underpants still on. A mad pair! That's how I knew what to expect when I got Ali Shir in bed. Didn't your parents have enterprising servant girls?"

"None who'd teach me anything," Hürü said.

"How surprising," the Sky-Wolf said. "Where I come from, most young girls practice on each other. Of course, it's all preparatory. Not the real thing, like ours."

But Hürü wondered if this were the real thing. Her feeling for Selim had been different, though never put to the test. He would've filled all her orifices at once and engulfed her absolutely. She imagined she'd be like a nutshell riding a storm, a mouse in the coils of a serpent; she'd have died giving herself up to a force more powerful than her own. With the Sky-Wolf . . . well, it was contemplative: tender, mutual, vulnerable. The Sky-Wolf seemed to guess her doubts.

"You've been in love with a man," she said. "What was he like?"

Hürü admitted to thinking she'd die of love for an omnipotent man who made up the rules; who was morose, surly, demanding, self-centered, and condescending. He was not, as she'd witnessed when he made her watch, even a good lover. Yet, she'd wanted to melt in that man's forge, beaten red hot under his enormous hammer.

"He's six-foot-four, forty and even crueler than he thinks he is," she announced.

"Ah," said the Sky-Wolf, "but, of course! He's the sleeping demon in your song!"

"Yes," Hürü said. "But he never knew how I felt. I was too afraid and helpless. Besides, dressed as a boy, I had no access to other women, even if I could've trusted my secret to one."

"Hmm," the Sky-Wolf mused. "I never had an honest conversation with another woman until I arrived at this house to live with Zubaida and Amine. Yet one can talk to women about other things than men, you know. After all, sex isn't our only function."

"Now," Hürü observed, "both those ladies are seriously compromised."

Despite the danger of not showing up at court, Hürü didn't stir out of the house. Let the Caliph find himself other entertainment! A whole month went by on wings. Hürü, who stopped scraping her head at the Sky-Wolf's request, grew a soft red halo. The new growth came in curly which dismayed Hürü, used as she was to thinking of her hair as smooth and silken. But the Sky-Wolf was delighted with the new commodity of curls. Sharing the business of taking care of themselves, and the monstrously large house, they spent their afternoons in the gardens, or sat in the shaded courtyard, palm trees rustling in the breezes, as Hürü plucked the lyre and sang. The Sky-Wolf embroidered curtains as she listened, evaluated, praised her lover's inventions. Early in the morning, they sprinted in the gardens, fenced in the salon or wrestled on the thick rugs. No honeymoon was ever as sweet or bathed in silver light as the name of that short segment of married life implies. Here, in this tranquil place, neither lover felt compelled to prove anything; neither was afraid to ask and take "no" for an answer; neither sought to lose herself in love. And, the special delight: both relished a love that was more than sexual.

The Sky-Wolf said she feared Abd-es-Samad the Magician might succeed in snatching Hürü forward to her own time, before they had enough of one another. She wished she could enjoy the present simply, without asking for more, but she couldn't forget this wasn't Hürü's time. In Hürü's present, the Sky-Wolf was a woman dead for several centuries, so dead, in fact, not even her bones remained. For Hürü, the Sky-Wolf was already a bag of dust.

"Whatever happens," Hürü said, "you won't die. Not really. Because you're the Sky-Wolf. You're not only my wife Safiye in Baghdad but also a legend that will live long after I'm gone."

Still Hürü admitted to feelings of guilt for loving the Sky-Wolf physically. This cloud of having done something terribly wrong hung over her head as if, any minute, retribution would come knocking on the door.

"Why is love wrong?" the Sky-Wolf said. "Loving you pleases me, and it pleases you. Who do we harm? Why should we have to pay?"

"What about God?" Hürü said. "You mustn't forget Him."

"If God is omniscient," the Sky-Wolf said, "He already knows the capacities He's built into us. I refuse to believe God's a spoilsport."

There was a loud knocking on the door, a clatter and voices. As Hürü quickly got into her trousers, put on her boots and donned her turban, the Sky-Wolf went to answer the door. It was only Lady Zubaida come calling with her retinue. Not a band of God's harsher angels. The first lady of the realm dismissed her retinue and joined them in the courtyard. She sat at the Sky-Wolf's embroidery frame, idly fingering the designs.

"I'm very upset," Lady Zubaida said suddenly, pulling a handkerchief out of her sleeve. "I came to have my hand held."

"What is it?" the Sky-Wolf asked, taking her hand. "You look ashen."

"Harun," Lady Zubaida said, sobbing, "had Jafar Barmaki crucified. He had the lovely old man hung on a cross right in the dungheaps. As if he were a common criminal. Harun got up in the middle of the night and had it done. When I woke up, it was all over."

"But I thought the Caliph's threats to have Jafar done in were just idle jests," the Sky-Wolf said. "Or just unpleasant humor. It was a running game between them."

"So everybody thought," Lady Zubaida said. "But Harun really went and did it this time—without even giving himself time to reconsider. I knew Harun was morose the past month, but I had no idea what was brewing. I thought he'd get better if I left him alone."

"Has the Caliph gone mad?" the Sky-Wolf said angrily. "Not only did Jafar Barmaki absorb the Caliph's worst mistakes in governance, his compassion softened the Caliph's blows against the people. God! That old man bore Harun's stupidest whims with the patience of Job! Now the big ass has no other but his own dunderhead to listen to, seeing he's already murdered the entire Barmaki family. Where's he going to find himself another capable Chamberlain?"

"I don't know," Lady Zubaida said.

"What will you do?"

"The time has come," Lady Zubaida said, "to reinvest my fortune elsewhere—if I can get my cash assets out of the country. I'm looking to the East. Great energy accumulating there in the steppes of Central Asia. Your former subjects, I hear, have united with other Turkish tribes and are progressively taking over Persia. I've been approached to finance their move West, as they battle their way through, under their sky-blue banner with the wolf's head."

"Ali Shir!" the Sky-Wolf cried.

"He calls himself Ali Khan, the King of the World," Lady Zubaida said. "I think I'll just buy myself a piece of the action."

"So!" the Sky-Wolf cried. "My children grew up!"

"What children?"

"The Karaman," said the Sky-Wolf pensively. "They've chosen the way of the world: high finance, imperialism, religious hegemony."

Lady Zubaida turned to Hūrū, who was listening with her mouth open. "Tell me, please, who succeeds Harun-er-Rashid."

"El-Amin," Hūrū said automatically. "Wait! Yes, yes, I'm pretty sure it's El-Amin, Lady Amine's difficult horse-face husband. But he rules a scant four years."

"And then?"

"El-Mamun, El-Mutasim, El-Wathik, El-Mutawakkil," Hūrū reeled off the historical names she'd learned so reluctantly. "But they all serve short terms. Then, the Mongols take Baghdad."

"And what do they do with it?"

"The Mongols burn all the books," Hūrū said, "and destroy your Abbasid civilization."

"Just as I feared," said Lady Zubaida, swallowing hard. "I didn't make a good alliance. But the wifely woes of a woman called Zubaida are faint in comparison to the catastrophe that awaits the Abbasid Empire. Even now, I see the handwriting on the wall. Jafar hanging dead on a cross casts a very long shadow on Harun's reign."

"What did I tell you?" Hūrū said to her wife. "God is too a spoilsport!"

Part Three

RETURN

*Hürü is snatched back into real time
and a life waiting to be lived*

Chapter 16

ℱACE TO ℱACE

Hürü wakes up
in the courtyard of Shahrazad

A blue thunder and a trumpeting reopened the ambages of time, sucking the traveller through its circuits like a human fish. What did you think? Of course, it hurts! They say you don't remember a thing. And you don't. But, sometimes, for an instant, you hear the summons and answer the call from within your body. You were born before. Yes, and you once lived someplace else. No, it wasn't a dream. Time had substance and viscosity in an elastic pull. It was nauseatingly familiar and, at the same time, only a strange throb in the plumbing. Don't fool yourself, it's not just the radiators knocking, steam hissing through the valves. You are troubled by something that went on before, by its aftermath; meaning will soon become manifest. But it doesn't. Not quite. Whatever it was, it merely takes another turn; here you are, smoking. You know it's bad for you. Yet, you still smoke because you see the substance of your breath in the smoke you make. You are definitely here: your breath. The radiator knocks, the mailman rattles the lid to the mailbox. Letters have been addressed to the name you now carry gingerly; when you say it aloud, your name seems to belong to someone else in another time and another place. You remember suddenly that the Arabic name for womb also means *compassion*.

Hürü sat up, holding onto her turban for dear life. The same courtyard, but changed. The mansion is older now: there are cracks in the stone walls and the doors fit less snugly into their hinges. Pots of red geraniums sun themselves around the fountain. The roses are all gone. Geraniums are the flowers of humbler people. And Hürü doesn't know why Jafar Barmaki got himself crucified.

"I told you," Hürü repeated. "God is too a spoilsport."

No answer. Water splashed in the fountain, enlarging the sensation of tranquility. Not only were Lady Zubaida and the Sky-Wolf nowhere to be seen, the person Hürü addressed, a big black ogress of a woman, lay unconscious beside her. Once the negress came to, she was even less help than she'd been as a deeply fainted person. Now, at the brink of hysteria, her voice gargled in the back of her throat at a great expenditure of emotion.

"Glugh-glugh-glugh!" the Negress said.

Making this sound seemed to cost her so much effort, the whites of the woman's eyes popped out of their black lids, which seemed too fragile to withstand the stress.

"Cat got your tongue?" Hürü said, only to instantly regret her trite and downright cruel question. In the darkness of the ogress's open mouth, Hürü recognized a red and scarred stump beating uselessly against uvular points of articulation. The poor giantess was a mute! Her tongue had been cut out to discourage her from spreading abroad evil stories.

"I'm truly sorry, Madam," Hürü said.

"Glugh?" the negress responded. "Glugh!"

"My entrances," Hürü said, "cause great distress to those who happen to be standing around where I enter. I don't know what happens to people who must suffer my exits. Perhaps they don't even notice I'm gone. Or maybe my vanishing act causes a sensation like the missing persons of our dreams who also can't be quite recalled but keep nagging us."

The discussion on missing persons seemed to bring the big negress to her senses. Whereas she'd been terrified before, now she lifted Hürü by the ears as if she were a kettle with two handles, or a puppy dog, bringing her to an elevation where Hürü might be properly scrutinized.

"That smarts!" Hürü cried, laying a couple of punches on the ogress's lantern jaw. "Leave off, you brute! Put me down! Help! Oh, help, Moslems! Oh, Christians! Oh, Jews! Someone! Help! Fire!"

Four little schoolgirls rushed out into the courtyard and, seeing Hürü dangle by the ears, filled the air with peals of laughter.

"Hey!" Hürü shouted. "Call her off, will you? My ears won't take much more of this!"

The schoolgirls conferred among themselves in whispers, not about to do a thing on Hürü's behalf who, apparently, they thought was more fun than a barrel of monkeys. The ogress, having seen all the Hürü she wanted, didn't quite drop her but, almost gently, floated her down. As Hürü sat rubbing her ears, a woman who walked like a lioness claiming her territory with each step, came out of the sliding door to the marble salon. Brows knit, she approached swiftly, skirts billowing. In her hand she held an inkstained plume, a quill for writing.

"How can Mama do her work?" she scolded the four little girls. "Come on, all of you, back in the schoolroom!"

The little girls neither moved nor answered but pointed at Hürü, who was trying to make herself scarce behind the black ogress's voluminous skirts. The girls giggled, jostled, shrugged playfully.

"Who have we here?" asked the formidable mistress of the house. "A lad or a lass?"

"Oh, Camphor," the mistress said, addressing the negress. "How many times must I tell you that I need some privacy in the morning? Now, take this person to the kitchen and feed him or her. Then, get rid of the person: there's a good Camphor."

"Pardon me, Madam," Hürü piped up, "for invading your privacy. But I used to live here, once."

"Did you, just!" the mistress said. "And were you a male or a female when you lived here, once?"

"Both," Hürü said. "Or neither, as the case may be."

"And when did you live here, if I may ask?"

"During Harun-er-Rashid's time," Hürü said. "I don't know what time this is, of course. But judging from the way you've let this mansion run down, I guess it's much later. I must've arrived fast-forward."

"Just tell me who put you up to this?" the mistress said, laughing. "My husband? Oh, he must think it an excellent jest. Harun-er-Rashid's time, indeed! Tell me, did Shahriyar send you?"

"Must be Abd-es-Samad," Hürü said. "But I'm sure he didn't intend for you to be my destination. He must've screwed up again. The first time, he hurtled me into a vat of hot candy. Between us, Abd-es-Samad has less control over time than he thinks."

"What are you babbling about?" the mistress asked impatiently. "What Abd-es-Samad?"

"*The* Abd-es-Samad," Hürü said. "He's the Maghrabi hot-shot alchemist—or a mage; I'm not sure. But he's certainly the one who commandeered the kohl-pot, the magic sword, the signet ring and, most deplorably, the celestial planisphere, while I'm the one who helped him get his fat fingers on all that. Last time I saw Abd-es-Samad, he couldn't decide whether to keep the four magic objects or exchange the lot for a book called *The Stories of the Ancients*, subtitled *The Thousand and One Nights*."

"Jaudar?" the mistress of the house said in amazement. "Is that who you claim to be? But Jaudar was definitely a young man."

"I've been called Jaudar," Hürü said, "though that's not my true name. A very special sweetmaker used to call me that. But he turned me out of his heart as well as his sweetshop."

"Now I know in whose pay you are!" the lady said, knitting her handsome brows in earnest. "You're the sneak who's been reading my manuscript on the sly! And I know just who you're spying for, too! You can tell that Al-Masudi that his version is only an interpolation. Mine is the authentic account. He doesn't even know the difference between authoring and scribbling."

"Please, lady," Hürü said, "I don't know any Al-Masudi. Besides, I've never laid eyes on your manuscript, neither on the sly, nor in broad daylight."

"Oh, Camphor," the lady said, "throw this person out. And don't spare the boot!"

"Wait!" Hürü said. "I can prove I'm not lying. Somewhere in this house is a Lyre made of stone. It's mine. But I failed to re-arrive with my Stone Lyre. See, the instrument is a mute. It won't play for any but me."

"We know nothing," the mistress said, "of any Stone Lyre. The only mute around here is Camphor, the poor dear."

"But, Mama," one of the little girls said.

"In the storage vault," said another.

"It won't play," said the third.

"Won't get broken, neither," a fourth confessed.

"It's a magic Lyre," Hürü added.

The Stone Lyre, recaptured once more, seemed to sulk in Hürü's hands. The couple of times Hürü struck the chords, the strings harped back at her, scolding willfully like an abandoned wife. She sweet-talked the balky instrument, plucking it tenderly in hopes of reconciling the sore strings to the flight of time. The Lyre whined and complained some more, but finally offered up a wet trickle of sound, as if it had caught cold from being held captive in a damp storage vault. After running through an arpeggio—somewhat apologetically— Hūrū began to sing of the pleasures of sweet madness which are known to none but lunatic lovers.

"A very old song," the mistress of the house commented. "But I've always liked it well. So well, I let Ali Shir sing it when he loses the slavegirl and goes off his skull. One needs add some embellishment to old tales, show off the redactor's scope and refinement. Yet, when rendered on the flat page, the song loses its spirit."

"But this isn't an old song!" Hūrū said. "I composed it only yesterday, right here in this courtyard. Yet, you tell me it's travelled the centuries intact."

"Tell me," the mistress said, "how does a Stone Lyre sing? I make stories of the vague apprehensions of my life which need characters and dialogues to unfold. I'm just a maker—forever peeking over the wall, so to speak, envying poets their task. In poetry, there are no lies."

"I don't understand," Hūrū said. "What lies?"

"Pleasant lies," the lady said. "Fictitious tales."

"I still don't get it," Hūrū said. "To me, poetry and fiction are the same thing: speech that has something wrong with it. So why envy the poet's lyre which is so tense, and dense, the strings have turned to stone?"

"Because," the lady said. "I am forty years old."

"What if you can't sing? So what?" Hūrū said. "You have a houseful of little girls. Aren't children enough?"

"Yes," the lady said. "And no. Nothing will suffice but that which is more than sufficient. You don't understand because you're half my age and blessed with the truths of your heart you don't have to comprehend. For you, apprehension is all. Come in my study, and I'll show you. Can you read?"

"Well," Hūrū said, "I think I can. But I don't understand everything I read. In other words, I'm no scholar."

"The story of Ali Shir," the lady said, "and his forceful slavegirl won't strain your knowledge or imagination. I knocked it off in the last couple of days. The prose shows the haste, too. I have a feeling, though, this story isn't Baghdadian in origin."

"I have a feeling," Hūrū said, "I already know this story."

"Of course," the lady said. "So does everyone else. I bank on your memory."

"Who are you?"

"Call me Shahrazad," the lady said.

"Shahrazad Who?"

"Plain old Shahrazad of Baghdad."

"In that case, I am Hürü of Istanbul."

Shahrazad's study was the marble hall where, formerly, guests were entertained. Hürü, who thought that studies rated rooms no larger than broom closets, understood that for Shahrazad work was paramount, entertainment negligible. More library than study, the shelves on the walls groaned with bound manuscripts, but musty and pungent with the ink hot off the paws of the scribes. Stacks of parchment had accumulated on her low writing table at which she must sit crosslegged, scribbling like a common scribe, day in, day out.

Obviously, Shahrazad was a woman of means, though the furniture and the hangings had acquired, over the centuries since Hürü had seen the hall, a genteel shabbiness. Yet, the literary industry of this woman seemed inexhaustible though thankless, considering how, these days, so few people were either literate or willing to expend energy on reading. Who would want to read when somebody could just tell a story? The written word had gotten calcified. On the other hand, word-of-mouth tales always kicked with immediacy, with laughter and the current meanings which suited the times and the talents of the teller.

Shahrazad studied Hürü's face intently as Hürü read *The Story of Ali Shir and His Slavegirl*. Hürü wished Shahrazad wouldn't hang on so! Watching for some reaction, at least a smile. But she supposed the writer, too, longed for a little praise for a work whose scope and intentions were so gigantic that even the perpetrator couldn't see her work whole. Accordingly, Hürü forced a smile when the dinner guests at Sky-Wolf's monthly feast imagined that eating sweet rice brought, along with nourishment, the penalty of death.

Shahrazad didn't seem to really know the Sky-Wolf. For one thing, she had given Safiye the Sky-Wolf a name befitting a slave. She'd called the wonderful Amazon and fabled artisan by a name that in Arabic means Emerald, a precious stone the possession of which is fraught with danger. Shahrazad had told the tale from an omniscient vantage, as if she sat on both Emerald's and Ali Shir's shoulders. In this writer's version, Emerald revealed herself to her lover, left her kingdom with practically the whole treasury of the realm loaded on camels and pack mules, and set off for Ali Shir's native town, where she became the mother of his children. Shahrazad made no mention of the Sky-Wolf's kingly difficulties which necessitated the self-exile the marvelous Amazon had endured. As the slavegirl called Emerald, the Sky-Wolf lived and died an unexamined life.

"Why is Ali Shir worthy of Emerald?" Hürü asked the writer. "He's a singularly unresourceful person."

"He doesn't have to be resourceful," Shahrazad explained. "In the interests of Baghdadian realism, he's the perfect lover. He bears the pain of separation with patience and constancy. But, instead of solving their dilemma, the lovers pine away, ready themselves for love-death. Love, in this form, is a final condition. Don't you see?—a state that admits neither change nor fulfillment. So, the unrequited lovers usually suffer, sing and die. The twist in my story is that Emerald, obviously not native to Baghdad, proves so heroically resourceful. She wrests Ali Shir away from the love-death to which he's so charmingly inclined."

"But I personally know this lady you call Emerald," Hürü said. "I know she married someone else. Ali Shir was nowhere around, being, at the time, the Viceroy in Karamankand in her stead."

"What kind of ending is that?"

"The truth," Hürü said.

"Then tell me your account," Shahrazad said.

"First a bite to eat," Hürü said. "I don't know about you, but I'm starving. You get mighty hungry travelling through the centuries."

"Ah!" Shahrazad said, striking her forehead with her wrist. "I get so carried away, I forget to eat lunch."

"Maybe that's why you don't get fat," Hürü suggested.

As big Camphor served lunch in the library, Hürü studied Shahrazad, who ate lightly, explaining that anything more than a couple of poached eggs made her placid. Shahrazad glowed with an inexplicable fire, as if she consumed herself for fuel, though her countenance was pale as the winter. Her dark brown hair tumbled down her back in wild cascades, not being, as it wasn't, dressed according to any fashion. The only jewelry she wore was a plain wedding band. Her gauzy vestments hung loosely about her body which, as she walked, was revealed to be firm and delicate as a maiden's. Shahrazad's clear and strong voice amplified her small stature. That facile tongue had never been at a loss. As Shahrazad talked rapidly, she'd turn a common phrase on its ear, disturbing

Arabic grammar's long sleep, poking the language awake as it were. Hürü preferred her confabulation to her fables. Shahrazad liked laughing. Yet, her teeth were bad. Spotting a missing canine in Shahrazad's mouth, upper left, Hürü thought she could grow fond of that gap, where once an eye-tooth must've gleamed as dangerously as the one left intact, upper right.

Hürü was surprised how easily Shahrazad accepted her as an equal, as if Hürü weren't the waif blown inexplicably into the court-yard, but was a friend Shahrazad had known all her life. She sup-posed Shahrazad wasn't used to long preambles and tests before she made friends. As a young girl, she must've been something of a prankster. Wasn't that true?

"Yes," Shahrazad said. "And something of a liar too."

Not given to false modesty, Shahrazad said she'd known her mind since she was four years old. And, when she couldn't carry pranks far enough in the actual world, she perpetrated pranks of the imagination. Maybe this strong imagination was the place from which her charisma arose. Shahrazad's charisma was palpably there. De-spite her small person, her presence seized her audience. Hürü realized that she salivated as she listened to Shahrazad speak. Still, there was something in Shahrazad, Hürü thought, that was inclined to outrage others, a drive that had been harnessed to a vehicle called Storytelling.

Hürü learned that Shahrazad had not only given birth to four daughters; her three sons were all away at boarding school.

"A little tribe of savages," she said fondly. "But I'm glad they all arrived in the world, all unplanned of course. If it were up to me, I'd have never thought of bearing children. Fortunately, God knows better."

Once, Shahrazad intimated, she'd been engrossed with people. She'd loved throwing parties and fetes for her husband's set.

"Are you a widow then?" Hürü asked.

"Practically," Shahrazad said, "although Shahriyar still lives." But, nowadays, Shahrazad would rather gossip about storybook char-acters than about people she'd known. She'd rather ponder than go travelling abroad. She liked routines and the familiar precincts where she was in total control. When her work went well, she couldn't wait to get up in the morning and start digging at the mines. When it didn't, she ventured out to make things happen. She created scenes that challenged the local customs of Baghdad. Shahrazad forced life to imitate fiction. And how was that done, Hürü wanted to know.

"You'll see," Shahrazad said mysteriously.

It seems this Shahriyar, Shahrazad's so-called husband, lived in his own palace where he pursued his own interests. As Hürü learned, Shahriyar's palace was none other than the old Barmaki place, confiscated from the family once good old Jafar was crucified. The husband and wife had become good friends ever since Shahrazad moved into her own mansion here. This might seem strange to Hürü, but Shahrazad actually *liked* her husband, now that she'd moved out. Even his faults endeared Shahriyar to her these days, so long as she didn't have to hang around, nattering at him, giving him advice, telling him exemplary tales.

"This place belonged to my mother's family," Shahrazad said. "But it hadn't been lived in for quite some time. I love living here. And I no longer have to compete with Shahriyar, nor live through him. What he does with himself is his own business. But I don't have to stand behind the throne, exercising my will through his so-called authority."

Shahriyar's business was to rule over Baghdad and its domains, the remnants of the Abbasid Empire. If Shahriyar could be said to rule. He was more a caretaker, a diligent lawyer, whose task it was to reconcile the will of the Mamluk Sultan to the welfare of the people. Shahriyar was an intermediary who translated the bidding and the forbidding of the foreign master to the subjects at the peril of his subjugated head.

Shahrazad wished her husband could express himself. Like any man, Shahriyar deserved to be judged on his own merits and faults. But she didn't see how he could move. Shahriyar was stuck. Yet he'd accepted his fate of being stuck with a certain grace. Shahriyar had a good ear for listening, a talent for organizing information, and for holding his own with his Mamluk master who couldn't bother with the details of administration. Yet, sometimes he resented his powerlessness: no army, no neighboring countries. He was a king without a kingdom, a husband without a wife, a father without children and, above all, a professor with no students. It seemed to Shahrazad her husband's greatest talent was for teaching.

"The ways of the world are strange," Shahrazad said, sighing. "I would have wished none of this on Shahriyar, even when I was most angry at him. His whole history, I suppose, has conspired to give him potency within impotence."

She explained how the Mamluks were brought into the land as
slaves. In fact, *mamluk* had once been synonymous with the word
slave. Imported from Circassia and Central Asia as praetorian guards,
the Mamluks had in time replaced the native Arab soldiery. Being
slaves, they had been well suited to taking orders, for the organized
death of warfare, for rigid hierarchies. The Arabs had been all too
willing to let their slave armies do their dying for them, to do their
work for them and, eventually, to do their thinking for them. Now the
Mamluks were the masters and the Arabs the slaves. Rubbing Arab
noses into Arab excrement was a favorite Mamluk pastime. Gone
were the golden days of Harun-er-Rashid!

"Arabs have been brutalized," Shahrazad said. "I suppose that's
why my tales recreate a time that was golden. I brush off Harun the
sort of shadows that fall on any prince. I polish the picture of a
Baghdad that was prosperous and brilliant."

"Forgive my ignorance," Hürü said, "But who the hell do these
Mamluks think they are?"

"Hmph!" Shahrazad said haughtily. "They're some kind of Turk."

"Ah!" Hürü said.

"Sometimes I think Turks were put on this earth," Shahrazad
said, "to spoil things for everyone. What, I ask you, have they ever
added to the world's intellectual history?"

"I'm sure I don't know," Hürü said. "Because I just happen to be
a Turk. And dumb as a rock."

"Oh dear!" Shahrazad said. "And have you come to spoil things
for me?"

"First, tell me today's date," Hürü said. "I don't even know if I'm
here for real—let alone if I spoil things for you."

Shahrazad informed her that it was the first of Shafar, the nine
hundred and twenty-second year of the Prophet's Flight. Hürü wanted
to know what that translated to in Infidel Time. Shahrazad shuttled
through her writing table and came up with the date of January 29,
1516.

"Wow!" Hürü exclaimed. "Then, I'm here for real. This must be
my destiny because I'm back in my own time. This must be the end
of the Road to Baghdad. Tell me, is this the end of the road?"

"How should I know the end," Shahrazad said, "if I don't know
the beginning and the middle of your story?"

"Then I'll tell you all," Hürü said.

For three days, Hürü told her story, resorting to song and rhyme when reason wouldn't suffice. Like the Asiatic minstrel that she was, she made no distinction between what's prose and what's verse, what's profane and what's sacred, what moves forward and what returns and recuperates. She gave it to Shahrazad just below the tension of the Stone-Born Lyre. Not at a fever pitch. Her voice flowed over the images as a brook does over pebbles and stones.

And Shahrazad was right there with the flow at every turn. Without making interruptions, she affected the story's course because, in the whole world, never was there a better audience. At midnight, the third night, Hürü fell silent. She was done telling. Not quite all, as she'd promised. She'd held something back, something that felt like guilt. Hürü didn't tell Shahrazad about her passionate, and inexplicable, love for Selim the Grim. She was too ashamed to admit her love.

Shahrazad, too, sat studying her hands. Extolled be the Perfect for He alone is Eternal. When she looked up, her eyes seemed to know Hürü's burning questions.

"Amazing performance," she said at last, "for a mere kid like you. So much promise! It just goes to show that poetry comes naturally to the young. And you do extremely well with the line, the image, with the natural given rhythm, the meter and the reflexive moment."

". . . But," Hürü said, sensing a reservation.

"But," Shahrazad said, "your story line is somewhat uneven. You can't apprehend the stars. You have to scrutinize the heavens to find the pattern in the constellations. The story exists to fulfill an expectation. Or to alter it. Or to disappoint. The story must be spellbinding. It must fill the emptiness of our lives. It must console, cajole, argue, trick, enchant and recreate us. Like the ventriloquist, the storyteller must draw our attention elsewhere while executing the mechanics of magic. The telling of stories depends on sham. Don't you see?"

"Gosh!" Hürü said, her hazel eyes widening. "You must be the Teacher I once asked for in the rose garden. You're the one Hidir-Ilyas had in mind for me. You're the one who knows the Beginning, the Middle and the End."

"You certainly went to school long enough."

"Yeah, but," Hürü said, "who ever learns anything at military school?"

"Nobody ever learns what's important in school, Hürü," Shah-

razad said. "You learn the truth by looking in your heart. And you
have. What amazes me is how clearly you speak your own heart.
Your voice is a wind, the breathing of God. The breathing will not
last but it touches a center that is speechless, as dark as the womb.
When breathing dies, so dies the prophet, the beating of your heart.
No illusions, no tricks, your poetry is benign only because of the
terrible truth of which it speaks."

"Wow!" Hürü said. "And what terrible truth is that?"

"Death," Shahrazad said. "Death."

"Wow!" Hürü said again. And she shivered.

Chapter 17

THE FALSE CALIPH

Life in the realm of fictions

Sickness is for the body," Shahrazad said, opening the largest of her black Abbasid trunks, "as madness is for the mind. Art is for the fragile sanity between what decays and what remains."

"Does that go for poetry, too?" Hūrū said. "I always thought poetry was just one damn thing after another."

"Tonight," Shahrazad said, ignoring her question, "we must understand the hyperbola of the 'False Caliph.' I'm the False Caliph, you are the False Jafar Barmaki, and Camphor gets to play False Mesrur, the Lord High Executioner. Here are your clothes. These were actually worn by the historical Jafar."

"That's right," Hūrū said. "Last time I saw him, he wore this cravat. Did you know that it was Jafar Barmaki who invented the necktie? Seems that as a young man, he was quite a dandy."

"Right," Shahrazad said. "Now we must send word to Shahriyar. He, too, must dress up, as the Real Caliph, disguised as a merchant. His righthand man gets to play the Real Barmaki, disguised as the second merchant. And the Chief Justice of the realm, who happens to be black, is the Real Mesrur, also disguised as a merchant."

"But how are those men to know what you have in mind?"

"Ah, that part is easy," Shahrazad said, eyes sparkling. "'The False Caliph' is an odd bit of fiction everybody knows. They all know it, but they don't get it. That's the trouble with the story, you see. It is a parable whose message has been buried under many layers of traditional Harun-er-Rashid lore. I always thought it was ruined by its ending. Tonight we'll recreate the story's true meaning. I'm going to send Shahriyar word to have his Chief Teller retell him the story of the 'False Caliph.' He'll know what to do then."

"Gosh," Hürü said. "Will Shahriyar be game?" Hürü asked.

"Why not? Seeing mine is the only game in town?"

"Somehow," Hürü mumbled, "I had the impression that Shahriyar was a . . . a crashing bore.

"Oh, he is! Yet he's also quite exciting. You see, he, too, wants to understand something about himself."

"Then, give me the story quick," Hürü said, "so I won't be the only dummy in Baghdad."

"Let's see," Shahrazad said, sitting on the trunk. "'The False Caliph' opens with Harun-er-Rashid suffering one of his nocturnal depressions. He calls in Mesrur, and he has Jafar Barmaki, his wise old Chamberlain, summoned out of his bed. Disguised as three merchants, the trio descends on Baghdad. Night life in the streets takes them to the banks of the River Tigris. There, they see an old man sitting in a rowboat. They ask him to take them for a ride.

"The old boatman refuses flat out. Not safe, going pleasure boating on the Tigris anymore, he tells them; the Caliph has taken to cruising downstream in a splendid barge. Every night. Not only that, he's forbidden all other night traffic. The penalty for disobeying is heavy. The Caliph will have your head. 'Here comes the Caliph's barge now!'

"'Good heavens!' cries the disguised Caliph. 'For two dinars, old man, row us under the arches of the Middle Bridge. Let's take a closer look at his Nocturnal Caliph!'

"Well, two dinars! The old boatman takes a chance. He eases his boat under an arch and covers his passengers under a black tarp. Peeking from under, the real royal company take a good look at the splendid barge. At the stem, a man holds a torch made of red gold feeding the flame with Sumatran aloes. The man wears a short cloak of red satin; over one shoulder runs a ribbon of yellow silk embroidered with silver; the turban on his head is made of the finest muslin. At the stern stands another man, in like dress, holding a similar torch.

"In the middle of the barge, two hundred slaves stand at attention on either side of a raised throne of gold. On the throne is

a young man, handsome and elegant, who is clad in the garments of
the Abbasid Caliphs: black stuff embroidered with gold. In front of
him stands a grand personage who seems none other than Grand
Vizier Jafar. Behind him looms a black eunuch with a naked sword in
hand, no doubt the person of Lord Mesrur.

"The bright pleasure barge with its extravagant lights cruises
by. The real Caliph, hidden among the shadows and the black shapes
of masonry, watches his double go on his way, enthroned in a blaze
of light. Harun is amazed, but being who he is, and so sure of himself,
he's not even angry at the young man who apes him. In fact he is
immensely excited by the sight of his double.

"'Did you see what I saw?' Harun cries. 'There went the living
image of the Caliph! You, Jafar, seemed to stand in front of him. And
you, Mesrur, behind.'

"Intrigued, the trio go to watch their doubles again the next
night. Harun is no longer bored. This time, they follow the False
Caliph to a stately house where a banquet is in progress. They
manage to slip in so easily, you wonder if they weren't expected, if
this isn't a trap to catch the Real Caliph.

"The trio is given food and drink, but they keep their eyes on
the pretentious young man. Presently, under the influence of songs
about unrequited love, the False Caliph gets up to rend his clothes
to bits. He faints, four times over. On his milk-white skin are deep
scars. Somebody's beaten the hell out of the False Caliph.

"Who? And why? the True Caliph must know. The False Caliph
tells all. Turns out the False Caliph has been wooed and wed by a
lady who wears the family jewels, if you know what I mean. This lady
happens to be Jafar Barmaki's half-sister, and she's wildly jealous.
During her frequent business trips out of Baghdad, she wants her
young husband to stay put in the house. Or else! Being the handsome, elegant young man he is, the False Caliph has attracted the
attention of Lady Zubaida, the Caliph's formidable wife. He's been
unable to refuse Lady Zubaida's invitation to a party at her private
quarters. But, on his return, his wife finds out he's been stepping out.
Furious, she has him beaten to within an inch of his life and throws
him out on his elegant ear.

"But the False Caliph confesses he's still crazy about his wife.
Not only that, he implies he's guessed the real identities of the
merchant trio. He says he puts on the dog every night just to impress
the people of Baghdad, thereby drawing the Real Caliph into his own

story. His object, so he says, is none other than begging Harun-er-Rashid's help. Will the Real Caliph make his wife take him back?

"Well, Harun doesn't resist the course of True Love. He makes the disagreeable Barmaki woman take her pussy of a husband back. You wonder why, don't you? What a let-down! Such an extravagant beginning and a shabby little end.

"That's what we will explore, Hürü girl. Why must Shahrazad put her signature on a seamy little domestic drama? We will wear the Abbasid black and go down the Tigris in splendor tonight!"

"Why?" Hürü said.

"Why, oh, why!" Shahrazad cried impatiently. "Because Shahrazad always wanted to wear the pants and masquerade as the Caliph. That's why! Does that satisfy you?"

"Plenty," Hürü said. "So hand me Jafar's trousers. I'll wear them."

"And tie on this long white beard," Shahrazad said. "The Chamberlain who plays the Real Jafar wears the real thing. A trim white beard. He's my good old Dad."

"Your Dad!" Hürü cried. "Your Dad runs around Baghdad putting on shows? Wow! What a family!"

"Thanks to me!" Shahrazad said. "Without me, they'd all try being consistently themselves all the time. Rigid as hell. What's the fun in being tied down to a single persona?"

"Some of us would like to construct one," Hürü said. "Some of us don't even have a reliable persona yet. Me, for example."

"That's what I like about you," Shahrazad said. "You're still somewhat unpredictable. My husband, too. Just as you think you have him figured out, he says something surprising. Or he'll go do some damn thing."

Baghdad nights were still enchanting. And fraught with danger. Cruising down the Tigris in a blaze of lights wasn't half bad either. On a borrowed barge. And a cast of out-of-work actors. Not only did Hürü get to see Shahriyar, she saw the deep scars that marred Shahrazad's strong back. And she wondered. How could these two be so civilized and yet . . . And what about Shahrazad's Dad? This slim and elegant old man who so reminded Hürü of her own father. Why did he go along with these shenanigans?

Shahriyar looked mild. Tall and red-bearded, not your hook-nosed swarthy Arab at all. His skin was tenderly white and his fingers long, cool and clean; he said little and what he said was not idle. He paid Hürü no attention . . . as if his wife's new student didn't exist, or if she did, she didn't matter. He intimidated Hürü, who liked to think of herself as an intrepid person. Perhaps because she knew at once that she bored Shahriyar. He wasn't the image of kindness either, the way he walked—like a big cat, a panther perhaps, with something sinister lurking in his feline strength. He played panther to Shahrazad's wolf. Cat and dog. Hürü liked Shahrazad instinctively, despite the bad press the wolf gets.

Who knows what Big Shahriyar learned from the theatrics. He seemed to have a good time though, almost as good a time as did Big Camphor, who played the black executioner as if she'd known Mesrur personally. When Shahriyar left—after filling his face with the food Camphor had prepared—he was still in character.

"Hah!" cried Shahrazad, trim and vigorous in her skinny black trousers, flowing black silk shirt and black leather boots. "I'm Shahrazad the Termagant, a vociferous and turbulent Arabess whose words are noxious as her farts! No wonder! In poisonous air like that, even a palace is too narrow a house for *two* Would-be Caliphs! Perhaps, now that I've renounced my false bid for the Caliphacy, Shahriyar can get on with the business of becoming the Real Caliph."

"Oh, pooh!" Hürü said.

Before she could say more, a loud knocking at the door stopped Hürü. On the doorstep towered an extremely tall woman, heavily veiled and cloaked. In her hand was a heavy braided leather crop. Obviously she'd been riding some poor horse.

"Welcome home, my Beauty," the False Caliph said, advancing, arms open. The haughty dame swished the riding crop with a dangerous snaky motion. But, familiar as you please, up the stairs she went to the master bedroom. The feline way the strange woman walked, gracefully muscular, reminded Hürü of someone else. Oh, my God! Must be Shahriyar himself, in drag! Playing this time Jafar Barmaki's sadistic sister.

No wonder the cries that emanated from the master bedroom kept Hürü up all night. A couple of animals, she thought. Tearing each other apart.

"I, too, was born in a famous city," Shahrazad said as she breakfasted. "And I, too, was born to a big beautiful woman! Safiye, the big blond Amazon who repeats herself in my family every third generation. Next, Safiye will be born to one of my daughters."

"Oh," Hürü said, "wish I could've seen her! But I must be out of sync with her incarnations."

"Safiye was so successful," Shahrazad said, "she didn't need to stand in her daughters' way, Dunyazad's and mine. But Mom died young. Dad was addicted to books, to the liberal arts, to intelligent company. He loved showing me off. I was a child prodigy. Since Dunyazad wasn't born until I turned nine, I had all the time in the world to imagine the world.

"Soon I outstripped my tutors. I had to dress up as a lad and go down to the city Seminary. I loved college, you know, being one of those lucky kids who bypass the boredom of secondary school. By the time I turned sixteen, believe me, I was the most educated person in all of Baghdad.

"But I'd lost my woman's place, without truly gaining the world of men. For example, who would I marry? Aside from a certain professor of logic, a man in his late sixties, no man pleased me halfway. Besides, who'd marry a girl who was such a royal pain in the ass?

"No matter. I'd stay a maiden. And become a loving aunt. Dunyazad, that plump darling, had no inclination for anything besides her own sensuous body. Even as a baby, she sat with one hand always toying with the little wedge between her legs. She'd suckle Mom's nipples as if she intended to consume that beautiful lady in her infantile passion. In the schoolroom, Dunyazad only used the feather end of the quill, dreaming hotly, quim wet, lips half open, gasping shamelessly as she came. Bless her voluptuousness, that one had no use for the quill's point.

"I met Shahriyar at the Seminary. He was doing post-graduate work. So was I, still passing myself off as a young man. He challenged me to a verbal duel. Well, I beat the pants off the Crown Prince. He took it like a sport, and soon we became fast friends. But I always evaded physical contest with him, turning his boisterous challenges to jokes. I teased him for pissing farther, for the size of his mantool, for his crapulous nights in the company of whores.

"'A Sissy is what you are!' Shahriyar teased back. 'Your balls have retracted into your head!'

"He was pleased, though. His physical prowess proved an equalizer. One day we were watching some wrestlers in the field. Shahriyar suddenly seized me by the nape, threw me down and locked me in some fancy hold. Not knowing what to do, I tried twisting away. Well, he managed to tear away the front of my suit. As he pinned down my shoulders, he saw my two naked breasts. There could be no

moment more inflaming! and we didn't put off the urge either. Right
then and there we went at it, wrestlers gaping at us and all. And most
tiptoed away, not wanting to embarrass the Crown Prince. But who
was embarrassed? We made love until the cows came home. And you
know the cows don't come home by themselves. Oh, there was war
in our embrace. All night and most of the next morning, too.

"'I wondered,' Shahriyar confessed, finally sitting up, 'if I was
turning queer or what . . . the way I felt about you. This sure takes
a load off my mind. My balls, too!'

"'We could get married,' I suggested.

"'Why not?' says Shahriyar. 'I always wanted a girl who'd do my
reading and writing.'

"What does a woman do when in doubt? She marries. Now that
the truth was out, I couldn't even land a job teaching at the Seminary.
So why not get married? Landing a job as the Queen wasn't all that
bad, either. But marriage wasn't as much fun. Shahriyar didn't much
like it, either.

"'A big mistake,' he said, 'marrying a girl who would be king.'

"Was is just me? Or were men and women basically incom-
patible? I still don't know the answer. When I asked Shahriyar for a
parallel existence, I hadn't written anything more inventive than a
shopping list. Or more exciting than a term paper. Fear of the
unknown beset me.

"'You're leaving,' Shahriyar said sadly. 'Clearing out for good.'

"'I've done some terrible things.'

"'Don't tell me,' he said, placing his forefinger on my lips.

"'You feel sorrow for me,' I said. 'Is that right?'

"'Maybe,' he said. 'But perhaps it's something else. For example,
love.'

"And I moved in here. The walls of this hall were lined with my
library, the boys settled in boarding school, Camphor retained. Then
a huge silence fell over the house. A mute presence inhabited it
which was as pervasive and obdurate as Camphor. Giving life to a
suspended house didn't quite take my own life out of suspension. I
had a good cry. I had two good cries. And I enjoyed both tremendously.

"I was free at last to do as I liked. But what did I really like?
Mohammed prescribed spinning to women. 'Sitting for an hour
employed with the distaff is better for women,' Mohammed said,
'than a year's worship. For every piece of cloth woven of the thread

they've spun, women shall receive in Paradise the reward of martyrs.' Nice, eh? But I hadn't had a proper girlhood. I could only spin with words. And my only distaff was the intellect. But what words should I spin? And in what order?

"Somewhere under my hand must be a full storehouse of words —if only I had the serenity to apprehend the treasury. 'Open Sesame' might enrich Ali Baba, but for me the key word didn't crack open a sesame bun. I was sitting in the library, and thinking that I needed a *jinn* or a *jann*—some supernatural power like in the old tale about Aladdin's Lamp.

"'Jann Baath!'" I cried passionately. 'Where the hell are you when you're really needed?'

"No sooner were the words out of my mouth than a creature materialized right out of that bookshelf there. The one devoted to the fables of the ancients. The outlandish creature gained substance right under my eyes. Not only did he look like a real man, he was the spitting image of Shahriyar. Just dressed oddly in a skimpy shirt and even skimpier trousers which showed most of his well-muscled legs, and tan as a sailor, too. Something free and easy about this creature who stood before me. And why not? I had called for the Spirit Reawakened after, Jann Baath.

"'You called?' he said, pleased as a cat who got away with something good. 'Can I really believe my eyes? You are Shahrazad, aren't you? I was on my boat talking to a friend. I had just said, "Even Shahrazad has run out of tales . . ." when you called me by my name. And here I am, at your service.'

"'Jann Baath? That your name?' I said. 'So you're a *jann*. And are you quite sure that you're not a *jinni*?

"'I'm no *jinni*—unless, of course, you consider that our English word for *genius* comes from your Arabic word, *jinn*.'

"'So you admit to being a genius?' I said. 'I'll be damned!' He blushed, high velocity and deep crimson. I liked him right off.

"He seemed to be under the impression that we spoke English. I'd never even heard of this language. His tongue was translated into Arabic as his person was translated to Baghdad. But I believed him when he said he came from the Antipodes. As I said, he could have been Shahriyar's twin, but he was also, in some essential way, different. Light skinned like my husband but more rosy, as are people who eat too much beef, the translated man's tonsure was smoother than a honeydew melon settled into a soft crescent of wispy red-gold hair. Over his shy smile grew a thatch of manly bristle. I like modesty in men, especially in one so tall and, obviously, devilishly clever. We fell to exchanging stories. He said he too was a writer of fictions, like me. Pray tell, what fictions did I write?

"'Your *Thousand and One Nights*, he said. 'Your work, although not read as much in the particular future I come from, has never been off my desk.'

"'That's nice, dear Jann,' I said. 'But what are the thousand and one nights?'

"'*Alf Laylah Wa Laylah*,' he insisted.

"This Jann Baath really held forth. Turns out he was professorial as they come. He praised, invoked, recited; he apostrophised, philosophized, rhapsodized; he harangued me 'til I finally understood I was meant to write an opus that would survive for all time. Not only that, I already knew all the stories I was to pen. The material existed in the popular domain. I was shocked. How vulgar! Me, Shahrazad? Put over a bunch of tales told to children and dim-witted adults? Never! Hardly a story existed in the bag, I told him, that one might repeat in good company!

"On and on, I scolded the genius. I had one of the best minds of the age, I said; I wasn't about to waste my intellect on a mishmash of tales that evolved among illiterate peasants from the land of the Maghrabis all the way to China. Misapprehended, annexed from one culture to another, the tales were so punky that not even a desert Bedouin could stand the stuff. No psychological verisimilitude, no philosophical grounding, no fresh insights about the way we live now, the stories were empty shells. Besides, they were so often such bad replicas of each other that reading all the tales was like sitting in the barber's chair and having all one's teeth extracted. I congratulated Jann Baath on his patience and generosity. Turns out, however, that the structure of the tales was what intrigued this genie. 'Oriental' he said, naming the structure. 'Patterns within patterns.'

"'I don't know from Oriental,' I said. 'Oriental as opposed to what? But tell me, what glue holds the patterns together?'

"'Your own life, of course,' Jann Baath said. 'The ultimate ransom: your own life, dear girl.'

"Was I amazed! Couldn't Jann Baath see I was a woman practically his own age, with a tribe of children of my own, and a disastrous marriage behind me? Perhaps he was only perceiving the Shahrazad in his own mind's eye. He lectured the student-princess in his imagination. So touching. So wonderful. I wanted to know more.

"Apparently, this Shahriyar in the story enjoyed a new Moslem virgin every night. And he had her destroyed in the morning. Women being the faithless sows Shahriyar thought they were, he didn't want them putting the horns on him. The carnage of virgins went on until, one night, Shahrazad arrived on her verbal charger.

"At the peril of her own life, Shahrazad told the misogynist king stories every night, but didn't divulge the ending. To hear the end, she had to be spared for another night when, just as she was through telling, she began a new story and stopped again at daybreak just before the climax. The king had to tune in the next night, that is, if he were to get his jollies. So Shahrazad went on for a thousand and one nights, staying her own execution, making babies and gaining time both for herself and for Shahriyar. Shahriyar, too, needed time to get himself domesticated into a loving husband. Not bad! Not bad, at all!

"'So,' I said lightly, 'I get revenge on Shahriyar, after all!'

"'Your motive isn't revenge,' said Jann Baath. 'Don't you see? Although writers often avenge themselves on the villains of their real lives, your motive is to *redeem* Shahriyar. You woo him away from his misogyny, bless your gentle heart. You save him from having to live out his life as the caricature of an Oriental potentate.'

"'And how did I get such a gentle heart?' I said, though my heart wished that I were suddenly granted a heavenly commodity of goodwill.

"'Ah, by writing *as if* you already have a gentle heart!' exclaimed the Jann, his bright eyes twinkling goodnaturedly. 'And, thereby, creating an audience of gentle hearts. That's the magic of art. If art cannot redeem the barbarities of history or spare us the horrors of living and dying, at least it sustains, refreshes, expands, ennobles, and enriches our spirits along the way.'

"'As if,' I said.

"'As if,' repeated Jann Baath.

"And, with that, the said Jann disappeared into the same shelves from which he'd appeared. Did I really see him? Or was he a projection of my mind? Did I invent him as the Good Shahriyar? Shahriyar as I'd like him to be? Or was he supernatural? Maybe he was a real *jann* who provided me with an idea. I don't know. And, ultimately, it doesn't matter.

"Maybe, I thought to myself, just maybe I can produce a work that's out of this world. If I could only reopen our verbal treasurehouse for the cynical and brutalized citizens of Baghdad, I could perhaps alchemize their souls again. Yes, I'd spring the Flying Horses from the storehouse, the Enchanted Princesses, the Love-struck Princes faithful even in adversity. I'd remind the reader of hardboiled merchants who still could navigate wondrous worlds beneath their daily lives. Maybe I, too, could recreate a race of ennobled Arabs.

"After all, the written charm is known to be more potent than the spoken one. Some feel that writing is magic that heals, fixes and protects. Self-knowledge unlocks man's better nature, especially the nature of those occupied with power and responsibility. Of course, I have Shahriyar in mind. My husband, my patron and, of course, my Caliph. I'm crafting this book for his eyes, though he says he cares little for escapist literature and will not read it. Do you realize how much it will cost to reproduce a book this size? I can't even afford publication. So, why do I keep writing?"

"I'll bet," Hürü interrupted, "Abd-es-Samad has something to do with your compulsion. Last time I saw him, he was dying to get hold of your book. I think that old fart has put the hex on you."

"The hell with magicians!" Shahrazad cried. "I don't care who exploits the book. All I want is to write it well. No, Abd-es-Samad is nothing to me."

"You don't know this Abd-es-Samad," Hürü said. "He pinches everything."

"Then he's welcome to everything!" Shahrazad shouted. "After all, who am I? Someone who's never travelled outside Baghdad. An obscure writer. I couldn't even keep house at a mediocre palace where I alternately played the bitter queen, the inept mother and, most lamentably, the failed thinker.

"I am also the thousand-and-one persons I have hallucinated. I am Sinbad the Sailor. Yes, my mind has travelled to that splendid showplace of death called the City of Brass. I've seen kingdoms under the sea, kept company with vagrants, outcasts, criminals and rogues in contexts both dirty and clean, abandoned myself to a hundred love-deaths in Baghdad, to a hundred-and-one infidelities in Cairo. I've put demons and warlocks under control, been flown on *jinn* to China and back. I've been transformed into birds, beasts, into saints, Jews, Christians, into wags, ghouls, merchants both prudent and imprudent, into wastrels, hunchbacks, imps, into enchantresses with menageries of lovers, into kings whose reigns are golden.

"But what's my mettle? My substance? That is precisely what I want to know. I long to exhaust all the shapes of my being. As each tale falls away from me, so does another guise, another need, another dream. Someday the shell called Shahrazad will be so empty, I will see the face of God."

Shahrazad fell silent.

"Wow!" Hürü cried. "Is that how it's done? Can you really see the Face by exhausting all faces?"

Chapter 18

EARTHLY MARRIAGE

*Hürü weds Selim the Grim,
Sultan of the Ottomans*

*B*efore Shahrazad could reply, Camphor flung open the doors to the library. In strode Shahriyar in a swelter, red beard uncombed, black turban askew.

"Gather the girls," the Big Caliph said, breathing as if exercised hard. "We have to get all of you to a safe place . . . if there's a safe place left."

"I can't leave now!" Shahrazad said, indicating her writing table. "You know my work . . ."

"Selim the Grim," Shahriyar said, "just took Aleppo. He devastated the Mamluks before the city gates. And the Grand Mamluk himself lies dead on the battlefield. Seems the Old Man was so upset, he died of a stroke."

"So old Al-Ghawri is dead!" Shahrazad exclaimed. "Poor bastard!"

"Was he the same Grand," Hürü wanted to know, "who had Shahriyar by the short hairs?"

Casting Hürü a baleful look, Shahriyar turned back to his wife as if Hürü hadn't spoken. And Hürü wished she hadn't.

"Listen," he said to Shahrazad. "Selim marches. This very minute he's upon Damascus. A messenger's just ridden in, bringing me word that Selim the Grim summons me before him in Damascus, fast. So, Shahrazad, this might be the final goodbye."

"Shahriyar!" Shahrazad cried. "I'm coming along! Whatever fate Selim metes out, I will share it with you."

"But your work . . ."

"The hell with my work!" Shahrazad cried, throwing her arms around Shahriyar.

The endangered monarch took his estranged wife's hands into his big paws. The two sat down together, looking into each other's eyes—as if time were granting them a moment of tranquility.

"You must live, Shahrazad," the Caliph said. "I never discovered my own heart's desire. I never produced something both *interesting* to me and *useful* to others. You have. I know I've teased you too much about your work, about spending your life on pleasant lies. But I've also cherished you for your steadfastness. Live, Shahrazad, and bring your labors into fruition."

"I'm coming along anyway," Shahrazad insisted.

"Be reasonable," Shahriyar said. "There's a good chance I'm a condemned man."

"Not necessarily," Hürü piped up, unable to contain herself any longer. "I happen to know Selim quite well. He's not always unreasonably cruel, and usually there's a method to his cruelty."

"Is *It* a girl or a boy?" Shahriyar said contemptuously. "And what is *It* babbling about?"

"*She*," Shahrazad said pointedly, "is an old friend of Selim's, it so happens. And *her* name is Hürü. She's had to put on masculine attire, obviously, because she's been on the road. That's how she's been able to arrive in Baghdad intact, body and soul, unmolested by some rapacious dunghead. Now, Hürü's offering you an inside look at Selim. If she says Selim is not always unreasonably cruel, that's a plus. Take advantage of it."

"Maybe I can be of some help," Hürü said. "I'd certainly like to try."

Shahriyar groaned.

"Sometimes," Shahrazad said, "you've got to put your trust in frail vessels."

Once persuaded to include Shahrazad and Hürü in his entourage, Shahriyar departed posthaste to his palace to change into some attire appropriate to the dreaded audience with Selim, and to see if he could scare up enough thoroughbreds at the stables. No one in his entourage was going to ride some miserable nag if he could help it. He wanted Selim impressed. Now that Selim the Grim had begun to dismantle the rule of the Mamluks, he might see fit to retain Shahriyar as the Vassal Prince of all Araby. And why not? There was no other Arab prince with a more legitimate claim. Sure, being Selim's vassal was dangerous, but, without putting one's head in danger, there was no getting ahead in this world. Yet, he was afraid he might not pass muster. Shahriyar just wasn't set up to provide Baghdad with a majestic fall. There were no armies to face Selim. Baghdad had to fall whimpering like a kitten.

In the meantime, Shahrazad opened again her Abbasid trunks stuffed with costumes from the past. In broad daylight, wrinkled and frayed Abbasid velvet didn't look so rich.

"Good grief!" said Shahrazad. "I don't have a thing to wear."

Sighing, she put on a white satin undergarment, stained with the marks that inexplicably appear on finery shut up in trunks. Over the white gown, she slipped a black velvet robe embroidered with real gold, though it seemed ready to crumble, and let the embroidered motifs fall where they would. On her lovely dark brown cascade of hair she placed a diadem of emeralds.

"A paste copy," she explained to Hūrū. "The real gems were disposed of long ago."

After all that careful dressing up, Shahrazad covered the whole effect, shabbily royal, under a black drapery that enveloped her whole person. Her beautiful, intense features were obscured behind a black muslin veil that hung to her waist.

"Now you look like Death's bride," Hūrū said.

"I feel like her, too," Shahrazad said, sighing once more. "Now you choose something from the trunks. Or will you go looking like a street boy?"

"Time has come to put on something feminine," Hūrū said. "Selim will recognize me, of course. And when he sees that I'm a girl, he wouldn't hold me to some god-awful punishment, would he?"

"You tell me," Shahrazad said. "I don't know the man. You really shouldn't take a terrible risk like this . . . not on our account. Maybe you ought to stay back, Hūrū. After all, Baghdad isn't your problem."

"But Selim," Hūrū said, "is my problem. He must see and recognize my face."

Hūrū took from Shahrazad's trunks some silken pantaloons the color of the sky, a gauzy blouse of fine muslin, and a little vest of black velvet embroidered with golden birds of paradise, unmistakably Safiye Sky-Wolf's handiwork, perhaps made for a daughter some

six centuries ago. A great sadness filled Hürü's heart: how sad that
a flimsy bit of embroidery survives the robust beauty who created
it.

"You're remembering," Shahrazad guessed, "your wife."

"Yes," Hürü said. "And what a beauty she was. Would you care
to see the spitting image of Safiye Sky-Wolf?"

"Let's see it," Shahrazad said, curious.

Hürü took out of the lining of one boot the Golden Lady that
Selim had hammered out of his heart's innermost desire. Poor Selim.
He's never to lay eyes on his dream girl. Dead for six centuries. Count
on Selim to desire only the impossible!

"Ravishing," Shahrazad said, returning the golden image.

As Hürü put the medallion back in her boot, Shahrazad brought
out of another trunk three winding sheets, and three fine burial
outfits, one for herself, one for her husband and one, God forbid, for
young Hürü.

"Why so pessimistic?" Hürü said.

"Arab custom," Shahrazad said, shrugging. "Besides, I've never
been on a trip before. Who knows. Maybe some traveller will have to
bury us. We'd better have our own grave linen."

Shahriyar rode up with a small escort, provisions and two
riderless Arab thoroughbreds, one chestnut and one black. Shahrazad, of course, would ride the dark horse. As Shahriyar offered to
give Hürü a leg up, she noticed the cleverly worked patch on his
black Abbasid robe. She was so touched, she accepted his assis-
tance. And she, too, felt like weeping as the two parents bid their
four little daughters farewell, remembering her own parent's departure—for good as it turned out. The four little girls sobbed on Big
Camphor's bosoms.

"Take care, Camphor," Shahrazad said. "And remember to summon Dunyazad if anybody gets sick. God bless you and keep you."

Joyless as a funeral procession, they set off towards Damascus.
On her part, Hürü considered, with some trepidation, the meeting
with Selim. Her female guise might just move Selim's disposition to
chivalry, which if not real, was at least inspired by his taste for
chivalric romances. Besides, by this time, with all the glory that
crowned him now, you'd think Selim would no longer care about
getting even with the Bald Boy. She, too, must trust Selim's better
nature. After all, on this dangerous mission her friends from Baghdad
trusted her even though she was their historic enemy.

Reflecting on Shahrazad's apprehensions about the battle of the sexes, Hürü now decided that compassion must, of necessity, start with the female of the species. Shahrazad's life, fraught with both success and failure, was a shining example of self-creation. So why should she, Hürü, relegate Selim to history as the caricature of an Oriental potentate? She must woo Selim away from his misogyny as well as his misanthropy. Selim must not be allowed to live and die as a warlord who never really knew the value of human hope and despair. Someone must translate some miraculous burst of color into Selim's black and white world; someone must become his *discriminating* eyes. Clearly, Hürü had already elected herself for this task, though she had no clever stratagem for how to start something.

But how was she to save Shahriyar's life? Spare Shahriyar, she'd say to Selim, for this man supported a woman who wrote the book that crowns Baghdad's lost glory. Yes, she'd beg for Shahriyar's life, not as the father of the seven children who awaited him, but as the protector of literature. In all likelihood, Selim was, after all, interested in art.

They rode west across the desert lands of Badiet-esh-Sham, scorched by the sirocco that raised the sand and forced the travellers into mohair tents where they huddled, waiting for the storm to pass, and where, at night, water in the bladders formed ice crystals. Bitten by sand fleas, every orifice full of sand, Hürü could now understand why sedentary Arabs hated travel. It just wasn't any fun. In the morning, up again, under the pounding sun, they rode westwards.

As they thought themselves nearing Damascus, they realized it wasn't the wind that raised the sand in the distance but the multitudinous armies of Selim the Grim. The army moved like the wind. Undaunted by the venture across such an unfamiliar and inhospitable terrain, this great war machine moved with amazing speed once the drums sounded, never breaking step, never stopping, unified under one will in its perpetual readiness for battle. And, since heavy artillery wouldn't be necessary to take the ill-defended desert cities, Selim's armies could move lightly armed; in one night, they'd travel the distance that would take, say, Christian armies, three days and three nights.

As Shahriyar's group also moved forward, in the pale distance, Hürü made out the column of Selim's cavalry brigades winding around the dunes like a magnificent, flowing serpent.

"Good heavens!" Shahriyar exclaimed, squinting under the hand that shaded his eyes. "Is this a human army? Or is it the hosts of the infernal regions?"

He reasoned that Selim, obviously impatient in Damascus, was probably chafing to reach Baghdad, the plum that topped the sandy desert Selim was so anxious to wolf down. Careful now, Shahriyar had his standard unfurled and hoisted up a white flag for good measure. He urged his entourage to make haste; one must not make this fellow wait. And don't anybody say or do anything dumb!

When they met up with Selim's advance guard, whose role, as Hürü had been instructed once, was to open the country before a projected attack, Hürü couldn't resist resorting to her native tongue.

"Well met, good brother Akinji," she said to the captain, amazed how good the flow of language felt on her tongue. "How does the conquest go?"

"With sand in every crack, sister," the captain of the Akinjis said. "But the enemy is nothing but a nest of lice."

Hürü was glad Shahriyar didn't understand; hearing himself described as a louse might hurt Shahriyar's feelings. But Shahrazad, who was conversant in Turkish, groaned under her veil. It was surprising that Arab nobles, under the domination of their foreign rulers, had never bothered learning the official language. Shahriyar knew no more of the Turkish mind than what was directly translatable; he was ignorant of the cultural logic that springs from the relation of noun to verb. Selim, on the other hand, intimately knew the language, as well as the manners and superstitions of the peoples he meant to dominate, never underestimating the significance of the smallest sign. Shahrazad, too, never underestimated the secrets of language. Having been raised by a Turkish nanny, she'd heard the tales from Central Asia in the original versions and intuited the impulses that inspired the telling. Shahrazad, too, was a person who'd deliberately prepared herself for her fate.

Once explained Shahriyar's mission, the cavalry scouts escorted the travellers to the Sultan, who rode forefront, accompanied by the awesome music of the Mehter ensemble, the greatest, perhaps the first, marching band in the known world. European armies scattered like fledgling birds before the sound.

"Good heavens!" Shahriyar said once again. "That music does strike terror in a man's heart. Poor old Al-Ghawri didn't stand a beggar's chance! Thank God, one is under no obligation to fight against this! I'd have a stroke at my age."

Hürü's heart too was in her throat with anticipation and also with a strange sort of pride. Even nostalgia. Before Shahrazad veiled herself tightly, Hürü noticed the great lady's pallor had increased at the sight of Selim's she-wolf, who lunged at once, recognizing Hürü's smell without, however, showing any affection. Hürü's horse, terrified of the wolfish sniffling at his genitals, reared. Hürü hung on the shivering nag's neck, making clicking sounds to calm both animals. Finally, the wolf sat on her haunches and minded her manners.

"There's a good girl!" Hürü lied to the wolf.

"Ho!" Selim cried, bringing his foamy white stallion to a stand-still.

The legions behind Selim halted abruptly as if ten thousand troops were one muscle. In the discipline of the silence that fell over the desert, you could hear the grains of sand shift. Now that the she-wolf had drawn Selim's gaze to her, Hürü was being intently studied by those predatory gray eyes whose focus couldn't be discerned.

"Why, my Lady!" Selim gasped. "It's you!"

"That's right," Hürü said.

The Sultan sprang off his mount, making Shahriyar follow suit with the haste of a falling rock. Selim advanced to Hürü's side, holding out his hand so she might use it to dismount. But Hürü wasn't going to step into any Sultan's hand; she leaned forward in the saddle and pumped instead Selim's outstretched hand.

"And these," she said in Arabic, "are my good benefactors, Shahriyar and Shahrazad of Baghdad. They've come all this way to present you the keys to the city."

"Fine," Selim said, nodding to the royal pair. "Now, we won't have to waste our time on Baghdad. We will proceed at once to Jerusalem. But," he went on, switching to Turkish, "first I will bed you, elusive Lady."

"No wed," Hürü said, "no bed."

"So, I will proclaim the banns," he said.

"Marry you?" Hürü said. "In a place like this?"

"They say," Selim said, "for the lover, the desert is Baghdad."

"The same people advise against mentioning Baghdad to the lover."

"We will restore Baghdad, then, so no lover need weep any-more."

"No lover ever wept," Hürü said, "because Baghdad is in ruins."

"Why then?" Selim said, enjoying himself tremendously.

"You know very well why," she said. "Love is ruinous."

"Not mine!" Selim said, confident now. "My love was inspired from Heaven. I was sent your image as I tasted the water of a salty lagoon in the woods. As your face shimmered in the ripples, I thought you must be my demon love; you disappeared from my sight, tempting me to quest after you. But, at the time, I couldn't abandon myself to the salt taste of love. Still, your image remained with me, bringing flavor to the blandness of routine. So, imagine my joy in finding you in the desert, not only a daughter of man but also a gentlewoman of my own race."

So, it wasn't the Bald Boy Selim recognized in Hürü; he recognized an idea in his own head, that of the perfect woman whose formalized beauty he'd embossed on a piece of gold which, even now, chafed Hürü's heel. No one should be so unlucky as to be someone's idea of perfection.

"What makes you think I'll accept you?" Hürü said. "I might already be married. Have you considered that?"

"Are you?" Selim asked, his countenance clouding immediately. "For your troth's sake, I hope not! I will not be thwarted!"

"See?" Hürü said. "How quick you are to threaten! If you loved me the way you say, inspired from Heaven and all that, would you think of harming someone to whom I've made a promise before God?"

"Well," Selim said, "the troops wait. Are you married?"

"As a matter of fact," Hürü said, "I am."

"This is turning into an ordeal," Selim said. "And I don't much care for ordeals of love. Who's the louse you married?"

"My beautiful wife," Hürü said, "joined the majority some five centuries ago. I'm what you call a historical widower."

"You like to joke, I see," Selim said, laughing unconvincingly. "I like humor in a woman, turns out."

"But I'm not putting you on," Hürü said, slipping off one boot. "Let me show you my wife's likeness which I carry in the lining of my boot. Here. Not only was my wife a king, she was a great beauty."

"That's mine!" Selim cried, snatching the amulet. "My lady."

"Not so," Hürü said. "She was my wife."

"But I made her!" Selim said. "And lost her."

"But I married her," Hürü insisted. "Isn't that a kick in the head? But then, that's life for you!"

"I give up," Selim said, handing back the amulet. "You must've married yourself. There's no other explanation."

Shahriyar, who didn't get a word, shifted from foot to foot. But Shahrazad had thrown open her veil; her luminous eyes studied the verbal duel, delighted with the revelations of time budding, flowering and ready to bear fruit—Shahrazad's presence might yet make things come out all right. Maybe writing was magic. Maybe Shahrazad could move the very constellations in the interests of love, constancy, truth. Left to Hürü, love might just bleach out whiter in the desert than a horny skull. Hürü could easily sacrifice Selim's intentions, as she baited him now, with a shocking failure of humanity. How to surmount the corruption of the moment? One cruel and cold child asks another cold and cruel child: Will you marry me? Someone must take the moment out of the children's hands and save them from taunting love away, slap for slap, lie for lie.

Selim, too, seemed to feel the magnetism that pulled him to the lady who sat on a dark horse, her veil thrown off her pale face, her melancholic brown eyes lit with intelligence. He walked up to Shahrazad and placed his forehead on her saddle like one in supplication.

"Intercede for me, Lady Shahrazad," he said. "I can't win the cruel girl on my own."

"Yet they call you Selim the Grim," Shahrazad said.

"Yes," Selim said, hanging his head.

"To match you," Shahrazad went on, "Hürü has to be twice as grim."

"Hürü?" Selim said, the name dawning on him. "Hürü!" he called out. "Hürü," he whispered.

"Here I am," she said, "Sleeping Prince."

"I won't ask you questions, Hürü," Selim said, suddenly breaking into purple flowery Persian, "neither your name nor your mouth, nor stern wit are Hers whose reflection fell into the lagoon. My lips on Her cold, briny mouth, I neither knew Her from before nor felt Her rise again in my dreams. Yet, She was real. She was real. Perhaps, sceptered and crowned, she lived long ago and surfaced as one who has died of the secret between you and I, Hürü, of a promise made before we were born, a promise of Hers who touched us both, the memory of Her eyes that we both met, Her lips we both kissed, Her name we both never knew. She became You. And You became Her.

"I will wait for you to speak," he went on. "If you keep silent, I'll abide by your choice. If you want to break my heart, it's yours; break it! I'll take my soldiers and go, without hindering you or your friends. If you wed me, I will be steadfast, without dishonoring the promises you yourself have made. This I swear by God and my honor as the Sultan of the Ottomans, even though you will, I know, prove a difficult wife. I will hazard my manhood, my sovereignty, my life. My body and my fame, my heart and my goods, they're yours to treat or to mistreat, to save or to squander, to have, to hold, to affect as you will as long as I live and even after death."

"Don't disappoint me now, Hürü!" Shahrazad cried. "Match him!"

"I can't match his pretty speech," Hürü said. "I'm only a dumb musician. But I can match his ardor! Selim!" she cried, "I will have you for my husband, come hell or high water."

"Mostly high water, then!" Selim said, back in Turkish, guffawing. "Because I promise to flood you with more spunk than Noah ever sailed on, more seed than womankind ever received or their men spilled, more semination than God intended or the saints believed. I will have you panting in oceans of sperm!"

"And I'll take all," Hürü said, "and ask for more."

"Quick!" Selim cried to his aides. "Get the clergy before I die of surfeit!"

Chapter 19

HONEYMOON AND BETRAYAL

Selim cannot be housebroken,
Shahrazad is not to be trusted

Shahrazad and Shahriyar accompanied the newlyweds to Jerusalem. Then to Bethlehem and the Gaza. The land of the prophets, which had swallowed up centuries of Crusaders, was now Selim's for the asking. Everywhere, open and decorated towns yielded Selim the role of the Deliverer from the hated Mamluks. And he fit the part of the Deliverer, not only because his true wife rode with him now, but because his fury, which had devoured Persia, had miraculously abated. Historically speaking, Selim proved true to the promise he made Hürü: You win, I'll go easy on the Arabs. No more senseless killing.

In every way, Sultan Selim cut a benign figure on his long-maned, milk-white stallion. In Jerusalem, he made a pilgrimage to the tombs of the Jewish prophets and to the Rock of Abraham. What's more, the awe Selim felt on his pilgrimage was so sincere, even the local Jews couldn't help being drawn to him. Treating Arab princes only as nominal vassals, he begged them, for his own sake, to free those incarcerated and to stop the trade in Circassian slaves. It behooves us good Moslems, he told them, to show tolerance towards the Jews and the Christians.

"Let's open up the Holy Lands to all pilgrims," he suggested to the sheiks. "What do you say? If the Holy Lands belong to all the peoples of the Book, we can't very well stand between the seekers and the sought, can we now? Let's show the world our compassion."

That's how Selim accomplished the reduction of taxes, tariffs and fees for the pilgrims to Jerusalem. He interceded on behalf of the friendless, the neglected, the sick and the aged, the disenfranchised, the disappointed, the unlovable. Nowhere had the Arabs seen a sweeter conqueror than Selim the Resolute. That's right! Not Grim. Resolute.

All wasn't quite as friendly as it seemed, however. One disgruntled and disenfranchised man travelled with Selim. His name was Shahriyar. Selim, whose predatory eyes never missed anything, appreciated Shahriyar's disappointment. But he made no effort to alleviate the man's unhappiness. Selim liked someone around who could be taunted. Taunting Shahriyar made Selim's day.

Was it so unreasonable for Selim to become Shahriyar's true friend? It wasn't, but it didn't happen. Selim immediately appointed a blood Turk the Viceroy of Araby, a prince called Tuman. Shahriyar wasn't even consulted. Selim placed great value on Shahrazad, but her husband he took lightly, as if Shahriyar were an oaf to be tolerated only because he came with the unusually talented lady. He refused to see the true nature of Shahriyar: a good manager of a dynasty, a state, a culture. He had already proved how well he husbanded meager resources, the way he took care of Baghdad with thrift and wisdom. But he had no flamboyance, and Selim liked style, arrogance and temerity.

So, Selim embarrassed Shahriyar. He interrupted Shahriyar's observations in mid-sentence by the mention of something trivial. He ordered Shahriyar around in the presence of other Arab princes. He treated the man without protocol, as if Shahriyar were his Bald Boy. He praised the man's wife too much.

Hürü supposed that Selim was testing Shahriyar's mettle. But Shahriyar was not someone who performed on cue. He prized himself on thinking for himself and hated to act according to someone else's expectations. Shahriyar knew Selim thought him an asshole. And he didn't like it. Hürü cautioned Selim: why make Shahriyar feel so powerless?

"Because I hate assholes who are enfranchised," Selim said. "Guys like Shahriyar take things for granted just because they're well-born and well connected. Complacent bastard! Let the Asshole work his way up, if he can. I don't think he can."

There must be a way of allowing Shahriyar to discharge himself honorably. If Selim respected only those who had the effrontery to tell him off, and since Shahriyar couldn't come through with a Bald Boy act of his own, then Shahriyar wasn't worth considering for the job as the Viceroy of Araby. Yes, Selim knew about Shahriyar's secret ambition; he thought it very funny.

"I'd appoint your wife Viceroy in a' minute, Shahriyar," Selim said, laughing uproariously. "But she won't take the job."

They were in Acre, spending a few days at a local prince's summer palace on the ocean. Selim didn't know how to enjoy himself at the seaside—except by making everybody miserable. Hürü felt as if she'd been hit on the head with a frying pan.

Shahrazad, protected by her work, would escape to a quiet room, where she was writing the sequence of Prince Kamar-ez-Zaman of Persia and Princess Budur of China. It was a fairy tale about a marriage made in heaven with all the romantic trappings: the Persian Prince falls in love with the image of a princess who looks enough like him to be his twin.

Hürü went into the royal suite to wrest with Shahrazad's strange tale. Lying down in the darkened bedroom, she heard Selim down in the courtyard, inviting Shahriyar to a wild-boar chase.

"No, thanks," Shahriyar said petulantly. "I don't feel any compulsion to spill blood."

"Well, now!" Selim taunted. "What do you have against manly sport, Shahriyar? Or can it be that you're afraid of the wild boar?"

"Wait for me!" Hürü heard Shahrazad say. "I'm coming along."

There goes Shahrazad! Hürü thought. She's drawing Selim's attention away from her husband. How well she performs the sleight-of-hand, in life as well as in fiction. And on the hunt Shahrazad would insult Selim to his spurious heart's content, further captivating Selim with her mysterious power over language.

The unemployed Caliph stayed on the beach where he was teaching himself how to swim. In dealing with Selim's insults, his only right was to protest. Shahriyar took criticism to heart: if he were disapproved of, then Selim must be right in disapproving.

Watching him dog-paddle, getting nowhere in the vastness of the Mediterranean Sea, Hürü's heart broke for him in sympathy and recognition. Shahriyar, too, wanted to make an exit. But he had no place to go. He couldn't even go to jail. Or get his head chopped off. He was, in a curious way, Selim's guest in this world. And Shahriyar's energies were sapped resisting Selim, so as not to be annexed under his personal hegemony. His realm had been annexed politically. He'd rather have Selim's trust—one king to another—but Selim didn't trust him because he didn't consider him his equal. Hürü felt she was exactly in the same place with Selim as was Shahriyar. She had been annexed, too, and she didn't like it a bit.

Only a couple of days earlier, when handing out further appointments to all kinds of Arab sheiks, with a bunch of greasy lowbrows in attendance, Selim had offered Shahriyar the office of Warden at Baghdad Municipal Jail.

"Us bad guys," Selim commented to Shahriyar as the latter winced, "set the tone in this world's jailhouses. But it's you good guys, Shahriyar, who maintain the system. You keep those who defy Our authority locked up."

"With your permission, my Lord," said Shahriyar, employing good manners that are designed to deal with situations like this, and kissing the hem of Selim's robe, "I'd beg off. My Lord, I'd rather not ever see Baghdad again than be Baghdad's jailkeeper."

Tell Selim off but good! Hürü thought. Spit in his eye! That's what he likes! She was about to say something scathing on Shahriyar's behalf. But she noticed Shahrazad's face, grim and white. She signaled Hürü to hold her tongue: Don't fight Shahriyar's battles for him, for God's sake! Leave him alone! So Hürü said nothing until she was in the bedroom with Selim.

"The man's a dullard!" Selim roared. "He's a blight on that clever lady's life."

"I wish poor Shahriyar were someplace else," Hürü said. "I wish we all were."

"So why doesn't he strike out on his own?" Selim wanted to know. "What does the fool wait for? For the axe to fall?"

God knows the husband and wife tried to leave. But Selim wouldn't let Shahrazad go—not before he could absorb into his own existence the essence of Shahrazad's nature which so impressed and baffled him. How could a mere woman persevere so with her own occupation? Why was Shahrazad so complete in herself? Selim must know. He must devour Shahrazad so that he could absorb her. That was Selim's way. He had to devour what he needed to know. The way he did with Persia—a country that also baffled and impressed him.

Selim's terms were quite clear: there was one way of learning a woman: he must have her.

"Besides," he confided to his new wife, "I like Shahrazad's tits. So pointed. At her age, too! Look here, Hürü girl, you arrange a threesome for us. And you've got yourself a great time in the sack!"

"She doesn't even like you!" Hürü said, shocked and hurt.

"She would like this!" Selim said shamelessly, pointing to the hard-on towering in his groin. "I'd enter her through the back door, if you get my meaning. Bet you that's how she likes it too. I'd bugger her like the man she really is!"

Maybe he thought if he were vulgar enough, he could chase her away. Maybe he wanted Hürü to make tracks, too. And he insulted her and insulted her because she failed to understand? Maybe she was not supposed to survive her nuptial night—was that it? But why? When Selim held her in bed he still quivered with emotion. He murmured in her ear that he'd waited for her all his life. He called her his arm-melter, his cock-coddler, his sweet ball-banger. Her cunt was manna, her mouth honey, her saliva the spring of Paradise. He could stay in her for all eternity. Sometimes Hürü fell asleep as she sat at the dinner table with food in her mouth, he exercised her that hard in bed. Then he would lift her in his great arms, put her in bed and tell her he was bound to her as she was bonded to him. They were husband and wife, but also blood-brothers. And when he made her weep, he kissed away her tears. "Don't fret, my darling, Selim is here. Don't you fret, my sweet."

Yet, he numbed her with his inconsistencies. His will to wound reared up suddenly and with great violence. Was Selim trying to show his new wife she must not put such implicit trust in matrimony? Did he want to set her free of the conventions of marital love. Or what?

How could he involve Hürü in his hankering for Shahrazad? Did he wish to kill the love between the two women? That was Selim, all right. And Shahrazad? Would she take Selim on? Naah! Not Shahrazad.

Hürü remembered she had held back only a piece of her heart from Shahrazad: she'd never admitted to having always been in love with Selim. Inexplicably, shamelessly, inexorably. She was bonded to him.

So Shahrazad didn't know Hürü had married Selim for real. She still thought Hürü had married Selim to help them save Baghdad. As if Hürü would make a gift of her life for any cause, let alone Baghdad's. Did Shahrazad think Hürü a whore? One who would sell her integrity? Perhaps she should tell her friend the truth. But it was embarrassing, in front of Shahrazad, to admit to being in love with a man like Selim. It was so . . . what could she say? . . . so stupidly woman. Instead, Hürü kept up the masquerade. She was still the insouciant boy-girl who extracted from her older husband the price of his passion for her youth. Shahrazad, who was of the same generation as Selim, thought she understood the appeal of Hürü's innocence.

"Poor Selim," Shahrazad said archly. "He's at an age when one yearns for a rose-petal-filled bower, dandling a boy-lover to transport him to Paradise and back. Of course, it never works out in reality. Believe me, I know. I've tried it, too."

So, Hürü put off telling the smart lady the truth. She couldn't very well confess to being desperately in love with a man who'd reached his midlife crisis.

At night, she dreamed Selim was dead. A premonition. As if she'd known in the dream Selim had been dead for a long time. Waking up, she lit a candle to make sure Selim lived. His sleeping face inspired such unwarranted tenderness! Just the pleasure of seeing his smooth-shaved cheeks! His long moustache drooping on the pillow!

Yet, after breakfast, he quickly managed to alienate her again. He first demanded of Shahrazad that she let him see the story of Prince Kamar-ez-Zaman and Princess Budur, which she had just finished. As he read Shahrazad's new work, the extremely complex fairy tale, he dipped his quill in ink to correct the occasional spelling error. How dare he! Even if it meant proofing copy, he had to control everything. He must even boss over the realm of a fairy tale. He must be responsible for all events, make them his own . . . such as the two Queens in the story who fall in love with their half-sons.

"Tell you what," Selim offered Shahrazad. "I'm willing to give both you and Hürü a son each. When the boys reach an age when they can get their cocks up, you two rape each other's sons. How about it? I wouldn't mind at all. You two can go ahead and enjoy the boys to the hilt."

"Cynicism," Shahrazad said coolly, "is the opiate of the emotionally dead."

"What's your cunt like?" Selim said, sizing her up. "Does it have big sails? Bet it does! Virtual widows like you often go to sail, I know. You beat the meat too much. Right?"

Shahrazad blinked rapidly several times before she regained her composure.

"I see," she said, "that you try to be rude. But I am not offended. In fact, I like it rude. Still, you don't come up to my standards. You aren't rude enough. So, if it's not too much effort to think, what did you think of my story?"

"Uneven," Selim said, yawning crassly. "Which is to say a woman wrote it."

"Then why did you want to read it?" Shahrazad said, "knowing, as you did, that it would be 'uneven.'"

"Oh, I thought I'd find some juicy information about you," Selim said. "And I've found you out, Shahrazad. How long have you been a Lesbo? And how often do you molest your sons? O-ho, blushing, eh? I found out what I wanted, so I don't have to read the rest."

"Perhaps," Shahrazad suggested, "your attention span is too short . . . as is your you-know-what!"

"Mine is at least a span long," Selim said, tugging at his fly. "Want to see him? You won't be frightened too much, will you? I know you're used to a three-inch fool."

"Cut it out!" Shahrazad cried, leaving the room.

Hopeless, that's what it seemed to Hürü. The pursuit of the Sweet Life in the manner of gentlepersons, this art of living graciously at the seaside, remained an art far out of reach. Whatever the requirements of gentleness, the essence of such a life couldn't even be approached with an animal like Selim around. Shahrazad's Genius from the Future didn't put in an appearance to teach everyone how to conduct himself. Besides, Hürü felt poorly. She couldn't keep food down, especially breakfast. Something was poisoning her from the inside. Something was conspiring to kill her before Selim called in the executioner. Should she resist death? Or comply? And whose story was this, after all? If it were Hürü's story, then why was she running after Selim in order to transform him? Hürü was the heroine to be transformed, not the skeleton strewn on Selim's way.

She confessed to Shahrazad that she wasn't long for this world. Perhaps Selim was having slow poison administered into her food. Or, perhaps, the nature of the sickness arose out of an existential dread. Whatever it was that ailed her, Hürü was expiring from the dry heaves.

"You're pregnant," Shahrazad said. "That beast knocked you up, I'm afraid. No mysterious ailment. And the first few months can be fierce."

"But I thought," Hürü said, "pregnancy was a state natural to women. I'm revolted all the time."

"And losing weight," Shahrazad said. "My poor baby, I wish I could take you to Baghdad for your confinement. At least there you wouldn't have to put up with Selim's ravenous assaults."

But I want his ravenous assaults, Hürü thought; I just wish I weren't pregnant so I could take more. But she said nothing. Instead, she intimated to Selim that she carried his baby.

"So what?" Selim wanted to know.

Hürü had never thought she'd hurt so much in her whole lifetime.

About an hour's walk from the summer palace, in the hills beyond the beach, there was a cedar forest in which was nestled a one-eyed tower. Perhaps an old windmill. Perhaps a watchtower left from the Crusaders. Hürü thought there might be a very fine view from up there: that's why, without Selim's permission, she had walked out to the tower. Here was a place to do some reflecting, a vantage point to view the world around her and her life.

Some stone steps up to the battlement on top of the tower were broken and missing and there was a decaying stench everywhere. Seemed like people never came in the tower—except to relieve themselves. But once out on top, the world receded and a golden shower of light, made clearer by the cedar freshness of the woods, came rushing in. Being so high was like dreaming an interior landscape. The blue of the Mediterranean joined with the blue of the sky, and air and water became one continuous material. The buzzing of a fly was a key that opened the meaning of life. These ancient lands! Time seemed to open its navel here and offer up all of eternity.

Hürü took off her richly bejeweled turban. She shook her red-gold hair loose. Her hair had grown long enough to play freely about her neck. Selim would never see her as she was now, hair on fire under the brilliance of the sun. That color-blind Selim! Here I am, Hürü thought, on my honeymoon. And I am not free to give myself up to love. I must go away. I must vanish as if the earth had opened and swallowed me.

A doe walked out of the woods and gracefully bent down to drink from a little stream. Beside the stream was a carved stone seat, ancient and weatherworn. The tranquility of this scene made Hürü feel she'd walked into a storybook so golden that happiness would certainly find its way into the ending. Suddenly the doe took fright and hurtled deep into the woods. Then Hürü heard the sound of horse hooves up the forest path. Before long, a pair of galloping steeds came to view and the riders stopped abruptly by the stone seat below. Hürü drew back. The two riders were none other than Selim and Shahrazad.

Now, what were those two doing up here? Maybe they, too, wanted to look at the view. Hürü should make her presence known before they came up the steps, and she would have rushed to the parapet and cried out and waved had she not heard the very tone of *intimacy* in Shahrazad's laughter. A tidal wave of jealousy suddenly rose in her heart. Unable to resist the demands of that awful feeling of wounded possessiveness, she stuck her head up between the battlements to spy on the two with whom she was in love.

Selim had already dismounted. He held up his arms so Shahrazad might slip in them down to the ground. But once he seized Shahrazad by the waist, slowly and sensuously he guided her lithe body against his face, and, for what seemed an eternity, sniffed her crotch, then he buried his face in her bosom, and then slowly he slipped her body against the length of his hard body until Shahrazad's feet gracefully rested on the ground. The gentleness of the motion, and the sexual power it exerted, took away Hürü's breath. My God! Hürü thought: they're courting!

The lovers stood briefly against each other. To gaze in Selim's mad gray eyes, Shahrazad, who was at least a foot shorter than Selim, had her head thrown back, her dark hair cascading down her back in wild waves. When Hürü stood so against Selim, her eyes would be in direct line with his mouth and her hipbone right up against his hipbone, since Hürü was, for a woman, so tall and her legs so long. Hürü had always thought she was well matched with Selim . . . she could take all he gave, his awesome length and thickness. Could Shahrazad? Another wave of jealousy rose into nauseating heights.

Releasing Shahrazad, Selim went back to his white stallion. Out of the saddlebags, he pulled a picnic lunch. Wine, bread, a roasted fowl, grapes. A light picnic lunch. Here was a monarch who didn't want to eat too much, for obvious reasons. He spread a cover on the green sward beside the stream. And he turned to hold his hand out to Shahrazad. His gesture was that of a shy swain.

"Come," said he. "We have to do this right. Just because we've had to wait so long for this appointment, it doesn't meant we have to hurry now. I want you always to remember this peak, Shahrazad. Passion between equals must, of necessity, be contemplative. And tranquil."

"You are such a sentimentalist, Selim," Shahrazad said, flirting. "But then, so are most of you tough guys."

"I've been aching for you, Shahrazad," Selim said. "Like in stories. You just ache for the hero to get into the heroine, don't you? But something always prevents it. Then, when they finally make it, you get a hard-on just from reading. That's the kind of story I like. Passion between people who want each other so much."

"So, let's go," Shahrazad said. "Please, Selim. Already I'm so greedy for you, I must have you at once."

"No, not so quick," Selim said. "I won't take you fast. I will give you sweet ecstasy, so gentle and measured, you will remember. And when you write about it, and I know you will, your readers will always be moist and ready to be taken, forever and ever. Everytime someone reads about this fuck, I will be eternally making love to Shahrazad."

So! Hürü thought. Selim wants his mantool celebrated in literature! The vanity of this man! Passion between equals, eh? Well, good for them! She would have liked to get away, but it was too late, now that Selim sat facing the door to the one-eyed tower. But Hürü couldn't be privy to the rest of what was to follow, not without doing herself irreparable damage. So she withdrew inside, into the stone stairway, and sat down on a worn step. She put her fists over her ears and shut her eyes tight. She wished she could stop breathing as well. But she couldn't. In the one-eyed tower, the stench of shit was like a physical blow. Then, inexplicably, she fell into a merciful sleep, and woke up feeling refreshed.

When she dared look down the parapet again, the afternoon sun had dipped toward the horizon. The Mediterranean was brilliantly embroidered with sequins of light on the gentle afternoon ripples. What an amazing setting! As if it had all been staged for Hürü's benefit—so she might learn from her vantage point the strange and terrible unfolding of destiny. She felt like a tutelary deity, hovering over a pair of lovers. Somehow, during the merciful nap in the heavy stench of excrement, it seemed that some divine power had elevated her above her own miserable situation.

Looking around, she thought she recognized the person of her guardian, the Green Old Man, in the form of a majestic cedar that grew slightly leaning toward the tower. Though she didn't remember the tree being so close to the tower, this was indeed the sort of spot the Green Old Man liked hanging about.

"Come on out," she whispered. "I see you, Old Man."

Nothing. The cedar just stood there, dumb as a tree. Perhaps, Hürü thought, I'm past the age of magic. Fabulous demesnes are now closed to me, or else my eyes no longer perceive the marvelous. No longer a child, in me I carry a child.

Yet, without a doubt, she had been changed in her sleep. As if the jealousy in her breast had been arrested, neutralized and then resolved. Who else but the Green Old Man could have guided her to her release from knee-jerk possessiveness. Yes, Selim was compulsive, and of course, he'd be compelled to get Shahrazad. And Shahrazad, equally curious as he, saw no virtue in denying her desires. The two were well-matched because they were made of the same stuff that makes monarchs. So this tryst, as if prearranged from the very beginning, was inevitable.

That the inevitable had happened did not make Hürü feel less a woman or person. Clearly, Hürü had two choices. She could join the fallen world of vanity: jealousy, malice and revenge. Or wake up refreshed. In her sleep, she'd chosen the latter. But this didn't seem like a dream. For here she was, wide awake to the utter truth of herself, in a one-eyed tower where the smell of the fallen world was so strong.

It was as if she'd been bidden to remain innocent. As if someone were cheering her on. Even as she triumphed over her wifely pride, without tears, it was as if she were being supplied with strength from inside . . . Of course! Someone was present who wanted her to remain steadfast, clear and fair: the magic child she carried under her heart. Her son. She owed him her innocence. She would not break away from the source of eternal Love.

Below, the picnic lunch eaten, the love-making done, the pair of equals were fast asleep under a silken coverlet of royal purple. Obviously, they had not come here to betray Hürü. They'd come to douse the fire that had raged between them—these two matched opponents. They'd made war and then made peace. So predictable, if you looked upon them from the elevation of the tower. They'd merely taken care of pending business. Yet, these two formidable personages of history had no more choice about mating than a pair of rutting beasts. Only Hürü, young nobody, had been blessed with a choice.

Well, Hürü thought, now is the time to get away unseen: and she ran down the one-eyed tower, down the forest path and towards the summer palace. When she entered the courtyard all out of breath, she was sorry to see Shahriyar reading by the fountain. She couldn't bear to look him straight in the eye. Maybe she could sneak into the royal suite without attracting his attention. But poor Shahriyar seemed to have been waiting to pounce on Hürü.

"You know, don't you," he said gruffly, "your husband's planking my wife."

"Shahriyar!" Hürü cried. "You are indeed an unfortunate man! Nobody needs you to reveal an open secret. It's in bad taste, and redundant besides."

"Then wear your horns in good health!"

"You too!" Hürü spat.

News arrived from Cairo that Prince Tuman, who enjoyed the job Shahriyar so much wanted, had declared himself independent. Thumbing his nose at Selim who was busy honeymooning on the seashore, Prince Tuman had declared himself the new Mamluk Sultan and successor to Al-Ghawri, as if Selim had not already broken that succession.

Well, Selim must go about his father's business. His job was to rout defiance and rebellion. Besides, he was awfully good at crushing rivals, in fact, second to none in all of history. Selim chortled that Tuman had grown too big, too fast, for his breeches. Good thing Tuman was making such a nuisance of himself. This would be a splendid opportunity to trample the grass that had begun to grow under his feet. Besides, Selim was not unaware that his honeymoon fell short of the mark.

His troops, too, had been aching to sack Araby, which they considered battle booty of which, so far, they'd been cheated. In the name of compassion and brotherhood with the Arab nations. Hooey! Everyone knew Arabs were incapable of fidelity and brotherhood. If they wanted to go along with Prince Tuman, good! Let the bastards enjoy what was coming to them.

As Selim once more set his armies in motion, as he activated his bards and historians, readied his troops of Janissaries, hired his polyglot irregulars, his mute executioners, his advance guards who were truly insane and ruthlessly fearless, the household also sighed a sigh of relief: Thank God, he's going—before something really goes wrong.

"Your condition," Selim told Hürü, "is too delicate for you to follow camp. Best you go back to Baghdad with your friends."

"Fine," Hürü said.

"What? No tears? No remonstrations? No clutching and kissing?"

"Nope," Hürü said. "No promises neither."

That's how Selim consigned Hürü to the care of the couple from Baghdad. Just to insult everybody, he promised Shahriyar material reward, maybe even a throne. Who knew. Maybe a kingdom out west: Hungary, Serbia. Even Greece. All were Selim's to bestow on whatever rascal Selim chose.

"You might like to lord it over some shepherd nation, Shahriyar," he said. "I know for a fact Shahrazad would benefit from a change of scenery. She's a great broad. But this desert climate leaches her sap, you know. I'd like to see her Queen of Hungary, for example. She'd show a thing or two to the so-called aristocracy there. Did you know that grandees in Hungary still pick their noses in public? And they never bathe, either."

"We don't need any rewards, my Lord," Shahriyar said politely. "Your friendship is reward enough."

Yeah, yeah. But, Selim would like to make a gift of Hungary to Shahrazad. He searched Shahrazad's face for the effect of his promises. Of course, everyone present was onto Selim. He might remember Shahrazad tomorrow. But then, he might not. He might make her the richest woman in the realm. Or have her head cut off. Still, at this particular moment, he seemed to need some kind of concession from Shahrazad, some sign of complicit recognition. But the Storyteller from Baghdad kept her face closed, conceding nothing to Selim the Grim.

So, Selim promised he'd be in Baghdad quicker than the Angel of Death. Don't anyone fret. And, even before the prayers for his speedy victory were done at the Grand Mosque, Selim headed his armies across the Sinai into Egypt. Watching him rush off for the land of the Pyramids, Hürü felt purged, but also inconsolable. Selim, too, must know that the only good widow is a war widow. If Selim survived his war, Hürü didn't think he'd ever look her up in Baghdad.

Growth and change might enhance the values humans hold dear, enlarging and giving solace along the difficult road of experience, but there was something purifying in the pain of failure. Hürü's hope for a future with Selim was bleached out on the desert like the horned skull of an animal: pure, white and dry.

Part Four

FREEDOM TO LIVE

Facing the terrible and
wonderful music of the world

Chapter 20

GESTATION
AND GERMINATION

*Life and work go on
in womanhouse, Baghdad*

The old mansion in downtown Baghdad became the site of much domesticity. At first, Big Camphor fussed over Shahriyar, pleased to have a man around again for whom to cook big meals, a fine custom so long neglected by the mistress of the house. But when he moved in on the huge kitchen, Camphor didn't like one bit sharing her realm.

"Glugh! Glugh!" she scolded her ex-king, mopping up madly.

"Damn it, woman!" Shahriyar cried. "Let a man be!"

Shahriyar was engrossed in his first project in wood: a writing table for Shahrazad, replete with many compartments, sliding surfaces, built-in grooves for her quills, her inkwell, shelves for her reference books, a book-holder for reading without losing the place and pretty carvings for Shahrazad to contemplate when she took her eyes off the page. He didn't start from scratch. Instead, he found several broken-down pieces of furniture, and other odd ends of wood already fashioned, and he married disparate styles and woods together into a new idea, a novel idea. This was a *desk* for sitting at—in a *chair*. Hunched over a low table, her legs crossed under her, Shahrazad's blood must go to sleep, he observed; wouldn't it be better to devise a way to make herself more comfortable as well as smarter by improving the circulation? The notion of a chair was inspired by the campstool that travelled with Selim on his campaigns so he might stretch his legs as he studied maps and recorded in his war-diary the exact course of action. One didn't need a throne to sit on, Shahriyar reasoned; one could, just as well, sit in a chair.

"I wouldn't know where to start with virgin wood," he said, lovingly stroking the various grains. "Too much freedom there for a beginner."

Shahrazad appreciated Shahriyar's retirement, a state, she said, he'd somehow been preparing for all his life. Never was there a man more suited to being kicked out of office. Shahriyar fairly hummed as he rubbed his wood into a soft glow, as he experimented with resins and thanked God often he no longer had to enact another piece of legislation. Yet, money was tight in the household, now that both husband and wife worked furiously but produced no income. Without their boarder, Hürü, who kicked in a generous share, they couldn't have made ends meet.

"When she and I," Shahriyar said, "will end up looking exactly alike."

Besides, there were all the children to educate. Shahriyar confessed he'd rather wander the world, though he'd settle for a workshop of his own, properly fitted out with good tools. His former self stalked him in Baghdad. Oh, to wander in places where he had no history.

"That's what I'd really like," he said. "I'm a runaway at heart."

But, he sighed, running away was just not possible. He was a man who took refuge in his formerly spurned wife's house, having to be grateful to the house-ogres for a corner in the kitchen, however ungraciously yielded. No, he wasn't asking for sympathy, either. So, don't anybody say or do anything condescending. You, too, Camphor, you better hold your tongue!

"But I can lend you the travel money, Shahriyar," Hürü said, bringing out the iron casket within which was much Ottoman gold, stamped with Selim's signature—Selim's idea of alimony.

"No," Shahriyar said. "Thanks, anyway."

Did Hürü think she could get rid of him as easily as all that? Besides, a man was entitled to his pipe dreams without some woman forcing on him the means to kill the dream by fulfilling it for real. And Hürü must husband her fortune, what with the baby coming any day now. He'd heard Selim was already back in Constantinople. But no sign of any hard-riding messengers arriving to invite Hürü to the fabled Palace of the Cannon Gate. No, he didn't want to be the in-house pessimist, but why should anyone get up and cheer because Selim got his own way, all the way?

News reached Baghdad that Selim, as he'd promised, had defeated Prince Tuman in two battles. Selim had the rebel's head still hanging at the city gates to impress the Cairenes with the price of defiance. Now, Selim owned the Standard and the Cloak of the Prophet, symbolizing his spiritual as well as political sovereignity over all Islam. Shahriyar wasn't impressed. Selim might claim what he liked, but he'd never be the True Caliph in the eyes of the Arabs who, when you came right down to it, owned Islam by virtue of their language. After all, it was Arabic that got a rise out of God. Did God communicate a single word to Selim in his native tongue? Not bloody likely! Shahriyar was sure that many minor gods had died trying to make sense of that impossible series of sounds called Turkish. Hürü must forgive him, but her mother-tongue sounded to Shahriyar like a chorus of animal noises. And Selim, too, would die, for all he cared, barking and braying, friendless, graceless, sick and old, illegitimate and brutal. No, there just wasn't anything to recommend Selim. The fact was that Selim was as wall-eyed as a pike.

"Not wall-eyed!" Hürü said in defense of her absent husband. "A *shah*'s gaze, that's what it's called, meaning a king's deep and mysteriously intent look."

"I do sympathize," Shahriyar commented. "To give up the exhilirating life of love is difficult."

Shahriyar, during his term as the highest official in the realm, must not have made any friends either. Wherever other highups also forced into early retirement hung out, none ever came to look up Shahriyar, to talk shop, to praise the good old days and denounce the new. Of course, he didn't exactly put out any invitations either, having boarded up the windows that overlooked the street, as if some natural calamity were expected.

"Keeps the house cooler," he said, to explain the barrier between himself and the citizenry. He began taking his meals in the kitchen.

Hürü, besides hearing the little girls' lessons, had committed herself to read Shahrazad's long book so that she might create original verses and songs for the text. Shahrazad felt Hürü's contribution would make all the difference between her version of the tales and Al-Masudi's. The time for recapturing the old tales out of thin air must be ripe, Shahrazad reasoned: the material freely floating for centuries, and altered according to the time, the place and the talents of the teller, hence forward would be locked up in Al-Masudi's and her versions, static and unalterable as to content, the written word. Al-Masudi called his version *One Thousand Nights*. Which version would survive? Well, Shahrazad's title seemed the more attractive package with its promise of extra pleasure: *The Thousand and One Nights*. One more night is all we ask for, she reflected, crowning perfection with pleasure.

"But don't knock yourself out laboring over the verses," Shahrazad cautioned Hūrū. "You're already very full up, which could mean hard labor."

But Hūrū felt robust, though heavy on the stairs. Camphor was very solicitous, preparing dark brews for her to drink, shooting baneful looks at Shahriyar, who made light of the ogress's medicine. Hūrū was obliged to taste teas concocted from the nastiest roots out of Africa, plus who knew what extracts of animal glands and assorted human parts. Big Camphor had remedies for everything, most of which didn't work, not only because the influences in the air opposed Camphor's art but because she had no speech through which to educate her patients as to the nature of the cure. Without words to stimulate the imagination, her craft lost much potency. But that didn't stop Big Camphor from trying.

It was discovered Camphor was slipping the excrement of a certain kind of African cobra into Shahriyar's food. An itinerant druggist hawking his mysterious wares showed up to make Camphor a delivery, explaining, at Shahriyar's insistence, the nature of the purchase. The dry snake turds came from a cobra which could shoot its venomous spit some six feet, thereby immobilizing its victim. Everyone in the house hoped Shahriyar hadn't been harmed by ingesting the stuff, which Camphor had been purchasing, of late, in larger quantities. Shahriyar thought it unconscionable that he supported the ogress's nasty experiments out of household expenses. As to why Camphor laced Shahriyar's sustenance with snake shit, that could not be understood, Camphor being unable to express the reasons why she did anything at all.

"Malicious black lardbag!" Shahriyar said. "She hates me."

"Maybe the remedy works through the rule of opposition,"

Shahrazad suggested. "If the cobra can immobilize with what comes out of his mouth, then what comes out the other end might mobilize. I think Camphor wants you to get a job."

"You don't know that!" Shahriyar exclaimed, scowling. "Yet, explanations just come shooting out of your mouth, aimed at your victim some distance away."

"Makes me a good storyteller," Shahrazad said, raising her eyebrows, "but a miserable wife."

"If you want me out of your house," he said, "just say so! No use us both being miserable."

"I didn't say that!"

"I'm sick of eating manure," Shahriyar said.

He abandoned Shahrazad's desk just as it was almost completed. He took up brooding instead. First he stripped the kitchen of his chisels, scrapers, resins, rottenstone, his planer, drill, hammer and saw; then he lowered the lot, carefully, down the well. He burned his memorabilia, his genealogical pedigrees, his marriage contract and looked around the house for other objects that betrayed his existence there. It was surprising, however, how little Shahriyar had actually accumulated during his administrative stay in Baghdad. Once he had disposed of his clothes, Shahriyar took to wrapping himself in a big white sheet, and sat listening to the termites devour the woodwork. He didn't notice Big Camphor burn myrrh all around him. From where he sat in his room without moving, he didn't even notice his little daughters include him in their games, decorating his unkempt beard with ribbons and beads. He was paying his dues to misery in a big way.

Hürü tried engaging Shahriyar in conversation, so he might not lose character, this man who, through his wife's efforts, would certainly become an immortal. But he wasn't having any. Impatient with his truculence, she told him that total irresponsibility towards those around him was neither appealing nor was it a method for saving one's soul. If one felt useless, the best solution was to admit one's uselessness and see what followed. Shahriyar didn't signal whether he heard the lecture or not, but rose from where he sat and, not bothering to clutch his sheet around him, peed on his bedroom wall. All of us want to impart a bit of wisdom to make someone snap out of a foolish enterprise, Hürü thought, but often our advice fails since it's easier to be wise than helpful. On the whole, it seemed more practical to leave Shahriyar alone.

So, Hürü went back to reading. In the stories, she found out how some of her friends and acquaintances from the past had ended up. The fate of Sweet, otherwise known as Bedr-ed-Din Hasan, came clear as a bell when the pompous young boy with whom Sweet had fallen strangely in love turned out to be none other than Sweet's own son, conceived during the single nuptial night Sweet spent in Cairo. Sweet wasn't the unnatural lover he feared he might be but the natural father, drawn, as Shahrazad put it in a winning formula, by the ties of blood. But Hürü still didn't understand why Sweet had taken such visceral offence when he learned Hürü was a Turk. Why had he booted her out of his sweet shop? In Shahrazad's telling, all traces of Hürü had been erased.

Looking through the text for other acquaintances, Hürü found her alter-self, the one known as Jaudar, had also fulfilled the good luck destined for him, but only for a short time. The Magi called Abd-es-Samad presented him with one of the four powerful talismans, the magic ring. Yet, the magic ring eventually became the death of Jaudar.

"But, whatever happened to Abd-es-Samad?" Hürü asked, tugging at Shahrazad's sleeve. "He was, in his repulsive way, very good to me. You don't mention how Abd-es-Samad dealt with the potent magic he acquired."

"Not Abd-es-Samad's story," Shahrazad said, shrugging.

This was, however, too important a detail to be shrugged off.

"Just imagine, can't you?" Hürü begged. "As if Abd-es-Samad were the real hero . . ."

"Let's see," Shahrazad said, scratching her nose. "Abd-es-Samad experiments with his Celestial Planisphere which can bring him images of far away lands and their inhabitants. He enjoys his farvision, or television, watching world events as he sits eating his lavish dinners.

"But he's dying to find out if the Celestial Planisphere also works as the ultimate weapon. He's not exactly a monster, so he chooses an uninhabited desert island in the Circumambient Oceans, and directs the Celestial Planisphere's destructive energies to that atoll island. At once, he sees on the Planisphere's televisual eye the island burned to a crisp. Abd-es-Samad has satisfied himself that his wonderful toy also functions as a working Doomsday Machine.

"But, he's also seen unimaginable destruction wreaked upon the island: creatures of the wild are grilled alive, the island is utterly stripped of its vegetation for all time, and Abd-es-Samad's machine has boiled mountains of fishes in their watery habitat.

"Abd-es-Samad feels bad. And he's surprised at himself, considering the promise he's made science never to flinch at results, fair or foul. In order to warn future possessors of the Celestial Planisphere, he writes a treatise. It gets published for the edification of the scientific community. But, alas, instead of deterring anyone, the treatise incites universal desire to get hold of the Celestial Planisphere.

"Abd-es-Samad is hounded and threatened daily by spies, terrorists, agents of governments engaged in hostilities. All manner of thieves and kings vie with each other to nab the Celestial Planisphere. That's how Abd-es-Samad's private life of inquiry is destroyed. He spends much time being abducted from one country into another. And, in order to make him spit out his secrets, he's so terribly tortured that he's finally driven mad.

"But, before going mad, Abd-es-Samad's had the foresight to entrust his terrible toy to the care of his remaining brother, Solomon the Jew. So, to this day, the Celestial Planisphere is at the discretion of the Jews."

"Does that mean," Hürü asked, "when the Jews are good and ready, they can burn the whole globe?"

"Makes a good ending," Shahrazad said, shrugging.

"It manages to depress me," Hürü said. "Who wants to bring a child into such a dreadful place? I know my luck won't hold out beyond my youth. I miss my stupid youth already. I miss the clear voice with which I sang. My voice is already murky from having been through the world's shithouse. Maybe I won't ever hit another true note again."

"Your voice will return," Shahrazad said. "Trust me."

"And will Selim?"

"Who knows?" Shahrazad said. "And who cares?"

I do, Hürü thought. Selim is the man to whom I plighted my troth. Troth meaning Truth.

She searched *The Thousand and One Nights* for another friend, the Green Old Man, known as Saint Hidir. But search as she might, she found no trace of the Green Old Man, nor his Blue Brother, Saint Ilyas. If only she could confirm the truth of her old friend in the pages of Shahrazad's encyclopedic work. All she found there, however, were abstruse references to the Good Brothers. Shahrazad seemed to assume the Brothers belonged to the domain of imaginary beings.

"The Good Brothers," Shahrazad told her, "are devices in folk-lore. They exist in order to be invoked whenever some pious character is in need of a quick solution."

"Still," Hürü insisted, "I feel the presence of the Guardians."

"Come off it!" Shahrazad said. "You're a big girl now."

She doesn't know everything, Hürü thought. But that doesn't make her less of a Shahrazad.

Although she learned much about telling stories, Hürü didn't think she could ever practice the art of fiction. She was always after simple and immediate truths. Not elaborate lies.

A fiction was like a machine, sometimes simple as a baby's toy. A fiction remained true only to its own internal logic. Fiction cared not a whit if real life models were manipulated or destroyed just for the sake of producing an effect.

"What a rotten way to get at the truth!" Hürü cried.

"Truth, truth!" Shahrazad snapped back. "Can't you concern yourself with anything else?"

"I think not," Hürü said. "Your treatment of Jafar Barmaki, for example: you reduce that grand old man to a mere possession of Harun-er-Rashid. The restless monarch constantly threatens him with the cross, the gallows, the executioner's sword."

"Foreshadowing," Shahrazad said, "the Barmaki's ignominious death."

Yet, all Hürü found on Jafar's death in *The Thousand and One Nights* was an anecdote. It opened with this curious statement:

"When Harun-er-Rashid had the Barmaki crucified, he ordered that anyone who wept or mourned for him would be crucified, too; so people refrained from lamenting."

But a Bedouin poet from a distant desert had not heard the edict forbidding mourning for Jafar. This desert poet was in the habit of bringing Jafar an ode every year. Since the ode was in praise of Jafar, Jafar awarded the poet a thousand dinars. The money saw the poet and his family through the year—and in fine Bedouin style, too.

So, the poet arrives in Baghdad with his yearly ode. As he is about to enter the city, he sees Jafar Barmaki at the dump, hanging on a cross. Shocked and inconsolable, the poet throws himself before the cross and recites his ode to the dead man. Then, overcome with grief, he weeps and weeps until he falls asleep from exhaustion.

In the ensuing dream, Jafar Barmaki appears to the poet.

"Go to the merchant called Fool," the dreamfigure instructs the poet. "Tell him hello and read him your ode. Then, ask for a thousand dinars for your pains, *by the token of the bean*."

When the poet awakens, he locates the merchant called Fool and subjects the man to the ode.

"Pay me a thousand dinars," the poet says, "by the token of the bean."

The word *bean* sends the merchant into such a state that he too dares to lament and weep for the crucified man. Not only does he award the poet the thousand, he throws in another five hundred on his own.

"Bring me an ode praising Barmaki again next year," he tells the poet, "and every year after that. Consider this a lifelong grant."

"What's the deal about this bean?" the poet wonders.

Well, once the merchant was a mere bean vendor. He cried his beans up and down the streets of Baghdad. One bleak and rainy day, he was passing by a pavilion where Jafar Barmaki sat watching big sheets of water that fell from the sky. Sympathizing with the vendor's plight, Jafar had the man invited inside. And for every measure of bean vended to his household attendants, Jafar filled the vendor's cup with gold. Finally, no beans remained in the kettle, save for one bean stuck to the bottom. It was this bean that Jafar plucked himself and broke into two. He gave one half to his wife and kept the other half.

"'What'll you give the man for half a bean?'" Jafar asked his wife.

"'Why, twice what he's already got!'" cried Mrs. Barmaki.

"'For my half,'" Jafar Barmaki said, "I'll double the sum my wife has doubled."

The bean vendor left, a rich man. In time, he capitalized on ventures so lucrative, he was now drenched in gold.

"'By the token of the bean,'" says the merchant, "'praise be Jafar Barmaki, living or dead. And may the Mercy of God, whose name is Exalted, be on Jafar now.'"

This anecdote about Jafar seemed to be the only true account of the man in the entire *Nights*. Yet it was almost thrown in as an aside.

"Why in the world did you make Jafar a coward and weakling," Hürü asked, "who always beats around the bush?"

"Not necessary for an anecdote to be true," Shahrazad said, "for it to be exemplary. As to the character called 'Jafar Barmaki,' the officious and ineffectual high bureaucrat, I didn't invent the character. The character rose as such out of the popular imagination. For the sake of the stories in the Harun Cycle, you see, nobody must detract from the wisdom, the nobility, the splendor of Harun-er-Rashid. As his foil, Jafar has to be something of a weakling."

"So Jafar gets crucified in literature, too!" Hürü cried. "But the real Barmaki was a wonderful old man."

"I beg to differ with you," Shahrazad said. "The historical Jafar was only thirty-seven at the time of his death. That's right. As you said once, he invented the wearing of a neck-tie. You know why? Well, he had an exceedingly long neck, and it bothered him. So he thought he'd hide his ungainly neck under a tie. He was something of a fop about town. On the positive side, he was gifted as an eloquent speaker, he was learned in astronomy, and the elegance of his penmanship was unequalled. Other than that, he impresses me as the arrogant younger son of a family that bred prime ministers. Besides, he wasn't above competing with Harun. For example, Jafar Barmaki's name appears on some gold coins of the time. So, I interpret the minting of his own coinage as a sign of Barmaki Trouble within the Abbasid Empire. Also, some historical whispers are heard concerning Jafar's sexual preferences. Some say he rose to power so fast because, as well as sharing the duties of state, he shared with Harun the royal bed."

"I don't believe it!" Hürü cried. "Both those guys were straight."

"Besides," Shahrazad continued, "for the sake of historical accuracy, I must mention that Harun didn't have Jafar crucified. He had his head cut off. Later, Jafar's body was severed vertically in half. His head was impaled on the Middle Bridge, the two halves of the body on the other two bridges. What do you say to that?"

"I still don't believe it," Hürü said doggedly.

"Then read for yourself," Shahrazad said, handing Hürü a thick volume. "It's in the *Ib'n Khallikan*."

Hürü drank in the information like one who's parched. Still, she was unconvinced. Should she trust her own two eyes? Or could she believe authority? Historians, too, might be fabricators who didn't bother to dignify their work as fiction. If so, history was no place to settle an issue. She still didn't know why Harun dealt death to Jafar. Was it over a bungled affair of state? Over Jafar's alleged activities as a fire worshipper? Or over a lover's quarrel that got out of hand? The pages were rife with speculation and innuendo.

"I met a venerable old Barmaki," Hürü said, "who gave every

impression of being the real Prime Minister. The man I met was not some long-necked fruit."

"You saw the man you expected to see," Shahrazad said. "After all, these popular tales have reached the less civilized parts of the world. As a child, you must've heard part of the Harun Cycle, or all."

"Is it possible?" Hürü mused. "Does the eye see what the mind expects? If he was not the lovely old man I saw, how can I mourn for his death?"

"Why so bothered," Shahrazad said, "about the Barmaki? Your own husband changes grand viziers oftener than he changes his undershirt."

"My own Grandfather," Hürü said, "was such a disposable Vizier. Perhaps I imagined my own Grandfather in Jafar Barmaki."

"So?"

"And I'm a disposable wife," Hürü said sadly. "Easily obtained, easily replaced. Nobody takes me seriously. Nobody bends over to maintain my friendship. It's assumed I will be all right, no matter what I have to endure."

"But you have a robust soul," Shahrazad said glibly. "As a matter of fact, you're my only friend who isn't a neurotic."

Hürü, stunned and angered, caught Shahrazad by her slender wrist. She had half a mind to hurt her.

"Not neurotic, eh?" she said, twisting Shahrazad's arm only a little. "Is that the same as saying 'uninteresting'? Do you assume I'm emotionally retarded? Or an incurable Good Girl?"

"Frankly," Shahrazad said, "I don't much think about you. I don't have to. You are exactly who you seem to be. One doesn't worry about your secret motives. You don't have any. You are marvelously transparent."

"All you're seeing, Shahrazad, is the clarity of my values. My personal ethics. You behave as if you're above a moral code, Shahrazad. And perhaps you are. On one hand, I admire you so much I could die of admiration—for your intensity, your intelligence, your charisma. But, on the other hand," Hürü went on, "I observe your petty thefts, your vanities, your cruelties. I see you laughing when someone falls down the stairs and lands in a bucket of water, even if that someone is one of your little daughters. Someone else has to pick up the child and take care of her hurts. But you laugh all the way into the library.

"I see you pinch stuff at the market. Small items of vanity. I see you draw the clerk's attention elsewhere while you pocket some trivial item. You seem to think folks are here to be your patsies. You won't pay your bills, for example. But people depend on you to pay.

"Your novelty as a woman with a superior mind fascinates Selim. Of course, you're flattered that the most powerful monarch in the world pants for you. How exciting to put him in his place! And what fun! So you fall in the sack with him. Why not? Who does it hurt? Not only can you appease your lust like a man, Selim's got nothing on you when it comes to looking after Number One. And if Shahriyar feels diminished, then too bad for him. He shouldn't be measuring his own worth through the fidelity of his spouse. Nobody should. For example, Hürü shouldn't mind, should she? If she does, then she's got a lesson coming."

"Well, then," Shahrazad said glumly, "do you mind?"

"The image of you and Selim under a purple cover," Hürü said, and her lip trembled, "doesn't hurt quite as much, now. I want you to know that if I don't show negative emotions, it's not because I'm a dunce. Or because I don't care. Or because I'm above the common herd. I chose to remain your friend, Shahrazad, though I hated your sneaking off with Selim."

"But why do you care? Not only is he the enemy of your family, you told me Selim's the enemy of love. And a misogynist to boot. I should think you'd welcome my victory over Selim. I seduced him, I subdued him and I rode him until he cried out. That's right. And when I was done, it was I who pushed him away."

"That's why you are more dangerous than Selim," Hürü said. "He is a known monster. But you come off looking eminently human."

"And you think me inhuman? Just because I hit on Selim?"

"I am not without blame," Hürü sighed. "I misled you because I failed to tell you how I feel about Selim. And I was too embarrassed to admit the truth of my heart. I know Selim is cruel, depraved and cynical. Yet I've also seen that side of him which is unspoiled, tender and idealistic.

"His dual nature obsesses me, and I hate my enslavement. When I'm around Selim, my will deteriorates in romantic and unfillable passion for him. He's hypnotic.

"But he grew impatient with me, and laughed at me because I didn't leave. Many a time I tried to extricate myself, but then I lost heart as soon as I laid eyes on Selim. He never really disgusted or angered me. He merely wore me out. I ran away to Baghdad with you only because he managed to exhaust me.

"I am free of Selim only by admitting that I'm not free of Selim. That which binds, frees."

"My poor Hūrū," Shahrazad said. "Had I only known! For me, Selim was nothing but a challenge. I thought I'd pay him back in his own coin. But I couldn't bear him as a constant lover in my bed. He demands too much, and I can see how his dominance would destroy a woman's mind. I prefer my man detached from me."

"And Shahriyar. Is he truly detached?"

"I feel comfortable with Shahriyar," Shahrazad said. "We like each other calmly, as men do. I call myself a man of letters."

"And a liar," Hūrū said, "and a cheat. There! Now I've said it."

"Oh my dear Hūrū," Shahrazad said; flinging down her quill, she hurried to hold Hūrū and kiss her closed eyelids. "I know it hurts. And it will keep hurting for some time. I too hurt with too much worldly vanity. My brightest moments come when I allow myself some small pleasure. Like taking tea infused with jasmine, or watching a child sleep. Or lying in and listening to Baghdad."

"Oh!" Hūrū cried, holding herself. "Oh-ho! Ho!"

"Hey, Camphor!" Shahrazad called over her shoulder. "Start boiling water, my big girl. And let's get our Hūrū to bed."

"Is it time?" Hūrū said.

"Don't be afraid." said Shahrazad.

Chapter 21

INTERRUPTED JOURNEY

Hürü cannot take
her beloved Baby Osman home

*H*ürü fell in love at once with the toothless and bald princeling, born with the immediate danger of blood, into the merciless house of Osman. Whenever a prince of Osman made it to the throne, out the back door came tiny coffins. Or small sacks sank (off Seraglio Point) into the Bosphorus, whimpering. As for survivors who achieved manhood before the death of their reigning fathers, they often rebelled against the brother who ascended the throne, knowing full well that the odds were against their survival. Defeated, captured, they succumbed to greased nooses in dark dungeons. Even those pacific princes who devoted themselves to theology or the arts couldn't escape with their lives: the nature of a royal brother was considered coequal with that of a snake in the grass. How many half-brothers did Hürü's baby have? No matter. Even one was too many. Selim must have bastards everywhere as well as legitimate sons. And the Crown Prince killed first and mourned later. In our great uncertain world, humans were in such desperate need for absolutes that even a paltry absolute like the divine right of sovereignty hardened the heart against the blood that flowed through the hearts of Osmans, hearts as brittle as dynasties.

Hürü hoped she could keep her mouth shut. Best that this little prince never know his true identity. If he grew up thinking himself an ordinary youth, he might learn to think of other interesting things beside his potential as an absolute monarch. She wondered how other mothers in the Seraglio stood it, watching doomed sons sleep. Perhaps in the hearts of those women flourished the hope that someday, against all odds, their sons might live and rise, taking their mothers along to the top where a woman, too, might enjoy respect and personhood, as well as the absolutely corrupting power of being the Queen Mother.

Hürü thanked God for keeping her and her son well out of it. Here in Baghdad she'd given birth to a virtual orphan. Yet, grudgingly, she named him Osman, a name common enough to be shared by both bootblack and prince. For his surname, she bestowed on him half of her maiden name: Kara. Osman Kara, then, a name given with blessing. But she ended up nicknaming him Karajuk, the diminutive Kara, the Little Black One.

The baby wasn't dark as his nickname implied. He turned peaches and cream once the high color of birth subsided. He was robust, already temperamental and quickly growing a full head of red-gold fuzz. In his eyes, Hürü thought, she recognized the unfocused gaze of Selim's, gray and mysterious. But Shahrazad assured her that all babies spend some time being cross-eyed. Hürü was too embarrassed to confess that she actually hoped the baby would retain his father's defect.

Once Karajuk reached the age of six months, he began to look like the golden prince he really was, chubby, dimpled, joyous, hungry for what was offered him on his silver spoon. Hürü longed to show him to her parents, to share her pleasure with those two dear persons who were so cruelly cut off from their hopes for the future. Each day, more and more she dreamed of arriving at the gate of her home, handing Karajuk to her good father and lady mother. She imagined them trembling and tearful with the enormity of this unexpected happiness.

It bothered her that Karajuk would say his first word in Arabic, spoken at him incessantly by Shahrazad's daughters, who were delighted with the big living doll, although, when Hürü wasn't looking, they were not above pinching him, or giving him lizard broth and scorpion eggs to eat. Another reason to leave was Shahriyar. As an authority figure, Shahriyar just didn't make it, sitting mute and immovable in his bedroom. Hürü thought it unwise to bring up a boy in a houseful of women.

"The time has come," Hürü told Shahrazad, "to take Karajuk home. Sometimes I burn with homesickness as if with fever. Strange. For so long, I seemed to have forgotten the very existence of hearth and home."

"You're better off here with us," Shahrazad said, "and without Selim. So, I wish you'd stay. But once you're gone, I will soon forget."

"Won't you miss me, at least?" Hürü said. "I wish you'd miss me."

"I shall miss you terribly," Shahrazad said; "and yet, I won't miss you at all. I live with those I love around me, but, as you know, I live alone."

"In either case," Hürü said, "I must return home."

"Ah, travelling's so dangerous," Shahrazad said, "too dangerous."

"I've made part of that journey before," Hürü said, "though the more difficult leg was made for me with the help of Abd-es-Samad flinging me across time and space. But, now, I have Karajuk to worry about. Why can't I hire myself an escort of some sort? Half a dozen men or so."

"Trustworthy persons are so hard to find these days," Shahrazad said. "I wouldn't know where to begin looking."

That's when an unexpected offer materialized in the form of Shahriyar who, unbeknownst to the inhabitants of the mansion, could overhear conversation through the woodwork. Having pulled his sheet about him, or having pulled himself together into his sheet, he stood at the doorway to the library, listening in person.

"How about me?" Shahriyar said in a rusty voice, speaking for the first time since he'd contracted the existential snits. "Constantinople. I'd like to see that town."

"Istanbul," Hürü corrected him, in a sudden fit of chauvinism.

Signing Shahriyar on as chief escort certainly seemed a good idea but embarrassing as all hell. Hiring an ex-king as a menial? Hürü was mortified as they formalized the contractual document, all signed, sealed and notarized as to the nature of Shahriyar's duties and Hürü's responsibilities as employer concerning salary, benefits and travel expenses. The contract was drawn with such loving precision that Hürü could see why he'd once been such a good administrator. Shahriyar was comfortable when things were down in black and white.

"That way," he said, "we won't quarrel over expectations in our own heads. Formality releases both parties from the unexpected."

The former king of Baghdad seemed not at all humiliated by

taking a job. His desire for travel was so overriding, he jumped at the chance to get out of the house where his only function had been to sit heavily on the other inhabitants' consciences. Seeing him all hustle and bustle, Hürü completely delegated the hiring of an escort to Shahriyar, who made a list of former faithful retainers, now probably all out of work and down in the heel. He was in such a hurry to get everything done, he was halfway out the door before he realized he was clad in a sheet.

"Get a man something decent to wear!" he roared at Camphor.

But, since he'd burned all his own apparel, he had to make do with the uniform of a *mamluk* slave Camphor dug up in the storage room. This didn't put off Shahriyar in the slightest. He went out the door like a shot. Hürü wondered what they'd think in downtown Baghdad.

"He's finally mobilized himself," Shahrazad whispered, hugging Hürü. "Thank God! And thank you, dear one!"

Despite Shahriyar's impatience, preparations took almost two weeks. Setting an army on course was easier than travelling with a baby. Shahriyar goaded and bullied Camphor in the kitchen, Hürü over the trunks, Shahrazad over her weeping in the library where her work had come to a grinding halt. The way it was those days, when one said goodbye to a friend, one said farewell until we meet again in the hereafter. With his first wages, Shahriyar proudly paid off some outstanding household bills.

"Tell my wife," he said to Hürü, since he still wasn't speaking to Shahrazad, "that I don't want to hear another word about money troubles."

"Tell my husband," Shahrazad said, "that money isn't something I worry over."

"Tell my wife," he retorted, "she'd better. I'm leaving the house in reasonable shape. She's got to try keeping finances balanced until I return."

"Tell my husband," she said, "my prayers are with him and his grave linen is in his left saddlebag."

"Tell her it's not all that easy to die," Shahriyar said.

"Tell him I hope he comes back home."

She kissed Shahriyar and clung to him. He accepted Shahrazad's physical embrace and even returned it; he wasn't cross with her body: he was cross with her words.

Shahriyar had chosen an escort of six men: three blacks, one

Turk—all former slaves of Shahriyar's, now freemen—and two free-born Arabs. He'd drawn up contracts favorable to the escort, accustomed as one in charge of public funds to spending money not his own. Oh, Hürü didn't mind throwing money around; she wanted the best available protection for the sake of Karajuk.

The infant on her hip, the Stone Lyre in one saddlebag, the casket of Selim's gold—now not quite as full—in the other, Hürü set forth. As soon as she mounted, the baby, perhaps sensing the excitement, filled his diapers. Everyone had to dismount, wait for the infant to be washed and changed; Karajuk had established his pattern on the road. Every morning, Karajuk waited until everyone was mounted before he besmirched himself. And he let everyone know how much he missed his crib, a hand-me-down from Shahrazad's children; he fussed and bawled, and wouldn't sleep in the little hammock rigged up for him at resting places. Instead, he demanded Hürü's bedroll, appropriated her pillow and kicked her face away with his soft pink feet. Her milk gave him the colic and the nightmares, and he woke up with a start, terrified. On the whole, Karajuk seemed to hate travel. Hürü hoped she would continue loving him without resentment; after all, that's what mothers are for. God, in his wisdom, made the babies adorable. Otherwise, how could a mother's heart be made to behave against her own self-interest? Hürü lost much weight.

The journey, although difficult, was unmarred by the usual nasty events, such as being set upon by bands of robbers, contracting some dread disease, getting thrown in some local jail because the village police didn't care for the looks of their faces. Seemed like Selim the Grim's rule deterred folks from taking chances with the law. The worst that ever happened was not getting a decent meal at some inn, or being set upon by bedbugs, fleas and lice. In and around Syria there lived a certain kind of mite, called little Tartar, whose bite gave people running sores that marked the victims forever with a scar known as the Aleppo button. Hürü, hoping to protect Karajuk's tender skin, stifled herself and the infant under mosquito netting through the hot Syrian nights.

Shahriyar, too, had his own method for avoiding hidden agues and assorted miseries. It was all in the water, he said. Drinking water one wasn't accustomed to would make the travellers prey to all the local plagues. The best course was to drink wine and other fermented brew, he advised, and took his own advice too liberally. The kindest way of describing Shahriyar's constant condition, and that of his men, was to call them dead drunk. The seven men started protecting their health well before breakfast and didn't spare preventive medicine till they dropped off into oblivion. A good thing, too, their oblivion! Pleasantly soused in the morning, maudlin at lunch, by mid-afternoon the escort was so crapulous that the fierce argumentation among them was intolerable. At night, even less tolerable were their lustful glances at Hürü, busy comforting her child, as if she were just a woman instead of the Boss.

This state, Hürü assumed, was what was forbidden about wine: the state of abject compliance with the demon in the bottle. Shahriyar's drinking capacity proved to be incredibly high; yet, although he handled himself better than his men, Hürü didn't think he was doing the sightseeing he'd originally taken this appointment to do. Instead, he concerned himself almost exclusively with the virtues of the wines made in various locales. He began by sipping and tasting, in order to praise or condemn the vintage; by nightfall, he could've drunk vinegar and not known it, immobilized as he was both in tongue and wits. Why would a man like Shahriyar—a good man, really, under his gruffness, his morbid spells, the flinty conversation—so methodically drink himself into a shameful state?

Three sheets to the wind as he was, if Shahriyar didn't mind not seeing the world, that was all right with Hürü. So long as he kept his men under control. For the longest, agonizing period of time, she gave no advice; nor did she plead for moderation, seeing Shahriyar preferred going to hell without any help from his friends. She didn't even pull rank. But she couldn't help casting chiding glances at him.

"Here, Prude, have yourself a quaff!" he guffawed, passing her the flagon. "Enjoy yourself a little!"

"Look here, Shahriyar," she said finally, after weeks of exasperation. "You have a contract to fulfill. You signed and sealed a document which binds you to deliver my son and me, safe and sound, at my father's door."

"So?" Shahriyar said. "Has any harm come to your precious brat's hide or hair? Or yours, for that matter?"

"But something might come up. And you're always drunk on the job. You're never in any condition to discharge your duties as stipulated in our contract."

"Let's see that contract," Shahriyar said. "I don't remember any clause about sobriety."

"But sobriety is assumed!" Hürü cried.

Obviously, a nasty surprise awaited Shahrazad on Shahriyar's return to Baghdad. Her husband was hardly himself, crowned as he often was with the grape leaves of the wine-god. On her part, Hürü would prefer a sober antagonist, a husband crazy from too much life rather than too much drink. Ah, too bad for Shahrazad. Her man behaved more like a wild satyr than father, husband, householder in downtown Baghdad.

Hürü wasn't enjoying herself. Seemed if she worried terribly, everything might go well, especially since the escort hired to do the worrying avoided worries completely. Once they crossed the Arabian badlands and started gaining elevation in the mountains of southern Anatolia, she breathed easier. Not only did she understand mountains, the clean clouds on the purple peaks loaned her spirits some buoyancy.

"See?" she said to Karajuk, holding him up to the sky. "These are the ranges of your homeland!"

Sweet mountain streams flowed so clearly from their hidden sources, she pointed out to Shahriyar, he need not fear that hidden plagues boiled unseen in the water.

"If you don't mind crow-crap," he said, "and otter-water."

Four grizzlies walked away from the travellers; a fifth, a mother bear with two cubs, considered the party briefly before following her young, who, fortunately, scampered the other way. Hürü didn't think her escort, drunk or sober, was any match for a hulking grizzly, having once seen a soldier left over from such a mother bear. But, seeing how no wild animals came after them, she thought Hidir must be keeping watch again. Then, one morning, they found a pack mule had been torn up in the night by what seemed, from the tracks, a leopard. Wilderness was also there, watching. She clutched Karajuk to her bosom, giving neither the infant nor herself any rest, listening to the unearthly howls of the wolves, the hysterics of the hyenas, the chilling commentary of the hoot-owls.

"When you are a man," she advised Karajuk, "never underestimate nature because nature always brings forth the unexpected."

She was, however, glad she hadn't released the escort as she'd contemplated doing ever since they entered the mountainous terrain. There was, at least, some safety in numbers. Then, the terrain opened up to the vast central plateau. They were nearing Konya, the home of her ancestors.

When they arrived at the piney woods where so much had happened to her in the past, she requested that they camp there. This was the spot where she'd met Hidir, the shepherd who'd traded clothes with her, where Selim had apparently seen her reflection in the salt lagoon and fallen in love, where she'd been flown on mules with Abd-es-Samad, where she'd lifted the four magic talismans and kept the Stone Lyre from the Treasury of the Tallest of the Tall.

"This place," she told Shahriyar, "is laden with the unseen."

"Will the unseen show itself then?" Shahriyar bantered, chugging up a whole bottle of *mavrodaphne* wine, sweet and dark, made by the Christian winemakers of Konya.

"If you can manage to stay awake," Hürü said curtly. "In wilderness, survival is the first necessity."

"Survive what?" he said, looking up at a ray of light that penetrated into the woods. "Nobody ever survives."

Shahriyar and the men settled down to some liquid picnic fares, telling tales about shooting wild animals whose luminous eyes blanked out when shot at the right moment, or those that would drag themselves into forests, lost because the wounded animal wouldn't die properly. Someone ought to tell these men they, too, are animals, thought Hürü. No one ever had.

She loosened her hair and stripped down to her chemise behind the berry bushes that grew at the edge of the lagoon. Karajuk, naked and joyous, crawled on his stomach on the sand, making straight for the water. The infant babbled at his image on the calm surface. What felicity! Hürü thought as she slipped into the cool water under which a whole treasury was submerged. Holding Karajuk carefully, she showed him how to float.

Too bad she couldn't persuade Shahriyar that the crystal lagoon wouldn't dry up if he stood in it, that the trees were friendly spirits, that the blue sky was the tangible guardian of the place. He thought the lagoon nothing but a body of water that demanded its quota of drowners, taking a cue from the sweet sticky wine where only his personal sorrows drowned. Help was everywhere, but invisible. Yet Shahriyar didn't know he could be cleared of the bruises of his past. Right in the crook of Shahriyar's arm could be some luminous green, luminous blue person who would not allow himself to be seen.

While the infant and Hürü cleaned themselves in the clear, salty water, the company soused itself, laughing and quarrelling. Hürü decided it really was high time that she sent the lot packing. She

quickly dressed herself and Karajuk, thinking of the words she'd use
to dismiss the escort and Shahriyar. She was combing her hair when
Shahriyar came to her uninvited and plunked himself on a stump,
gesturing wildly with his bottled hand, watching her with all too
familiar an interest. Hürü quickly twisted her hair into place and
covered her head with a kerchief.

"Don't cover up," Shahriyar said. "Ever since your hair reached
your shoulders, you've been looking almost beautiful."

"Look here, Shahriyar," she said; "I've been thinking. I can make
it home from here by myself. There's no reason to keep you and your
men any longer."

"My contract says all the way into Constantinople," he said.
"And I'm going to uphold my contractual obligations, by God! Besides, you and I could benefit much from each other's company. I'm
a fool for having neglected you for so long."

Hürü chose not to understand him.

"On the contrary," she said, "you've been awfully kind."

"Don't contradict me!" Shahriyar said belligerently. "I've suffered
from one contradictory woman long enough!"

"Would you like some tea?" Hürü said.

"Tea and sympathy I can do without," he said. "But I'm dying
for a piece of tail. How about it? No harm in a bit of sport between
two good friends. Nice fresh air like this—it must make your juices
flow. Besides, widowhood must be awful hard on a young woman."

"No, thank you," Hürü said. "Sexual life can be so demeaning to
a woman that it's best to renounce it altogether. Besides, not even a
whore would want you in your present state."

Something in the resolute tone of her statement seemed to
irritate Shahriyar so much, he snatched the infant out of Hürü's
arms. And she, not expecting such a frontal attack, released Karajuk
to him without a fight. It took her a moment to realize what had
happened. She still couldn't believe that Shahriyar had so rudely
yanked away her child. Karajuk, unused to being manhandled, bellowed angrily.

"Dammit, Shahriyar!" she said. "Hand the baby back!"

"I will," he said. "But first, you give me what I want."

"Don't do this to us, Shahriyar," Hürü said. "It's neither becoming nor in good faith. I'm not the one you want to harm."

"You'll do," he said.

"We're friends," she begged. "Don't ruin our friendship."

"I have no friends!"

"Yes, you do!" she said. "I am your friend."

"Undress!" he roared. "Or I'll fling this pup in the lake."

"I will not undress," Hürü stated. "And you won't fling anybody anywhere."

"Won't I, now?" Shahriyar said, dangling Karajuk by the collar of his shirt over the water. "I will, by God!"

"I don't bluff easily," Hürü said. "You won't harm my son because you, too, are a father and a decent man. You're just senseless drunk. Go sleep it off. I won't even demand an apology in the morning."

"Don't tell me what to do!" Shahriyar said, his face turning high purple. "I won't be told!"

And he tossed Karajuk into the lagoon.

Like a sequence in a dream, one's arms and feet seem so absolutely weighted that one can't move to save oneself. She watched her son float briefly like a waterlily in his gauze shirt; then, she watched him sink like a stone. As ripples grew out of the spot where the baby vanished, Hürü came to her senses and flung herself into the water. But Shahriyar was hard behind her.

He wrestled her in the water. Maddened with drink and resentment, he bore on her like a grizzly bear. But Hürü, maddened with anguish over her son, fought him like a she-wolf and bit one ear lobe clear off. Shahriyar, stunned with the blood that came gushing out of his ear, began to bellow so hard that the men came running, and saw Hürü land a knee in his groin. Just as she released herself from her assailant, now doubled over and bleeding, several men were on her, holding down her arms, feet, one sitting on her chest. One of the men stood off, just watching.

"Brother!" she called out in Turkish to the disinterested man. "Don't let these filthy Arabs do this to your countrywoman! Help me!"

"I have no country," said the ex-slave, shrugging. "Besides, there are six of them and only one of me."

"Shahriyar!" Hürü said, appealing for mercy from where she lay spread-eagled. "Don't do it! Let me go! Let me go after my son!"

"Bloody bitch!" Shahriyar said, binding a length he cut off his turban over his ear. "Look what you did to me! Where's my ear lobe? Did you swallow it? Accursed and bloodthirsty nomad-women!"

"Let me save my son," Hürü begged, weeping. "Don't detain me any longer."

"The Ottoman whelp's long drowned," Shahriyar said. "Now, it's your turn. Your body or your life; I will have one!"

"Why are you doing this?" Hürü said, appealing to reason now. Shahriyar shrugged.

"What is it you really want?" she said. "If it's money, all I have is yours. Think of your own wife. Would you have a bully do to her what you're doing to me?"

"Maybe she'll get lucky," he said. "She's not going to get it any other way."

"Your ear doesn't hear what your mouth says," she said. "Please, don't think of me as Selim's wife. Think of me as I am: a person called Hürü who's been a steadfast friend to your family."

"With friends like you," he said, "one loses ear lobes. Forget friendship!"

"If I am your enemy," she said, "don't trifle with me. Humiliating an enemy makes a trifle of one's dignity."

"Will you shut up?" he asked. "Or shall I shut you up?"

She couldn't believe any of it. She stayed quiet for a moment, gathering her wits, composing herself before she made another serious mistake.

"All right, Shahriyar," she said. "You win. I prefer that you kill me. But, first, I must ready myself for my death. Allow me a few minutes of prayer and reflection so I may face God as one who's made peace with life."

"My Lord," said the drunk black who sat on Hürü's chest, "let the woman perform her last rites."

"All right," Shahriyar said. "Go ahead, pray!"

"But I can't pray like this!" Hürü said. "Give me some privacy. My God! Have you no decency, Shahriyar?"

"Be quick about it, then," Shahriyar said, signalling his men off her. "We still have the rest of the world to see."

"Thank you," Hürü said, rising. "God, when he judges you, will remember the little respite you allowed me."

"Are you still talking?"

Quickly, Hürü ran behind the thicket of blackberry bushes. She was bleeding from cuts she hadn't noticed before. She kneeled for a second to catch her breath. Her mind raced. There was no way Shahriyar would leave her alive now; raped or not, she'd have to be murdered. Shahriyar couldn't allow the mother to breathe a word to Sultan Selim about the way his infant son had met his untimely death. Hürü was shocked she could so clearly apprehend her situation when her son was at the bottom of the lagoon—as if a sudden burst of cool reason were suddenly granted her. As if it was needed that she survive!

"Shh!" a voice said behind her as a hand cupped her mouth. "Don't scream. It's your old friend, the shepherd. Promise you won't scream."

Hürü nodded madly. And once released, she turned around to see her old friend, the shepherd, older now and more substantial.

"Need a quick change of clothes?" he whispered.

"Thank God, it's you!"

"Nobody but!" the shepherd said drily. "Hurry. Here's my cloak. Get out of those fancy duds before those godless men fall on you again."

"What about you?" Hürü said. "They won't be kind when they find out you've traded clothes with me. They're contemplating rape."

"I'd like to see the big guy try and mount me!" the shepherd said.

They exchanged clothes quickly.

"Ain't I dainty in these veils?" he said. "For you, I just happen to have another sheep's bladder. You want it? When I saw you and your rough company ride into the woods, I thought sooner or later you'd be wanting to cover your head. So, I came prepared."

"Give the bladder here," Hürü said, pulling it over her hair with ease, the long practice of concealment coming back to her.

"Brung your horse, too," the shepherd said, clicking his tongue to the white mare that had come through the thicket. "See? That's the white I seen you ride on."

"Bless you!" Hürü said, springing on the mare. "And give my regards to your pretty girl."

"We's all married now," the shepherd said, shyly hanging his head. "And three young ones, too! Them earrings of yours, remember? I had enough to pay her father the bride-price."

"Oh, my God!" Hürü said, "I can't have you risking your life! Not now that I know you're a husband and father! Those seven men are very angry and very drunk."

"Don't worry about me," he said. "I'll tell them I'm still Hürü, but Saint Hidir, seeing my plight, changed me into a man. How's that for a good line?"

"How did you know my name?"

"Don't know," he said. "Just came to me, I guess. It's this place, you know. Even I turn smart when I step into this blessed wood, like suddenly I know stuff, and everything. Feel better too."

"And yet . . ." Hürü said, her heart burning in her mouth, ". . . my boy. My poor little boy . . ."

"All I know is, you've got to live," the shepherd replied. "You've got to get away. Even if you ride into madness."

"Got to get away," Hürü whispered into the white mare's ear, urging her to take wings, "got to live."

Chapter 22

TRANSFORMATION AND MADNESS

In true voice, Hürü becomes the Entranced Baldie

*I*f she unnumbed herself, she'd go mad. Perhaps madness was what was now being offered her. Some insistent voice inside kept warning that she must resist; she must not be driven insane. Somewhere else, way off, other whispering voices beckoned, melodiously tempting: *surrender*, said the susurrant voices, *surrender now*. They were the soft voices of animals and vegetables that surrender their fruits to an order that plucks only the very young, the very tender and the most succulent. Louder and louder she heard their seductive sibilance, melodiously beckoning; fainter and fainter the pedantic resister inside. She stopped the white mare with the gray stripe down her back. Her eye fell on a smooth and white oval of a large marble, about as long as Karajuk, embedded in a patch of clover and whimpering in the drizzling rain. She gathered up the stone, brushed away the soil that clung on the underside.

"Hush, little one," she whispered, kissing it. "Mama will clean your little behind and dress you in something dry and warm."

She swaddled it in crib clothes, tied a lacy bonnet on its head. She pressed the stone baby to her breast. She knew both that it was a real baby and that it was not. As she rode with her hard bundle tight against her bosom, the stone gained in warmth and presence. She sang it lullabies so sad, the stone sighed and moved in its sleep.

Passing through towns whose names she didn't bother ask, folks put her up in front of their hearth fires, gave her gruel and solace for the sake of the babe. She seemed to remember she had some currency somewhere about her, but not finding any in the saddlebags, assumed she was mistaken. She must've always been a poor person who only imagined having lived a life full of earthly comforts. She wasn't even sure, anymore, whether she was a man or a woman.

"Young man," she was often asked, "how is it your babe never cries?"

"Because," she said, "my love gave him to me."

And she sang lullabies so sad, the baby sighed in its sleep. Folks flocked to town squares where she sat under an old and gnarled oak that always marked the center of every town and village, her legs extended, a pillow under her feet, rocking the stone baby. Her voice was equal to the tension of the Stone Lyre. She was smelly, dressed in the mean clothes of a shepherd, her head covered with a pestilence that strips off hanks of hair and puckers the scalp something awful. Yet, folks had never heard a clearer voice; never were lullabies so overflowing with the agony of life; never were babies better advised that they begin to die the moment they draw their first breath.

Other minstrels were driven to song by the loss of love, loss of freedom, loss of faith, finding again in song what's been lost. God had given this poor minstrel a riddle so entrancing, he'd lost his wits. Everything about the young minstrel was of stone; Stone Lyre, stone baby, stone face. For it never took folks too long to guess that a stone was wrapped in the baby's swaddling clothes. Yet, they indulged the mad minstrel, gave him thin soup for the baby, a few coins, a place to bed down for the night. They listened to stone winds whistling inside the backbone, a void filled with dead stars, petrified oceans, ships with marble sails, granite kernels on which hermits crack their teeth: a matter so immovable that even the Angel of Death couldn't travel through its dense substance. A man could open the minstrel's lullabies only in his own ear from which there was no translation. Stone silence, that's what it was, wrapped around stone sleep.

They called the mad minstrel whose fame preceded his arrivals Entranced Baldie. But she didn't know who this Entranced Baldie might be whose name folks thought she ought to know. She didn't even know Baldie played a Stone Lyre so mean, folks turned into stone, entranced. So she passed through the countryside, scarcely aware of the beating of her heart, let alone where she came from and where she was going. The mention of Baghdad made her weep. But she didn't know why. At every village and town, every tent and campfire where she stopped, she remembered having once left someone behind her, someone who didn't exist but who was the cause of everything, an invisible absence who could escape between the bars but who would not. Was it a he or a she? Or was it the absence of itself? What beat against the grating as if it had material wings? It would neither show itself nor leave off.

She remembered speaking in another language which would not manifest itself on her lips; nor would it stop hurting for a loss of words. A hush fell over her dreams as if the dreams were expecting someone. The missing presence didn't show up. But then, a voice spoke: "Habibi," it said: "would you care for a black olive? Or just the pit?"

"Where am I?" she sometimes queried. "And what year is this?" She was always answered by someone kindly. But she couldn't hear. On newly minted coins dropped into her palm, she sought to read the name of the place of issue, the date, the name of the issuer. But she couldn't read. Only the sensation that she could lingered. She must've only dreamed of having once read something clearly, like the aftermath of a dream of flying. Her hand drew charcoal marks on whitewashed walls; the handwriting was there, but between the writing and the reading someone had made a choice. She floated on choices partially made. She swallowed the pit and threw away the bitter black flesh. She hugged the stone which had been punished by being turned into a baby.

Once she mislaid the horse, she set forth on foot, wore through her boots in which the golden lady was still concealed. But she remembered neither the horse nor the golden lady. Then she walked barefoot; her feet bled on the blue thistle, on rocks, on ice. She saw the baby and the Lyre through blizzards, torrential rains, through parched terrain; no harm must come to either, for both had to be delivered intact. Babies and magic lyres couldn't be kept but must be returned to Distance. She passed by quietly, undistanced from everywhere and everyone.

"A town like Baghdad, there is no other," a popular ditty moved on her lips, "in true love, none like your mother."

She supposed she was on the road to Baghdad where her mother had died. But who was her mother? A brindle cow. Yes, that's right. Yet she couldn't remember where she'd last seen her mother, couple-colored and full of milk. Folks guessed her destination from her lullabies and, in the morning, turned her squarely on the road north, gave her brown bread, a pouch of sour curds and a pocketful of carob beans. Sometimes another pedestrian took the provisions away from her. She didn't mind. She ate broom seeds and the roots of dandelions, sucked a drop of nectar from the honeysuckle, chewed on the tender hearts of bunches of wisteria. Sometimes she even ate someone's haughty rose and was severely chastised.

And, at times, she met up with other wandering minstrels who, having heard of Entranced Baldie's obsession, improvised lullabies for the stone baby's sake. She didn't fail to hear their lullabies, but their melancholy seemed, somehow, not to echo her history. So she sang the lullaby and passed it on. As she forgot the courtly songs that required at least three languages for courtliness enough, a forthright voice and plain rendition colored anew the old lullaby.

Breaking the shell, this voice came from the marrows. It was essence and word fused. The singer didn't know about the folk-love for old values, but the lyrics found a home in folks' hearts. Her breath drove the words without itself being apparent. Had she been sensible to her training, she would've faltered. But, blessedly, she'd forgotten how to discriminate between what's paltry and what's rich. Now, she sang without even submitting to the magic Lyre. Chest stuck out, she sang with a voice robust as the hills, a human voice rising from the noblest, the most magical of instruments.

No one would've imagined that once she sang in sophisticated meter, that once she talked falconry and strategy to Princes, apologetics to Ayatollahs, affairs of state to Sultans, affairs of God to Caliphs. Had anyone ever guessed she was the legitimate Sultana of the realm, he would've been neither surprised nor any kinder to the unfortunate minstrel with scrofula going wild on his scalp, syllables of lullabies on his lips. In those days, folks made much over those whom God elects by bestowing divine madness upon them. Hell is always there, but it's only the entranced who go through it lovingly. And had they guessed the wretched wanderer had once been lawfully wed to Sultan Selim, they would've believed that, too. Folks would have had no trouble believing that their Sultana had been transformed by despair into an Entranced Baldie, now singing lullabies for a crust of bread. Those days, when folks wanted to curse someone, they'd wish him intimacy with Sultan Selim.

"May you be Vizier to Selim!" they cursed.

Then, too, they would've wished the office of queenhood on some offensive woman. But no one had so far imagined the nature of that office because of the secrecy with which it was practiced.

Reaching the shore of the sea which becomes a river that separates two continents, she didn't know she beheld the slender minarets of Istanbul. She thought she'd arrived by good fortune. Not only did a boatman row her across, for the sake of a lullaby she made up for him, he gave her a copper coin. She wouldn't take it.

"Take it," the boatman said. "You paid me already in gold."

The boatman landed her at Seraglio Point, saying something about sightseers, pockets full of money to throw at prodigious talents; the minstrel might find a spot there to practice his trade. Who knew. Maybe his strong voice would be heard from within the Palace gate, land him a job lulling Palace babies to sleep. She both heard the boatman and didn't hear him. She said nothing in reply but clutched the stone baby to her bosom because he'd begun to fret.

"Good luck," the boatman said, indicating the tall stone wall of the fortified Palace.

She joined the traffic in this unknown city. Things were very loud here. A certain smell of milk being boiled rose from the streets, as if a thousand puddings were being made in a thousand houses. From the minaret of the largest mosque in the quarter, the *muezzin* called the faithful to a funeral prayer. She hung around the mosque courtyard until the prayers were done. Then, she saw the coffin draped in green, borne by a thousand friends and relatives. The pair at the tail end of the mourning thousand kept hurrying forward and shouldering the coffin; the pair at the head shifted to become the second, and so forth. The number of the living was in pairs; the number of the dead remained odd. Always the One Thousand-and-First, the dead went alone.

She followed the procession, making an odd number of the living as well, a straggler who neither carried the odd fellow in the box nor was carried away by the throng. As the procession passed by a side street, she stopped dead in her tracks. Although she'd never seen the gate in front of her, nor ever heard it described, she recognized immediately the wood arches eaten away by sea-salt, charred wood lattices, the gutted balconies of sandalwood. Suddenly, she could read once more as she looked at a most pitiful sign tacked on the gate: *For Sale*.

There had been a fire in this house. She sat herself down on the front step and watched the funeral procession turn the corner and disappear. A beggar approached and eased himself next to her, scratched himself luxuriantly and, from a dirty pouch, extracted a vial.

"Here," the beggar said. "The physician who used to live here gave me this salve once. For my head pestilence. Cured it right up."

Seeing the afflicted one didn't take the medicine, the beggar put away his salve.

"Suit yourself," he said. "You must be the kind who has to see the physician for himself. In that case, young man, I'll tell you. Take the road to Eyub where the Saint lies interred. He ain't an unfitting saint for the likes of you. He loved his misery, they say. He sat there, day in and day out, leprous as anything. Whenever a maggot fell off his rotting flesh, he picked the feeder off the ground and put him back on the spot. Folks say he did it because he had compassion for all creatures who must feed to live. But I think it was on account of something else. You want to hear what I think?

"Well, I'll tell you anyway," he said, getting no response. "I think Saint Eyub was so sensitive a man, he knew he felt better with the maggots on than off. The maggots cleaned out his body rot, if you get my meaning. I ain't no physician, but I've noticed a thing or two. There must be good reasons why God created the maggot. As you can see, I'm a small-time philosopher. Begging is a drag without some philosophy attached to it. And, I suppose, philosophy could be a drag too without some begging out on the street. Folks feed the beggar's body, and the beggar provides folks with food for thought. So I part with a crumb of wisdom or two."

The beggar put his hand on the baby in swaddling clothes.

"Don't your baby feel well?" he asked. "Good God, he's stone cold! What's the matter with the poor tyke? Hurry up, young man! The funeral procession will lead you to the physician's door. Just before you arrive at Stonesville—that's my little joke—you'll see a house built of stone, the door painted black. The physician's sort of a recluse. Lost both his children. He likes to watch the cemetery, all day long, the potter's field, you know. But knock on the door anyway. You'll be kindly received. I can't promise he'll heal your baby. As he'll tell you himself, the physician no longer practices."

To the beggar's surprise, the youth responded by dropping a copper coin in the beggar's tin cup. He threw the coin back on the youth's lap.

"Look here," the beggar said, offended. "I don't take from other mendicants. Have my professional courtesy, you know. Come on, get up! Otherwise, the funeral'll be too far ahead to take you to the physician's door. From the chill I felt on your baby, you don't have a moment to lose."

Still the unfortunate youth sat without moving, as if glued to the step. Suddenly, the beggar's eyes lit with recognition.

"I get it!" the beggar said. "You're a dumb mute! Guess I'd better lead you there myself. Come on, wretch, take my hand. I'll take you there, don't you fret."

The beggar hurried her down the street and turned the corner where the funeral procession had dropped out of sight. Seeing his charge was having a difficult time carrying both a stone musical instrument and a sick baby besides, the gruff philosopher offered to carry the whachamacallit.

"What's it, anyway?" he asked uselessly. "Seems like the statue of a string instrument. What on earth is it good for?"

Beyond the City limits, the mourners moved into the open countryside, falling back in pairs as they advanced; the burden of death lightened. The beggar stopped near the edge of the cemetery which was distinguished by the presence of a real Saint. They stood in front of a stone house with a black door. It was the only house on the hill which overlooked, on one side, the potter's field where headstones were planted haphazardly. From the other side, you could see an inlet where the water was alive with boats and barges, fish leaping out for silver seconds. Noticing the wretched youth was unable to tear his eyes from the water beckoning with the urgency of life, the beggar thought he'd enlighten the dumb-mute with the name of the limpid inlet.

"That's the Golden Horn," he said.

Somehow she heard the name sung in her ears for only a second. Then, she remembered a cow, taller than a horse. Remembered the smell of a man's boot, the smell of wolves and road dust. A dog ran ahead of the marching soldiers. A young man, who was not a man, played a martial pipe. He was dressed in a uniform that smelled of mohair tents and deep snow. Then another odor rose, a mixture of odors so subtly precise that it must have been a thousand years old: spirits of camphor, eucalyptus and alcohol on hands so clean that behind the spirits lingered the smell of soap made of gum-arabic. She remembered the smell of a touch like newly laundered bedsheets warmed before a fire. Then, it all came to an end, like a fairy tale. Maybe this was her country.

The beggar didn't have to knock on the door. Standing on the front steps of the stone house was an old man, wizened beyond belief, yet his bones had yielded up their flesh to a sparseness that was like the beauty of an elm that has surrendered its leaves to winter frost. His full head of hair was so white, it shimmered like the pale mane of a horse. Beside him stood a stately matron, a head taller than he, completely veiled and covered by a black overgarment. The beggar approached the pair and doffed his cap, which caused a family of headlice to relocate elsewhere.

"I brung you a real sad sack, Physician," the beggar said. "I beg you, don't turn him away."

"But I no longer practice," the old man said.

"Just touch the baby," the beggar said. "That's all I ask."

The old man approached, light as a bird, so that his feet scarcely seemed to touch the cobblestones. The sight of him went through her like a transparent knife that revealed the wound as it cut. Her knees buckled. And she sank in the road. The Physician touched the bundle in her arms.

"Son," the old man said. "Accept my condolences. Perhaps birth is the Departure from the Source. And death the Return."

"Ahh!" she said.

"Come, my dear," the old man said to the matron. "Help me ease this young man into the house. You shall have water, son, and a refreshing bowl of yogurt, too, with leaves of mint and dill."

She handed the stone baby to the matron. The matron accepted the bundle without any hesitation. Placing the baby in the crook of her arm, she lifted the blanket off the baby's face. Then quickly, the woman swept away the veiling on her own face, looked intently at the baby as if to make sure she wasn't dreaming.

"Is he dead?" the beggar asked. "What's wrong with the tyke?"

"As a matter of fact," the matron said, "he's right as he's ever been."

"But the Physician ought to do something anyway," the beggar said.

"I'm sorry," the old man said. "But I no longer practice healing."

The beggar followed the Physician, his wife and the stranger with the odd baby into the courtyard. He had a question or two to put.

"Why won't you practice your healing anymore?" the beggar asked. "That's something I don't understand. If God gives a man the gift of healing, why would a man spurn the gift?"

"The Angel of Death," the old Physician said, "had made it known to me that I must no longer interfere with his Work. There's a gnashing in my bones, an invisible but discrete grinding before dawn. And I grow cold in my warm bed. The rooster crows in alarm, for it's the hour when the Angel of Death visits, looking to see if I'm ready to spit up my pit."

"Are you afraid, Physician?" the beggar asked.

"I'm waiting for a sign," the old man said, "from those who have died. They pass by, riding the shoulders of the living, quietly practicing in their coffins the task of Eternity. What's patient is the disease, not the man. The disease endures intact in the body until it's purified in a blinding light. I've stood too long, a bolt of shadow against eternal lightning."

"This baby," the matron said, "is perhaps the sign for which you wait, husband. Pray, take a look."

The old Physician took the bundle in his arms. He peered at the petrified infant with eyes like two very deep, very dark wells. Seeing the face of stony silence, the old Physician seemed terribly agitated. He began to shake like someone taken with a sudden fever.

"Ahh!" he said, sighing deeply. "Here's a baby without any crying."

"Poor youth," the beggar said, nudging the dumb-mute wretch. "Take your instrument. And I'll be gone."

Neither the matron nor the Physician knew what else to do but keep the deaf-mute. They were reconciled to the fact that their questions could not be answered. The mute had been sent by Destiny. God's guest in the house. That's how come the deaf-mute stayed on at the whitewashed stone house by the graveyards of Saint Job.

Once the wretched guest had delivered the baby to the lady, and the stone statue of a lyre to the Physician, he seemed to lose interest in them. The guest seemed much younger than his (or her) physical age. No, they couldn't agree on the sex of the stranger. They guessed the guest must be about twenty-one, but the way he sucked

one skinny thumb, as if haunted by long-lost senses, it was as if the
poor thing were an infant.

The Physician and his wife, whose name was Lady Gülbahar,
assured the other guests in the house that the mute understood
things, but simply could not speak. The two other permanent guests
took an immediate dislike to the new addition. One of them, called
Mistress Kevser, had been the tutoress of the hosts' lost daughter.
The other was a man of the cloth, the Imam who'd been their lost
son's spiritual guide.

Although much younger than the Physician, the Imam was
already prey to senility. The Physician saw how the Imam's mind
came and went, and knew his arteries to be as hard as stone.
Sometimes, the blood left the Imam's mind without a drop of sense.
It was during one of those times, in fact, that the Imam had set fire
to the Physician's elegant woodframe house by the Palace of the
Cannon Gate.

Now, one look at the deaf-mute, the Imam's blood rushed out of
his head, leaving him senseless on the flagstones in the courtyard.
Once revived, the Iman was boiling mad.

"Get that Green Devil out of here!" cried the Imam. "Can't you
see his ugly green skin?"

"That color is from starvation," said the Physician, who didn't
hold the Imam's disposition against him. "The youth suffers from a
hunger that's older than you and I."

"But he'll require care," the tutoress piped up. "Too much care."

"I'm sure we'll all do what we can," Lady Gülbahar said.

"Count me out," the tutoress chided. "If you want to saddle
yourself with more work, that's your business."

The tutoress could no longer take her body about the house.
She was fat as several mountains made entirely out of lard. So she
wanted to keep all the available love and care for herself. The
Physician and Lady Gülbahar didn't shun physical work. They still
kept the stone house shipshape, despite the inconvenience of living
so far from the City, and being too poor to have servants. But the
stone courtyard gleamed as if waxed because the Physician washed
the stones every day with soft oil soap. All around the courtyard, a
perennial border of flowers nodded in the breezes. Behind the house
was a well-tended orchard, a vegetable patch, a small vineyard and
a deep field of vulnerary and culinary herbs.

Thin, determined and industrious, the Physician could be heard

washing the dishes in the kitchen. As he worked he sang, especially
lullabies from the province of Karaman. Never did he hint to his big
and handsome wife that he was cleaning up for both of them.

"To put it kindly," the tutoress whispered to visitors, "the
Physician is not like other men, if you get my meaning."

Whenever the tutoress mentioned the Physician, she made a
cranking gesture up against her head. She gossiped that old age and
misfortune had made the old man peculiar. Just take the way the
Physician befriended Death out here by the potter's field! On her
part, the tutoress was no friend of Death's, being as she said she was,
of sane mind.

"True," the Physician said sadly, "our new guest will require
serious care. Just as I withdrew from the world of deep emotions, in
hopes of lightening my presence here, God sent me this creature
bearing stone that had once lived. Perhaps the beggar did right in
questioning me. Perhaps I was wrong in withdrawing prematurely. If
I were detached, I could go about without casting a backward glance.
Perhaps it's wrong to prepare for the Visitor who terminates delights
and separates companions. Perhaps we're all meant to leave this
world still furiously attached to it, and regretting it as we go."

"Haven't I told you?" the tutoress exploded. "And told you. Do
you listen? No. But let some beggar come around toting a strange
wretch, you're all ears."

The miserable guest downed a glass of water, but wouldn't
touch the bowl of yogurt with crushed leaves of mint and dill.
Instead, the guest sat before the bowl and stared at the pattern the
herbs made on top of the food. Lady Gülbahar picked up the spoon
herself and offered a tiny bit of yogurt to the starving youth. The
spoonfeeding didn't work either.

"Leave him be," the Physician advised. "He'll come around
himself."

But the guest wouldn't eat anything in the way of human food,
munching on the sly seeds off the kitchen broom, blades of grass,
domestic and wild flowers. This lack of proper appetite bothered
Lady Gülbahar. The good lady complained that she saw the guest
scoop a handful of earth into his mouth. Since they had no way of
learning the guest's name, they called the strange waif Camphor—the
name of a fugitive spirit. One dared not thrust a proper Moslem name
on someone who might, after all, be born into some other religion.

The elderly couple wanted to be careful about things. They'd had so much trouble and sorrow because, once, they'd failed to attend to small beginnings of large events. And Fate had responded by dealing them several hard blows.

"He's getting much better," Lady Gülbahar said hopefully. "He's getting better now that we've thought of calling him Camphor."

Both husband and wife saw that Camphor's state was no better at all. When Lady Gülbahar, in her zeal for cleanliness, tried to bathe him, Camphor flew into a tantrum, curled up tight as a spring on the stone floor of the bath. Holding onto the miserable rags that passed for clothing, he screamed wordlessly something that sounded like "Glugh! Glugh!" Like a person whose tongue is cut off, when he, clearly, had an intact tongue in his head.

"Camphor's terrified of bathing," she reported to her husband. "Of course, it's somewhat improper for me to bathe a male person. You try."

"Let Camphor be," said the Physician.

"Doesn't Camphor remind you of someone?" she insisted.

"Not much," the old Physician said.

So, they let Camphor be. And they were pleasantly surprised when Camphor took charge of the cabbage patch. Under Camphor's care, the rows of cabbages responded enthusiastically to existence, like a row of students under the tutelage of a patient master. Not a single pest disfigured their thick green petals.

"I think Camphor's headier than Camphor lets on," the Physician said. "See? He's at one with the headiest member of the vegetable kingdom."

"He's an idiot!" said the retired tutoress called Mistress Kevser.

Chapter 23

$\mathcal{A}$TONEMENT

*Hürü returns from the Dread Kingdom
and Selim the Grim redeems his heart*

$\mathcal{U}$nbeknownst to Lady Gülbahar, in the whitewashed stone house by the graveyards, the Saint who died of body-rot made the rounds, showing himself to the unfortunate deaf-mute. Sometimes, when the lady couldn't resist tempting Camphor with breakfast in bed—big slices of bread and cheese, topped with her fragrant jams (all of which she'd have to take away untouched)—she heard murmurings that stopped as soon as she opened the door to the trunkroom where Camphor slept. Camphor was talking to someone. But to whom? Or someone talked to Camphor. But who?

Often, Lady Gülbahar's memory seemed to be playing tricks on her. Seeing Camphor sleep, curled up on a mat in the corner, she thought she recognized the unfortunate waif's prominent cheekbones, the full lips and the pale wrists where the pulse beat with such intensity. Having no time for sentiment—what with the house to run, and looking to the welfare of the strange denizens that it seemed to attract—she didn't dwell much on the mumblings of her own heart. She reported to her husband that Camphor was stealthily conversing with someone. The Physician thought the poor sap was probably hallucinating. Which was a good sign.

"We're running a loony bin here," he told her. "I don't know about the other two, but Camphor's prognosis isn't hopeless. Camphor can instantly regain his memory and lost speech if something happens that is as cataclysmic as what made him lose his faculties. His case is complicated with a nervous condition called anorexia. It shows up in young people who've been force-fed ideas, emotions, as well as food. A form of rebellion that can starve the rebel to death. I've been watching Camphor's odd cravings. He eats only what's unacceptable to civilized people but eats just barely enough to survive. Anyway, since the condition rarely, if ever, manifests itself in males, I have my suspicions about Camphor's sex. He might be a hermaphrodite."

"Poor thing!" Lady Gülbahar said. "How do we know for sure?"

"We don't," he said. "You don't expect me to pull down Camphor's pants, do you?"

Mistress Kevser hinted, whenever she could, that the Physician took delight in impiety, in unregenerated ideas and hostility towards mosque and clergy. The Physician didn't take the retired schoolteacher's criticisms amiss. He felt the presence of a Power that might be called God. But, to him, God was the sum-total of all the collective Good in the universe. If that made him a heretic, well then, a heretic he was.

"The Imam and Mistress Kevser," he often reminded his wife, "are useful to us as agents of Chaos, lest we forget, in our orderly and hermetic lives, the powerful force of ignorant beliefs."

The Physician and his wife were attracted to Ideas. Sometimes they thought they were the only free thinkers left in the world. They had retained from the past a certain influence that had always been empirical: Sufi Thought. In the Physician's case it was the influence of the Bektashi, the teachers who were humorists and who were far too liberal to insist that God be Good. The Physician said that what goes on in our minds has always gone on. The ancients had been thinking unimpeded before the Big Religions set in. So, neither the Physician nor his good wife held any commerce with unexamined beliefs. Nor did they practice religion that manifested itself in brutality against others.

Without the presence of the two disgraceful permanent guests, they might become too smug and start thinking they were right without thinking. The disagreeable pair kept the Physician's mind alive.

The Imam, who seemed to be uncomfortable in the Physician's presence ever since the latter returned from Mecca, had perhaps taken refuge in early dementia so he could imagine the Physician dead. That's what the Imam thought as he blithered and peed in his bed; he thought the Physician was dead and buried. Then, during bouts of lucidity, he'd recognize the Physician's slight form and make a terrible face.

"Aren't you dead yet?" the Imam demanded of the Physician. In fact, it was the Imam himself who'd died several times from cardiac arrest, only to be brought back each time by the Physician thumping on his chest and blowing the gift of life into his gaping mouth. Each time, the Physician, slight and old, practically expired from the tremendous emotional and physical strength required to bring the Imam around.

"You cracked my ribs, you dog!" the Imam always scolded the Physician on his returns from the dead. "May God punish you for misusing a helpless man in his sick bed."

The Physician never told the Imam he'd died. There was no sense in bedeviling a demented person. After one particular episode that severely taxed the Physician in every way and left him gasping, breathless, cold and indignant, Lady Gülbahar helped her husband make a policy decision not to interfere with Death's work. The Imam didn't know that the next time he croaked, he'd stay croaked. In the meantime, the couple paid no attention to the Imam's proclamations, echoed by Mistress Kevser, that the Physician lived past the normal time allotted to men because the Physician was in cahoots with Satan.

"We're paying our dues to sentiment," Lady Gülbahar said, "that's what. We go to unreasonable lengths to keep our children's memories alive. Why else would we take care of their respective pedagogues? Especially when both are such pisspots?"

"Told you this is a loony bin," the Physician said. "Goes for you and me, too."

Obsessed as they might be with their private losses, the Physician and his wife still woke up each day, thankful for each day that life brings. Neither had any intention to die, although, in some remarkable way, they'd managed to make the Angel of Death an intimate of the household. Giving up his lifelong struggle to outwit Death seemed to give the Physician a new lease on life, a new interest in seeing how organisms behave if left alone. Never before in his life had he ever thought of leaving anything alone. He'd always been out there—push, push, push—all for the sake of health and order. Now, he was on his elbows and knees watching fungi, blights and molds. This was Chaos and it absorbed him. He began to think that certain blights and molds must also be present in the organism for it to keep itself organized. Scouring out Chaos to achieve perfect order now seemed to him a dangerous as well as a mistaken practice.

Take, for example, Camphor. The Physician serenely studied Camphor endure the unhygienic condition which the Physician made no effort to correct. He was beginning to trust that nature, with its balances of health and corruption, might be the only healer. Yet, he wasn't unaware of something about Camphor that demanded of him some involvement with Camphor's plight. If he succumbed to that demand, the Physician knew he'd be right in there, forcing on Camphor physical hygiene, and thereby destroying his chances for spontaneous emotional recovery. In a way, he was working desperately *not* to recognize Camphor. In his heart, he hoped something would happen that would snap Camphor back from the place where the youth had gotten lost.

So it was that on a fine day in the Fall when the pomegranates by the doorway came to fruit, there was a tremendous knocking at the Physician's black door. Amidst much clattering of horses' hooves on the cobblestones, military drums and bugles, rapid-fire commands, it was a great company come calling on the Physician. In fact, the company was no less than the entire Ottoman army: the infantry and the cavalry, the miners and the sappers, the artillery and the support forces, even the *bashibozouks*, the *chapuljus*, the lunatic fringe that preceded the regulars to battle for the express purpose of becoming cannon fodder; they'd all stopped by. Their colorful and intimidating presence covered the immense graveyards as well as the adjoining open countryside.

The old Physician had heard the armies were on the move again, this time to besiege and take Vienna, now that the East was secured. But he did not understand why he was being paid a visit by Sultan Selim's troops, unless they had in store for him an unpleasant surprise. Yet, it was safe to assume, a whole army wasn't needed to punish a mere physician living quietly in the countryside. Well, whatever it was, the Physician was ready.

"Yes?" he said. "What is your desire?"

The man standing in the doorway, a big light-colored bruiser whose high color betrayed his tendency for apoplexy, turned out to be the Sultan's brand-new Grand Vizier, an Arab who didn't know enough vernacular to say hello, how are you. Inquiring if the Physician understood the new Grand Vizier, the old Physician modestly replied that he spoke a little Arabic and less Persian. What was the Grand Vizier's pleasure, may he live longer than his predecessor.

"My name's Shahriyar," the regal bruiser said, "a noble son of the Arabs. I come to your door on behalf of Sultan Selim who's being carried in a litter to Adrianople. The Sultan is grievously ill, although the troops aren't aware of how mortally he suffers. You know how the troops are, chomping at the bit. They think they're on the move to Vienna. If they're not given a war, they'll revolt."

"You don't say!" the old Physician said.

The Grand Vizier called Shahriyar explained that, though the troops thought their Sultan was suffering from a minor discomfort, they expected he'd soon recover and lead them with his usual fiery energy and rapid destructive march. But Selim was in no condition to think, let alone move armies. The Grand Vizier confided to the Physician that though he was an experienced administrator, he had never been to battle himself. Selim must recover and take over the helm. But the Sultan, he whispered, was more like a wild animal who was mortally wounded and cornered. He would lash out furiously, intent on the senseless destruction of others. Only a few hours ago, on the advice of his former Grand Vizier, Selim had allowed the court physicians to lance the boil on his back, a large, five-cusped carbuncle which the physicians called Shir-Penche, or the Lion's Claw.

"Believe me," Grand Vizier Shahriyar said, "the boil really was in the shape of a lion's claw. But once the court physicians lanced the carbuncle, the pain drove the Sultan insane. He had the former Grand Vizier and attending physicians immediately put to the greased noose. Only five hours ago, I was appointed the new Grand Vizier. All those close to the throne having dispersed for parts unknown, the office fell to me, a foreigner, because I didn't know enough to make myself scarce. It was an appointment that couldn't be refused."

The Physician smelled the wine on the new Grand Vizier's breath and sympathized. One must lace one's head with enough painkiller before putting it into the lion's mouth.

"Aren't you apprehensive about your neck?" he asked the poor man.

"I'm not here to discuss my neck!" snapped Grand Vizier Shahriyar. "I'm here to ask you to help Selim, old man. You're supposed to be a legendary healer in your own time. Several ladies in the Palace say that you have a pact with Death, that if you see Death standing at the foot of the patient's bed, you can go ahead and save the patient."

"And what if I see Death clutching the patient's headboard?" the Physician said, amused. "Did they tell you what I do then?"

"Yes," Grand Vizier Shahriyar said, "you're supposed to turn the challenge down. That's why they say you've lived long as Methuselah."

"I'm not that old!" the Physician said. "But I no longer practice healing. Death makes no pacts with anyone."

"Have you lost your humanity?" Grand Vizier Shahriyar asked pointedly. "Even if Selim weren't your sovereign; you owe him something as a human being. Poor man is too pained to know where he is or what he is. Will you stand by idly while a man suffers?"

"Not idly," the Physician said. "But stand by him, I will."

"May we bring the Sultan inside then?"

"Suit yourself," the Physician said, shrugging.

Eight muscular black mutes brought into the courtyard a palanquin inside which a wolf seemed trapped. When Shahriyar lifted the drape, the old Physician saw his Sultan on whom he'd never before laid eyes. Strapped by heavy leather bonds to the litter, mercilessly oppressed and drawn, his strange gray eyes crazed with pain, his emaciated chest heaving spasmodically, there lay the Sultan of the Ottomans.

The old Physician felt pity for the pitiless sovereign under whose iron rule order both took its toll and brought prosperity and safety to the realm. Selim was the sort of ruler that's good for one—like bitter medicine. But here he was suffering mortal affliction, abject and chaotic in the Physician's tranquil courtyard. The old Physician didn't even have to examine the Sultan to see Death clutching him by the throat. But he must see this deadly boil, if only to satisfy his own curiosity.

"Turn the Sultan over," he said to the eight ogres.

The mute slaves, who heard but could not speak, held down the Sultan, losing ground despite their number, as they unstrapped the leather bonds. Quickly, they bound him again, now flat on his face. So much humiliation! the old Physician thought. Good thing the Sultan was hardly sensible. The Physician took a long look at the Sultan's wound. Just as he thought! The boil was not what the court

physicians said it was! The incompetents! Although the Lion's Claw
was a deadly enough disease, sometimes people recovered from it
through sheer physical stamina. But this was not the Lion's Claw.

"Ah!" the Physician said. "The tumor should never have been
lanced! The man suffers from the grip of the crab, not the lion."

"What crab?" Grand Vizier Shahriyar said. "Are you senile?"

"Cancer," the Physician said. "Ever heard of it?"

"Get rid of it then!"

"No one has discovered how," the Physician said. "Not yet."

"So!" Grand Vizier Shahriyar said. "How long has he?"

"Not long," the Physician said. "Sooner the better, considering
the torture he's going through."

"Can't you do something?" Grand Vizier Shahriyar said. "Put him
out of his misery then, at least. Administer some quick poison."

"I can't do that!" cried the Physician, recoiling. "I've never been
anyone's executioner."

"Husband," said Lady Gülbahar, who'd been standing wordlessly
at her husband's elbow, "you can do something for the poor soul. I
beg you, give the Sultan the drug of euphoria."

"What's the woman babbling about?" the Grand Vizier said.

"I do have in my possession a drug," the Physician said. "But I
have only a single draught which I was saving for myself, just in case.
My wife's only reminding me that a physician cannot hoard a precious dram for his own use. And she's right. The drug might give the
Sultan one lucid hour of relatively little pain."

"Then, don't stand around," the Grand Vizier said. "Give it to
him! Let the man regain his manhood enough to know he's dying. You
owe him that much."

As Lady Gülbahar helped the trembling Physician administer
the potent and irreplaceable drug, the infirm denizens of the household, sensing the ill omens in the air, pulled themselves together and
came one by one to witness the dying Sultan perform his terrible
task. First, Mistress Kevser waddled out and complained into Lady
Gülbahar's ear of the stench that rose off the Sultan's body. Then,
out came the Imam, his *Koran* under his arm, offering to help the sick
man depart with Faith on his breath. Then Camphor lunged at the
palanquin and, despite the Grand Vizier's glowering admonishments,
sniffed at the suffering Sultan's heavy-duty boots still on his feet.

Once the drug took effect, the Sultan began swallowing huge
gulps of air, which activity the Physician feared might stress the

Sultan's heart too much and kill him before the dying man could enjoy his final hour of lucidity. He calmed the patient with soothing words, massaged his wrists, called him endearing names such as might be used in calming down a skittish horse. Finally, the Sultan seemed able to see those gathered around him. Keeping his emaciated body still, he seemed to live, once more, inside himself. The Physician motioned to the mutes to undo the Sultan's bonds. The Sultan's eye first fell on Camphor.

"Ho!" Selim said. "So here you are at last, Bald Boy!"

As Camphor stared at the sick man with eyes as large as two glass globes in which soothsayers may see fortunes, the Physician and his wife could not help but show their surprise at the poor waif's seeming acquaintance with the Sultan. But still, Camphor didn't speak, though for a second he looked as if he might. But then he hung his head as if he'd done something to offend the Sultan.

"You're long forgiven, Bald Boy," the Sultan said. "But you look worse than you ever did. What happened to you? Got the scrofula again?"

"He doesn't speak," the Physician said.

"He never had anything to say anyway," Sultan Selim said.

The Sultan seemed to have woken up in a jocular mood. As his eyes scanned the courtyard, the next person he recognized was his Grand Vizier.

"You still here?" Selim asked his brand-new Grand Vizier. "Must be I only dreamed I'd had you strung up."

"Still here," Grand Vizier Shahriyar said, "and serving you."

"Good!" Selim said. "But tell me, Shahriyar, where the hell am I?"

"At this old Physician's dwelling," the Grand Vizier said. "The good old man gave you a healing dose of some drug he was saving for himself."

"Ah!" Selim said, turning his head painfully toward the Physician. "May God requite you, old man, for I have a feeling that I won't live to requite anybody. Tell me the truth now, how am I?"

"You're done for," the Physician said. "That's why I gave you the potion. I wouldn't give it to a man for whom there was the slightest bit of hope."

"Now, now, old man," the Grand Vizier said, "hold your tongue. Sultan Selim has places to go and peoples to conquer."

"I have no journey left to make," Selim said, "save to the

hereafter. Send word to Prince Suleyman; tell him Vienna awaits him, not Selim. Tell him he's fated to be the Second Solomon; tell him never to forget the wise king after whom he was named. Tell him to give law to the lawless, civility to the uncivil, tolerance to the intolerable. Tell him his father charges him to behave, in every way, against the example set by his father."

"On my head," Shahriyar said, swearing fealty, "and on my eye."

"And Shahriyar," Selim said, "I put my trust in you to make the transition smooth. Forgive me my past offenses against you. If I could, I'd kneel to you."

"It's I who must kneel to you," Shahriyar said, falling on his knees. "Forgive me my sin against you, Selim my Lord."

"You are, and always were, the more generous man," Selim said, "For what offense should I forgive you? What happened to my wife happened through no fault of yours, Shahriyar."

"Ahh," said the Grand Vizier, covering his face with his hands.

"Now, be that as it may," Selim said, "send for the Keeper of Royal Effects and have him bring me my *saz*. I wish to die singing, for I know not how to weep."

The imperial *saz* was brought so the Sultan could sing himself to death. Selim sat up in his litter, waited for Lady Gülbahar to plump up his pillows and took the *saz* in hand. He seemed to consider something that interested him briefly; then, surprisingly, he came up with a simple song. He sang a *türkü* that came sweeping through Central Asia into the Anatolian peninsula on nomads' breaths, though the Sultan, burdened with the pain of humanity, invented it in his last hour. As the old Physician put it later: Who would've guessed Selim had it in him? The *türkü* was called "Hürü's Lagoon" and was to be sung for centuries to come among plain folks, as one of unknown authorship, since Selim did not sign the verses by mentioning his name in the final stanza. He let the *türkü* go as it were. This is what he sang:

> For Hürü's Lagoon tastes salt and clear,
> My mermaid's drowned in watery vault;
> I lost my woman; Hürü's gone away
> Where her lagoon tastes clear and salt.
> In Hürü's Lagoon sleeps my son;
> As night won't come, she will not come.
> Come Hürü, come *türkü*, sleep come!

Her image fell down into blue water,
Her hair turned the ripples gold;
Fires of color bathed my grayling world,
For Hürü's Lagoon tastes clear and salt.
In Hürü's Lagoon sleeps my son;
As night won't come, she will not come.
Come Hürü, come *türkü*, sleep come!

Shahriyar blames our bad blood,
Shahriyar says Hürü was distraught—
Heart, don't take Shahriyar's word,
For Hürü's Lagoon tastes clear and salt.
In Hürü's Lagoon sleeps my son;
As night won't come, she will not come;
Come Hürü, come *türkü*; sleep come!

Come night, come Hürü, lull my heart
Made of flint and black basalt;
Bathe me in ancient seas and hush,
For Hürü's Lagoon tastes clear and salt.
In Hürü's Lagoon sleeps my son;
Won't you come as I am done?
Come Hürü, come *türkü*; sleep come!

The Physician and Lady Gülbahar could barely contain them selves, so excited were they to hear their lost daughter's name, so lovingly and insistently called. Yet it seemed inappropriate to question the Sultan as he lay expiring. In whispers they charged each other to put to the Sultan the question that might prove too painful for the dying man as well as themselves. Just as the Physician screwed up his courage, Camphor rudely reached over the Sultan's litter and plucked a string of the *saz*: Ping!

"Your song touched the poor young man," said the Physician, excusing the waif. "I'll see to it he keeps his fingers off your *saz*."

"Has Bald Boy never played for you?" the Sultan asked in amazement. "When he was with me, he was at his music all the time. His instructors got rid of his stuttering by using music as his reward."

"P-p-play . . ." Camphor croaked. "P-p-play . . ."

"Let the young man demonstrate his skill, Sultan Selim," the Physician said. "This might be the chance I've been waiting for."

"I don't mind," Selim said, handing over the *saz*.

"What will you play for us, Camphor?" Lady Gülbahar said, at the edge of her seat.

"The addle-brain can't play!" Mistress Kevser said in a stage whisper. "The rate he's going, we shall never get out of here."

"I'm in no hurry to get anywhere," Selim said earnestly. "Take your time, Bald Boy."

So, the strange musician took the imperial *saz* in hand. This is the song that came pouring out to break Camphor's silence:

> He stirred in pain of his demon sleep
> Enchanted Prince, his half-sleep he slept.
> Despising tears he caused and love he spurned,
> The demon-sleeper within dreamless wept.
>
> It's She inside who says her Nay!
> Demands your life with willful glee.
> Call her forth by her true name,
> Awake the demon-woman free!
>
> He and She are One in human soul's
> Looking-glass, the snake around the well,
> The well around the snake, the friend, the foe,
> Heaved and heaving, its heaven and its hell.
>
> It's She inside who says her Nay!
> Demands your life in willful glee.
> Call her forth by her true name,
> Say Hürü; say Hürü is Free!

The listeners were surprised that the verses were constructed in the high-flown and chimerical language in which highbrow poets talked to each other; Arabic in text, Persian in ornamentation, set in motion by verbs in Turkish. One would've had to be an accomplished linguist to get the meaning. Even if the idea had been less complicated, the listeners would've had a hard time getting all the words since the song hadn't yet been translated.

"Bosh!" Mistress Kevser decreed. "Never heard such nonsense."

"I believe it's a song to wake the Prince's sleeping soul," Lady Gülbahar said simply.

"I get it now!" the Physician said excitedly. "The male is the body, and the female the soul. Is that right?"

"I don't think that's quite right," Lady Gülbahar said. "I think both are, you see, both."

But, it seems, Sultan Selim understood the song. Half-asleep and half on his death-bed, he sank back into his pillows in an agony that was clearly not physical alone.

"My Hürü wrote that for me," Selim moaned. "I just know it! Yet, she never sang it for me. During our brief time together, she never did sing."

"Can she also be our Hürü?" the Physician wondered aloud. "Our Hürü was such a simple lass."

"Simple as Satan!" the Imam said. "Music is Satan's bait!"

"Why is Hürü's name being bandied around?" Grand Vizier Shahriyar wanted to know, not having caught the vernacular drift. Everyone was too devastated to answer Shahriyar, brand-new Grand Vizier as he was. The implacable ghost of the lost woman, the lost child, the lost bride, seemed to demand propitiation from all those present.

"Tell us where you learned that song," the Physician said to Camphor. "How is your history entwined with that of the girl called Hürü? If you can't speak, sing us something we might understand. Sing, for example, your own song."

"So I will," said Camphor, talking up a storm. "But first, all the doors must be barred. And with each refrain, the mutes must perform what the song demands."

"Bar the door," Selim said. "And listen well to the refrain."

So, the musician once more took the imperial *saz* in hand and sang:

> The Imam veered off the holy path,
> Assaulted Hürü at the public bath.
> Corrupt Kevser his panderer became;
> Bind the Cleric, bind the ugly Damè,
>   Oh, bind!

The eight mutes immediately bound the Imam to the doorpost where he gibbered and blithered pitifully, having lost his speech along with his wandering mind. Since Mistress Kevser collapsed into a fat puddle on the flagstones, the eight mutes bodily lifted the foul-mouthed bawd and bound her to the same post by the neck. Nobody wanted to hear Mistress Kevser's loud demand for justice, her admonitions that she was innocent until proven guilty; nor did anybody believe her litany of good deeds performed before she came to this unexpected pass. Once more the Sultan ordered silence, the musician took *saz* in hand:

> My brother bound me to an ancient pine,
> Wouldn't tell the nature of my crime,
> Left me for the sake of Karaman's name;
> Bind my brother, for he is to blame,
> > Oh, bind!

The eight mutes looked around for a brother. But one cannot bind the dead anywhere, let alone blame the dead for the hold they have over the living. But, being resourceful mutes, they went through the motions of binding an invisible someone to a cedar tree that grew in the middle of the courtyard. So the musician took the *saz* in hand once more:

> Hidir led Selim to my hiding place,
> But Selim didn't know my scabby face.
> I played his fool, Bald Boy by name;
> Bind the Sultan to his mortal fame,
> > Oh, bind!

The mutes, being literal-minded as well as imaginative, bound the Sultan to his royal palanquin; seeing the Sultan didn't object, they tightened the leather straps. So the musician took *saz* in hand.

> Shahrazad has wonderful stories told,
> Telling how wine renders Arabs bold.
> The baby's life did Shahriyar claim;
> Bind the Arab to his reckless shame,
> > Oh, bind!

For Grand Vizier Shahriyar's place of bondage, the eight mutes chose a huge storage amphora that stood in one corner, inside which the Physician's grapes were fermenting. They bound Shahriyar to his future intoxications. The noble Arab seemed to sense the game was up, but he didn't offer any excuses. So the musician took up the *saz*.

> My parents, they are kind and astute;
> They bind with love both loud and mute,
> But believed against me a foul claim;
> So bind them together just the same,
> > Oh, bind!

The eight mutes must've thought the Physician and Lady Gül-bahar were the most likely candidates for parenthood; but instead of binding them to posts, they bound the couple together by the wrists, seeing how parenthood is no crime. Now that the courtyard was no longer a court but also a hall of detention, those listeners bound by manifest restraints both understood and did not understand their condition. Something, however, stirred and muttered inside them, now that the anesthetic was wearing off, like a fairy tale that comes to an end.

That was when the musician stood up and pulled off the head pestilence which appeared to have been, all the time, the foul bladder of a dead sheep. The unfortunate He was at once trans-formed into a fortunate She. Swiftly, she unbound her red-gold hair which came tumbling down her shoulders in waves silky and free. Don't ask me how that abundant hair was kept clean and shiny under the despicable bladder; in revelations like this, finicky questions aren't appropriate.

"HÜRÜ!" gasped everyone, besides the mutes, in mixed unison. "We knew it was you all the time!"

But, they hadn't known! Since when have people known what's in their best interest to know? "I knew it all the time!"—That's our common chorus whenever the obvious can no longer be avoided. Like the nature of our existence, for example, bound and hood-winked, prisoners and slaves in this restricted place. Yet, during moments of revelation, in what appears to be the best of all possible worlds with its comforting philosophies about the time to sow and the time to reap, suddenly we discover ourselves confined beyond all tolerance. Without knowing, we're already on the road to some-place else. Death, we know in our hearts, is only the half of it.

Whatever acknowledgement Hürü had made to existence, in madness and in health, now she approached her dying husband and unbound his stays. She crawled into the palanquin next to him under the fur coverlet, and lay herself down next to Selim's violent shiver-ing.

"You're dying, Selim," she said.

At this joke, Selim laughed as in the old days when he roared with gusto at ironies beyond himself. Soon the husband and wife were laughing together irrepressibly as the restrained onlookers tittered uncomfortably at the inappropriateness of the humor. Selim and Hürü sat within the circle of each other's arms, shaking with the

same violent tremor, cheeks pressed together, like a pair of storybook lovers who were, at last, totally and terminally wed. As the
Physician knew well, having administered himself the dram of merciful lucidity, Selim was on the Road to Bliss. Now that he'd tasted
atonement, he'd never return to life where light is obscured by
ignorance, truth by desire and joy by pain. Selim would not—he
could not—hang onto his raging, tortured, mortal shell. He'd follow
lucidity to its logical conclusion. Already on Selim's lips was a
whispered song. He put his last breath into a wish that was merci-
ly granted.

"Comes Hürü, comes *türkü*. Sleep comes."

And so Selim's stranded refrain bid this world good night.

The monarch who'd squandered mercy in his life preserved
mercy for those he left behind. And so, Selim, with light under his
eyelashes, his breath foundering in the scent of roses and bergamots,
fully awake now, fell fully asleep. True, he was forty-seven, six-foot-
four and grim as the name he earned himself. But he didn't die a
painful death. Historians are so gleeful in reporting that Selim's death
was excruciating—as if a violent end were the just desserts of a
violent man. The joke is on the historians. Selim died serenely
singing.

Chapter 24

THE TURNING

Hürü sets out
on the road to Baghdad once more

*H*ürü didn't intend to keep all those people captive. Neither did she seek revenge on Mistress Kevser, the Imam and Shahriyar—just because fate had conspired to make the threesome the villains of her life. Her aged parents could not be blamed for tugging at her heart, around which they'd thrown an invisible lasso of love. She was no saint herself, Hürü figured.

Yet, it wasn't easy to let Shahriyar take a hike. Still tortured by Selim's death, and sobered under restraints, Shahriyar tried to make amends with Hürü, blaming the loss of Karajuk on accident.

"I know you can't forgive me," he begged her. "Let me, at least, be a slave to your father's household. I'll chop your wood and carry your water."

"Thank you, but no," the Physician said on his daughter's behalf.

"Go, Shahriyar," Hürü said, "and don't look back."

So, Grand-Viziered for a scant half dozen hours, perhaps having set a record for the shortest term of any prime minister, Shahriyar disguised himself as a lumberjack and departed on foot for parts unknown.

It's easier to report one's sins to the whole world than to tell one's parents one single unadorned truth. Hürü recited to her par-

ents her history as it now stands, embellished, inventive, provisional.
When she came to the part telling how Karajuk sank to the bottom
of the salt lagoon, like a water-lily in his diaphanous shirt, and then
like a stone, the old couple sobbed for the grandchild they'd never
seen. Yet, Hürü was tearless. Honestly, there was no wellspring
available. Instead, she recomposed her state of mind on Selim's
orphaned *saz*, in a song she called "Hürü's Madness." The Physician
and Lady Gülbahar patiently waited through their daughter's urge to
break into song. When "Hürü's Madness" was done, the old Physician
had an observation to make.

"Seems to me," he said, "you don't remember Karajuk very well.
He might've just as well been the hunk of marble wrapped in
swaddling clothes with which you came home."

That brought on the tears. Not the knowledge of Karajuk being
really dead. It was the grief of not having wholly known Karajuk while
he lived that made Hürü cry. She admitted, sobbing, that her memory
of Karajuk was not unlike that of a doll which had been, inadvertently, left out in the rain. She regretted him. But she didn't know
Karajuk.

"Perhaps you didn't forgive Karajuk," Lady Gülbahar said, "for
being the son of his father."

"Oh, no!" Hürü said, shocked beyond belief. "He was an innocent
babe, Mama! It's unreasonable to resent a baby for his father's
difficulties with life."

"And you are a reasonable woman," the Physician said with
irony.

"Right," Hürü said, "now that I've recovered my wits."

"Then, how do you account for the blind spot in your recita-
tion?" the Physician asked.

"What blind spot?" Hürü said tersely. "I told you everything."

"If I could perceive through your eyes," he said, "I'd tell you
what blind spot. But, then, if I saw through your eyes, I wouldn't
know what is missing either."

"Give the girl a chance," Lady Gülbahar said, "to recover from
her husband's death. Maybe the blind spot is the shadow of the dead
man."

"One thing is for sure though," Hürü said. "I'd better hit the road
soon."

"Why, but why?" her mother said. "Don't go, my darling."

"I have to," Hürü said. "Have to see what lies in my blind spot."

"And I have to lose you all over again?" said her lady mother, a small sob involuntarily escaping her lips.

The Physician went back to his reading, which he'd taken on with renewed devotion since he'd turned recluse. And Lady Gülbahar withdrew to do her weeping on her own time. Her tears fell in a pot of preserves she made every Fall, a jam made of unripe Seville oranges, dark green and bittersweet as the reunion with her daughter.

"I'll be at the graveyards," Hürü said, poking her head in the kitchen long enough to see how red her mother's fine nose had turned from weeping, "paying a visit to Saint Job."

"Ask him to grant you," Lady Gülbahar said, "a little patience."

The two guests chose this moment to put in their appearance. Lady Gülbahar had not seen hide nor hair of either criminal since Hürü's revelations. Both had made themselves scarce the minute they were unbound, neither able to examine their consciences nor look anyone in the face. Fuzzy though the Imam was about the details of the turmoil, he followed Mistress Kevser into the kitchen to tell Lady Gülbahar her hospitality was no longer acceptable.

"We're leaving now," she said to Lady Gülbahar, who was weeping over the hot stove. "Too many ghosts in this house and not enough understanding. The Imam's the only true friend a woman's ever had. So, I'm taking him along."

Lady Gülbahar tried to find out where the two were going, worried about them, since Mistress Kevser could hardly walk and the Imam think. Mistress Kevser shrugged as if she didn't have any idea of her destination.

"Seems to me I have a distant cousin in Smyrna," the mistress said in an effort to be precise. "Saint Hidir willing, I might find this cousin, for my distress is dire. And if you think we're absconding with anything of value, you're welcome to go through our satchels. I refuse to be called a thief, should anything turn up missing later."

Lady Gülbahar waved her hand as if to dismiss the idea.

"Please say something to Hürü as you go by the graveyards," Lady Gülbahar said, sniffling. "One moment of reconciliation is more blessed than a lifetime of teaching piety."

"So she can kiss me off?" Mistress Kevser cried. "Not on your life! I want her to feel the weight of having wronged me. I want her to remember how she ruined our lives, barging in here with a bunch of allegations and not a shred of evidence. I want her suffering her guilty conscience."

Lady Gülbahar sadly regarded the Imam, who was salivating, his eyes on the plump green globes she was stirring in the tart syrup.

"About time you went then," Lady Gülbahar said.

"Say goodbye," Mistress Kevser instructed the Imam.

"Say goodbye," the Imam said.

And that was that. The two unfortunates hit the dusty road, creeping at two snails' paces, without having uttered a word of thanks to the Physician.

After a few weeks of having her parents all to herself, Hürü, too, begged their leave. Where would she go? What would she do? Of course she was still too young to contemplate the graveyards day in and day out, though she'd already suffered widowhood and the pain of surviving her only child. But wandering aimlessly throughout our virulent and wretched world also seemed an unfitting occupation for a young woman—unheard of as well as unproductive. That sort of drastic lack of domicile belongs to the wandering dervishes, to curiosity-seeking Western puzzleheads, to lepers and those God means to destroy.

Wouldn't she prefer, Lady Gülbahar wondered, to settle down with some nice scholar or a budding physician and raise a proper family? Granted, marrying a commoner might seem like a comedown, but there were men more princely than titled princes.

True, the Physician concurred. Selim had never been a fitting consort for a girl who'd been raised in a family devoted to freedom.

"When you say freedom," Lady Gülbahar chided her husband, "you mean freedom from interference. Truth is, the living get interfered with all the time."

"Ah, but one's still free," the Physician said, "when one understands where the interference comes from. Freedom is Conduct."

"I enjoyed your lecture very much," Hürü said to her father. "But now I must go."

"Each time has its Conduct," the Physician went on, as if his daughter had asked him the meaning of Conduct. "Each place has its Conduct, too. And each state of mind as well. Conduct is both the means and the end; it's the Journey and the Arrival. That's why I say Hürü can still be free, here in this narrow house, even with her interfering foolish old parents—while she, herself, will be interfering with our set old ways."

"Stay, Hürü," Lady Gülbahar said. "It's far better to bind your old parents with love than set free a thousand slaves."

"But I can't stay," Hürü said, "let alone understand what is meant by Conduct. Should I stay, I would still continue to conduct myself badly. So, I'm not yet free to stay."

"Go, then," the Physician said. "If this compulsion to leave passes, you might return of your own choice."

"It's all your fault!" Lady Gülbahar exploded at her husband. "You always put ideas in her head."

"That's what ideas are for," the Physician said. "The candle cannot illuminate itself."

"Others have their children around them," Lady Gülbahar said. "Most grandparents dandle their grandchildren on their knees. But I must abide like some dry old stick, watching funerals go by. What delight is there in this thing called Freedom of Conduct? Does freedom mean to give up everything that's delightful?"

"I am sorry," Hürü said. "I *am*."

"Since you're set on rattling around like a hollow gourd," Lady Gülbahar said, disappointed and angry, "no one here has any more advice to give you. But remember this, daughter: there's a big difference between being called an Adventurer and an Adventuress."

"Observe," the Physician said, "Conduct that was considered improper or impossible yesterday has become good and right today. Conduct that is judged wrong today will surely be esteemed right tomorrow."

"It's all your fault!" Lady Gülbahar reiterated. "My father, may he rest in peace, warned me about you."

"What about me?" the Physician said, amused.

"My father said," Lady Gülbahar quoted, "'Beware of the man who makes off with your wart because he'll soon oblige you to make do without other presences you're accustomed to; for example, your daughter.'"

"That's very good!" the Physician said. "I never dreamed your father truly understood me."

"Now that we all know whom to blame," Hürü said, "may I go?"

But no! She couldn't just leave without a purpose or destination! What was her destination then? Well, East. There was a certain salt lagoon in a piney forest, not too far from Konya; she longed to lay eyes on that lagoon again.

"Oh, no!" Lady Gülbahar said. "You can't mean to go back where the little one drowned."

"Why not?" Hürü said.

The Physician remarked that he wasn't aware of any salt la-
goons anywhere near Konya. He had, after all, grown up in that locale
without once coming across or hearing reports about such a place.
But he didn't argue with his daughter about the existence of the
beauty spot on the plain Konya steppe. He thought Hürü must've
imagined the place while she was out of her mind, but he didn't say
so. With that thought, the old Physician, who hadn't been to town
for quite some time, put on his turban—he disliked hats of any sort,
especially one that a mummy might wear to the grave—and prepared
to walk to the City. He'd inquire downtown and secure a place for
Hürü in an appropriate caravan of travellers. Hürü thought it unnecessary for him to go to all that trouble.

"Let me perform this one small service," the Physician said. "It's
really more for me than for you."

That's how come one sharp morning in December, Hürü set off
to face the long and harsh winter on the central steppe. Her place in
a mercantile caravan secured for a fee, she rode a company hack,
Selim's *saz* in one saddlebag, the mute Stone Lyre in the other. In her
girdle swelled a pouch of gold Lady Gülbahar had hidden, just in
case, on her husband's death, the state should decide to confiscate
the Physician's property. The gold was Lady Gülbahar's insurance
against a disagreeable, penniless widowhood. Who knew? she said.
Before one dried one's tears for one's departed helpmate, the offi-
cials were at the door, sealing it in the name of the Sultan. But, here,
Hürü, take the gold!

"I can't take it!" Hürü cried. "I won't!"

"But you must!" Lady Gülbahar said. "I can't send you off
without knowing there are a couple of gold pieces clinking in your
girdle. If you refuse, may you kiss my dead eyes!"

"I'll keep the gold for you," Hürü said, taking the pouch. Neither
could Lady Gülbahar prevent herself from burdening Hürü with
homemade preserves, meatballs, a couple of roasted chickens, stuffed
grapeleaves, meat pastries, crocks of olives, cheeses, boiled eggs,
loaves of bread, all of which required the hiring of a pack mule to
carry the excess baggage. That Hürü would eventually run out of
provisions and have to depend on her own skills didn't seem to have
occurred to Lady Gülbahar; nor was it any concern of hers that Hürü
would've preferred travelling light. She loaded the hired pack mule
with two huge wicker hampers. Finally, she pressed on her daughter
a sheaf of poems bundled in a yellow silk napkin, those fateful poems

the Physician and Lady Gülbahar had fired at each other during their courtship.

"The poems were the only valuables I snatched from the burning house," she told Hürü. "It's the book of your parents' love. We call it *The Pouch*. Take it along."

Chapter 25

LIFE AND DEATH

*Now Hürü knows she's utterly alone
in this beautiful place, this awful place*

*H*ürü would've preferred treading
alone this same road she seemed
destined to travel back and forth, each time feeling she hadn't yet
learned what she'd set out to learn. But she was no longer the young
girl so full of trust and expectations, so prone to remark on the
inconsistencies in what other people say and do. She felt like the
sorry hack she rode: tired, scathed and bruised.

The care she took to keep to herself, avoiding easy acquaintance with those she met, guarding her energy and her self, as it
were, reminded her of Shahrazad's aloofness. She remembered Shahrazad's pale and wan face as the writer peered inside herself, trying
the puzzles of her own heart, as she breathed her own life and wit
into old plots. How carefully Shahrazad husbanded herself! Now,
Hürü, too, took care not to inspire in her travelling companions any
friendship or hostility as the caravan slowly wound along the steppe
for an entire month.

Under the rule of her stepson, Süleyman—who was, in the
future, to be known as the Magnificent—bandits, rapists, cozeners
and other assorted malfeasants seemed to be lying low. Hürü heard
from the travellers that Sultan Süleyman's arm was swift and long;
detailed laws were being drafted for every little offense, insuring
folks their rights as well as their obligations. The rebellions of

330

fanatical Persian Shi'ites no longer paid off, nor could their sympathizers, the Redhead nomad Turks, raid landed peasantry whenever they felt like helping themselves to groceries or girls. Any good Sunnite, who minded the law and his own business, was free to pursue happiness. It bothered folks, however, to put up with so many rules. Like simpler folk everywhere, they were in favor of less government.

In February, when the bleak face of all ill fortune not yet suffered puts in its fangs, when old people succumb despairing of ever seeing Spring, when the young come down with fevers and everyone else with melancholia, when freezing winds hurry down from the north, houses burn and herds are lost in blizzards, Hürü quit the caravan. She left behind for the other travellers the mottled and bone-weary horse, the mule with the remainder of Lady Gülbahar's provisions and her gratitude for an uneventful journey. She departed wrapped in a heavy cloak, Selim's *saz* under one arm, the Stone Lyre under the other, the pouch containing her parents' courtship dangling from her girdle. There was much admonishment, as well as banter, concerning her foolhardy departure. But she paid no heed. She'd rather make the remaining couple of days' journey to the piney woods alone, not wanting the vociferous company of travellers to intrude on the peace of the woods. Besides, once he became aware of the site, the caravan-master might return there routinely, making those magical woods a dump for what travellers cast away. Perhaps she was wrong in concealing her knowledge of the piney woods. Perhaps everyone needed a chance to visit such a mysterious and uncharted ground. No one knew for sure who might benefit from a chance encounter with the unknown. But Hürü was in no mind to share her discovery.

Upon arriving at the woods, she walked to the ancient pine tree to which she'd once been tied, only to find herself bound to a green sage dressed in a robe of shimmering, luminous green. The same tree where she'd met Selim; the same tree under which the formidable Abd-es-Samad had performed his art of drying up the lagoon, whose sandy bed had concealed the portals to the Treasury of the Tallest of the Tall; the same tree in whose presence she'd seen her infant son drown. She sat under the ancient pine, which gave no sign now of ever having been the old sage.

The flora and fauna in the woods were luxuriating in high summer, though the adjoining steppe was blanketed with snow and scoured by icy winds. The lagoon was warm and calm. For two days, she sat comtemplating and fasting, waiting for a sign. No signal came. Not even the shepherd put in an appearance, to exchange with Hürü his humble apparel. For two days it was just Hürü, the limpid lagoon, the scolding squirrels, the hurried drilling of the woodpeckers, the dense field of shasta daisies, the pines and the berry bushes, small and vulnerable beasts enjoying their perpetual high summer. On the third day, a very old man showed up. He wore a tattered robe, leaned on a staff and carried a gourd which served him as a bowl. He made toward Hürü as if he knew this was where she could be found, sitting under the pine.

"Ah, there you are!" the dervish said. "Have you been waiting long?"

"This is the third day," Hürü said.

"And you're getting headier and headier, too," the dervish commented, "from lack of food! Perhaps you might share with me some of the victuals your mother prepared."

"How did you know?" Hürü asked in amazement.

And the next minute, she recognized the dervish who'd once taught her how to grow cabbages for the Mevlana Institute. Then, the master of horticulture had been dressed in the impeccable fashion of the brotherhood and carried himself with the certainty of one who's privy to the Truth. But now, he wandered in the tattered robe of a mendicant, uncertain of where his next meal might come from or his shelter for the night. She bowed to him and kissed his knuckles, which shook on the staff.

"Forgive me, Master," she said. "I didn't know you at first."

"No harm done," the dervish said. "Let's eat some of the goodies Lady Gülbahar so carefully prepared."

The dervish scarcely touched the cheese, which had turned somewhat moldy, or the meatballs, which were now dark and shriveled marbles. But he drank a gourdful of salty water from the lagoon. Despite the Master's lack of appetite, Hürü discovered she was ravenously hungry and didn't mind the mold or the age of the edibles. As she ate, the dervish related that since she'd last seen him, he'd been called forth to wander in poverty, to live without the safety of the order and the brotherhood. He didn't comment on how he'd been called and to what purpose.

"Come, play us something sprightly," he invited Hürü to perform. "I haven't heard any music since I left the Institute."

"Forgive me, Master," Hürü said, "but I can't. My hand is too heavy on the *saz* and too light on the stone lyre. I can perform on neither. As for my voice, I haven't heard myself sing for months."

"Was Selim worthy of your love then?" asked the dervish, who seemed to know all that happened to her since she deserted in Konya without bidding her favorite Master farewell.

"Oh, yes!" Hürü said. "Yes, yes!"

"Selim died in grace," the dervish informed her.

"I know," she said.

"Good," the dervish said. "But now, I must travel on."

"So soon?"

"I don't have much time," the dervish said. "There's a certain shepherd, one who's well known to you, whose hut I must burn down."

"Don't do that!" Hürü exclaimed. "He's a good man. You must not burn him out!"

"Things aren't often what they seem," the dervish said.

"Why must you burn down his hut?" she insisted.

"Pay it no attention," the dervish said. "But before I go, I have a favor to ask you."

"Fine. Just don't ask me to get you the kindling!"

"Tomorrow," he said, "it has been revealed to me, you will return to this spot about midday. And when you arrive here, you will find me dead under this ancient pine. So wash me, wrap me in the shroud you'll find bundled under my head, and, having said a prayer to comfort my soul, bury me in the sand. Then, take my robe, my gourd and my staff. Towards dusk, someone will come and ask for the articles. Hand these objects over to him."

"Why?"

"Self-evident," the dervish said. "He's to succeed me."

And touching Hürü on the forehead, he took off on his feeble legs to requite the kindly shepherd with calamity. Hürü could imagine how quick the shepherd would be to give the dervish food and shelter. She could still run after the dervish and detain him. How easy it would be to overpower the will of the dervish until, as promised, he died midday tomorrow! But she just couldn't bring herself to do it, her heart divided between the dervish and the shepherd. When in doubt, she reflected, an unenlightened person like me takes refuge in inaction. Will I never see the light?

She fell asleep with the birds, exhausted from the chiding she'd

given herself, and dreamed fitfully all night of Mansur al-Hallaj, the
martyred Saint, whose crime was integrating Christianity into Islam.
Over and over, she had the same dream until she quite memorized
it: al-Hallaj is exposed to an angry mob. When both his hands are cut
off, the Saint shows no sign of pain. Then the crowd stones al-Hallaj.
Great bloody wounds open like red roses on the Saint's person. Still,
he remains impassive, inward. Then the master of the cabbages
enters the dream. He approaches al-Hallaj and strikes him with a
rose. Mansur al-Hallaj screams like one subjected to extreme torture.

At break of day, she awoke to a whiff of smoke, and knew the
dervish had accomplished his mission. Perhaps folks and theologians were right in their warnings about Sufi dervishes, accusing
them of apostasy and heresy. Once, in the vegetable garden, she'd
asked the Master of Horticulture what Islam was and who were
Moslems.

"Islam is in the books," he had replied; "the Moslems are in their
tombs."

She'd thought the Master meant that organized religion has a
way of freezing into unregenerate recipes and forms, but she couldn't
be sure, considering the Master often spoke cryptically about com-
monsense conduct. But sinning against God is one thing; sinning
against Man must surely be worse.

Following the trail of smoke, she reached the edge of the
summery woods; out on the open and frozen terrain, in the bleak
distance, she spied the source of the fire. So that's where the
shepherd lived! Or used to. She began briskly walking towards the
site of the arson. The hut, by the time she reached it, was totally
gutted. In front of this burned-down dwelling stood the shepherd
tearing out his hair as his animals bleated and lowed in the pen.
Around him were gathered his children, his pretty wife and—surprise
of surprises—Shahrazad herself! Her face and hair were exposed to
the winds and she seemed to have escaped with only her life.

"My friends!" Hūrū cried, running toward the survivors. "Are
you all right?"

"She asks me if I'm all right!" the shepherd said. "I'm alive, aren't
I?"

"Hello, Hūrū," Shahrazad said calmly.

"Praise be the Merciful and the Compassionate," the shepherd's
wife thanked.

"Satan take that dervish, though!" the shepherd said. "I don't serve God like a laborer, expecting my wages. But I don't need repayment from men, either. We gave the man food and lodging for the night. This morning, he torches the hut."

"Where's the dervish now?"

"Vanished," the shepherd said, snapping his fingers. "Just like that. Didn't want to stick around, I guess."

"Sure must've been a holy man, though," his wife said. "Should'a seen how he faded away."

"He seemed to," Shahrazad said, "vanish."

"But what are you doing at a place like this, Shahrazad—and all alone?"

"I was sleeping over," Shahrazad said, "on my way to Constantinople, looking for you. Yes, I'm alone."

As Shahrazad and Hūrū fell into each other's arms and then to talking, the stricken family dejectedly scanned the rubble for any articles that might have survived the fire. Hūrū wept freely as she told Shahrazad how she'd lost Karajuk through an accident by water. Her tears released the stone hand that had gripped her heart for so long. But, fearful of wounding Shahrazad more than necessary, she glossed over Shahriyar's unforgivable brutality.

"Where was Shahriyar as the baby drowned?" Shahrazad asked in great consternation, as if she already guessed something she must face. "He taught himself to swim, remember?"

"Yes, I remember," Hūrū said. "He was just standing around, dead drunk. His henchmen prevented me from going after the baby. Shahriyar wasn't responsible for his actions, believe me. Though I shall never understand."

"So!" Shahrazad said, intuiting all, as she covered her pale and wan face with her two trembling hands.

"I wished you'd never know."

"Somehow, I knew," Shahrazad said. "Something told me things went wrong. Did I turn my husband into a monster, Hūrū?"

"Why must you think of yourself as causing every turn in a plot, real or imagined?" Hūrū felt an odd jealousy flaring up. "Are you God?"

"Of course not!" Shahrazad cried.

"Well, then?"

"It's just that I cannot fully comprehend myself," Shahrazad said, "so long as Shahriyar remains an enigma to me. Who is this man, after all? He must've come into my life for some reason. I've guessed the puzzles in the hearts of a thousand and one fictional characters, but I know nothing about the man to whom I'm forever bonded."

"Who does?" Hürü said.

"Take the dervish," Shahrazad mused. "Last night, he seemed like such a mild person. He said some bizarre things, just to make himself interesting I thought; being a guest, he felt obliged to entertain the hosts. He declared, for example, that stone-eating was forbidden. I asked him why he mentioned such a ridiculous prohibition, considering stones are just not on people's food list. 'No one mentions such a prohibition,' he replied, 'because not eating stones is what may be called a common habit.'"

"Too much!" Hürü said, chuckling despite herself.

"Not setting fire to people's homes, too," Shahrazad added, reflecting, "is also a prohibition obvious to the ethical person. It might be said that most of us are in the habit of *not* setting fire to our host's hut. But I didn't know, last night, what the dervish was in the habit of doing—or not doing. So, to humor the old man, I asked if he could give us an example of what he meant, using some illustration that had a basis in reality. 'Judging from the indented, ink-stained middle finger of your right hand,' the dervish said, 'I guess you're a righthanded person who's in the habit of scribbling.' I agreed I was given to writing a great deal with my right hand. He then put me a curious question. 'Do you own your habit?' he asked. 'Or does your habit own you?' I replied that, to my mind, I'd chosen my habit; so, I must be said to own it. 'Ah!' he said, 'the curious thing about habit is that though sometimes you kick a habit, it more often kicks you.' I was up half the night, wondering if I wrote out of some habitual compulsion; then, I fell asleep for a few minutes—only to wake up to a hut on fire."

"Well," Hürü said. "Did you decide? Do you write out of habit or choice?"

"Don't know," Shahrazad said. "Yet one thing is sure; if habit it was, then it was certainly broken for me. My manuscript burned along with the hut. The whole thing. I can't imagine ever rewriting the whole of *The Thousand and One Nights*. Pouf! It's all gone! The manuscript was too precious, you see, to leave behind in Baghdad where I left my beautiful children."

"Good God!" Hürü said. "Didn't you have a copy made?"

"Who could afford it?" Shahrazad said. "Now it's obliterated."

"I cannot believe the dervish did such a terrible thing for sport or malice." Hürü said. "I used to know him when he had his senses about him. He was a famous teacher of horticulture. And now he's ruined your life's work, and the shepherd's life, too."

"That's what I call," Shahrazad said, "roasting two habits with one fire."

"You seem unreasonably calm," Hürü commented.

"Well," Shahrazad said. "Remember how I was visited by the Future? Well, the Genius doesn't drop around anymore, having other irons in the fire. But this morning, I think I was visited by the Past. Listen to this. As the hut burst into high flames, a fat little man appeared out of nowhere, riding a tall, white mule. He dashed right into the fire, mule and all, and emerged a split second later, unscathed—with my book in his pudgy hands. 'I got it!' he cried. 'I got *The Thousand and One Nights*. I got the better of the Most Profound, the Guardians and even you, Shahrazad! But, don't worry, old girl! Your book will be preserved, albeit under my name, in the past. And the future will remember me as the owner of *The Thousand and One Nights*.' He cackled and chortled as I stood by dumbfounded. Still laughing, the greasy bandit disappeared as his mule sort of hovered and then seemed to take wing. Can you believe that?"

"Tell me," Hürü said.

"Did the man who captured your book out of the flames wear a gorgeous Maghrabi's habit?"

"Yes," Shahrazad said.

"Were there a pair of extremely handsome saddlebags hanging on his mule?"

"Yes."

"Did he have slit eyes, a bulbous nose and a huge mole on his chin?"

"I didn't notice a mole," Shahrazad said.

"Well, anyway," Hürü said, "it sounds like Abd-es-Samad. Funny you didn't recognize him since you yourself described him so well in the 'Story of Jaudar from Cairo.' All the psychological ordeals I went through, lifting the magic objects from the submerged treasury and earning the Stone-Born Lyre, must have been arranged, after all, just so Abd-es-Samad could get me to compose the lyrics for your book. But, of course, at the time your book didn't yet exist. But the four brothers, the three Maghrabis and the Jew, were already fighting over ownership. They each knew parts of the contents though they couldn't grab the text out of thin air, the spirit of the time. Abd-es-Samad was ahead of himself since he was always interfering with Time. A foolish enterprise because, besides suffering from time lag himself, he's made it impossible for future scholars to date your book precisely."

"I didn't expect him to turn up in real life," Shahrazad said. "So it's not surprising I didn't recognize him. And I'm not even sure I saw him this morning. The shepherd and his wife didn't. Nor did the children. But the shepherd's big wolfhound bitch must've felt the pirate's presence. The dog's hair stood up and she dashed at the Maghrabi as if to stop him from absconding with my book. She even tore a bit off the saddlebags. Here it is, a piece of fine morocco leather embroidered with pearls and gold."

Digging into her girdle, Shahrazad produced a piece of the gorgeous saddlebags in which so much rich food was concocted for the insatiable Maghrabi.

"That's the stuff!" Hürü cried. "Dripping with conspicuous consumption. I wonder, though, if the hole in the saddlebag ruins the magic chef's talents. Poor Abd-es-Samad might have to learn to cook."

"But did my book go up in flames?" Shahrazad said, neutral as if she were discussing a moot point. "Or was it saved for the past, the present and the future?"

"I'd say the book exists," Hürü said, "but it's out of your hands."

At that moment, they heard the shepherd call out for everyone to come and help him. He'd come across an iron trapdoor in the foundation still too hot to handle; but, all together, they could lift it with a lever. Everyone must put a shoulder to the task. Groaning and hopping about in the embers, trying not to burn themselves, they finally managed to raise the metal trap. A few steps leading down into a dugout came to view. The shepherd, in peril of scorching himself, descended at once—and climbed out almost as fast with an earthen crock in his hands.

"Cool as anything down there," he said. "And look what I found! There's more of it where this came from, too!"

The crock was chockful of gold, pagan currency that had been sleeping cool and safe for some centuries.

"Hadrian," Shahrazad said, reading the inscription on a gold piece, "the king who minted the coins. The profile is of the god Apollo."

"He a true god?" the shepherd said, recoiling from his treasure.

"Of course!" Shahrazad cried, lifting her arms toward the sun. "Isn't the sun true? Doesn't it give light and warmth and growth and health? Apollo is the sun: beauty, form and harmony! He heals and whispers in our ears that the universe is true and good."

"Goodness!" the shepherd's wife exclaimed. "Let me see the face of light and wisdom."

"That sneaky dervish!" the shepherd whistled. "Bet he knowed the treasure was in there all along. He's gotta have torched the hut so's we'd come upon the metal trap."

"He didn't have to burn us out of our home, did he?" his wife complained. "Could've just told us."

"But, then," the shepherd said, having regained his balance, composure and, with it, his sagacity, "he'd have to put up with our fawning all over him, for making us rich. Don't you know nothing, woman? These holy fellows, they like doing their work in secret. They don't want folks beholden, see?"

"If you know so much," his wife came back, "how come's you were sending the holy man to the devil before?"

"I was a poor man then," the shepherd said.

"I wonder," Shahrazad said, "for the sake of what truth the dervish made me lose my manuscript."

"Gosh, Lady," the shepherd said. "If I give you one of them crocks chockful of money, will that make it up to you? You lost something precious so's I could find me my fortune."

"No," Shahrazad said. "But thanks, anyway."

"See what I mean?" the shepherd asked his wife. "Folks don't like handouts. What did our wise man of Konya say? Charity is bad for the giver and bad for the receiver, unless it's all done unknown-like."

◆

It turned out, however, that the shepherd was counting his chickens too soon; the rest of the crocks, though similar on the outside to the first, were crammed with some sort of yellow clay. No one had seen clay that yellow before, shimmering with flecks of gold.

"Some sort of fool's gold," the shepherd said, crestfallen.

"See what I mean?" his wife retorted. "I bet, each time you badmouthed the holy man, the gold in another crock turned to fool's dirt. That's what happens when you go shooting off your mouth!"

"How would you know?" the shepherd said, annoyed with his wife's wisdom.

"Maybe," Hürü offered, "you weren't meant to get in the habit of finding gold."

"Guess not," the shepherd said, still unreconciled to his loss.

The shepherd's children, however, were quite satisfied. Dumping the yellow earth on the worn-out, bleak square of a courtyard, where the soil had been tramped down hard as stone, they began playing in the mounds of the strange substance which, for them, became cities and kingdoms, castles and magic mountains. Once more the shouts of children rang in the frozen countryside, and laughter was heard among the ruins. The big yellow wolfhound came out of the sheep-pen where she had been sulking, no doubt still spooked by the fire and the mysterious mule-riding thief, and raised her tail like a flag.

Watching the children at play, the adults began discussing how they, too, might delight their own hearts. Shahrazad, who didn't know what else to do but to return to Baghdad, said maybe she could learn to find happiness in her children, watching them grow.

"Baghdad ever get cold like this?" the shepherd wanted to know.

"No," Shahrazad said. "But sometimes it gets hot as the devil's cauldron."

"Why should we put up with miserable cold?" the shepherd said to his wife. "Let's go bake our bones like them rich folks."

"We's rich folks now!" his wife said.

That's how the shepherd and his wife decided to leave for Baghdad, accompanying Shahrazad to her native city, which everybody's heard so much about for centuries. They'd tidy up, find some sort of conveyance and, in the morning, say goodbye to their former existence on this harsh steppe. The shepherd told anyone who'd listen how his forefathers had always been tied down to this little plot of land, grazing their animals on soil that didn't even belong to them. One never knew when some influential person might lay claim to God's great pasture-lands, doing the shepherd out of his livelihood. He'd always lived— blessed be the Merciful—a free man but yet in danger of having to become an indentured servant to some big landowner. Now, he'd be free of that danger. Besides, the world was there to be seen.

Hürü could think of no other course either but to get back on the Road to Baghdad. Suddenly, she remembered, however, the duty she owed the dervish. The sun was creeping up to its zenith.

Explaining that she had a mission to fulfill, she told the others they could find her by the limpid lagoon in the morning.

"Hope you won't be wanting another quick change of clothes," the shepherd teased. "All my spare duds went up in smoke."

Hürü took off, feeling blessed for having been granted this reunion with true friends. Now she might be allowed to keep the companions of her heart. About midday, she reached the spot where compassion was eternal. She found the dervish under the ancient pine, his head resting on his neatly folded shroud. Not yet cold, he appeared neither contented nor discontented. He was merely in repose: never again would he have to wander hither and yon, gourd slung on his back, leaning on his staff, his tattered robe catching on brambles. Death *was*; no more and no less.

Next to the dead man lay the articles Hürü had left on the spot: Selim's *saz*, the Stone-Born Lyre, the little pouch containing her parents' poetry, the remnants of her mother's provisions. First she must eat something so she'd have the strength to perform the dervish's last rites. She ate slowly a crust of moldy bread. Then, as she was about to pop a black olive into her mouth, she remembered the voice: "Habibi, would you care for a black olive?"

"Beloved," she responded to the voice now. "I'll take the pit!" And she spat out the bitter nourishment. She swallowed the pit.

She undressed the old man. He was even leaner than he appeared to be under his robe. Then she carried his frail body to the lagoon. The dervish weighed no more than a child, as if he'd taken care not to make himself a burden on his undertaker. Suddenly Hürü was excruciated with the thought of her own father's impending death. She'd left him high and dry. He'd have to be lowered into his grave by strangers. The image of her father walking light and spry as a woodthrush came to her like an agony without a name. Was her father also dead?

Then she remembered that she had no soap about her. With what would she soap the old dervish's hair and beard? But, wait! In her pocket she had a handful of the yellow clay the shepherd had found in the crocks; she remembered hearing how some kinds of clay, in conjunction with salty water, would serve as soap. She scrubbed the dervish's body with the yellow substance which bubbled in the lagoon, turning his hoary beard into silk.

She recalled the last time she'd sponged another old man, so angry and disgusted that she'd tried to boil the Imam alive. But now, she bathed this dear dead old man with care and obedience which was more like love.

And she was into the blind spot in her vision. The lacuna was filled with a sudden flash of light; there she saw herself tenderly gathering to her bosom the bony, wrinkled body of an already decaying mortal. A dead old woman. Herself. Tears that were like a mother's sorrow and pity welled in her eyes.

But her robust youth did not flinch. Her heart filled with compassion for her own mortal body whose task was to wear out on its journey towards death. I will die, she knew; I will achieve death.

She dug a grave in the loose sand with the shovel she brought from the shepherd's sheep pen. Once the hole was big enough, she wound the grave-linen around the dervish's spanking clean body and lowered him into his sandy resting place. The wrapped human form, solitary beyond any companionship now, receded farther away from existence, down into the eternal abode where no light reached, nor kind words. Would this holy body, too, rot? But then she remembered the dervish had once told her that Matter was indestructible; that what looked like decomposition to us was, in reality, transmutation. Every speck in our bodies, he'd said, had been here since the beginning and would continue for eternity.

"You left," she chided the form in the grave, "after you took care of everybody and his brother. But what about me? You didn't even bother to explain why bliss is withheld from me. You elected me only to witness your death."

And she closed the grave as easily as she'd opened it; recited the *Fatiha* to ease the passage of the dervish's soul. Then she settled down to wait. On one side of her, she piled the musical instruments (both the immutable and the mutable), the collection of love poetry; on the other side, she put the staff, the gourd and the robe. She'd sit keeping vigil until the chosen person put in an appearance.

Still, she was of two minds. One hoped the promised person would not appear so she could retain possession of the dervish's effects. The other wished to be rid of these tools of dervish trade so that she, too, could be on her way with her instruments and poetry. If only she could surmount the barrier that kept her from singing and playing, she knew there were yet many songs to sing.

But, then, perhaps the dervish left the articles to test her heart. Suppose the dervish's successor failed to materialize. Would she don the tattered robe, prod her way with the staff and drink out of the humble gourd? Perhaps the dervish, who'd once offered her discipleship, had put the tools of trade under her care, only to call her indirectly to the realm of Sufi Conduct. Hürü felt there was some sneaky plan afoot. For one thing, when she was a mere slip of a girl, she'd been protected by Hidir-Ilyas, the unseen Guides of the Sufis. But for what end? What task was it that she'd been elected to perform? Hürü didn't know.

She had a notion by now that the dervish, her former Master of horticulture, might just be the Teacher of the Age. He'd always seemed to have his finger on the pulse of the vegetable kingdom. Not hard to imagine he'd arrived at the highest sphere of being, not through music and dance like Mevlana, but through the love of cabbages and roses, and the rest of creation that had hearts of green. In her dream, she'd seen the dervish strike the martyred saint, al-Hallaj, with a sweet rose. The dying saint in her dream screamed, not out of pain, Hürü now understood, but ecstasy.

Now, here she was waiting for the next Teacher of the Age. In every age, there was a Kutub, the magnetic pole of human questing, who drew to himself those for whom it was possible to apprehend the true nature of experience. The elected were called, mysteriously, the Near Ones. Of necessity, no one knew who was the Kutub, or the Teacher of the Age.

The dervish had once explained that Nearness was communicated by direct succession of Being—whatever that meant. She had complained that Nearness then, was an elitist estate, like nobility of birth or comeliness of person or genius of mind, reserved for the few at the expense of most.

"Why not?" the dervish had wanted to know.

Why not indeed? Knowledge had no relationship to social justice. By its nature, knowledge yielded only to those who yielded to knowledge. So why should knowledge spread itself around equally for the sake of fairness to all mankind?

No wonder, then, those who sought shortcuts to illumination often found themselves sitting at the feet of some unregenerate person. Hürü now realized the vanity of pouncing on the dervish's effects and styling herself a Near One. The effects were intended for someone else. She could not elect herself.

Of the two careers, whose instruments were piled on either side, she could choose neither. Neither chose her. She was barred from Nearness; she'd been abandoned by Poetry.

"I am stuck, Old Man," she said to the ancient pine against the crusty bark of which she pressed her spine. "I've been elected to get stuck in this compassionate, verdant and changeless place."

Then, out of the corner of one eye, she saw someone approach in the last rays of the sun that barely illumined the forest. She took the approaching person to be a woman from the way the person walked, hips swinging from side to side with crass invitation built into the gait. As the person came nearer, she saw it was a young man dressed as a woman, waist up. Not only was he draped with beads and baubles, his long fair hair was fashionably coiffed, his fingernails had been dyed with henna, his eyebrows plucked into thin arches, his lashes thickened and curled with mascara. He must be a professional dancer, Hürü thought, the kind Arabs call *jink*, whose finger-cymbals went jink-jink-jink.

"Sweetheart," he lisped, "are you the woman called Hürü?"

"That's my name," Hürü said.

"So give me what's been entrusted you, my dear," he said, grooming his hair flirtatiously, "and I'll be on my way."

Not *him*! Hürü thought. God forgive me—he looks like the sort who sneaks into garrisons when the soldiers are hard up.

"What, then, had been entrusted me?" she asked the fay youth.

"Garment, gourd and staff," the effete person said. "Does that satisfy you, Sweetheart?"

"Who told you about the garment, the gourd and staff?"

"I only know one thing, Sweetie," he answered. "Last night, I entertained at a wedding which turned out to be a super bash. I spent the night in wine-and-roses, so to speak; at dawn, I was having a catnap in the company of a lover when I felt the presence of someone standing over my head. I woke up and heard a voice, one that belonged to none of the carousers, for sure. 'Know that the soul of the Teacher of the Age has just now returned to the Source,' the voice informed me; 'and you've been elected to take his place.' So, here I am."

"But you didn't answer my question," Hürü said. "*Who* told you?"

"I don't know *who*!" the young dancer said. "But the voice went on and on. It gave me instructions on how to get here, described you down to your name and history, told me to receive from you the gourd, the garment and the staff. 'For,' the voice said, 'the Kutub left those articles for you.' Can you beat that?"

"Here are the articles reposited for you," Hürü said. "Enjoy them in good health."

"This it?" the young dancer said.

"That's it."

"Thank you, Sweetie," he said, batting one eyelash. "I think I might just put on this robe."

As the young man put on the tattered robe over his outrageous finery, Hürü thought she saw a luminous green in the lining shimmering through the tattered holes. She put her hand out to adjust the collar for the young man, but instantly drew it away from the intensity of what felt like green-hot fire. This robe wasn't, in fact, what it seemed.

"Ahhh!" said the young man, transported in bliss. "I could faint from this excruciating pleasure."

"Are you all right?" Hürü said in alarm.

"Quite," the young man said. "It's like bathing in fire that does not burn. If the boys could just see me now!"

"Wait a tattered minute!" Hürü exclaimed. "This is the beginning of the rest of your life. You can't go back to your old ways!"

"Who says?"

"Well . . ." she said, "dancing, in the way you do, isn't exactly a seemly occupation for the next Teacher of the Age."

"Who says?"

Hürü couldn't imagine Who Says, unless it was Everybody and his Brother plus herself. But she was angered by the young man who took the greatness thrust on him so casually.

"Don't forget," she said, "I know who the Kutub of the Age happens to be. There's no reason why I shouldn't blab around."

"You *are* impetuous, Sweetie!" the young man said, laughing. "Go on and tell everybody that the Magnetic Pole is a female impersonator who dances at the local tavern. People will either laugh at you, thinking you're mad. Or else, taking you for a storyteller, they'll give you presents for telling them pleasant lies."

"Or worse," she said, "they'll throw me in the loony bin."

"That's about the size of it, Sweetie," he said.

And he picked up the staff and the gourd, leaving her alone at the site, for some reason she couldn't name, weeping.

Chapter 26

THE ULTIMATE BOON

Hürü regains the human heart
and Shahrazad beholds the Face of God

She woke up to bleatings and the high-pitched screech of the wooden wheels of an oxcart. A pampered lambkin nuzzled her hair which had tumbled into a bed of true-blue forget-me-nots. Ferns and pink ladyslippers tickled her face. The sound of tortured wood wheels stopped beside her piney bed.

"Up, up, sleepyhead!" she heard the shepherd call out. "The sun's already up the length of two grains."

There they were, the shepherd and his family in a ramshackle oxcart with Shahrazad in the back, swinging her shapely legs over the tailgate. And, in her tattered Abbasid garments, she looked quite the nomad queen. The shepherd's flock, too, was accompanying the travellers on the Road to Baghdad. The big yellow wolfhound, full of importance, ran herself ragged keeping in line the fat-tail sheep and their sweet little lambs.

"An oxcart!" Hürü cried, already complaining about the accommodations. "The trip will take an entire century. And where are all these sheep going?"

"Couldn't very well leave the animals behind," the shepherd said, "could I? Not at the mercy of wolves and strangers."

"Where's the cow, then?" Hürü asked. "Where's Lady Gülbahar?"

"Didn't I tell you? Couple of weeks back, the old lady died of a

346

croupy cough. I think, though, she died on account of . . . a broken heart. Wolves carried off her calf."

"I wonder . . . if my mother's all right," Hürü said, the words getting stuck in her throat, feeling a sudden premonition. She knew full well that the correspondence between the cow's name and her mother's was entirely accidental; to imagine a cosmic connection between the two Lady Gülbahars was not only a form of superstitious feeblemindedness, it was downright insulting to her Mom, that excellent lady who was anything but bovine. Yet she couldn't dispel the constriction in her chest: that feeling that she had abandoned her aging mother. The lady had to live beside a graveyard in Istanbul when she could have dandled grandchildren on her knees, nothing to show for having been a mother so good that she'd been able to let her daughter go. A stout heart could not be put on the mantelpiece. Now Hürü feared that death might arrive on its own time, not for her good old father first and then, years later, for her big, handsome mother. Death wasn't interesting in timeliness. Fear suddenly reverberated through her body, her fingertips went icy despite the sweet summer air that bathed her in fragrant mercy.

"Hurry up, then!" chided the shepherd. "Let's get a move on!"

"What an incredible place!" Shahrazad gasped; slipping off the oxcart, kicking off her shoes, she approached tentatively the edge of the lagoon.

"Now what?" the shepherd sighed. "You seen the water. Now let's go!"

"It's June!" exclaimed Shahrazad, gesturing with her sturdy walking stick to the eternal garden all around the lagoon. "And the wild callas are in bloom!"

Hürü joined her ecstatic friend and slipped her hand into Shahrazad's. Now they were two women, neither of whom any longer tried to avoid her fate, standing together, contemplating the water which shimmered green-blue, fresh as if it were created only yesterday.

"What is this place?" Shahrazad said with awe, breathing softly. "Have I seen, or imagined, anything like this before? Looking, I'm taken with spasms, with a fever of discovery. Yet I know this place has always existed. My nose has always been pressed up against the opaque glass door behind which lay I knew, without knowing, my future. This place. Don't you see? Here, one can live without any reason to be. Here, one has the freedom to live. Without any compulsions. Without having to write, to introspect, to read even. Without having to be anybody's daughter, wife or mother. In a small hut by the water, built right, a woman can abide on her own. This place must be where the unseen world touches the one we know, yes? Oh, my, yes! Don't you wish you'd be allowed to stay?"

"Not me!" Hūrū said. "I'm not delighted by this delightful place anymore. It's laid hold of me long enough."

"I wish it would hold me," Shahrazad said. "Space, silence and time. Like existing forever in my long book. I only dipped into something like this lagoon, and I wrote too many pages. I'm grateful to your fat friend for taking the *Nights* off my hands. I am a woman freed. Or am I?"

"*Shahrazad, approach!*" a voice said.

"How strange!" Shahrazad said. "Did you hear that?"

"Hear what?"

"I'm being called by name."

"Pay no attention," Hūrū said with alarm. "Believe me, this is a treacherous place."

"*Shahrazad,*" the voice insisted,"*abide!*"

"There it goes again! I'm being told to abide."

"Let's beat it," Hūrū said, "before it's too late! As if the place hadn't already claimed enough, now it's after your soul!"

"*Shahrazad*" the voice commanded, "*attend!*"

"I am," Shahrazad answered the voice rapturously, "listening."

Hūrū guessed the wood was speaking to Shahrazad. But was it the voices of nature which are familiar speakers in a poet's head? Or some other enchantment? Hūrū thought she saw in Shahrazad the signs of something so laden with meaning, it was ominous. Something awesome was about to happen. Hūrū stood aghast. Shahrazad's face, turned up to the light streaming into the woods, seemed to be freed of the heaviness of flesh. No longer merely rapturous, her eyes aloofly regarded the light of eternity. Shahrazad's expressive face had taken on another beauty, a transparence, which revealed the beauty of her skull. As if light had already consumed the living mask, Shahrazad reposed in her own radiance. Her eyes, luminous as the lagoon, were lit from behind with all the power of her soul. And already the skeleton of herself, like a skull bleached and purified on the desert, the structure of her bones was manifest in her pellucid face: so terrible was this new Shahrazad's beauty.

There must be a way to safely extricate Shahrazad from the

dangerous voyage inwards, madness and death. No fun and games, as Hürü knew from experience. And death was no escape. She tried to attract Shahrazad's attention, but the writer's eyes remained fixed on an object somewhere in the middle of the lagoon.

It was then that Hürü's eyes fell on the Stone-Born Lyre, which the shepherd was busy packing on the flatbed oxcart. All right, then! That should get Shahrazad's attention.

Hürü pulled the Lyre out of the shepherd's hands. As she struck the stone strings with impassioned vigor, the mute instrument yielded up all its terrifying sound at once. And milk gushed forth from Hürü's breasts.

She stood aghast.

The awesome sound of the Lyre disengaged Shahrazad's preoccupation with the unseen. As she refocused her gaze on this world, Shahrazad regarded Hürü dispassionately, witnessing the young bard's amazement with her plight. There stood Hürü, the maker of songs, one foot in the lagoon, staring at the heavy wetness spreading down the front of her shirt.

"I'm lactating again," Hürü groaned. "And like two faucets, too!"

"Strange," Shahrazad said. "How strange!"

Perhaps the time was ripe to return the Stone-Born Lyre to the source, for such things could not be kept. With all the power in her forearm, Hürü flung the Lyre, still vibrating, into the middle of the lagoon. The magical instrument once more sank away from human sight, perhaps to await the arrival of the next foolhardy minstrel who'd play the unplayable.

"Here, take your Lyre!" Hürü commanded the unseen guardians of the place. "And give me back my son!"

"Good heavens!" Shahrazad said.

"What'd she go do that for?" the shepherd disapproved.

"Wants her son back," the shepherdess explained.

From then on, events happened in such quick succession that, later, none of the witnesses could agree on which came first.

An infant appeared, a big chubby darling, riding in a reed basket on the becalmed surface of the lagoon. Not only did the infant coo and chortle joyously, but he seemed to be singing himself a fine lullaby.

Hürü was perceived to dive precipitously into the lagoon and swim towards the infant with the speed of a water *jinni*.

And, supposedly, Shahrazad, dropping her walking stick on the bank, was seen to walk resolutely and deliberately, as if she had an appointment to keep with someone or something far ahead, into the lagoon until the water completely covered her and she vanished from sight.

Sometime in the course of all these happenings, the ancient pine that stood leaning over the water crashed down. Not as a tree, mind you, what with branches and needles still intact, but as a log. The log floated out rapidly, as if driven by some intelligent life force. As if it meant to offer safety to a drowning person.

Many years later, the shepherd's children had quite some story to tell their children and grandchildren. According to them, first one great lady dove into the water, for no apparent reason at all, and, as she flailed about, the second lady had walked in to help her. But the second lady too, although much younger and quite athletic, was dragged in by the undertow, herself in imminent peril of drowning. And that was when the baby showed up, riding in a basket and singing himself a lullaby. The younger lady held onto the reed basket, which, amazingly enough, could keep both ladies afloat.

The children saw the sudden appearance of another person, neither man nor woman, who approached the scene dancing to the percussion of his finger-cymbals: jink-jink-jink. Dressed in a robe of shimmering luminous green, and making enough whoopee to raise the dead, this strange person also jumped into the lagoon. But once the green dancer struck the surface of the water, a pine log appeared in the person's place.

The two drowning ladies managed to cling to the transformed log and, together, they worked the log towards the opposite shore. The infant in the basket just followed in the log's wake, as if it were a dinghy being towed behind a boat. The shepherd's children always marvelled at the lesson they learned that day: a thing doesn't necessarily have to be one thing; it can also be something else.

The shepherd said it was the tree which fell to its death first. According to him, just as Hürü had reached Shahrazad and began dragging her friend back to land, the ancient pine had fallen flat on the water and conked Hürü on the head, preventing her from saving Shahrazad's and her own life.

The shepherd, in an effort to understand all the magical events that he'd witnessed in his youth, decided to go in for education in a big way. In those days, Baghdad was just the place to do it, too, what with schools of philosophy promising enlightenment on every street-corner. Now that there was no need for him to rescue Hürü, or, for that matter, work for a living, the shepherd could put all his energies into his academic pursuits. Turning the day-to-day troubles of life over to his wife, he became that sort of scholar who's never seen buying a loaf of bread or choosing a new shirt. Utterly insulated from vulgar notions, not only did this excellent man, who once had enough trouble speaking Turkish, manage to qualify for a doctoral program in Baghdad, but soon he was publishing his homework, penned in his own brand of hard-hitting and no-nonsense Arabic. Of course, at the time, he was studying at the School of Hard to Believe. Once granted his union card, however, he founded his own school of hard-headed realists, who study theories of Cause and Effect, and who deny the magical.

To his dying day, the great man insisted that neither Shahrazad nor Hürü survived the catastrophe on the lagoon. His wife, now a senior faculty wife herself, questioned the acuteness of her husband's perceptions. In private, of course. She maintained that it was Shahrazad who began marching into the lagoon even before the infant appeared. According to her, Hürü had dived in to save her friend first and only later became aware of the floating babe. She kept on telling him that Hürü recovered the baby, swam ashore and, holding her son to her breast, vanished into the wintery countryside.

But Queen Shahrazad herself, the wife argued, rode ashore on the log which travelled with the speed of lightning.

Her husband often used the example of his wife to teach his students how not to be deceived by appearances. He concluded that his wife had needed a miraculous ending for the Good Sisters, Hürü and Shahrazad, who, as anyone could see, had come to the end of the road.

"So," he said, chuckling professorially into his beard, "my wife willfully imagined the wondrous rescue."

And many in Baghdad, who remembered Shahrazad and disapproved of her antics, thought this realistic end for their former First Lady made a fine cautionary tale for their children: don't mess with big ideas and big bodies of water, boys and girls; and don't you dare get too big for your pants, either.

Yet the shepherdess was no fool, although she didn't dare repeat her story in front of strangers, let alone for the ears of her husband's uppity students. But when her favorite granddaughter began to put on masculine attire in order to sneak lectures down at the seminary, she gave the girl a thick and heavy book, just made available in Baghdad through a Maghrabi publisher: *The Book of A Thousand Nights and One Night*; in Arabic, *Kitabi Alf Laylah Wa Laylah*.

"Here's a gift that cost an arm and a leg," she said to the girl. "Your poor Grandma can't read a word of it. But you can! So, happy eighteenth birthday, sweetheart."

"Wow!" said the girl. "Just what I wanted! Thanks, Grandma!"

"I knew Shahrazad who hunted up the stories and captured them for all time in her own life," the old lady said. "And I knew Hürü who breathed into the book the lyrics of her soul. Both were queens. And women of extraordinary talents. Now, it's all up to you, my girl. Understand these tales and commit them to memory. The Maghrabi who owns this book couldn't memorize the whole; so he published it. He didn't understand it well enough to confide it to memory, or to learn from it. It was not his story. It was the story of a woman. He was frantic only about possessing it—to stamp it with his imprint."

"Gee, Grandma!" the girl protested. "Shahrazad is only a figure of literary tradition. A figment. And I don't know anything about this Hürü character. Who was she anyway?"

"Yourself," the old lady admonished. "Pay attention!"

"Grandma!" the girl reproved. "What's got under your bonnet this morning?"

"Memory," the old lady said. "But it's up to you to pick up from my memory and go on from there. Shahrazad still exists. In a changed form to be sure, but she exists as an aspect of the Invisible Teacher."

"Invisible Teacher?" the girl said. "I hear him mentioned. He must be the name of an idea, I suppose, that comes out of the Sufi Tradition. But nobody will tell me who he is for sure. Who is he, Grandma?"

"He is she," the old lady said, "and she is he. Pay attention! A teacher who is enlightened has no self and, therefore, is invisible. Like a piece of glass that has no impurities, the Invisible Teacher's self is transparent enough for Light to come through undistorted. If a teacher is visible, then he is not enlightened."

"But Grandpa is a great teacher, too," the girl said, her lower lip trembling a little with the pain that comes with sudden understanding. "Isn't he?"

"And a wonderful man," the grandmother said, hugging her. "Now I will tell you the end of the Good Sisters' story. But, when the time comes, you must tell it to one of your granddaughters. Tell it to the one who understands. Promise me now."

"I promise, Grandma. But what if I have no granddaughter?"

"Then tell it to your grandson," her grandmother said. "I saw it all happen with my own eyes, believe me, and heard with my own ears.

"When Hürü's baby floated back from the unknown in a basket of reed, I swear to you, he was singing himself a lullaby. A mere infant, already singing like an angel! Was he a human baby, or a demon? A changeling? If he were a *jinni* of some sort, Hürü was in for a lot of trouble. If he were human, then, by the grace of Allah, he was sent back to breathe into our ears the wind of truth.

"And if the baby was really the son Sultan Selim begat on Hürü, then you know the little fellow was half-brother to the reigning Sultan, Suleyman the Magnificent himself. And you know the Magnificent wouldn't have allowed his infant brother to live.

"So, after Hürü took her baby and ran—and who can blame her?—I saw Shahrazad ride that old pine log as if it were an Arabian stallion. The log and the woman travelled ashore faster than light, it seemed to me, though I caught just a glimpse. I saw what went on, if you get my meaning, and didn't see.

"Hardly trusting my eyes, I, too, ran down to the lagoon and saw Shahrazad pull herself panting onto the bank. But the log, once it bumped on the beach, turned into a green-robed youth who also came ashore. His wet green robe, which streamed with water, dried even before I heard the personage speak.

"'May I have the next dance?' the green youth said. 'Come, Shahrazad, let's give it a whirl.'

"Then, the green dancing boy was changed, this time into an unbearably brilliant green light. And where Shahrazad stood, a blue light appeared, growing in intensity and brilliance until the two prodigious lights merged into one single blue-green fire.

"I could no longer bear to look on this dazzling light. My hands shielding my eyes, I stood there as if I'd taken root, unable to move or cry out. When your Grampa finally arrived to fetch me, I flung myself on his breast, tears pouring out of my eyes. I couldn't have said if the tears I shed were of sorrow . . . or of joy."

"And then what?"

"That's it," her grandmother said. "You see, my darling, Sufi knowledge is as silent and secret as our woman knowledge. On the path where Hürü vanished, she can no longer be followed through ordinary learning. When your footing is sure, I hope you can track down Hürü—and her son . . . who returned from the world navel singing."

AFTERWORD

*H*ow is it we understand such a strange tale? Despite this narrative's eccentric and concentric subject matter, its foreign garb, its translation from languages unpleasant to our ears, its journey over great distances and the time warp across which it comes, we get the meaning. How come? We don't even understand the Modern Arab. Yet, here we are, having travelled on the Road to Baghdad.

Shahrazad, of course. The Invisible Teacher. The quirks of her personality burned out in a blue blaze of light, Shahrazad illuminates a thousand and one manuscripts, tablets, writing tables and now, monitor screens. But Shahrazad's manuscript either went up in flames, or it was pirated by an overzealous magician who played tricks with space and time. Obviously the text was both lost and saved, magic that isn't hard to imagine anymore. If you know how, you can even retrieve an irretrievably lost file, this imaginary electronic stuff that can be burned up at a touch, sometimes inadvertently, from the robot mind of your word processor, your personal *jinni*.

As a woman writer of the last quarter of the twentieth century, I accept my responsibilities. I come from a country where the oral tradition is still not dead. Somewhere deep inside, I must have known I would someday have to retrieve Shahrazad and her tales from the treasury where they were reposited.

After four years of research, dreaming and writing, I don't know any more what parts are historically true, or what parts are accept-able to those who travel on the Sufi Path. And I don't distinguish between parts that are highway robberies of others' literary property and those that are inventions of my own. History, plunder and inven-tion help each other to make one palpable text which comes, after all, from a sub-aquatic storehouse which is of no use—unless trespassed.

And, as you've suspected all along, I am Hürü and Shahrazad and Abd-es-Samad the fat and unscrupulous alchemist, as well as all the known and unknown writers who participated in authoring and reauthoring *The Thousand and One Nights*, not to mention the cast of historical and fantastical characters. So don't try to pin me down on what's real and what's irreal. In other words, any coincidences or resemblances to persons, living or dead, or any plagiarisms, outright or thinly disguised, are purely intentional, that is: fictional.

Our revels have certainly not ended. For one thing, we want to know what happened to Hürü and her re-materialized kid. We under-stand that she exchanged the Stone-Born Lyre for the Water-Born Boy. Or some other being quite different altogether?

Once, I briefly saw a dilapidated and anonymous manuscript which dealt with a history I suspect tracks down the vanished minstrel and her son. My guess is that the manuscript was the work of none other than the shepherd's granddaughter. Or a great-great granddaughter.

But, the first and only time I was privy to the history, I never dreamed that I might need to study it more carefully some day. All I have is a remembered impression from my early youth when I used to have, more or less, a photographic memory which, alas, disap-peared once I learned to reason. The history in question, penned in Arabic script, has also disappeared. Since I couldn't yet read, the text was read to me by my dad. I still cannot read Arabic script, which was banned in modern Turkey. But the manuscript I saw only once was, for a time, photographed in my memory as if I were a Polaroid camera. The photograph has not survived the passage of time: the trouble with instant pictures.

The last time I saw the manuscript, it was among my dad's medical textbooks (also in the Old Script) which he was storing in the countryhouse in the Turkish hinterlands that was his home. Turns out all his papers were sold (by feckless cousins) to a can-dymaker who later admitted that he transformed each page into a paper sack to vend children afterschool treats.

I remember, however, the spirit, if not the word, of the obscure manuscript.

The infant, registered under the name of Osman Kara, grew up to become the Minstrel of the Age. My obscure source hints that he was none other than the Pir Sultan Abdal. This great sixteenth century sage-minstrel lived in Anatolia, now called Turkey. He lived during the reign of Suleyman the Magnificent who was, of course, Selim the Grim's son and heir. The great minstrel's pen name, probably bestowed upon him by his fans, roughly translates as Sage Sultan the Fool. Divine Fool, of course.

Not much is known about this king among the poets. All that remain are his songs of Magical Protest. In his songs, the life of the spirit marries the life of the senses in such ecstatic purity that to hear, just once, only one deathless song, believe me, warrants the hardship of learning Turkish. Too bad for you, the songs must remain hermetically sealed! And too bad for me. Not only is the job of translating the Fool beyond me, it's downright dangerous.

The Fool fell in love with Love.

The Fool's songs are called Breaths, as natural to man as is breathing. Their truth was so dangerous for the social and political establishment of the time, alas, the Fool was hanged on the gall-tree for breathing so dangerously. But his corpse proved even more dangerous. He was crowned Sultan in folks' hearts. On that throne, there is no death, no deposition. Who can murder immortal ideas? Freedom, for example. Justice, and Love.

The Fool's Breaths reveal his comprehensive education. But he breathed in such a simple and direct manner that even the rudest shepherd's heart was transported, his spirit ennobled. For the felicity of speaking directly to the simplest soul on the street, the Fool chose to remain hidden in an obscure town, speaking beauty into an obscure language. He never was a servant to Fame.

As it is with all the Teachers, the Fool's personality, too, is burned away. Of course, so were his manuscripts. But the strange thing is, Breaths cannot be destroyed by fire. Breath is the same as Spirit. Folks learn Breaths by heart.

Had Süleyman the Magnificent lent a perceptive ear to a single Breath that wafted from the Hinterland, his empire would not have decayed in such shameless tyranny. The Magnificent was only interested in the material world. And his hold on this world was magnificent. Not the soldier Selim the Grim was, nor the hellmaker, he was interested in legislation and collecting revenue on his father's conquests. The Magnificent stuffed the treasury full, he paved campaign trails with gold. But the big spender still couldn't conquer Vienna, outside the gates of which he died an old man. He had no heart.

I imagine the Magnificent as an overdressed, bilious man. He fell prey to his Russian concubine, Roxanne, on whom he fathered an idiot prince. During his incredibly long reign, he didn't manage to bring up a proper heir because Roxanne made sure her idiot son would succeed and raise her so high that when she defecated, she'd miss no one. With a mother like that, who needs enemies? The Empire stopped dead in its tracks, to babble, rave and masturbate compulsively. And it served the House of Osman right. All they'd required of women was that they be beautiful and they bear sons.

Odd that the Magnificent and the Fool were brothers, both Sultans of their own realms. I am willing to wager that the Fool knew the Sultan of the world was his half-brother because Hürü wouldn't have kept the truth from her son. What if the Magnificent had known the true identity of the Fool? Ah, believe me, he'd have inflicted two consecutive death sentences on his brother: the first for breathing seditious songs and the second for the crime of being born a brother.

The Fool's Breaths are still laden with danger in that small and obscure republic called Turkey, the remnant of the mighty Empire of Osman, or Ottoman. There, even today, minstrels who awaken the Fool's Breaths know that the Truth that sets you Free can also land you in jail. Or worse. But we're not here to talk about what's worse.

Sage Sultan the Fool is supposed to have drawn his last breath in a Breath. Personally, I have no difficulty believing it. After all, even his father, Selim the Grim, who knew the possibility of the Perfected Heart all his life but mocked it, died singing. Selim's path was also another route to Felicity.

This big book you hold in your hands is about, among other things, Felicity. Felicity, as I interpret it, means true happiness. But what is true happiness? And how are we to distinguish it from happiness that isn't true? A Chinese wisdom has this to say about the subject: if you want happiness for a day, get drunk; if you want happiness for three days, kill your pig and eat it; if you want happiness for eight days, get married; but if you want true happiness, plant a perennial garden. Not bad. Not bad at all. But what I really like is Aristotle's word for Felicity: *evdaimonia*, classical Greek for "being under the watch of good demons." The Good Brothers and the Good Sisters, in other words. So how do we get hold of these good demons? We don't. They come entirely on their own.

Plutarch, in his biography of Demosthenes, cautions us that we mustn't assume a lack of fame is necessarily a lack of Felicity—as Plutarch's big city friends seem to have done. To think that living in a hick town inevitably leads to a truly unhappy life, Plutarch says, is like thinking that you cannot be a truly happy person if you arrived in this world out of a small and plain-looking mom.

Besides, our heroine *was* born in a famous city. And she was born to a big and beautiful mother. So, neither Istanbul nor the grand matriarch who gave her birth can be held accountable for our heroine's difficulties in making a name for herself. Her difficulties with fame must be attributed to, or blamed upon, something else.

I'm disturbed that Anonymous was a woman. Come right down to it, I'm worried sick. We all are, those of us who think Feminist Thoughts. And here's why: Maybe things haven't changed all that much for a woman with extraordinary talents. Hürü threw away her gift. But did she have a choice? Or, worse yet, the conflicts in Hürü's life seem more insoluble than I believed when I first heard her story from my father's lips.

Then I was a child and depended on the word of mouth. What absorbed me then was how Hürü would woo and wed her difficult Prince. Foolish child! Romance, it turns out, was only the half of it. On the road to fame and fortune, the abandonment of a gift, no matter how prodigious, seems minor compared to the survival of the human heart. Humanity is all. Is that it? Tsk, tsk, tsk. I live in a time and place where people opt for fame and fortune at the drop of a hat! Glitter is all, in my time.

I too want my heart to survive. Yet, I'm a person of my time: I adore glitter. So I want my name to survive as well. Is that too much to ask? I'd like to make it big in New York. I'd like to lunch with the Glitter Set. I'd like to be On the Road to L.A. with a Hot Property. But, instead, I've been on the Road to Baghdad, on the trail of a sixteenth century heroine who, despite talking and acting like an American college girl, will not make me a famous author.

Yet, on the Road to Baghdad—despite my longings for fame and fortune, despite my feminist lingo, despite the many forms of chauvinism from which I suffer—I've been taken beyond myself. As if some good demon's been dictating to me the true voice of my heart.

We all hope to speak more beautifully than we do now. Take me, for example. I'm always casting about in history to find myself appropriate paragons. In my readings I've discovered that although beautiful speech is quite difficult, industry is no mean virtue for one who'd speak better, as Demosthenes proved amply. Demosthenes was a terrible stutterer, of course, an affliction parallel to our own Hürü's and which they both overcame.

Necessity forced Hürü to free her tongue and unlock her imagination. The girl had gall! Not only did Hürü equal her fate, she transcended it—like her mentor and friend, Shahrazad of the Thousand and One Nights fame. Because Hürü—let's get on with it, shall we?—Hürü was the girl who dared to seize the lyre that had belonged to Orpheus and then to Homer.

As to Sage Sultan the Fool being born to an immensely talented woman (in the famous city of Baghdad), the name of Hürü Osmanli *nee* Karaman isn't listed under the Great Composers of the Age. Not surprising. I've finally figured it out. She's the matrix of her son, see? Instead of making a name for herself, Hürü wanted her personality burned out of history. Get it? Because she's one of the Invisible Minstrels, Hürü sings deep in the choir of our hearts.

Through the course of telling Hürü's story, I have intruded myself into Hürü's persona when the temptation was all too great. I freely admit she is my invention embellished over her fairytale history. I've entered her time, her space and her consciousness like the bandit alchemist you've met on the Road to Baghdad. I've taken you on flights of Time in creaky space warps and exposed you to lapses of memory where historical persons—as well as a famous author who's alive and well in Maryland—are trapped in fictional time. For these irregularities, I ask you, good reader, your indulgence. What can I say? I've robbed history blind. I'm just another time bandit looking for a good time. I have to: I live in a small town where nothing much ever happens and where, as Plutarch said about himself, I'm willing to abide, considering that my moving away would make the place even less populated.

Remember Plutarch, my exemplary chronicler, who felt, with good reason, that true happiness, like a hardy perennial, survives in any old place. As he thrived in his obscure hometown in Boeotia (long after the Glory of Greece had faded away), he hoped that any deficiency in his heart would not get blamed on his birthplace or, I surmise, on his mother tongue.

Plutarch discovered happiness through a foreign tongue, in his case, the perennial language of the Romans, which revealed itself to him late and after much travail. Strange but true, Plutarch muses: it was not through the knowledge of Latin words that he came to understand things, but through his experience of things that he came to understand Latin words.

I take Plutarch to heart as I take my own father, though I know nobody reads him much these days. Nobody reads my father, either. But, should you read me, take a look at Plutarch again. See how he can both burn himself into the text and also burn himself out. That's what I call the true happiness of authorship. Writing not because he had to. Writing because he was free to. You can see through Plutarch because his personality doesn't obscure the Face of God—which is a dramatic way of saying: the truth behind things, or ideas.

I, too, have translated my experience of things into a foreign tongue; in my case, English, which I consider very big and so very beautiful. But more than that, although I'm stuck on Fame, now I'm informed of the Invisible Teachers who instruct my heart. As I wrote this book, I lived under the watch of good demons, all those Good Sisters and Good Brothers who, for reasons of their own, have allowed me to pass on to you, good reader, the Felicity of travelling with you on this Road to Baghdad.

Oberlin, Ohio
1990

HISTORICAL NOTE

*H*ürü (the virtuous daughter, wife and mother) comes out of a folk tale localized to Kalejik, a province of Ankara—perhaps localized even more specifically to the household of the Aga of Kalejik, grandfather of the author. Two things interested the author in the character of Hürü:

1) the heroine solves her travelling problem by turning herself into an orphan boy, Keloglan, a well known hero in Turkish folktales, the Bald Boy: an old but sophisticated storytelling device through which one fictional character impersonates another. As a folk hero, Keloglan goes back to tales told by the Turkoman, a term that denotes all the Turkic tribes that spread out of their original home in Central Asia.

2) the heroine regains her family, husband and child through the harmonious magic of her musical inventions.

The author invented a history for Hürü which is in keeping with the actual historical time through which she is set in motion. As a fictional vehicle, she carries her Turkish author intrepidly into the Arabian Nights Tales. Scholars inform us that the tales found their final shape as The Thousand and One Nights in the early sixteenth century when the Ottoman Turks conquered the territories that belonged to the Arabs. The author theorizes that it must have been the Turkish political annexation that stimulated the Arab culture to define and formalize its fictional heritage. Shahrazad is seen, in this light, not only as the sort of author who transforms autobiography into fiction but also as a bluestocking queen who takes on the job of ennobling Arabs, who now feel impotent before their Turkish conquerors, by telling them the tales of their golden past, especially the reign of Harun-er-Rashid, the Abbasid Caliph who ruled in Baghdad, A.D. 786–809.

Since Turks, Arabs and Persians live in roughly the same area of the world, and they practice roughly the same religion, their ethnic qualities are blurred so much in the Western Mind that often they are thought to be identical. In fact, not only are these peoples of different racial backgrounds, their languages are not at all related. Turkish is a Ural-Altaic language, Persian an Indo-European and Arabic a Semitic one. If language patterns thought, it must, therefore, shape the culture in which that language is spoken. The behavior, the ethics, the esthetics of these peoples are as different as their languages. The author makes an attempt to distinguish these differences by identifying the sources of some of the Arabian Nights tales. For example, much value is put on chivalric romance in tales of Persian origin. Tales of Baghdadian origin are full of lovers who fall in love, sing, suffer, and die in purity, whereas the versions of the same tales which come through Cairo have a more cynical attitude towards love-death, often told with ribald overtones. Tales that involve mercantile settings are obviously what entertained the middle class audiences that populated the major Arab cities of the time: Baghdad, Damascus, Aleppo, Basra, Cairo.

In tales that have a Turkish origin, even under the superimposed Islamic coloring there are elements that harken back to a pantheistic religion, a love of the great outdoors, of animals, of travel, of the seasonal joys of a nomadic life. The women aren't sedentary but take an active role when hearth and home are threatened; they ride, wrestle and shoot arrows for the sheer pleasure of it. Chapter 14, "Lady Safiye's Tale," for example, is based on a version that appears in *The Thousand and One Nights* called "The Story of Zumrut." This tale is so imbued with Turkish values that the chance to use the material to contrast these values with those of the Arabs and the Persians proved irresistible. These national differences made a formidable soup that always seethed in the uneasy melting pot called the Ottoman Empire. Of course, the Turks had other difficulties in Eastern Europe with other subjugated nations, but these don't seem to be subject matters of the tales.

Hūrü has been given an aristocratic background as a princess of the Karaman, one of the ten Turkish "Oghuz" tribes which, in the ninth and tenth centuries, migrated westward from the region of the Altai Mountains and Lake Baikal, the lands east of the Caspian Sea (now in the USSR). On their march westward, since these lands were then under the control of the Caliphs of Baghdad, they came under the influence of Islam, and Oghuz warriors served as crack troops, generals and military advisors for Arab forces. Still moving westward, the Oghuz tribes were united under the banner of the Seljuk family, who conquered Iran in the eleventh century and Anatolia in the eleventh and twelfth. Once the Seljuk Empire began breaking up into princedoms, of which Karaman was one, the Ottoman dynasty (another Oghuz tribe) gradually took over Anatolia in the thirteenth century, constantly putting down the rebellious principalities. By the time Hūrü's story takes place in the sixteenth century, Istanbul Turks no longer thought of themselves as "Oghuz," but as citizens of a very successful conglomerate empire.

During Hūrü's fictional childhood in Istanbul, the reigning monarch was Sultan Bayezid II, the rather passive son of firebrand Mehmet I who conquered Constantinople in 1453. At the time, Prince Selim, the youngest and the most warlike of the three sons of Bayezid II, was the governor of Karaman at Konya, former capital of the Seljuks, where the great Sufi Teacher known as Mevlana Rumi had lived and taught during the political and cultural zenith of the now defunct empire of the Seljuks. Selim managed to wrest the crown from the heir apparent, his elder brother Ahmet.

At the time, the Shah of Persia was Ismail, who became known as the Great Sufi, famous in Bektashi literature under his pen name of Hatayi. His heterodox beliefs won great support among the Turkomans throughout eastern and southern Anatolia. The nomadic tribesmen resented central authority, aimed to tax and control tribal autonomy. That's how come the rebellious Turkomans wore red hats, the official headgear of Shah Ismail's troops, and hence came to be known as "Redheads," religious fanatics disloyal to Ottoman order. While Bayezid II himself had mystical inclinations and was sympathetic to the doctrines of Sufi philosophy, he couldn't allow a foreign monarch to use Sufism to subvert Ottoman subjects. His favorite son and heir, Prince Ahmet himself, had turned heretic and donned the Red Hat. The price of mysticism and religious freedom seemed too high. The Ottoman armies gave chase to Shah Ismail but couldn't bring him to battle—that is, not until Prince Selim became the Sultan and defeated Shah Ismail disastrously, earning himself his awful *nom de guerre*, "the Grim."

Yet Selim's treatment of the Arabs, once he conquered Arabia, was mild. Even kind. In less than a decade he doubled the territories of the Ottoman Empire, which, at his death, stretched from the banks of the Danube to those of the Nile, from the coasts of the Adriatic to those of the Indian Ocean. His son, Suleyman the Magnificent, whose accession in 1520 coincided with a turning point in European history (the golden light of the Renaissance), ruled during the golden age of the Ottoman Sultanate.

Pir Sultan Abdal, the great mystic bard from the interior province of Sivas, lived during Suleyman the Magnificent's rule. Nothing is known about his childhood and early life, as if he appeared in this world out of Nowhere. Obviously a Redhead sympathizer, opposed to oppression, in love with God, he was involved in a "heretic" Shi'ite uprising and hanged. His poems, which were immensely popular throughout the Empire, are incandescent with a very sophisticated social and political protest but are written in the simple spoken Turkish of the time.

Sufism is the essence of the Turkish heart. Never quite reconciled to Islam, a monotheistic religion which requires total submission, the freedom-loving and pantheistic Turks found hearth and home in the philosophies of the Sufis, or gnostic and pantheistic mystics, of which there are many schools but of which the Bektashi order, founded by Haji Bektash Wali, and the Mevlevi, founded by Mevlana Jalal-ed-Din Rumi, are mentioned in this book.

LIST OF CHARACTERS

and historical figures,
place names, special terms

[a]—Characters in ON THE ROAD TO BAGHDAD
[b]—Historical figures
[c]—Place names
[d]—Special terms or words from other languages

Acre [c]—Seaport in the eastern Mediterranean, now in northwest Israel.

Abd-es-Samad (the Maghrabi) [a]—An alchemist and magician; original publisher of *The Thousand Nights and One Night*.

Ahmad-ed-Denef Gang [a]—The Forty Thieves.

Ahmet, Prince [b]—Governor of Amasya, middle and favorite son of Bayezid II.

Ajib [a]—Son of Bedr-ed-Din Hasan, the candymaker.

akinji(s) [d]—Irregular or volunteer cavalrymen.

Aleppo [c]—Haleb, a city in Syria near the Turkish border.

Al-Ghawri [b]—Last Sultan of the Mamluk Empire.

Al-Masudi [b]—Compiler of one version of The Arabian Nights under the title of *The Thousand Nights Tales*.

Ali Shir [a]—Persian live-in lover of Lady Safiye Skywolf.

Amazons [a]—The Three Ladies of Baghdad, Lady Zubaida, Feisty Amine, and Safiye Skywolf.

Amin (Prince El-Amin) [a,b]—Husband of Amine, son of Harun-er-Rashid.

Amine, Feisty Amine [a]—One of "The Three Ladies of Baghdad," who marries Prince El-Amine.

Anatolia [c]—Asia Minor, the central plateau in present-day Turkey.

Antioch [c]—Ancient city, now Antâkya, on the Orontes River in southern Turkey.

antipodes [c]—Parts of the globe diametrically opposite each other.

ayatollah [d]—Islamic "bishop" of the Shi'ite sect.

Baby Osman (Karajuk) [a]—Hürü's son.

Badiet-es-Sham [c]—Desert in Iraq.

Baghdad [c]—Capital of the Abbasid Empire, principal city of modern-day Iraq.

Bald Boy [a]—Hero of a Turkish folktale, one of the disguises of Hürü.

Barren Aunt (in Turkish *Kisir Teyze*) [a]—Turcoman character in Lady Safiye's Tale.

Barsoom [a]—See Rashid-ed-Din.

Basra [c]—City on the Bay of Basra in the Persian Gulf.

Bayezid II; Old Man [b]—Son of Mehmet I, ruled from 1481–1512.

Bedr-ed-Din Hasan [a]—Given name of the hero of the "Tale of Two Vizier Brothers," also called Sweet, the Candymaker.

Blowing Bull (in Turkish *Esen Boğa*) [a]—Turcoman character in Lady Safiye's Tale.

Boghaz Kesen Castle [c]—Fortification around the city of Istanbul.

Bosphorus [c]—Strait between the Black Sea and the Sea of Marmara, separating the European and Asian parts of Istanbul.

Bursa [c]—Town in northwest Turkey, formerly Brussa.

Byzantium [c]—Later called Constantinople, now Istanbul, capital of the Byzantine or Eastern Roman Empire from the 5th to 15th centuries until the city's destruction in 1453 by the Ottoman Turks.

Camphor (Big Camphor) [a]—Black slave woman in the household of Shahrazad.

caravanserai [d]—Middle-eastern inn, halting place for caravans.

Caucasus Mountains [c]—Mountainous region between the Black Sea and the Caspian Sea, now in USSR.

Circassian [c]—An individual or a group of tribes inhabiting the Caucasus, of Caucasian race but not of Indo-European speech, noted for physical beauty.

Damascus [c]—Ancient city, capital of modern-day Syria.

"Dastur Ya Mabarak" [d]—"Quarter ye Blessed!" A phrase used to ward off the mischievous influences of *jinn*.

Day of Judgment [d]—End of Islamic time.

Deli Kachar (Turkish for "Crazy Fugitive") [a]—Name of a horse in Lady Safiye's tale.

dergah [d]—Dervish convent; a school of theology; a seminary.

Divan [d]—Cabinet of Ministers (or viziers) presided over by the Grand Vizier; Council of State.

divan [d]—Classical Ottoman poetry; body of poetic work arranged alphabetically; form of Turkish music.

Dunyazad [a]—Sister of Shahrazad.

Faghfur, fağfur [d]—Chinese Emperor; also Chinese porcelain of the Ming Dynasty.

fatiha [d]—Opening chapter of the Koran.

ferman or *firman* [d]—Imperial edict, command, order.

Friend [d]—Fellow mystic.

Gaza (in Arabic *Ghazze*) [c]—Seaport on the Eastern Mediterranean in Palestine, also the coastal district surrounding the city.

ghazi [d]—Veteran; survivor of a holy war or *jihad*.

The Godly Prince [a,b]—Son of Harun-er-Rashid.

Gog and Magog [d]—Pair of mischievous tribes, allied with each other; referred to in Ezekiel XXXVIII and also Revelations XX.

Golden Horn [c]—Inlet of the Bosphorus forming the harbor of Istanbul; famed in Ottoman times for its summer palaces.

Good Brothers [a,b]—Hidir-Ilyas (Green Old Man/Blue Brother), the Guardians from the spiritual universe.

Grand Vizier (Vezir) [d]—Prime Minister.

hadid [d]—Arabic for iron, a metal odious to *jinns*.

hadji [d]—Pilgrim; one who has completed the Hajj, the pilgrimage to Mecca.

Haji Bektash Wali [b]—Sufi master who founded the Bektashi order (1242–1337), one of the most important non-conformist orders of the Ottoman Empire known to drink "wine" and practice equality with women.

Hallaj, al-Mansur [b]—A mystic who sought to unify Christianity and Islam and who was put to death for apostasy.

Harun-er-Rashid [a,b]—766–809, Caliph of the Abbasid Kingdom, Defender of the Faithful, known for his night adventures in disguise in the city of Baghdad.

Hidir [a,b]—The Green Guide, the special guardian or teacher of wandering Sufi mystics; see also Good Brothers.

House of Osman [b]—The Ottoman Dynasty.

hurafa [d]—Similar to "hogwash": pleasant lies, fictions.

Hûrû [a]—The heroine of a Turkish exemplary folk tale; in other dialects, "Hörü" or "Houri".

Iblis [d]—The Devil.

ifrit [d]—An "upperclass" jinn, like a "colonel" or a "baron" among monsters, frightfully ugly.

Ilyas [a,b]—Elijah, Elias, the Blue Guardian. See also Good Brothers.

Imam; *imam* [d]—Chief religious leader of a mosque; a preacher or minister of Islam.

Immaculate Ram (in Turkish *Tam Koç*) [a]—Turcoman character in Lady Safiye's Tale.

Isphahan [c]—City in Persia, known for its rose gardens and rugs.

Istanbul [c]—Formerly Constantinople and Byzantium, the capital of the Ottoman and the Byzantine empire; largest city in modern-day Turkey.

Jafar Barmaki [a,b]—Grand Vizier to Caliph Harun-er-Rashid and a companion in his night adventures in Baghdad.

Janissary corps, Janissaries [b]—Ottoman standing army, comprised of Christian boys drafted from European provinces; assassinated Karaman Mehmet Pasha.

jann [d]—Another form of *jinn.*

Jann Baath [a]—John Barth, American writer.

Jaudar [a]—The hero of the "Tale of the Dutiful Son;" also a name assigned to Hûrû by Sweet, the Candymaker.

Jawan the Kurd [a]—Senior member of the Ahmad-ed-Denef Gang of Forty Thieves; enemy of Lady Safiye.

Jelal-ed-Din Rumi, Mevlana [b]—Sufi Teacher; founder and master of the Mevlevi Order of "whirling dervishes" at the Mevlana Institute in Konya.

Jem, Prince [a,b]—Son of Mehmet I, the Conqueror of Constantinople; brother of Bayezid II; known for his poetry, his tenure as Governor of Konya, his political defection to the Knights Hospitallers of Rhodes, and his assassination at the hands of the Vatican in Naples.

jink [d]—Dancing boys made up as girls; transvestite dancers.

jinn (pl.); *jinni* (s); *jiniye* (female) [d]—Class of spirits supposedly able to assume human or animal forms and exercise supernatural powers; the spirits may be summoned by a magician to serve their master; different ranks among the *jinn* include *Marid*, who are like lords and *ifrit*, who are like barons.

junk (chang) [d]—Persian musical instrument.

Kamar-ez-Zaman; Prince/Princess Budur [a]—Hero of the "Tale of the Prince and the Princess," a tale of Persian origin.

kanun [d]—A Persian musical instrument, zither-like, with 72 strings.

Kara (Turkish for "black") [a]—Last name of Hürü's son; Karajuk ("little black").

Karaman [c]—Principality of the Seljuk Empire unified under the Ottoman Empire; the name of a Turcoman tribe; a dynasty in the 14th Century with its capital in Konya; an obsolete Turkish dialect written in Greek characters.

Karaman Mehmet Pasha [b]—Father of Turhan Bey, murdered Grand Vizier to Mehmet the Conqueror; Hürü's (presumed) grandfather.

Karamankand [c]—Invented name for the Central Asian capital of an invented princedom in Lady Safiye's Tale.

Keloğlan [b]—Hero of a Turkish folktale, the Bald Boy.

Mistress Kevser [a]—Hürü's tutoress.

kiosks [d]—Summer palaces.

kohl (Arabic *kuhl*) [d]—Preparation used to darken the edges of the eyelids.

Konya [c]—Capital of Karaman; city in central Anatolia where Mevlana Jelal-ed-Din Rumi founded his spiritual order and School of Theology; capital of the Seljuk Empire, formerly known as Iconium.

Koran [d]—Holy Book of Islam, inspired by Allah in Arabic verse and recited by Mohammed, his Prophet.

Korkut, Prince [b]—Eldest son of Bayezid II.

Kutub [d]—Teacher of the Age.

Latif (formerly Sam) [a]—Zubaida's first husband.

Lion's claw [d]— *Shir-i penche* (Persian); a carbuncle; cancer.

lokum [d]—"Turkish delight," a sweet gum drop of sorts, usually cut into squares and dusted with powdered sugar.

maghrabi [d]—Berber, inhabitant of the Barbary coast (Tunisia, Algeria, Morocco), speaker of an Arabic dialect, Maghi.

Mahmut Jan [a]—Hürü's half-brother.

Mamluk or Mameluke [b]—Ruling Turkic dynasty of Syria during the period 1250–1517.

mamluk (*mameluk*) [d]—Fighting (Turkish) slave recruited by Arabs and converted into Islam.

mathnawi [d]—A long poem in rhymed couplets of the same meter, but with a different rhyme for each couplet.

Mehmet I, the Conqueror [b]—Bayezid II's father, the conqueror of Constantinople.

Mehter Ensemble [b]—First fighting military band known in Europe, used by the Ottomans to scatter the enemy as well as to regulate the marching of troops.

Mesrur, Black Mesrur [a]—Lord High Executioner to Harun-er-Rashid, the third companion in the night adventures.

mizmar [d]—Wooden flute.

Mohammed [b]—570–632, Arab founder and Prophet of Islam.

Mount Kaf [c]—Mythical mountain thought to surround the world and to bound the horizon on all sides; (obs.) Caucasus.

odalisques (in Turkish *odalik*) [d]—Woman slave in a harem.

Oghuz tribes [b]—Ten Turkish tribes from the area called Turkistan in today's USSR; *oghuz*: ox, (Modern Turkish: *öküz*)

Osman I [b]—From Othman (Arabic), thereby Ottoman (European corruption of the name), son of Orhan, the commander of the Oghuz tribe who died en route to Asia Minor from Central Asia; first ruler of the Ottoman dynasty who gave his name to the empire.

Osman Kara; Karajuk [a]—Hürü's son.

Ottoman Empire; Ottoman dynasty; Ottoman Sultanate [b]—1295–1920, very durable dynastic Turkish empire that stretched from Europe to Asia and Africa.

oud [d]—An Arabic musical instrument, a lute.

Palace of the Cannon Gate [c]—Topkapi Palace or the Grand Seraglio, started in 1465 on the pivotal site of the former Byzantine Acropolis, the promontory commanding the confluence of the three seas— the Golden Horn, the Bosphorus, and Marmara that surround Istanbul, which became known as the Seraglio Point.

Palace School of Pages [d]—Form of university during the early Ottoman Empire used mostly for civil service.

Phoenicians [b]—Inhabitants of an ancient country on the coast of Syria, its chief cities were Tyre and Sidon; Canaanites of Semitic stock; a people noted in antiquity for their purple dye and fabrics, colored glass, and abilities as navigators, colonizers, and international traders.

Pir Sultan Abdal [a,b]—16th century mystic poet from Sivas about whose life little is known. He lived under Suleyman the Magnificent, was involved in a Shi'ite uprising, and was hanged.

The Prophet [d]—Mohammed, the founder of Islam.

Rahmeh [a]—Daughter of Abd-es-Samad; a *jinniye*.

Rangy Flower (in Turkish *Banu Çiçek*) [a]—Female character in Lady Safiye's Tale, noted for her military prowess; also a character in the *Dede Korkut* cycle of Tales from Central Asia.

Rashid-ed-Din [a]—Alias for Barsoom, a Christian slavedealer and mortal enemy of Lady Safiye.

Redhead; Red Hat [b]—The Kizil Bash, related to the Alevi Order of Shi'ite Moslems.

Rock of Abraham [c]—Presumably where Abraham brought his son Isaac to sacrifice him to Jahweh; a sacred site in Jerusalem.

Sacred She-Wolf [a,b]—A deity of the tribes of the *Gök Türk* Empire in Central Asia, in the area now called Turkestan in USSR.

Safiye [a]—Third Amazon in the cycle of tales known as "The Three Ladies of Baghdad" in *The Thousand and One Nights*.

Saint Eyub [b]—Saint Job, an Arab saint, Eyyub-u Ansari (historical) name of an Arab commander, reported to have died outside Istanbul. The saint seems to have had leprosy which he bore with legendary patience; the district of Istanbul at the tip of the Golden Horn.

Sam [a]—See Latif.

sam'a [d]—In Sufi teaching, an ecstatic state.

saz [d]—Stringed musical instrument, shaped something like a mandolin, played by plucking. The 12-string *saz*, called the *divan saz*, was played by Sultan Selim, the Grim.

Selim, Prince and Emperor [a,b]—Son of Bayezid II, also called The Grim, Selim I, Yavuz (the Resolute), who ruled the Ottoman Empire from 1512–1520; husband of Hürü and father of Karajuk.

Seljuk family; Seljuk Empire (1071–1243) [b]—Took Anatolia over from Byzantium and established a number of sultanates, notably that which succeeded to the dominions of the Caliph of Baghdad. They met and mostly defeated several waves of crusaders; were eventually unified under the Ottoman Empire.

shafar [d]—Islamic month.

Shah Ismail (of Persia) [b]—The Grand Sufi, a Shi'ite mystic who proclaimed himself Shah of Persia in 1502 claiming direct descent through Mohammad's son-in-law, Ali; he proclaimed Shi'ite Islam as the official religion of Persia.

Shahrazad (in Turkish *Shehrazad*, in European *Scheherazade* [a,b]—Friend and mentor of Hürü; (historical) Queen of the Abbasid caliphate, who supposedly survived by telling tales to her husband, Shahriyar, thereby staying her execution and making *The Thousand and One Nights* tales into a serial—perhaps the first serial—that saved her life.

Shahriyar [a,b]—Husband of Shahrazad; (historical) the legendary Abbasid caliph who took a virgin bride to bed every night, only to have her executed in the morning to avoid getting cuckholded, but who was saved from his misogamy by Shahrazad and redeemed as husband and father.

shalvar [d]—A baggy trouser worn by Turkish peasants.

Shams Tabrizi [b]—Mevlana Rumi's great love, who was considered by others to be a charlatan.

Shia; Shi'ite [d]—Branch of Islam, official religion of Persia.

Sindbad the Sailor [b]—The Odysseus-like hero of a cycle of tales in *The Thousand and One Nights*.

Solomon the Jew [b]—Merchant brother of Abd-es-Samad.

Stone-Born Lyre; Stone Lyre; Lyre [a]—The mythical musical instrument which belonged to Orpheus and then to Homer, the blind Bard, and, in this book, to Hürü.

Suleyman the Magnificent [a,b]—Son of Selim I who ruled from 1520–1566, also called Suleyman the Lawgiver (in Turkish Kanunî).

Sultan [d]—King, sovereign ruler, prince; precedes a masculine name, i.e., Sultan Selim; follows a feminine name, i.e., Selimé Sultana.

Sunni; Sunnite [d]—Orthodox Islam, which supported the claims of the Ummayad family to the succession to Mohammed; the predominant religious faith in Turkey and most Arab countries.

Sweet [a]—See Bedr-ed-Din Hasan.

Sweet Idiot [a]—Affectionate name bestowed on Hürü by her father.

Tallest of the Tall [a]—The arch-magician whose mummy is in possession of the objects desired by Abd-ed-Samad, the alchemist.

Tarsus [c]—City in the south of Turkey.

Taurus Mountains [c]—Mountain range in the South of Turkey.

The Thousand and One Nights; The Book of the Ancients; *Alf-Laylah Wa Laylah, Kitabi Alf-Laylah Wa Laylah* [d]—A collection of cycles of Arabian Nights tales, often stories within stories, in repetitions of forms known as arabesques, compiled in the 16th Century in roughly the same form as it exists today.

Tiberias [c]—Ancient town on the western shore of the sea of Galilee.

Tigris River [c]—The great river that, along with the River Euphrates, defines the fertile land called Mesopotamia, the fertile crescent, the cradle of civilization.

Tuman, Prince [b]—Appointed by Selim I as the governor of Egypt, but proclaimed himself Sultan Tuman, the Ruler of Cairo; defeated by Selim near the Pyramids and hanged at the city's gate.

Turan [c]—Turkestan area that extends from the Ural Mountains southeast to the Altai mountains north of India.

Turan [d]—Older language classification which refers to Ural-Altaic languages, of which Turkic languages are members, also called Turco-Finnic languages (i.e., Finnish, Hungarian and Mongolian), ultimately going back to Hunnish peoples of which Atilla's hordes were one.

Turhan Bey [a]—Physician, Hürü's father, fictional son of Karaman Mehmet Pasha, the heir to Karaman, prince of the Seljuk Empire.

Turkistan; Turkestan [c]—Central Asian areas inhabited by Turkic peoples, the Turcoman.

Turkish [d]—One variant of the Turkic languages, as it is spoken in Asia Minor by a people who define themselves as Turks.

Turkoman, Turcoman (in Turkish *Türkmen*) [d]—Turkic peoples of Central Asian origin apparently so-named by the Chinese: *Tü Kei*, "the people of the helmet." Among them are the Azeri, the Özbek (or Uzbeck), the Kirgiz, the Uigur (in China), the Kazakh, the Kipçhak, the Yakut, and many other fighting cousins always making war on each other.

türkü [d]—Turkish song.

Two Brothers Festival [d]—Festival of the Sixth of May, celebrating the Good Brothers, Hidir-Ilyas.

Üsküdar [c]—Scutari, the opposite shore in Istanbul, the Asian side.

Vezir, vizier [d]—Minister of state.

Yunus Emre [b]—Mystic folk poet and minstrel who lived in Anatolia and wrote poems of incredible purity.

Zubaida, Lady [a]—One of "The Three Ladies of Baghdad." The author conjectures she must also be the historical personage, Queen Zubaida, the main wife of Harun-er-Rashid, known for her "shrewish" personality in *The Thousand and One Nights* tales.

zulumat [d]—According to Islamic cosmography, a place of difficulties in the southeastern corner of the world, beyond The Sea of Darkness, where the fountain of youth springs eternal. It sounds curiously like Tierra del Fuego.